The Fatal Series by Marie Force
Now available in ebook and print #5
Suggested reading order

MARIE FORCE

Fatal DECEPTION

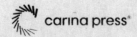
carina press

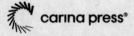

carina press®

ISBN-13: 978-0-373-00420-1

Recycling programs
for this product may
not exist in your area.

Fatal Deception

www.CarinaPress.com

Printed in U.S.A.

Fatal
DECEPTION

ONE

"CAN THERE REALLY be this many kinds of mac 'n cheese?" Lt. Sam Holland asked U.S. Senator Nick Cappuano.

Sam's normally unflappable husband looked somewhat flapped as he contemplated the wide array of choices. "How do we know which one to get?"

There were spirals and shapes and something called "Easy," but Sam was certain it would be easy for everyone but her. "Maybe we should wait until Scotty gets here and let him pick out his favorite kind."

"I want him to have what he likes in the house. How hard can it be?"

Sam scanned the shelves once again and decided it could be quite hard. "You don't suppose there's this many choices for chicken nuggets too, do you?"

The question seemed to suck the life out of Nick. Sam pushed the grocery cart aside and reached for him.

Surprised by her rare public display of affection, Nick returned the embrace. "How am I going to convince him to come live with us permanently if I can't even handle mac 'n cheese for a three-week visit?"

"He's not going to care about the food, Nick. He cares about being with you."

"And you."

Sam took in the busy grocery store, overwhelmed by the task. Hunting down murderers was simple compared to this. "What're we even doing here?"

Chuckling, Nick kissed her cheek and stepped back from her. "We're doing what regular people do when they have a guest coming to stay with them."

"So we're regular people now, huh?"

"For a few more minutes anyway." Nick took the box that proclaimed to be easy off the shelf and put it in the carriage. "Let's hope for the best."

"If he doesn't like it, I'll tell him it was your call."

"That's good of you, babe," he said as he steered the cart toward the chicken nugget aisle. "So I've been thinking."

Sam was busy enjoying the view of his denim-clad ass as she followed him through the store. He had rich brown hair that curled at the ends, hazel eyes and a mouth that was made for sin. And he regularly made sinfully good use of it. "About?"

"We need some help."

"With what?"

"Let me rephrase—we need someone to run our lives, especially with Scotty coming to stay with us. What if we get caught at work or something comes up that we can't get out of?"

Sam thought about that. "He could go to my dad's."

"True, but your dad and Celia have lives too. If Scotty lives with us, he's our responsibility."

"What do you think we need?"

"Someone to keep tabs on him when we're not home. To drive him to practice if we can't do it. To make sure the house isn't a wreck, the dry cleaning gets picked up, the bills get paid, there's dinner at night and some sort of schedule."

Sam rolled her shoulders, already chafing at the

thought of paying someone to boss her around. "I don't know about this..."

"Someone to buy the mac 'n cheese and chicken nuggets," he added with the charming smile that made her knees go weak. "You'd never have to step foot in a grocery store again."

"That's playing dirty, Senator."

"We need someone like Shelby." The tiny dynamo had put together their fairytale wedding in six short weeks. "Someone who can hold her own with you," he added, ducking as she took a playful swing at him. "Why does it have to be a her? I'm picturing a studly dude named Sven with muscles on top of his muscles."

Over his shoulder, Nick rolled his eyes at her. "It doesn't have to be a her. It has to be someone who can put up with you."

Even though he was absolutely right about that, she'd never tell him so. "You're skating on thin ice, my friend." She followed him up one freezer aisle and down another until he stopped the cart in front of a mind-boggling selection of chicken nuggets. "I wonder if Shelby would be up for a career change."

Laughing, Nick put his arm around Sam. "We could certainly ask her."

"She won't want to do it. She has a booming business."

"You never know. It's certainly worth asking. Maybe she knows someone who'd be interested."

"We're really doing this?"

"Let's ask around and see what transpires."

"You're sure this *she* of yours will know what chicken to buy?"

Nick opened the freezer door and withdrew a bag of

breast tenders, studied them and put them back. "She can't screw it up any worse than we are."

"That's for sure." Sam's cell phone rang. "Saved by the bell."

He frowned at her. Their rare day off together had taken a tremendous amount of schedule juggling to pull off, and she hoped this call wouldn't ruin their plans. They'd even declined the standing invite to Sunday dinner at the Leesburg, Virginia, home of his adopted parents, retired Senator Graham O'Connor and his wife, Laine.

Sam flipped open the phone. "Holland."

WHILE SAM TOOK the call, Nick studied the chicken tender options. He'd been nervous about Scotty's pending arrival for days now. The three-week visit was actually a trial run for all of them. The boy Nick had met at a campaign stop at a Virginia home for children in Richmond had become their close friend. When Nick asked him to come live with them permanently, Scotty's hesitation had surprised him. With hindsight, Nick could understand the twelve-year-old boy's reluctance to leave the place that had become home to him.

He'd been elated when Scotty mentioned a baseball camp in the District and suggested he might stay with them while he attended. Nick wanted everything to be perfect for all of them, thus the knot of fear he'd been carrying around. Nothing about their life was ever perfect. Most of the time it was a bloody circus—literally—with Sam hunting down murderers while he campaigned for reelection.

They were lucky to get ten uninterrupted minutes together on a regular day. What business did they have bringing a child into that madness? But what choice did they have? He'd become essential to them, and now Nick could only hope they'd become essential to him too.

"What's the matter?" Sam asked.

Nick dragged his eyes from the chicken nuggets and turned to her. "Was that work?"

She shook her head. "Tracy had another huge fight with Brooke." Sam's sister had been locked in World War III with her teenage daughter for months now. "It keeps getting worse."

"That's tough."

"Trace is a mess." She reached up to caress his face. "What has you looking so troubled?"

"I was thinking about Scotty."

"What about him?"

"What if this visit is a disaster? What if we blow our only chance with him?"

Sam stepped closer, placed her hands on his shoulders and looked up at him with potent blue eyes. "It won't be a disaster. It'll be reality. He needs to see what our life is really like—the good, the bad, the ugly. There's no sense sugar-coating it. If he comes to live with us, he needs to know what he'd be getting. He needs to know who he'd be getting."

Amused and touched by her efforts to bolster his spirits, he said, "And who would he be getting?"

"Two people who'd love him and care for him and support him—always."

"You're right. Of course you're right."

"I usually am," she said with a cocky grin that made him laugh.

"I refuse to dignify that with a response for fear of hearing about it for the rest of my life." Reaching into the freezer, he grabbed a bag of breast tenders and tossed it into the carriage. "Let's hope we got something he'll eat. If all else fails, there's always his favorite—spaghetti."

"Even we can't screw that up."

"Don't jinx us."

She took his hand and linked their fingers. "It'll be great. I promise."

Since his gorgeous wife was, in fact, often right, Nick chose to believe her. For the first time in days, the knot in his stomach loosened a bit. Maybe, just maybe, it would all be fine.

AFTER THEY STASHED the groceries at home, Nick went looking for Sam and found her in the study in front of the computer. "Um, excuse me. Day off. Remember?"

"I need to check in, and then I'm all yours."

He wrapped his arms around her from behind and stopped short when he saw that she'd rearranged his desk—again. "Really, Samantha? Every time?"

The kisses he placed in the most ticklish areas on her neck made her laugh even harder.

He reached around her and pushed the power button on the monitor. "You're done." With more kisses to sweeten her up, he said, "What do you think about a trip to Georgetown? I bet our workaholic buddy Shelby is at her shop today. We can stop in and say hello. If she isn't there, we can grab some lunch and do some window shopping."

She curled an arm around his neck and brought him down for a real kiss. "Am I only allowed to window shop?"

"Whatever you want, my love."

"Ohhh, I like the sound of that."

"Then let's go."

They grabbed a cab to the swanky neighborhood where Shelby kept a storefront bridal boutique. "Damn it," Sam said when she saw the closed sign outside the main door. "It was too much to hope that she'd be open today."

"Look." Nick pointed to a pink Mini Cooper parked across the street. "Who else could that belong to?"

"True."

"Call her. Maybe she'll see us."

Sam pulled out her phone and placed the call.

"Did you already blow it with the sexy senator?" Shelby asked when she answered.

"Ha-ha, no, I didn't already blow it with him," Sam said with a smile for Nick. "Thanks for the vote of confidence, though. We're outside your store. Got time for a quick visit?"

"For you? Always!"

Sam slapped the phone closed. "She's coming."

A minute later, Shelby appeared at the door to let them in. The tiny blonde, dressed in a pink silk jogging suit, greeted them with hugs and squeals of delight, though her face was puffy and red. "You guys look fabulous! Married life is clearly agreeing with you. Are you here about the replacement dress? Vera promised it by the end of the month. I still can't believe someone actually slashed a Vera Wang original!"

"What's wrong, Shelby?" Sam asked. "Have you been crying?"

"Oh no, no. Allergies." She led them back to her office. "They're a bitch this time of year."

Behind Shelby's back, Sam grimaced at Nick, letting him know she didn't believe Shelby's explanation.

When they were seated in pink leather easy chairs and holding glasses of pink lemonade, Shelby clapped her hands and let out another giddy squeal. "It's so good to see you! I'm thrilled you came by. The dress should be in any time. Unfortunately, we caught Vera in the height of the spring wedding season."

"Actually, we're not here about the dress, even though we appreciate your help in replacing it," Nick said, glancing at Sam. "We have a bit of an ulterior motive."

"What's that?" Shelby asked.

"We're hoping you might know someone who'd be interested in a job."

"What kind of job?"

"Basically, we need someone to run our lives." He explained about Scotty coming to stay with them, how they were hoping to adopt him and how they needed someone to see to the day-to-day details. "Do you know anyone who might fit the bill?"

By the time he finished speaking, Shelby had tears running down her face.

Alarmed, Sam looked at him and then at her. "Shelby, what is it?"

"I'm so sorry." Shelby tried frantically to deal with the tears. "I'm a mess lately. It's the hormones. They're making me into a wreck. And the business. I'm trying to figure out what to do, and then here you come and you're looking for—"

"We're looking for you," Sam said, "or someone exactly like you who is ruthlessly organized."

"And can handle her," Nick said, pointing a thumb at Sam.

As Sam scowled at her husband, Shelby laughed through her tears. "I should explain. I've been trying to have a baby. I know it might seem crazy, but I'm forty-two, and I'm tired of waiting for Mr. Right to show up. I really want a baby, you know?"

Nick reached for Sam's hand and squeezed. "Yes, we know." Thinking of the baby they'd lost in February was like reopening a still-raw wound.

"I see happy couples through the most wonderful day of their lives, wishing all the time that one of those happy days might be mine. Before you dropped by, I was sitting here by myself, mired in paperwork, weeping all over the place as I wondered how much longer I can do this. I was going to have to either give up on the baby dream or give up the business, because I can't continue to work with happy people while I'm crying my eyes out all the time."

Sam sat up a little straighter. "Does that mean you might—"

"It would be an honor and a privilege to work with you both—and to help take care of your Scotty, who is absolutely adorable."

"Really?" Nick said. "What about your business?"

Shelby shrugged as if it were no big deal to step away from a successful business. "I have people who could run it for me. I'd keep half an eye on it from a distance."

"Are you sure about this?" Sam asked.

"Your visit here today was the sign I've been waiting for. I need a change, and working with you again would be wonderful. As long as you won't be put out by some occasional tears."

"Not at all," Nick said.

Sam nodded in agreement. "How soon could you start?"

"How about a week from Monday?"

"Wow, that'd be great," Nick said. "That's the day after Scotty gets here."

"I'll have to deal with the weekend weddings I've already committed to for a few months. I hope that's okay."

"Of course," Sam said, still not fully sold on this plan of Nick's, which had fallen into place rather easily. She also wasn't sure how she felt about being around another fertility-challenged woman when she'd had her own difficulties in that area. "One thing I should mention is the uniform."

Nick looked at Sam. "What uniform? We never talked about that."

Forcing a blank look, Sam said, "Absolutely no pink allowed. I'm afraid this is a deal breaker for me."

Nick and Shelby laughed, as Sam expected them to. "I can't believe this has happened," Shelby said with another squeal. "It's like an answer to a prayer."

"For us too," Nick said as Sam's phone rang. "Crap," she said with a regretful look for him. "It's Dispatch."

"There goes our day off," Nick said to Shelby. While Sam was occupied, he talked salary with Shelby.

In a state of shock, Sam listened to the rote recitation of details from Dispatch.

Nick glanced up at her. "What is it, babe?"

Her voice was little more than a whisper when she said, "Victoria Kavanaugh has been murdered."

TWO

"Do you know what happened?" Nick asked as they raced to their Capitol Hill home in a cab, so they could pick up a car.

Sam knew he was thinking of his close friend, White House deputy chief of staff Derek Kavanaugh, and Derek's gorgeous, vivacious wife.

"Derek came home after weekend meetings at Camp David and found her on the kitchen floor. Hang on a sec." She held up a finger. "Cruz, we've got a homicide." Sam rattled off the particulars to her partner. "See you there."

"What about Maeve?" Nick asked of the Kavanaughs' baby daughter.

"She wasn't in the house."

"So she's…"

"We don't know. Victoria could've left her with someone or—"

"Technically she's missing then."

"At the moment."

"Jesus," Nick whispered. "Poor Derek."

Sam stared out the window as the city flashed by in a blur of buildings and people. A thick haze of humidity hung over the District. The locals called this time of year the dog days of summer. When the cab pulled up in front of their house, Nick tossed a bill at the driver. They rushed to his car, which was closer than hers.

"It took months for him to get up the nerve to ask her

out," Nick said as he drove the two blocks to the Kavanaughs' home.

Sam reached for Nick's hand and held it between both of hers. "I'm so sorry. She was lovely. I can't imagine what he must be going through."

He glanced over at her. "You won't look at him for this, will you?"

"I'll have to question him, but if he was with the president when she was killed, I'd say he's got a pretty solid alibi."

"And Maeve?"

"Finding her will be our top priority."

"Is it okay if I call Harry?" he asked of his and Derek's mutual friend. "Derek would want him there."

"Sure. I don't see any problem with that."

When they alighted from the car, a Patrol officer met them on the sidewalk.

"What've we got?" Sam asked.

"Lieutenant." The young officer nodded to Nick. "Mr. Kavanaugh returned home after two days at Camp David to find his wife dead on the kitchen floor. Their thirteen-month-old daughter was missing from the home. He's been calling the child's grandparents, aunts, uncles and family friends to see if anyone has her." The officer gestured to Derek, who was on the phone, pacing back and forth on the sidewalk in front of the house he'd shared with Victoria and their daughter.

"Thank you." She pointed to Nick. "The senator is with me."

"Yes, ma'am."

They went over to Derek, who visibly crumbled when he saw them coming toward him. He quickly ended his call.

"Someone killed Vic," he said, incredulous.

"I'm so sorry." Nick embraced his friend and held him as he sobbed helplessly.

Never comfortable with grief, Sam hung back and let her husband do what he did best while she itched to get inside and get to work. Nick held on to Derek for a long time, speaking softly, assuring him they'd do anything they could for him and Maeve.

"I can't find Maeve," Derek said between sobs. "No one has her. Vic said they were having a girls' weekend while I was working… If only I'd been here. Who could've done this?"

"We don't know yet, Derek," Sam said. "But I promise you we'll find out, and we'll find Maeve." She assured him despite the sinking feeling in her belly. The child could be anywhere by now. She pushed that depressing thought to the side and forced herself to focus. "I need your help."

"Whatever I can do," he said, wiping tears from his face.

"I have to go inside for a few minutes, and then we'll go downtown to talk."

"I'm not a suspect, am I? I never could've harmed her. She was my life."

"I was told you have a solid alibi."

Derek nodded. "I was with the president, the senior staff and the campaign leadership all weekend."

"Good." She glanced at Nick. "Stay here until I get back, okay?"

Her husband nodded, knowing she expected him to console Derek the best way he could while she viewed the crime scene.

The patrolman held up the yellow tape for her, and she

ducked under it. Inside she went to the kitchen in the back of the house where the District's Chief Medical Examiner Dr. Lindsey McNamara examined the body. Victoria's long, dark hair was fanned out on the floor. Bruises covered her face, and her lips were blue. She wore black yoga pants and a yellow T-shirt.

Sam grimaced at the sight of a woman she'd met many times in the months since she'd been with Nick.

Lindsey looked up, her green eyes brimming with compassion. "Beaten to a pulp and manually strangled," Lindsey said, gesturing to the bruises on Victoria's neck.

The kitchen bore signs of a struggle, with chairs toppled and broken dishes on the floor.

"Any indication of sexual assault?" Sam asked.

"Not that I can tell from visual inspection. I'll know more when I get her back to the lab. She put up a fight." Lindsey held up Victoria's right hand to show Sam the bruises on her knuckles. "I'm glad she got a few hits in."

"For all the good it did."

"Looks to be some skin under her nails too," Lindsey added.

Sam called for Crime Scene detectives and then took a walk through the well-appointed house that was full of photos of the blonde baby girl who was the center of her parents' lives. Mixed in with the family photos were pictures of Derek with his boss, the president of the United States, and other political luminaries as well as his parents and what looked to be his siblings along with their families.

His framed degrees from Yale University and Yale Law School hung in the study along with a certificate from the John F. Kennedy School of Government at Harvard and Victoria Taft's degree from Bryn Mawr. Sam pulled the notebook from her back pocket and made a note of Victoria's maiden name as well as the year of her graduation from college. On the shelves in the study were sports trophies that Sam took a moment to study. All of them were Derek's. Soccer and lacrosse had been his games at St. George's School in Rhode Island.

Sam thought it odd that she didn't find photos of Victoria with anyone other than her husband and daughter. In the master bedroom, which was done in shades of blue with white accents, she picked up a silver-framed photo of Derek, Victoria and Maeve and studied the woman who'd been killed, noting her serene smile and the happiness that sparkled in her brown eyes.

She thought about what she knew of Victoria, overall impressions, pieces of conversations from the last eight months. Sam, who'd always fancied herself a bit of a fashionista, had felt like an amateur next to Victoria, who did stylishly sexy with that effortless grace some women seemed born with.

Sam might've envied Victoria for that effortless grace if she hadn't been so warm and genuine and funny. Every time she'd been with Victoria, Sam had found her to be a happy, peaceful person who was clearly in love with her shy but accomplished husband and thrilled with her sweet baby girl.

A deep, penetrating sadness settled into Sam's bones when it dawned on her that Victoria might've made for a good friend if Sam had taken the time to get to know her better.

"We'll find your little girl, Victoria," Sam whispered, as the sound of a throat clearing caught her attention. She returned the photo to the bedside table and turned to face her partner, Detective Freddie Cruz. His dark hair was mussed, and he looked sleepy-eyed and rumpled. Ever since he moved in with his girlfriend Elin a few months ago, he always looked like he'd just rolled out of bed—and he usually had.

"What've we got?" he asked, taking in the spacious bedroom.

Sam walked him through what she knew so far. "Crime Scene is on the way," she said. The detectives would go through every square inch of the home looking for evidence.

"She was a friend of yours, wasn't she?"

Sam looked down at the photo. "We socialized occasionally. Her husband and Nick are good friends, but I didn't know her all that well. She always had the baby with her, so it wasn't easy to chat about anything other than Maeve." Sam didn't add that she'd been jealous of Victoria because she had the baby Sam had been denied. "I need to get Mr. Kavanaugh to HQ and get to work. Can you take care of the canvass and wait for Crime Scene?"

"I'm on it."

"Thanks." Sam went downstairs as Lindsey was overseeing the removal of Victoria's body from the house.

Derek's keening wail at seeing the body bag broke Sam's heart. She simply couldn't imagine what he must be feeling—and didn't want to. The thought of losing her wonderful husband so violently didn't bear considering.

Her wonderful husband was, at the moment, holding his friend up as he cried his heart out.

Across the street, photographers from the city's newspapers took photos of the two men.

"Get rid of them," Sam snapped at Freddie. "Heartless bastards."

Darren Tabor from the *Washington Star* crossed the street. "What've you got, Lieutenant?"

"Why do you vultures have to take pictures of a husband's unimaginable grief?"

"Because he's deputy chief of staff to the president, and he's being comforted by one of the nation's most popular senators." Darren shrugged. "That photo will sell a lot of papers tomorrow."

"It's sick."

"Maybe so."

Thinking of the promise she'd made to Victoria, Sam forced herself to make eye contact with the earnest young man who'd once done her a huge personal favor—one she was not likely to ever forget. "Put the word out that Kavanaugh's daughter, thirteen-month-old Maeve, is missing and presumed kidnapped from the scene."

"Holy Christ."

"Do it, Darren. The sooner we have everyone looking for her, the faster we'll find her. Cruz, go back inside and get a photo of the kid. Hurry up."

"On it."

"Get it out on the wires as fast as you can," Sam said to Darren, who looked a little paler than he had initially.

"I will. If you have anything else you can tell me, you know where to find me."

Sam left him with a quick nod and went back to Derek and Nick. Their friend, Dr. Harry Flynn, had joined them and was hugging Derek.

"We need to find Maeve," Derek said, hiccupping on a sob. "Whoever did this to Vic took her."

"We'll find her, but we need your help. I'd like to take you downtown to HQ now, but before we go, you need to call your folks and anyone who shouldn't hear about

Victoria's murder and Maeve's disappearance from the media."

"Oh God, my parents," Derek said. "When I called to see if they might have Maeve, I told them I couldn't reach Vic… I didn't tell them anything yet…because I couldn't… I couldn't get the words out…"

"Do you want me to call them for you?" Harry asked.

"Would you?" Derek seemed relieved by his friend's offer. "I don't think I could say the words… That would make it real…"

"What about Victoria's family?" Sam asked.

Derek shook his head. "She doesn't have any. Her parents died years ago, before I met her, and she was an only child."

"Aunts, uncles, cousins?"

"None that I knew of."

Sam thought it was odd that Victoria had no one, but she kept her expression blank so as not to add to his distress.

"Go ahead and make the call to his folks," she said to Harry, who took Derek's phone from him.

"Do I tell them about Maeve?" Harry asked.

"You may as well," Sam said. "I asked the *Star* reporter to put it on the wires, so it'll be on the news before too much longer."

Harry nodded. "I'll meet you at the station," he said to Nick. "I want to be there if Derek needs me." He walked away to make the call.

"Will you drive us to HQ?" Sam asked Nick as Crime Scene detectives arrived on the scene. "I don't want to give the vultures a photo of him being put into a police cruiser when he's not a suspect."

"Of course. Come on, Derek. Let's get you downtown so Sam can figure out what happened and find Maeve."

While Sam had a word with the Crime Scene detective in charge, Nick settled Derek into the backseat of his car.

Sam joined them a minute later, sending her husband a small smile of thanks for his help with Derek. Usually dealing with the grief-stricken fell to her, and she hated that part of her job more than any other. What did one say to someone whose life had been violently changed forever?

Using his elbow to flip up the arm rests that would block Derek's view of the center console, Nick reached for her hand and held it all the way downtown.

"I KNOW YOUR loss is unimaginable, and I'm truly heart-broken for you and Maeve," Sam said when she had Derek settled in an interrogation room at HQ, "but I need you to take me through the last few days. Your schedule, Victoria's, anything unusual that she or anyone else might've said or done."

Derek's light brown hair was standing on end, as if he'd been running his hands through it, and his brown eyes were red from crying. With his elbows on the table, he hung his head and was quiet for a long time.

Watching him and his terrible grief, Sam vibrated with tension and fury. Someone she knew and considered a friend had been murdered in her city, and she was pissed off. That anger would fuel her every movement until she found the person who killed Victoria and took Maeve.

"I didn't want to go to Camp David," Derek finally said, his voice barely a whisper. "It was Vic's birthday yesterday, and I wanted to be with her and Maeve."

"What was the reason for the weekend at Camp David?" Sam asked.

"We were fine-tuning the president's convention speech. The convention starts in two weeks in Charlotte." He glanced at her. "Nick's name came up as a possible keynoter." Derek huffed out a deep breath. "I was going to call him about it tomorrow." It seemed to occur to Derek right then that all his future plans had been altered.

Even though Sam was stunned to hear her husband had been considered for such an honor, she couldn't take the time to process that now when she had murder and kidnapping on her mind. "Was Victoria having any problems with anyone that you knew of?"

"No. You knew how she was, bubbly and friendly. Everything I'm not." As a fresh wave of sobs racked his muscular but wiry frame, he dropped his head into his hands. "I'm sorry. I know you need my help, but all I can think about is where's Maeve, and how am I supposed to live without Vic?"

Moved by his raw grief, Sam dragged her chair over next to his and rested a hand on his back. "I'm so sorry, Derek. I know this is a nightmare, but time isn't on our side where Maeve is concerned. I won't quote statistics, but it's imperative that we find her soon." She watched him make an effort to pull himself together. "You're certain Victoria hadn't had recent conflicts or problems with anyone?"

"Not that she told me."

"And she would have?"

"I think so. We're tight, you know?" His use of the present tense saddened Sam. Family members of murder victims almost always used the present tense when speaking of their loved ones right after they were taken from them suddenly and violently. Poor Derek had a long road ahead of him as his staggering loss registered. "I work a lot—too much, especially lately with the campaign heating up. So it's possible something could've happened and she hadn't had a chance to tell me."

"If something big happened and you were at Camp David with the president—"

"She would've called me. I might have an important job, but she knew that she and Maeve came first—always."

"I have to ask about your work and if there's anyone or anything you're involved with that might factor into this."

"That's my job," a familiar voice said from the doorway.

Sam bit back a groan when FBI Special Agent Avery Hill and her boss, Chief Farnsworth, stepped into the room. Hill had butted into an earlier investigation of hers before Farnsworth sent him packing back to Quantico.

"I've got this, Hill," Sam said in her best dismissive tone. "But nice of you to come by."

"Actually," Hill said in a honeyed Southern accent that no doubt worked on most women. Unfortunately for him, Sam wasn't most women. "Since I have a top-secret security clearance and you don't, I'll be looking into Mr. Kavanaugh's work and any tie-ins."

The guy was too handsome for his own good, and Sam hated to admit that if she hadn't been recently— and happily—married, she might've been interested in getting to know him better. He wore his golden-brown hair combed back off his face in a style he could pull off thanks to chiseled cheekbones and equally golden-brown eyes that zeroed in on her with laser-sharp purpose.

Of course Nick picked that moment to step into the room to see if Derek needed a drink or anything to eat. Over the last eight months, Nick had become an unofficial member of Sam's team. They'd all but deputized him a few times, so no one thought a thing of him coming into the room where his friend was being questioned. When Nick noticed her staring match with the agent, the subtle lift of one eyebrow was the only change to her husband's otherwise expressionless demeanor.

"Let's put aside the turf war," Farnsworth said with a warning look for Sam. "We all have the same priority—finding Maeve Kavanaugh and catching Victoria Kavanaugh's killer."

When the man that Sam once called "Uncle Joe" used that particular tone, there was no point in arguing. "Follow me," he said to her and Hill.

"Excuse me for a minute," Sam said to Derek, annoyed by the interruption.

On the way past Nick, she rolled her eyes. Farnsworth led them to a conference room where Special Victims Detective Ramsey waited with another officer.

He nodded to Sam. "Lieutenant, we meet again."

"Detective." Their paths had crossed right before Sam's wedding when she'd gone to him seeking information on an old case that might've been tied to her father's unsolved shooting. It had turned into another dead end.

"My partner, Detective Harper," Ramsey said.

The younger officer reached out a hand to Sam. "Heard so much about you, Lieutenant. Pleasure to finally meet you."

The sucking up earned him a scowl from Ramsey. Harper quickly pulled back his hand after Sam shook it.

Sam never had figured out what Ramsey had against

her. She'd decided he was put out by the fact that he was easily ten years older than her, but she had two ranks on him. Whatever. His fragile ego was the last thing on her mind at the moment.

"Here's how this is going to go," Farnsworth said as Sam's mentor, Detective Captain Malone, joined them. Farnsworth pointed to Sam. "You're the lead on the Victoria Kavanaugh murder. Hill's in charge of looking into any possible connections to the husband's work, and Ramsey is leading the investigation into the missing kid. Anyone have a problem with that?"

Sam had a problem with it, all right. Her team could easily handle every aspect of the investigation without assistance, but she held her tongue, knowing the chief expected her to do what she was told.

"Anyone who can't work collaboratively will be taken off the investigation and disciplined accordingly," Farnsworth continued.

Hill smirked at Sam, letting her know that he expected her to be disciplined before it was over.

Fuck that, she thought, determined to close her third of the investigation while the other two were still tripping over their own dicks. That thought made her smile as the chief made eye contact with her.

"Am I clear, Lieutenant?"

"Yes, sir," she said in her sweetest tone.

Unused to such easy capitulation, let alone sweetness, from her, Farnsworth eyed her suspiciously before he moved on to the others. "Ramsey? Hill?"

Both men muttered their agreement.

"Now, get to work, and keep me posted. Lieutenant, I'll need you to brief the media at zero seven hundred."

"What if we don't have anything by then?" Sam asked.

"Get something," Farnsworth said as he walked away with the other men in tow.

"Sure, no problem." When they were alone, Sam turned to Cruz, who had joined them. "Where are we with the canvass?"

"We checked the whole block and didn't find anyone who heard or saw anything unusual. Naturally, all the neighbors wanted the lowdown on what happened." People were always obscenely interested in crime until it happened to them. "Call in Gonzo, Arnold, McBride and Tyrone. We need all the help we can get on this one."

"And of course you'll want to close the case before Hill or Ramsey," Freddie said.

Sam rewarded him with a shit-eating grin. "Duh."

THREE

"TELL ME ABOUT VICTORIA," Sam said, once again filled with regret that she'd never taken the time to get to know the other woman better.

Hill stood inside the closed door to the interrogation room, observing the interview.

Sam went out of her way to pretend he wasn't there, which wasn't easy when he was staring at her the whole time.

"What about her?" Derek asked. He'd already answered a staggering number of questions about his daughter for Ramsey and Harper, who'd left to mobilize the entire Special Victims unit in the search for Maeve. Issuing an Amber Alert would be their first order of business.

"Where did she grow up? What do you know about her childhood?"

"Her maiden name was Taft. She grew up in Ohio with her parents. She didn't talk too much about her childhood. I got the feeling it wasn't particularly happy."

"What did she study in school?"

"History and political science."

"What did she do after college?"

"She worked for a lobby firm but quit her job when we got married. She couldn't do that while I was working for a senator, especially since he was running for president. It would've been a conflict of interest."

"Can you write down the name of the firm where she worked?"

Derek reached for the pad and pen she pushed across the table.

"Who were Victoria's close friends? Who did she see every day who might have insight into her activities?"

"I should know that," he said regretfully. "But I'm afraid I didn't spend much of the small amount of time we had together talking about who was in their playgroup."

"So she did belong to a playgroup?"

"A few of them, I think. She and Maeve kept busy with lots of activities."

"And she never talked about who she met through these activities?"

"Look, I know this'll make me sound horrible, but I didn't care about those people. I work so much that when I was home, I wanted to talk to her about Maeve and about us, and I wanted..." He faltered and again dropped his head into his hands.

"What did you want, Derek?"

"I wanted to be alone with her, to take her to bed..." His hands over his mouth muffled his voice. "I can't believe I'll never, we'll never... Ever again."

Sam ached for him. For the first time since they started the questioning, Sam took a tentative glance at Hill. She noticed the pulse of tension that ticked in his jaw before his eyes met hers, offering support that Sam appreciated in the face of Derek's terrible grief.

"We'll need her phone," Hill said. "The list of contacts will give us a place to start."

When the agent took the words right out of her mouth, Sam frowned at him, and the moment of unity was forgotten.

"It's probably in her purse at the house," Derek said. "That's where she kept it when she was home. I'm thinking now that her friend Ginger, who she met in the hospital when she had Maeve, might know her other friends."

"That's helpful," Sam said. "Excuse us for a minute."

Hill followed her out of the room.

"I thought you were going to stand there and keep quiet until I'm done," Sam said.

"Just trying to help," Hill replied with a charming smile that had the desired effect, even if Sam would never admit it.

"Do me a favor and don't. I've got this."

"Whatever you say, Lieutenant."

His condescension earned him another scowl. "Your husband sure is a lucky man," he said with a chuckle that grated on Sam's already raw nerves.

"Yes, he is," she said suggestively. Let him wonder how lucky Nick really was. If anyone had any idea, she'd be tagged a nymphomaniac. Under normal circumstances, that thought would've made her laugh. But nothing about this situation was funny.

"Would you like me to ask your partner to arrange for transport of the phone?" Hill asked.

"Sure, thanks." Since she was apparently stuck with the ingratiating agent, she may as well make use of him. "That would help."

"Wait for me before you start up again," Hill said over his shoulder as he headed for the pit to find Freddie.

Sam stuck her tongue out at his back, which made her feel much better.

"How's it going, babe?"

At the sound of Nick's voice, Sam turned. "Where'd you come from?"

"I saw you come out. What's with that guy Hill?"

"What do you mean?"

"He watches your every move like…" Nick looked past her as he seemed to search for the words he needed.

"Like what?"

Turning his potent hazel-eyed gaze on her, he said, "Like I imagine I do."

Sam stared up at him. "Are you jealous?"

"Do I need to be?"

"You've got to be kidding me. Our friend has been murdered, and we're talking about the way a fellow officer looks at me? As if I have any control over that!"

Shrugging, he said, "I don't like it."

Sam went up on tiptoes to kiss her husband, a rare deviation from her strict no-PDA-at-work—or ever— rule. "You're very cute when you're jealous."

His brows narrowed with annoyance. "Samantha…"

"Oh, sorry to interrupt." Freddie said when he came around the corner. "Hill said you want me to get Victoria's phone?"

Sam stepped back from Nick. "You're not interrupting. Get the phone to the lab. I want a call made to every contact on there, asking when they last heard from her or if they've seen Maeve today. Then we need a report on every number, as well as a log of all calls made and received in the last month."

"On it."

"Where are our reinforcements?"

"Gonzo and Christina are on a train back from New York City, where they were visiting his sister. He said he cleared the weekend away with you before he went."

"Yeah, he did. I forgot."

"Arnold is in Florida visiting his parents. He said he also cleared it."

"I guess he did, now that I think about it. What about McBride and Tyrone?"

"They're at Tyrone's brother's wedding in Baltimore. She said she can come in if we need her, but it'll be an hour or more before she can get back to the city. She said they cleared it—"

"All right already! They all cleared their plans with me, and I forgot! Sue me."

Freddie started to grin, but her frown discouraged him.

"Phone. Lab. Now."

"You got it, boss," he said as he scrambled off.

"Sometimes I feel sorry for him," Nick said.

"He's lucky to work with me, and he knows it."

"Sure he does."

"I have to go back in there and dig deeper into Derek's life when all I want to do is offer comfort to our friend."

"The best thing you can do for him is find his daughter and get the person who killed his wife. Harry and I will be there for him when you are done."

"Good," she said, squeezing his arm. "I'm sure he appreciates that you're here."

He gave her shoulders a quick, fortifying massage right as Hill reappeared in the hallway.

"Are you ready to get back to work, Lieutenant?"

Nick gave her one last squeeze and let her go, muttering "asshole" under his breath.

Surprised by the unusual and unwarranted hostility from her mild-mannered husband, she whispered, "That's no way to talk about an FBI agent."

"Since when do you need help from the Feds?"

"Since I don't have a security clearance and he does. Someone has to dig into Derek's work and any possible connections. Can I go back in there now?"

"Don't let me stop you, but stay away from that guy. I don't like him."

"So you said." Sam rolled her eyes at him and stepped into the interrogation room, where Hill was opening a soda for Derek.

He gestured to the diet cola he'd left on the table along with a can of lemon-lime-flavored water. "Drink, Lieutenant?"

"Don't mind if I do." Staring at the diet cola with lust in her heart, she chose the flavored water, but only because Nick might be watching in observation. She didn't feel like hearing it from him if she fell off the diet-cola wagon she'd been on for months now thanks to her damned stomach.

"Sorry to keep you waiting," she said to Derek when she sat next to him at the table.

"I'm going crazy wondering where Maeve is. There has to be something I can do. I should be out looking for her rather than sitting here answering endless questions."

"The best thing you can do is cooperate with the investigation. We've got every cop in the region looking for her."

"She could be anywhere. Who knows how long ago this even happened?"

"The medical examiner is working on getting us a timeline right now. In the meantime, take me through the last time you talked to Victoria."

"Last night. Late. I was finally back in my room after an eighteen-hour day."

"Was there anything unusual about the call?"

"No. We were both tired after the long day of political strategizing and chasing a toddler. It was a quick call."

"Let's talk about how you met."

"THEY TOLD ME I might find you in here," Harry said to Nick when he stepped into Sam's office.

Nick, who had his feet on the desk he'd spent twenty minutes cleaning, gestured for Harry to have a seat in the visitor's chair.

"What's the latest?" Harry asked.

"Last I heard, they're talking about how Derek and Victoria met."

"Remember how he was after he met her?" Harry asked with a small, sad smile.

"Yeah. A total disaster." Their shy, unassuming but sharply intelligent friend had been blown away by the dark-haired beauty. Nick had met Derek shortly after John O'Connor was sworn into the Senate and Nick became the new senator's chief of staff. Derek was an aide to then-Senator Nelson, who was now the president.

Nick ached thinking of the golden days when John was still alive and Derek was trying to figure out how to ask out Victoria. "How'd it go with his parents?"

"Horrible, as you can imagine. They're despondent about Maeve and heartsick over Victoria. I know how they feel. Who in the world would want to kill Victoria?"

"I can't begin to guess. Everyone loved her. Especially Derek." If Nick let himself think how he would feel if this had happened to him… He shook it off, refusing to go there. It was bad enough that he lived in fear of suddenly losing his wife every day of his life. "I was thinking about how long it took him to work up the nerve to ask her out."

Harry ran a hand over his face in a gesture of weariness Nick could relate to. It was all so hard to fathom. "The poor guy was so painfully shy, and she was so vivacious. We thought it would never work."

Sam stepped into the office. "Derek needs a minute," she said, looking battered by the grueling interview. Her eyes bugged out of her head when she took in the clean surface of her desk. "Every time? It's a sickness!" To Harry, she said, "Can't you prescribe something to cure his anal retentiveness?"

"No more than I can cure your messiness, my friend," Harry said with a smile.

Sam flipped Harry the bird.

"Do you want to sit?" Harry asked, offering her his chair.

"No, I need to pace."

"How's Derek?" Nick asked.

"He was doing okay until we started talking about how they met and got together."

"At the gym," Nick and Harry said together.

"We were there," Nick said, filling her in. "He was instantly attracted."

"But it took him forever and lots of urging from us to work up the nerve to ask her out," Harry added.

"I did some recon work for him and asked her if she'd consider going out with him," Nick said.

"Remember how mad he was with you about that? He said something about how this wasn't junior high, for crying out loud."

Nick smiled at the memory. "He was only mad until I told him she'd been waiting for him to ask."

"His parents desperately want to speak to him," Harry

said to Sam, holding up Derek's phone as Agent Hill appeared in the doorway.

"Do you mind if I take the phone in to him and sit with him while he calls his folks?" Nick asked.

"Go ahead," Sam said. "He's no help to us in his current condition."

Nick got up, pressed a kiss to Sam's forehead and gave her a quick squeeze that he made sure Hill saw before he left the office to go to Derek. He didn't like the way that agent looked at his wife. He didn't like it one bit.

"I WAS GOING to call you tomorrow," Harry said to Sam when they were alone.

Hill had wandered into the pit to make a call.

"What about?" Sam asked the handsome, dark-haired doctor with the adorable dimples. He'd become her good friend since she'd been with Nick.

"Close the door."

Wondering why he was being so secretive, she did as he asked.

"I had a note pop up on my calendar on Friday that your three-month birth-control shot is wearing off this week. You'll need to either renew it or be aware that you could conceive at any time."

Sam had managed to keep the looming date in a far back corner of her mind as she enjoyed the first few months of marriage without having to contend with "the issue" that hung over her the rest of the time. It had been a brief but refreshing respite from "the question" of what to do now that she knew the plumbing actually worked.

Before she suffered her fourth miscarriage in February after an altercation with a murder suspect, she'd been under the impression that she could no longer conceive.

That she was, in fact, able to get pregnant after all had been on her mind constantly since then.

"Sam?"

She forced herself to look at him, to answer. "Three months never went by so fast."

"Time flies when you're madly in love and newly married." He glanced at the doorway and then at her. "I know this is hardly the time or the place, but if you want to talk, you know where I am."

Sam nodded. "Thanks."

Nick knocked on the office door a few minutes later. "Come in," Sam said.

"Derek's off the phone." He took a closer look at her. "What's wrong?" he asked, glancing from her to Harry and then to her again.

"Nothing," Sam said, making an effort to shake off the ache that Harry's reminder had resurrected. As he'd said, this was neither the time nor the place.

Nick held out a hand to her.

She took it and let him lead her down the hallway toward the interrogation room. Since the area was mostly deserted that Sunday evening, she allowed him to get away with it.

"What's the matter?" he asked, his expression full of concern.

"We'll talk about it later, okay?"

"If you're okay, I'm okay," he said, but she could tell he was annoyed by her evasion.

"Oh for Christ's sake," Hill said when he stepped into the hallway and caught sight of them standing close to each other holding hands. "If you're quite finished snuggling with your husband, Lieutenant, do you mind if we get back to work?"

"Fuck off, Hill. The victim was a friend of ours."

Hill immediately sobered. "My apologies. I'll be in the room when you're ready to continue."

Sam leaned her forehead against Nick's splendid chest. "I shouldn't have said that. Now I'll have to apologize, and I hate that."

Nick chuckled softly and gave her a final squeeze. "You can do it."

She raised her head to look at him. "How'd it go with Derek's parents?"

"Terrible. They're beside themselves, of course. He was able to keep them from coming here for the time being, but they need to do something. I told them we'd call when he's done here. They'll come and pick him up."

"That's good. He shouldn't be alone right now."

"Isn't there something he could be doing to help find Maeve? It's driving him crazy that he's stuck here while she's missing."

"I can't think of anything, but the minute I do, I'll let him know."

"Thanks, babe."

"You could probably go home. We'll be wrapping this up soon, and his parents will come for him."

"I'll wait for you. I also want to be here for Derek if he needs me."

Sam patted his chest. "I'll be back as soon as I can."

"Take your time."

Chief Farnsworth approached them, looking frazzled. Sam couldn't think of a single other instance in which the chief had looked quite so undone.

"Sir? Are you all right?"

"I received a call from the president. Of the United States."

"Oh." Sam had met the president and first lady several times since she'd been with Nick. In fact, she'd gotten engaged in their rose garden. "What did he say?"

"He's very upset about what's happened to Victoria Kavanaugh and wanted to know what we're doing to find her killer as well as the baby. He also assured me that Mr. Kavanaugh was with the White House staff at Camp David all weekend, in case we were wondering."

"That closes the alibi loop," Sam said.

"Doesn't get much better than having the president vouch for you," the chief said. "He wanted me to convey his deepest sympathy to Mr. Kavanaugh. Would you mind?"

"Sure, go ahead," Sam said. To Nick, she said, "I'll catch up to you."

"I'll be here."

FOUR

THEY SEARCHED FOR Maeve Kavanaugh all night. Once the Amber Alert was issued, tips began pouring in. The Special Victims detectives investigated every one, but as the clock struck one the next morning, they had to admit they were no closer to finding the baby than they'd been hours earlier, and fatigue was making them all less than effective.

"I want you to go home, get a few hours of sleep and report back at zero six thirty," Farnsworth said to Sam, Cruz, Hill, Ramsey and Harper. "Turn everything over to third shift for now. Release Mr. Kavanaugh with orders to stay local and ask him not to do anything to find his daughter unless he clears it with us first."

Sam nodded in agreement.

"Thank you all for your good work today," Farnsworth said as he dismissed them.

Sam returned to the interrogation room where Nick and Harry were keeping Derek company.

"Anything?" Derek asked, standing.

"I'm sorry, but no," Sam said. "We've got tips coming in since the alert was issued, and we're following up on all of them. It could take some time..."

Her news deflated Derek, and he dropped back into his chair. "Which is the one thing we don't have." He turned to Nick and Harry. "What if she's dead too? What'll I do then?"

"Don't go there," Harry said. "There's no reason to believe she's dead."

"I've gone over it and over it in my mind," Derek said. "I can't think of anyone who would have reason to hurt us like this. Vic didn't have an enemy in the world, and I don't either. My business is rough and tumble, but I'm not. You guys know that."

"Sure we do." Nick placed a comforting hand on Derek's shoulder. "It might've been totally random. Someone who saw her somewhere... You don't know."

"In the morning, I've arranged for you to walk through the house with the Crime Scene detectives to see if anything valuable was taken," Sam said. "A robbery would at least give us a motive."

"Do you think this was a robbery gone bad?" Derek asked, seeming almost hopeful at the thought.

Sam weighed whether she should tell him the truth— that the walk-through was a formality—or what he wanted to hear. "I'm not leaning toward a robbery," she said tentatively. "Victoria was badly beaten, and Maeve was taken. A robber would want to get in and get out with the goods. He wouldn't beat her like that or take her child. This feels personal to me."

Derek's shoulders sagged at that news. "I can't think of anyone who hated us this much. I don't get it."

"Sam and her team will get to the bottom of it," Nick assured him.

"That won't bring Vic back," Derek said with a bitter edge to his voice. "Will it?"

His comment struck at the heart of what made her job so difficult. Sure, she could get justice for victims' families, but she could never bring back the person they'd lost or undo the damage murder had done to their lives.

"You're free to go for now, Derek," Sam said. "We'd like you to remain local, however, and if you take any steps to locate Maeve, we ask that you clear them with us first."

"Is my parents' house in Herndon local enough?"

"That's fine." She pulled a pad from her back pocket and produced a pen. "Write down their address and your cell number for me."

Derek wrote down the information and handed the pad back to her.

"I'll need to speak with you in the morning after you do the walk-through of the house," Agent Hill said to Derek. "We've got a lot of ground to cover on any possible tie-ins to your work."

Resigned, Derek grimaced. "Fine."

"I'll give you a ride to your folks' place," Harry said. "Save them the trip at this hour."

As Harry guided him from the room, Derek stopped in front of Sam. "Find my baby girl. Please find her."

Sam squeezed his arm. "I'll do my best and so will everyone in this department."

"Thank you."

"I'm here if you need me," Nick said, hugging Derek. "Anything you need. Any time you need it."

"Thanks," Derek said, his voice catching. "You've all been great."

"We're so sorry about Vic," Nick said. Nodding, he left with Harry.

"Hill," Sam said.

On his way out the door, the agent turned to her and raised an eyebrow in question.

"I apologize for what I said before and for being short with you. It's been a really upsetting day."

"No harm done, but I have to ask—should you be leading this investigation if she was a friend?"

"We weren't close. Our husbands are friends. That's how I knew her."

"All right, then. See you in the morning."

"See you then." When they were alone, Sam said to Nick, "That was uncomfortable."

"You handled it well."

"Let's go home for a few hours." Before him, she would've worked all night on a case like this. Now, knowing Nick wouldn't leave until she did, she put him ahead of the case. He had a busy week of work and campaigning before Scotty arrived and couldn't afford a night without sleep. Putting him first was the single biggest change she'd made to what used to be a one-track life.

With his arm around her shoulders, they stepped out of the chill of HQ into oppressive heat and humidity. The second they were outside, a pack of reporters descended.

Sam fended them off by telling them there'd be a briefing at zero seven hundred but nothing before then.

Nick escorted her through the mob to his car and held the passenger door for her.

"Vultures," she muttered as the reporters chased the car out of the parking lot.

"It'll be a big story in light of Derek's job," Nick said.

"Yeah," Sam said. The intense media interest would only make a complicated case more so.

All the way home, Sam replayed the last few hours, thinking over what she'd learned about Victoria, Derek, their routine, their lives. Nothing at all stood out as a thread that could be pulled to unravel the answers they needed to find a killer—and a kidnapper.

The thought of what that sweet baby might be forced

to endure made Sam shudder with fear and revulsion. She knew all too well how inhumane people could be.

"What's wrong, babe?" Nick asked, reaching for her hand as he drove them through deserted streets in the capital city.

She held on to his hand, comforted by his steady presence. "I'm thinking about Maeve. When stuff like this happens, it makes me almost thankful I've never been able to have kids of my own. I don't know how Derek was able to function the way he did tonight. I'd be out of my freaking mind."

"I'm sure he is. He's very good about remaining calm and composed. I've never seen him rattled, let alone totally unglued like he was today."

"The poor guy. It's such an awful thing."

"You really have no leads at all as to where Maeve might be?"

"Not yet, and with every hour that passes, it becomes less likely that we'll find her alive."

"God."

When they got home, Nick turned off the alarm and headed for the kitchen. "I don't know about you, but I'm starving."

"I could eat something."

Working together, they made turkey sandwiches. He poured himself a cola and an ice water for her.

"It's not fair that you get to drink that when I'm stuck with water," she said as she polished off the sandwich.

"I'm not the one who nearly blew a hole in my stomach mainlining diet cola for years."

"It's probably healed by now, so I could have an occasional one, right?"

"Once an addict, always an addict."

"Sometimes you're absolutely no fun," she said as she put their plates in the dishwasher.

His arms encircled her from behind as his lips found the spot on her neck that turned her to putty every time. "Other times, I'm a lot of fun. You've said so yourself."

Smiling, Sam turned and put her arms around him. Resting her head on his chest, she held on tight as he did the same. She breathed in his scent, the scent of home, thankful as always for everything he'd brought to her life. Knowing he was there to hang on to made even the most nightmarish days bearable.

They held each other for a long time before Nick kissed the top of her head, took her hand and led her upstairs.

"I need a shower," Sam said.

"So do I."

She eyed him suspiciously. "Is that right?"

"Yep," he said with a smile that was the picture of innocence. When he pulled off his shirt, the ripple of washboard abs had Sam licking her lips.

"What're you looking at?"

"One of my favorite things."

He rolled his eyes, embarrassed as always when she made comments about his supreme hotness.

"How about showing me some of my favorite things?" He tugged at her shirt, helped her out of it and then removed her bra with expertise and finesse that boggled her mind. "There they are."

"Nick…"

"Hmm?"

She followed him into the bathroom and shed the rest of her clothes while he adjusted the water. "Is it wrong that I feel so happy to be here with you, to be doing what we always do, when our friends' lives have been ripped apart?"

"It's not wrong, babe. You've spent hours doing everything you could for Derek and the case. It's okay now to take a few hours for you." He ushered her ahead of him into the shower and got busy washing her back. "You're no good to him or anyone if you're running on fumes."

"The whole time I was talking to Derek, all I kept thinking was what would I do if that ever happened to me, if I came home and found you..." She shuddered. It simply didn't bear thinking about.

His lips were soft against the back of her shoulder. "That's how I feel every time you walk out the door to go to work. I wonder, will this be the day I get the call that something has happened to you? And then I try to imagine how I'd ever live without you."

Sam turned into his embrace, clinging to him in a way she didn't usually, needing his reassurance more than normal. The loss of someone they knew, someone who'd been every bit as in love with her husband as Sam was with hers, made this case that much more personal.

"It's an awful feeling," she said.

"Yes, it is."

"I'm sorry if I haven't taken it seriously enough, that you have to live with worry the way you do."

"I knew what I was signing on for." He smiled down at her, seeming to study her face in great detail, before he placed one hand on her cheek and touched his lips to hers softly and reverently. "I'm thankful for every minute we get to spend together. Even when you're driving me crazy, which is most of the time, they're the best minutes I've ever spent with anyone."

"I feel the same way, even when you're driving me crazy with your anal-retentive freakazoidisms."

Laughing, he maneuvered her against the wall of the shower and kissed her with more serious intent.

Sam looped her arms around his neck, pressed her breasts to his chest and hooked her leg around his. She ran her tongue back and forth over his bottom lip, drawing a gasp from him. "Make love to me, Nick." As she said the words, Harry's warning from earlier made her question whether she was still protected. But at that moment, all that mattered was being as close to Nick as possible.

With his hands on her bottom, he lifted her and brought her down on his erection, filling her the way only he could.

Absorbing the myriad sensations, she let her head fall back against the wall.

He took advantage of the opportunity to make a trail of love bites from her throat to her ear.

She almost warned him about leaving marks but realized she didn't need to, because he certainly would've thought of that. He thought of everything.

With his hands still clutching her bottom, he took her on a slow ride.

She opened her eyes and found him watching her intently. Sliding her hand around the back of his neck, she drew him in for a kiss. "Nick," she gasped when he went deep again. "Faster."

He picked up the pace, and Sam had to remind herself to keep breathing as he drove her to a sudden, spectacular finish. She gripped his shoulders and held on tight when he pushed hard into her once more before shuddering in release. For a long moment afterward, he leaned against her, absorbing the trembling waves that continued to ripple through her.

"Sorry for being so rough."

"You weren't. I loved it." She caressed his face and traced the outline of his sexy mouth. "I love you."

"I love you, too. I don't know what happens to me when we're together like this, but it's never happened before you."

Sam didn't like to think about the women he'd been with before her. She didn't know any of them, whereas her ex-husband had caused them nothing but trouble since she'd been with Nick. "Whatever it is, the same thing happens to me."

He withdrew from her, and they finished their shower.

Sam dried her hair, brushed her teeth and got into bed a few minutes after him. As she did every night, she crawled into his arms and settled her head on his chest. She used to hate sleeping with someone else. Now she couldn't bear to sleep without him.

"Are you going to tell me what was up with Harry earlier?"

"Why can't you be one of those oblivious husbands who doesn't pay attention to anything unless he's getting laid?"

Nick laughed—hard. "Because you've already been married to that guy, and if I recall correctly, it didn't work out so well."

Sam poked him in the ribs, making him jolt. "That was a low blow."

"Am I wrong?" he asked with a cocky grin.

"No comment."

"So what gives with Harry?"

Resigned to being truthful with him when her inclination was to keep this—and almost everything else—to herself, like she did when she was married to passive-aggressive Peter, she said, "Harry was reminding me that the birth-control shot I had before the wedding is wearing off this week."

"Oh."

"Yeah. Exactly."

He combed his fingers through her long hair, which Sam found comforting.

"So…what're you thinking?" he asked after a long silence.

"It's all I've thought about for months, but I still don't know what to do."

"I think about it all the time too."

"I'm not as raw as I was right after it happened." Her throat closed a bit, despite her fervent desire to keep this conversation from getting emotional. How was she supposed to ponder a potential pregnancy when she couldn't even talk about it without bawling her head off? "But I think about our baby every day. I think about them all, but that one…"

"I know. Believe me. I know." He tightened his hold on her, with one hand on the back of her head to keep her snuggled into his chest. "You don't have to decide anything until you're ready."

"Well, we have to decide something or practice abstinence until we do."

"I do not know this word of which you speak."

Sam snorted out a laugh. "No, you don't, do you?"

"You've spoiled me rotten in that regard, and now I have rather significant expectations."

Sam appreciated the humor he was bringing to what was always an intense conversation.

"If you're not ready to figure this out, get another three-month shot," he said. "What's three more months when we've got a lifetime to look forward to?"

"You wouldn't mind?"

"I've told you before, and I'll continue to tell you, this is all about what you want. I want what you want."

"And I want to give you the family you've never had."

"I already have that, Samantha. If it was only you and me—and hopefully Scotty—I'd have more than I ever could've hoped for, more than I've ever had before." He lifted her head from his chest and turned to face her while keeping one arm around her. "I need you to believe me when I tell you that. I don't want you to feel any pressure from me on this."

"I don't. You've been your usual wonderful self about this situation from day one."

"Will you do something for me?"

"Of course."

"Will you talk to me about it and not keep it all inside like last time?"

Sam still felt guilty about getting the initial birth-control shot before she told him about it. But at that time, a few short weeks after the most devastating miscarriage of all, she hadn't been thinking clearly, to say the least. "I promise I'll talk to you. I'm sorry I didn't last time."

"That's in the past. All that matters now is the future."

"Until we decide what we're doing, we should probably, you know, refrain…from any further nookie."

"Wait…back up. What did you say?"

Sam dissolved into a fit of laughter at his horrified expression. "You heard me. If we decide to do this, I want it to be intentional and not something that happens by accident."

He moved so he was on top of her. "So what you're saying," he said, peppering her neck with kisses, "is that until we decide one way or the other, there's no more of this?" Flexing his hips, he entered her fully in one quick thrust.

"Nick!" she said, laughing. "We have to talk about this!"

"Yes, we do," he said, kissing the protest off her lips. "And we will. But if we're going on hiatus, I need one more dose to tide me over until we're back to business as usual."

Sam smoothed her hands over the firm muscles on his back, which flexed and strained as he made love to her. "Eventually we'll become like regular married people and stop wanting to do this every day, won't we?"

"God, I hope not."

Sam floated on a cloud of amusement and desire and love, marveling at how he'd managed to get her through this difficult conversation with more laughter than tears. That was definitely a first.

He leaned his forehead against hers as his hips kept up a steady rhythm. "I'd willingly sacrifice everything I have, except for you, of course, to give you the baby you want so badly."

"And I love you for that. If I didn't already love you for a million other reasons, that alone would seal the deal."

"Speaking of sealing the deal…" He hooked his arm under her leg, changing the angle. "What do you say we do this together?"

"I say give it your best shot." Sam arched into him as the now-familiar rush of desire moved through her in a flash of heat that settled between her legs.

"You know how I love a challenge."

And didn't he manage, through the creative use of every tool in his arsenal, to send them tripping into climax at the exact same instant.

Sam would be tired in the morning, but as she thought of Derek Kavanaugh and his horrible loss, she held her husband a little tighter, filled with the strength his love gave her to face whatever tomorrow might bring.

FIVE

LONG AFTER NICK was asleep, Sam thought about Victoria, Maeve, Derek, the birth-control dilemma and a hundred other things. When her mind raced like this, sleep was all but out of the question. Moving slowly so she wouldn't disturb Nick, she slipped out of bed and crossed the hall to her closet to find some sweats and a T-shirt.

With the help of her sisters, she was slowly but surely replacing the clothes—including her gorgeous, one-of-a-kind wedding dress—that her ex-friend Melissa had slashed during a recent investigation. Last she'd heard, Melissa was undergoing psychological evaluations to determine whether she was mentally fit to stand trial on multiple murder charges as well as breaking and entering, vandalism and a host of other counts. Sam had her doubts about the woman's mental fitness, but all she cared about was that Melissa was off the streets after she'd killed most of the people who'd "done her wrong" in her life.

As Sam went downstairs, she thought of that wild afternoon here in their house during which Freddie had discharged his weapon for the first time in the line of duty. He'd shot Melissa's hand right off her arm to keep her from detonating the bomb she'd strapped to her chest. Pouring herself a glass of ice water, Sam shuddered as she remembered that day. She and Nick along with her entire squad had nearly been wiped off the planet. Thanks to Freddie's quick thinking, they'd averted disaster and caught a killer.

"Just another day at the office," she muttered to herself, seeking to lighten her dark thoughts. In the study, Sam fired up Nick's computer and logged in to her MPD e-mail account to see if there were any updates from third shift on the search for Maeve. Nothing so far. "Damn it." The longer they went without finding the child… "Stop thinking that way. Being defeatist won't help anything."

Taking advantage of the quiet time to dig into the details, she began with the most basic tool available—an Internet search. She searched for Victoria Taft, Victoria Taft Kavanaugh and Victoria Kavanaugh. The first references to Victoria Taft came in press releases issued more than five years ago from Calahan Rice, a K Street lobby firm that catered to the automobile industry.

Sam wrote down the name and address of the firm and read through some of the releases that bore Victoria's name as a point of contact. The search engines also led to the announcement of Victoria and Derek's wedding in the *Post* and *Star*. Victoria's parents were listed as "the late Greg and Betty Taft of Defiance, Ohio." Sam took down their names as well.

The wedding had been at Sewall Belmont House, near Capitol Hill. Sam added a note to ask Nick what he recalled from Derek and Victoria's wedding day to her to-do list. Harry was Derek's best man, and a woman named Felicity Rider had been the maid of honor. Sam added her to the list of people she wanted to speak with.

She went next to the site of Bryn Mawr, a small women's college in Pennsylvania. Sam wondered why anyone would want to attend an all-female college, but she supposed it appealed to some women. Not her, of course.

When she read through the information about the school, the words became scrambled as her dyslexia reminded her that she was beyond tired. Locating the link to the alumni association, Sam looked for an e-mail address and dashed off a message indicating she was investigating a homicide and looking for information about Victoria Taft along with Victoria's year of graduation and fields of study.

When she'd read everything she could find about Victoria, which wasn't much, she switched over to Derek. The results of his search were many pages long, full of references to his involvement in legislation sponsored first by Senator Nelson and then President Nelson. Fighting her way through the jumble of words that swam before her exhausted eyes, she discovered that as the president's second-ranking aide, Derek served as the White House liaison to Congress.

From everything she read about him, he seemed well regarded by congressional members on both sides of the aisle and by his boss, who'd recognized him with several letters of commendation. Derek had been the White House's critical behind-the-scenes player in brokering the landmark immigration legislation that was the hallmark of Nelson's first term.

The Senate had been due to vote on that same bill, sponsored by Nick's then-boss Senator John O'Connor, on the day O'Connor was murdered. That was the same day Sam reconnected with Nick after a memorable one-night stand six years earlier. They'd been together ever since. *Hard to believe*, she thought as fatigue tugged at her, that was only eight months ago.

References to Derek dated back to his high school sports triumphs, his induction into multiple honor societies, four years as vice president of his class at Yale and a paper he coauthored while attending the JFK School of Government at Harvard. She found a link to his brother, Kevin Kavanaugh, a DEA agent.

"Wonderful," Sam muttered, expecting the brother to show up any second and insert himself into her investigation.

Only when she couldn't power through the dyslexia or keep her eyes open for another second did Sam shut down the computer and trudge upstairs. A glance at the bedside clock told her it was 4:13 a.m. Suppressing a groan, she stripped off her clothes and slid back into bed with her husband.

Curling up to him, she sighed with pleasure when he pulled her closer to him in his sleep, as if he needed her near him even in slumber.

As she tried to quiet her busy mind, she reviewed what she'd learned about the Kavanaughs. Odd, wasn't it, that the available information about Derek dated back to high school, whereas Victoria's life seemed to begin with a job at a D.C. lobby firm. Before Sam could ponder that thought any further, she dropped off the cliff into sleep.

"Sam, babe, wake up."

SAM COULD HEAR Nick trying to rouse her, but she was enjoying the sleep far too much for even him to convince her to give it up.

He kissed his way up her neck to her lips. "Babe, you slept through your alarm."

Her eyes flew open and landed on his handsome face, an outstanding way to start what promised to be a shitty day. "What time is it?"

"Six."

Sam groaned. "I've got to be at HQ in half an hour."

"Then you'd better get moving."

"Don't want to." Sam reached for him and let him surround her with his warmth and love. She'd give anything to be able to spend this day in bed with him.

"I know this is the last thing you want to hear," he said, his lips laying a new path of heat on her neck, "but don't forget tonight is Graham's fundraiser."

Sam moaned and pounded her fists on Nick's back. "It's not tonight! You said it was in a couple of weeks!"

"I said that a couple of weeks ago," he replied, chuckling.

"I caught a murder yesterday. I can't possibly go to a fundraiser tonight!" She thought of the champagne-colored gown that had been made for her by an up-and-coming Virginia designer who'd wanted to give it to her because of the publicity the event would garner. Apparently, on top of all her other roles, Sam was now a style icon too. Citing Senate rules about receiving gifts, Nick had insisted on paying for the dress.

"Samantha," he said in that stern no-nonsense tone he saved for the most important moments, "you have to go. I said from the beginning you had to give me a firm commitment on this one. They billed it as both of us, and I can't let Graham down."

His adopted father and mentor, retired Senator Graham O'Connor was still a bigwig in the Virginia Democratic Party. He was the reason Nick was in office, and his support had been critical to Nick's reelection campaign.

She wanted to weep and moan some more, but how could she do that when he was exactly right? He'd explained that Graham wanted to show his support for the campaign and had requested they both attend the event.

Since Sam had barely lifted a finger to assist in her husband's campaign, she'd thought at the time he asked that she could give him one night. Of course she could.

"So," he said, continuing to work his magic on her neck, "we're good, right?"

"Yes, we're good."

"And you'll be home by six and ready to go by six thirty?"

"Yes!"

"And you won't keep me waiting, wondering where you are and thinking you're standing me up when I ask so very little of my precious wife, right?"

More moaning because he did, in fact, ask very little of her. "Yes!"

"Yes, you're going to stand me up or yes, you'll be ready on time?"

She pushed at his chest when the last thing she wanted was to push him away. "Yes, I'll be ready on time. Now let me up, you heavy beast."

"I'm not done yet."

"I know what you're doing."

"And what is that?" he asked with a smirk.

"You're trying to piss me off and start a fight so we can have make-up sex later, but I'm wise to you, my friend, and I'm no longer easy that way. So you can try and try, but you will not make me mad."

"Samantha," he said, his tone thick with condescension, "I could make you madder than a wet hen in two seconds flat if I really wanted to. Lucky for you, I'm feeling generous this morning. As long as I know I can count on you to be here on time tonight, my work here is finished."

When he tried to kiss her mouth, she turned away

from him. "I'm not kissing you after that. No way. And as scintillating as this conversation has been, I gotta go, so if you could remove yourself from my person…"

"Not until you kiss me."

"You do realize I'm trained in all sorts of methods to get you off me, and if I chose to implement these methods—"

Flashing that half grin she loved so much, he kissed her into submission. "There," he said as he rolled over to let her up, "now I can let you go for twelve whole hours."

"I let you do that."

He sat up on his side of the bed to stretch. "Duly noted, my love."

Even though she so didn't have time for this, she crawled up behind him and pressed her breasts to his back.

He sucked in a deep breath, as she'd known he would, and his entire body went rigid when she dragged a hand down the front of him to stroke him back to life. "What're you doing?"

She stayed silent until he was good and hard, and then she released him. "Getting the last word," she said, kissing his shoulder. She bolted from the bed and made for the bathroom.

"I let you do that!" he called after her.

Laughing, Sam stepped into the shower.

As MUCH AS she'd loved the sparring match with her husband, she was now frightfully late with no time to eat. Her stomach growled with emptiness, so she decided to grab something on the way to HQ for the six-thirty meeting, which was in sixteen minutes.

From a lockbox in the bedside table drawer, she retrieved her weapon, cuffs and badge. She slid the weapon into a hip holster, clipped the badge on the waistband of her jeans and jammed the cuffs into one back pocket and her ever-present notebook into the other. Grabbing her phone off the charger, she pushed that into one of her front pockets.

Nick emerged from the bathroom with a towel slung low around his narrow hips. He was finger combing his wet hair, which made the muscles on his chest flex rather appealingly.

As usual, Sam was struck dumb by the sight of him. "You're staring," he said as he withdrew a suit from his closet. "And you're late, so get moving."

"You're very bossy this morning."

"You require a tremendous amount of supervision."

"Still not getting mad." She went up on tiptoes to press a lingering kiss on him. Patting his freshly shaven face, she said, "Nice try, though, Senator. Do me a favor, will you? If you have time this morning, shoot me an e-mail with everything you remember about Victoria from the day you met her. Tell me about their wedding and anything else that might give me some insight into her."

"Sure, I can do that."

"I can't find any reference to her online before she worked for Calahan Rice. That's weird, isn't it?"

Shrugging, he said, "Maybe she was low profile before then."

"I understand low profile. It's no profile I don't get. Everyone who's been alive in the last two decades has a past. If there's a paper trail of any kind, normally you can find it online. College degrees, licenses, that kind of stuff. There's nothing at all for her."

"And when did you make this discovery?"

Shit, she thought, wishing once again for the clueless husband who didn't see right through her. "Couldn't sleep," she said. "Why waste the time?"

His frown spoke volumes. "You'll be wiped out today after only a couple of hours of sleep."

"I'll be fine, perky and ready to play the politician's perfect spouse later."

He smiled down at her. "That'll be the day. Be careful out there today, babe."

"I always am. Will you be with Derek at all today?"

"As much as I can. I've got two committee hearings and a town hall meeting with constituents that we're doing via Skype this afternoon, so I can't get out of that."

"I'm sure he'll understand."

"Harry's taking the day off to be with him."

"Try to have a good one."

"You too. Find that baby."

"I'm hoping third shift got us a thread to pull. I'll let you know what I hear. See ya, babe." Sam went downstairs and was bolting down the ramp that led to the sidewalk a minute later. She drove much faster than she should have through Capitol Hill, which was still quiet at that early hour. Pulling up to a convenience store on D Street, she double-parked outside and ran in to grab a bagel.

She was standing at the back case, deciding between apple and cranberry juice while yearning for diet cola, when the reflection off the glass drew her attention to the front of the store, where a man wearing a heavy coat waved a gun around.

Fuck. As she dropped the bagel on the floor and crouched behind one of the shelves, it occurred to her that she was going to be late for her meeting. With her heart beating fast and hard, she dashed off a text to Freddie and Gonzo, requesting backup.

A woman lying on the floor gestured for Sam to be quiet.

Sam twisted her body so the other woman could see her badge and gun.

The woman's eyes lit up with relief.

With a finger to her lips, Sam urged the woman to remain calm and quiet as Sam crawled past her and an older man who was also lying in the bread aisle. Minutes that felt like hours passed as the clerk loaded money into a plastic shopping bag. His hands, Sam noted, were trembling.

The perp danced from one foot to the other, clearly high on something.

A young woman came skipping through the door, unaware she was walking into a potential nightmare.

Sam wanted to yell at her to get down, but when the perp swung his gun in her direction, she let out a scream and dove onto the floor. Smart girl. Whimpers and sniffs from the next aisle told Sam there were other civilians hiding there. At least five, Sam concluded as she watched the gunman return his attention to the panic-stricken man behind the counter.

"Hurry up!"

Sam made eye contact with the cashier, flashing her badge and gun, and encouraging him with the briefest of nods to stay calm.

Sensing something was happening behind him, the gunman twisted around to survey the rest of the store.

Sam ducked behind a display and held her breath. As long as he thought unarmed civilians surrounded him, they were probably relatively safe. If he caught wind of a cop in their midst, this could go bad fast.

After realizing he had help, the clerk seemed to calm down. His hands weren't shaking quite as violently, and his movements were slow and precise as he emptied the register.

Knowing her presence had calmed the man, Sam hoped she didn't let him down.

"What about the safe?" the gunman asked.

"I don't have access." He glanced again at Sam, which caused the gunman to turn again.

Seeing nothing amiss and everyone on the floor where they were supposed to be, he returned his attention to the clerk.

Now or never, Sam decided, springing to her feet and rushing the gunman from behind. She was a foot from him when he sensed her coming. He swung his arm back, and the gun caught her square in the face. Even though the blow knocked her senseless, she knew if she hesitated, she'd be the first to die.

"Stay down," she yelled to the other people in the store. Grabbing his arm, she twisted and wrenched it until he had no choice but to release the gun. As it clattered to the floor, she tugged his arms behind his back and had him facedown and cuffed within ten seconds. "Holy shit," the clerk uttered. "That was fucking amazing."

The rest of the people in the store surged to their feet and rushed her.

"She's bleeding," one of them said.

"We need a clean cloth and some ice," another cried.

By the time Freddie and Gonzo arrived with the cavalry, Sam was being tended to by seven of her new best friends.

"Don't let us interrupt the party," Freddie said drolly, even though Sam could tell he was relieved to see her alive and well and the gunman neutralized. Reaching for the radio on his hip, he called for transport for the perp and a bus for her.

"I don't need EMS," Sam protested, even though she was starting to have trouble seeing out of her right eye due to the swelling. To the citizens who'd come to her aid, she said, "I'm fine, everyone. Thanks."

Freddie leaned in and took a closer look. "Um, I hate to be the bearer of bad news, Lieutenant, but your cheek is laid wide open. You do need EMS."

"Oh, come on! I've got a homicide investigation to contend with. I can't spend half a day in the ER."

Her usually amenable partner shrugged. "You can't walk around with your face sliced in half either. You're scary enough as it is."

"It can't be that bad." To the clerk, she said, "Is there a mirror around here?"

He pointed to the back of the store. "In the restroom."

With Freddie in tow, Sam stepped over her abandoned bagel on the way to the restroom. She flipped on the light, took one look in the mirror and nearly fainted. "Oh shit," she whispered, remembering the fundraiser that evening and the dress she was wearing to help out one of Nick's constituents. She probably ought to give the designer the chance to back out of the arrangement.

"Told ya," Freddie said as he snagged a bag of powdered donuts off the shelf. As he ventured to the front of the store to pay for his favorite food group, Sam withdrew her cell phone from her pocket to call Nick.

They had a deal that he heard any unusual or upsetting happenings on the job directly from her as soon as it was possible for her to call. That deal resulted in frequent phone calls to her husband during crazy workdays.

"Didn't I just see you?" he asked when he answered.

As always, the sound of his voice calmed her. "So, okay, something happened, but I'm fine." She hated, absolutely hated, having to tell him things she knew would upset him. But she hated more the wounded look on his face when he realized she'd kept something major from him.

"Define 'something' and 'fine.'" Normally, his stern tone would make her laugh, but this wasn't the time for laughter.

As she took a moment to choose her words, she returned to the front of the store where Patrol was hauling the gunman off the floor and escorting him out the door. "I stopped to get a bagel at a place on D Street and interrupted a robbery in progress. I neutralized the gunman, and all is well."

"Define 'neutralized the gunman.'"

Sam gritted her teeth, knowing she owed him the full truth. "I jumped him from behind, and it would've been a perfect takedown if he hadn't smacked me in the face with the gun."

He gasped. "Jesus Christ, Sam. So you're hurt."

"Only a cut. They're taking me to the ER to get some stitches." She held up a finger to stop the paramedics from approaching her until she took care of her husband. "No biggie—and you do not have to come there. You've got a busy day with hearings and town hall meetings, and your friend needs you. I prohibit you from coming to the ER, do you hear me?"

After a long moment of silence, he said, "You can't tell me what to do. You know that, don't you?"

"I can in this case."

"Since you're being your usual mouthy self, I'll take your word for it that you're fine. However, I make no promises about coming to see for myself."

"I'll tell the doctors you're prohibited."

"Which will land our nonexistent marital troubles in the papers. Is that what you want?"

She couldn't deny he had a point.

"Only my wife could stop for a bagel and take a gun to the face. When I think about what a close call the gun to the face probably was… And you wonder why I'm always worried about you."

"Don't think about it, and don't worry. Everything is fine. I promise."

Since the paramedic in charge was getting pissed waiting for her and the rag they'd given her to mop up the blood had soaked through, she waved them over. "I gotta go. See you tonight."

"Samantha…"

Her heart never failed to skip a beat when he said her name in that particular way. "Yeah?"

"I love you. I'm glad you're okay."

"Back atcha, Senator. See you later."

SIX

BEFORE THEY'D LET her leave the scene, Sam received another round of profuse thanks and grateful hugs from the people who'd been in the store during the attempted robbery. The clerk was particularly appreciative and promised Sam free bagels for life.

The paramedics escorted her to the ambulance, where they applied medication to the wound that felt like they'd poured battery acid on her face. The pain was so ridiculous, she nearly passed out, and it was all she could do not to ruin her badass reputation by crying like a baby.

"Sorry," the lead paramedic said.

He'd probably enjoyed inflicting maximum pain to pay her back for making him wait.

Sam focused on breathing through the pain as they transported her to the George Washington University Hospital emergency department, where she'd been somewhat of a regular in the last year. At the hospital, she was whisked into a room and was grateful to see a doctor she recognized. Anderson, if she remembered correctly. Since she had only one working eye at the moment, she couldn't make out the name embroidered into his white coat.

"You again?" he asked with a grin.

"What can I say? The service is so great here, I can't stay away."

After the paramedics transferred her from the gurney

to the hospital bed and left, the doctor got up close and personal with her face, poking and prodding until Sam wanted to beg for mercy. By the time he was done, she was shaking and nauseated.

"That'll require a plastic surgeon," he declared. "Oh, come on! Why can't you sew it up and get me out of here? I've got a murder and kidnapping to contend with."

"Believe me," he said with a laugh, "you don't want me sewing that. A celebrity like you needs to be worried about a big ugly scar on her face."

"Those are fighting words," she growled. "For your information, I'm not a celebrity. I'm a cop, and I need to get to work."

"You may be a cop, but you're also a celebrity, and I ain't doing it."

"They teach you that grammar in medical school?"

"They teach you that charm at the academy?"

Despite the pain it caused her, Sam glowered at him, but he didn't blink. She hated when that happened. Her glower was rather potent, if she said so herself.

"I'll page plastics and be back to let you know how long you'll be our guest."

"Doc." She swallowed hard. "Will this require shots? In the face?"

"Couple of them, but they'll numb you up first. Don't worry."

Right, don't worry, she thought as her entire body *went cold with fear. The only thing that freaked Sam out more than needles was flying. No, needles were worse.*

Definitely worse. And needles to the face had to be the absolute worst. She'd rather take on ten gunmen single-handed than have a shot in the face.

Freddie came in with Captain Malone trailing behind him.

"I had your frequent-flyer card punched," the captain said. "So don't worry about that. You're one incident shy of a free ER visit."

"Very funny. I've got a dead body in the morgue and a missing baby, and I have to sit here and cool my heels until McSteamy can sew me up."

"Who?" Freddie asked.

"Plastic surgeon."

"The guy's name is McSteamy?" Malone asked, perplexed.

"Don't you watch *Grey's Anatomy*?" It was the one show Sam never missed. Didn't everyone know who McSteamy was? "You watch it, don't you?" she asked her partner.

"Sorry, far too busy for such foolishness," Freddie said.

"Right," Sam said. "I know what you're busy doing." She pushed a finger into her closed fist and waggled her brows at him, which made her face sting with the fury of a thousand fire ants.

With a mortified glance at the captain, Freddie slapped at her hands. "Shut up, Sam."

Naturally, his mortification made her laugh. Mission accomplished.

"Children," Malone said. "Keep your hands to yourselves."

Dr. Anderson returned to the cubicle. "It's going to be an hour," he said grimly. "Maybe two."

"Oh my God! I can't sit here for two hours when I've got a murdering kidnapper on the loose!"

"I'm afraid that's the best I can do," Anderson replied.

"There's no one else in this entire hospital who can give me some stitches and send me on my way?"

"Trust me when I tell you that you want the right guy for this job. When he's done, you'll barely have a scar. I'll be back. Sit tight."

"Sitting tight is not her strong suit," Malone muttered to the doctor's retreating back.

"I heard that," Sam said.

Her mentor, who was tall and brawny with wise gray eyes and close-cropped silver hair, sent her a smug grin.

"I can't sit here and do nothing." To Freddie, she said, "If I can't get to HQ, I'll bring HQ to me. Get everyone over here right away. Tell Jeannie to bring a dry-erase board. And if they can get out of there without alerting Hill as to where they're going, that'd be good. Hurry." As Freddie scampered off, Malone shook his head.

"You're too much, Holland."

"I've got shit to do and a deadline today."

"What deadline?"

"Fundraiser for Nick's campaign tonight. It's a big deal. He reserved me weeks in advance."

Malone hooted with laughter.

"What the hell is so funny?"

"Wait'll he gets a look at your face. Can I be there for that? Please can I?"

Sam attempted her trademark scowl, but that made the cut hurt like a son of a bitch, so she resorted to the old standby and gave him the finger.

"Don't let Stahl see you disrespecting a superior officer that way," Malone said of Sam's nemesis. "He'll convene an IAB hearing."

"Let him. It was worth it."

A nurse came into the cubicle, carrying implements of torture.

"What's that?" Sam asked, immediately on alert and anxious.

"I'm starting an IV so we can get some fluids into you."

"My mouth is working fine."

"That's the truth," Malone said.

Ignoring him, Sam said, "Get me a bottle of water. I'll drink it right down." Anything to avoid another needle.

The nurse held up the bag. "This is more than water. It's electrolytes that you need because of the blood loss."

"Get me a sports drink. I don't want that."

"Doctor's orders."

Sam crossed her arms tight across her chest. "No IV." The nurse glanced at Malone, who shrugged. "There's not much point arguing with her when she's in this—or any—mood."

"Lovely," the nurse said on her way out of the room. Sam nearly swooned with relief when she realized she'd dodged the IV bullet. A familiar whirring noise from the hallway had her sitting up straighter on the bed as her father turned his wheelchair into her cubicle.

Her stepmother, Celia, was right behind him.

"We came as soon as we heard you were here," Skip said, grimacing at the sight of her injury.

Sam was glad to see them but suspicious nonetheless. "And how did you know I was here?" she asked, even though she knew exactly how they'd heard.

"I can't reveal my sources," her father said. He came in as close as he could get for a look at her face.

In deference to his paralysis and his concern, Sam leaned forward to give him a better view.

He winced. "He gotcha good, huh?"

Shrugging, Sam said, "I got him better."

"I had no doubt, baby girl."

"She's giving the nurses a hard time," Malone said, probably in retaliation for the bird she'd sent his way.

"I don't need you ratting me out to my dad," Sam said. "Isn't it time for your morning donut break?"

"Oh," Malone said, his face lighting up, "donuts. Can I get you anything?"

The others demurred, and he said he'd be right back.

"Don't rush on my account," Sam called after him.

"Why are you giving the nurses a hard time?" asked Celia, a nurse herself.

"They want to stick me full of unnecessary needles."

Skip laughed at her petulance. "You look like you did at twelve when you crashed your bike and they wanted to give you a tetanus shot."

"Didn't need it then, don't need it now."

Celia reached out to brush Sam's hair back from her forehead and pressed a motherly kiss to her uninjured cheek. "Let them take care of you, honey. They know what they're doing."

Touched, as always, by Celia's sweetness, Sam said, "Why does everything they're doing have to involve needles? And why did my husband have to call you guys when I told him I was fine?"

"Because he was worried about you and couldn't get here himself to check on you," Skip said. "So he called in the next best thing."

"You don't have to stay. The plastics guy is going to stitch me up, and then I'm going to work."

"We'll stick around until you're done." Her father's blue

eyes, the exact shade of hers, allowed for no argument. He got a lot done with those eyes. "In case you need us."

WHEN CELIA STEPPED into the hallway to take a phone call from her sister, Skip turned those formidable blue eyes on his daughter again.

"What?" Sam asked, suddenly feeling the need to squirm. He was one of two people who had the power to make her squirm.

"I had dinner with Joe over the weekend," he said of his longtime friend, the chief of police.

An uncomfortable itch settled at the base of Sam's neck when she sensed her father was pissed about something. "That's nice. I know how much you enjoy seeing him." His former colleagues at the MPD had been endlessly devoted since the devastating shooting that left Skip a quadriplegic two and a half years ago.

"He mentioned something I was quite surprised to hear, especially since my own daughter was involved and never saw fit to tell me about it."

Yep, he was pissed. Sam wished she knew what he was talking about so she could prepare the defense she'd probably need. Whenever he got mad at her, it was usually with good reason. "What was that?" Sam asked, though she suspected she didn't want to know.

"The Fitzgerald case."

"Oh." Sam's stomach took a perilous dip. "That."

"Yeah, that. The cold case of mine that you reopened when I was hooked to a ventilator earlier this year and unable to tell you to leave well enough alone."

"You don't understand—"

"You're goddamned right I don't understand! I told

you once before to leave that one alone, and nothing has changed since then."

Sam stared at him, mouth agape, which caused more pain to radiate through her injured face. "*Everything* has changed since then. The day you told me to leave it alone the first time was the same day you were shot. We thought you were going to *die* when you had pneumonia. I wanted to get closure for you. I did it for you."

"Is that right? So when I didn't have the decency to die, why didn't you tell me you'd reopened my case without my permission?"

"I hate to tell you," Sam said, unnerved by his unusual hostility, "that it's not your case anymore. In case you've forgotten, I'm in charge of the Homicide division now, and all cases—hot and cold—are actually *my* cases." The instant the words were out of her mouth, Sam realized she'd said exactly the wrong thing.

The side of his face that wasn't paralyzed became stormy as he went from pissed to furious. "It's good to know you're not above pulling rank on your paralyzed old man."

"Oh, Jesus, Dad, you're going to play the paralyzed card on me?"

"I don't have many other cards in my deck these days. I can't believe you let me hear about this from Joe. Do you have any idea how embarrassing it is to hear from him what my own kid should've told me months ago? And then to see his surprise when he realized I didn't know? You promised you wouldn't keep shit from me anymore. I'm disappointed you broke your promise."

His words hit like arrows to her heart. She'd embarrassed and hurt him, which in turn hurt her. Sam couldn't find the words to respond. To hear him say he was disappointed in her was far worse than anything else he could've said, and he knew it.

"Here's how this is going to go. I understand you've caught a new case. So at your earliest possible convenience, I want a meeting with you, McBride and Tyrone. I want to know what they did, who they talked to and what came of it. Do I make myself clear?"

If he were any other past member of the MPD barking orders at her, she'd tell him to fuck off. But because he was her dad and one of the most important people in her life, she said, "Yes, sir."

"Good."

"I used the cold case as a way to get McBride back to work after she was attacked," Sam said sullenly. "And they didn't uncover anything new."

"I still want a full report—from them—and I want it very soon."

"Fine."

Sam was certain her expression was every bit as mulish as his. In their case, the apple and the tree were often one and the same. They sat in uncomfortable and unusual silence until Celia returned.

Her gaze moved between them, settling on her husband. "What happened?"

"Nothing," he said.

Before her stepmother could delve into their dispute, Freddie came in with McBride, Tyrone, Gonzo and Arnold in tow. Judging by the horrified stares each of her colleagues levied on her face, Sam deduced her injury was getting more spectacular looking by the minute. Great.

When McBride and Tyrone saw her dad in the room, Sam watched the partners exchange uneasy glances. *Oh, for fuck's sake*, Sam thought. What was that about? Sam wished she had time to dig into that situation, but right now their focus had to be on the Kavanaugh case.

"Do you want me to go?" Skip asked.

The question pained her. Of course she didn't want him to go. Without him, she never would've suspected Melissa was the one behind the killing spree earlier in the year. He was an invaluable member of her team, and he knew it. "No, I don't want you to leave."

Tuned in to the tension between father and daughter, Freddie raised a questioning eyebrow.

"I'll be in the waiting room if you need me," Celia said on her way out of the crowded cubicle.

"Hope you all had a good weekend," Sam said to her detectives. She took the dry-erase board Jeannie McBride handed her and launched into an update on the facts of the case, making notes on the board as she went. It was much smaller than her usual murder board, but it would do for now.

"Lindsey reported in early this morning." Freddie produced the medical examiner's report and handed it to Sam.

She took a quick scan. "Cause of death was manual strangulation. No sign of sexual assault. Lindsey was able to retrieve DNA samples from under Victoria Kavanaugh's fingernails, which she has sent to the lab for analysis." Sam was glad to know Victoria had fought for her life. "Doesn't give us much to work with, but at least there's hope we'll get a hit on the DNA."

"We never get that lucky," Freddie said.

"Where is SVU on the search for the baby?" Sam asked.

"Following up on all the tips that came in after the alert was issued," Gonzo said, "but nothing yet."

"If we find Victoria's killer," Sam said, "I bet we'll find the baby." Whether or not Maeve would still be alive by then was anyone's guess.

"First," Lindsey McNamara said from the doorway, "we need to figure out who exactly was killed yesterday."

The medical examiner's statement caught the attention of everyone in the room. Her long, red hair was pulled into the ponytail she wore to work, and her green eyes zeroed in on Sam. "Ouch."

"Forget about that," Sam said. "What're you talking about?"

"As a matter of routine, I run the prints of every victim through AFIS," Lindsey said of the Automated Fingerprint Identification System. "Our victim's prints came back with a hit for a Denise Desposito."

Sam's blood zinged through her veins as she processed what Lindsey was saying and absorbed the implications for the case—and for Derek.

"Desposito has a long criminal record, mostly fraud—Medicare, Social Security, Medicaid. She's been involved with one fraud after another and was finally put away for a long stretch about six years ago after the Feds cracked a scheme in Ohio. She basically defrauded the government for a living."

"Wait," Freddie said. "If our vic is Denise Desposito and she was put away for a long stretch six years ago, how is it possible that she was married and had a kid in that time?"

"She didn't," Lindsey said. "Thirty-six-year-old Desposito was killed in a fight in prison a month after she was sent away."

Sam exhaled a long, deep breath. "What the hell?" She shook her head in disbelief. "So our victim isn't Victoria Taft Kavanaugh, which explains why there was practically no sign of her online, and even though her prints match up with Denise Desposito, she's not her either?"

"That's right," Lindsey said.

"Then who the hell is she?"

SEVEN

"Everybody out," Dr. Anderson said a few minutes later when he returned with another doctor.

Sam and her team were still processing what Lindsey had told them.

"Cruz," Sam said, "go to Calahan Rice on K Street and find out everything you can about the woman who'd been known there as Victoria Taft. Gonzo, you and Arnold track down Felicity Rider, maid of honor in the Kavanaugh's wedding."

"What can we do?" McBride asked.

"You can get out so we can sew her up," Anderson said.

"See if you can track down a Victoria Taft from Defiance, Ohio," Sam said, ignoring the doctor. "Parents are Greg and Betty."

"Got it," McBride said, writing down the info.

"I'll be at HQ as soon as I'm done here. Meet me there."

"That's it," Anderson said, ushering the others from the cubicle. "Everyone out."

"My parents can stay," Sam said, suddenly filled with anxiety as the plastic surgeon approached and introduced himself as Dr. Simsbury. As they prepped her for the procedure, she wished she'd allowed Nick to come after all. While Celia offered a comforting and steady presence, no one could take his place.

"A quick pinch to numb you up," Simsbury said when he came at her face with a freakishly long needle.

It took every ounce of self-control Sam could muster not to scream or grab his arm to stop him—if she broke his arm in the process that would be fine too. The "quick pinch" burned like a fucking bastard, sending tears spilling from her eyes.

"You're almost there, honey," Celia said, squeezing Sam's hand.

"One more," Simsbury said.

This time Sam closed her eyes so she wouldn't have to watch the needle come toward her. It burned no less the second time around. She broke into a cold sweat and forced air into her lungs by sheer will.

"We're going to give you something to calm you down, Sam," Anderson said. "Your heart rate is through the roof."

Her eyes flew open. "No!" The medicine that would calm her would also ruin the rest of her day, and she couldn't afford to be muzzy around the edges today. Plus, it would require more needles. "Give me the goddamn stitches and get me out of here."

"This is going to take a while," Simsbury said. "You may as well get comfortable."

Sam wanted to take his head off. Did he really think she was going to get *comfortable* while he was sewing her face closed? But because the argument would take time she didn't have, she bit her tongue and closed her eyes to get "comfortable."

The next thing she knew, Celia was shaking her awake. "Sam? Honey, they're done."

What the hell? Did she sleep through the stitches? "What did they give me?"

"Nothing. You fell asleep."

"That's one for the record books." At least her face didn't hurt anymore. That was something anyway. "What time is it?"

"Noon."

Groaning, Sam sat up too fast, and a head rush overtook her. Celia's hands on her shoulders steadied her.

"You need to take it slow, honey. You've had a shock and lost a lot of blood. You're apt to be a bit woozy for the rest of the day."

"Great. Where's Dad?" The earlier disagreement with her dad came rushing back to remind her she had yet another matter to attend to today.

"In the waiting room. He couldn't bear to watch them sew up your face."

"Can you guys drop me at HQ?"

"I suppose there's no chance of talking you into taking the rest of the day off, is there?" Celia asked.

"No chance in hell."

"You can't leave until they discharge you with pain meds you're going to need when the numbness wears off."

"They've got five minutes, and then I'm outta here."

"You're a pain in the rear, you know that?"

"I hear that a lot."

Chuckling, Celia left the cubicle to go find the doctors while Sam looked around for her clothes. Her bloodstained jeans were on a chair in the room, but no sign of her shirt or bra. "Um, hello," she called into the hallway. "Where's my shirt?"

A nurse came in a minute later carrying a set of scrubs.

"Where's my stuff?"

"Ruined."

Damn it, Sam thought, she'd liked that shirt. She had

few enough clothes after the slashing incident that losing something she liked was a bummer. "What am I supposed to do for a bra?"

The nurse shrugged. "That's up to you."

Sam muttered at the nurse's back as she left the room. Since she couldn't very well go braless at HQ, and it was too damned hot to wear a sweatshirt, she was forced to go home and change before she went to work. This day was so fucked up! She wondered if someone had at least taken her car to HQ. Hopefully, Freddie had seen to that. "Change of plans," she said when Celia returned with Dr. Anderson in tow. "I need to go home before work."

"No problem. We'll take you wherever you need to go."

As Anderson launched into an exhaustive list of follow-up procedures, Sam rolled a hand in the air to move things along. "Cut to the chase, Doc. I gotta run."

His lips firmed with displeasure. "Cover it for the first forty-eight hours, and then keep it clean."

"I'll look after it," Celia assured him.

"Prescription for painkillers," he said, handing the slip to Sam, "and a follow-up appointment in two weeks with Dr. Simsbury that you will want to keep."

"Great, thanks." Sam grabbed the papers from him and made for the door, ignoring the swimming sensation in her head. "Later."

"See you soon," Anderson said with a mocking smile that earned him the bird from Sam.

FREDDIE TOOK THE stairs to the second-floor office building and followed the directions to the Calahan Rice offices. Inside the smoked-glass door, the reception area boasted the logos of each of the American auto companies with a buy-American banner above them.

Subtle, he thought.

"May I help you?" the dark-haired receptionist asked, giving him a not-so-subtle once-over. Ever since he'd started sleeping with Elin, other women seemed far more interested in him than they'd ever been before. Could they tell somehow that he was finally having sex, and lots of it? Didn't matter. Elin was the only one he wanted to have sex with, and it was better if he didn't think about her or having sex with her in the middle of his workday.

"Detective Cruz." He flashed his badge. "MPD. I'm looking for some information about a former employee named Victoria Taft."

"I've only been here a year, so I haven't heard of her. Let me get our managing partner. She'll be able to help you. She's been here forever."

"Thank you." While he waited, Freddie took a seat in the comfortable waiting room, picked up a sports magazine and flipped through the coverage of the D.C. Federals' magical season. The entire city was riveted by the young team's first winning season. Last year, the team had stooped to giving away tickets to get people to the ballpark. This year, tickets were hard to come by.

A cool blonde in a black power suit and sky-high heels strode into the reception area. "Detective Cruz?"

Freddie put down the magazine and stood. "Yes." He showed her his badge.

She took a good long look at it. "I'm Susan Jacobson, the managing partner. What can I do for you?"

"I'm looking for some information about a former employee."

"Victoria Taft."

"Yes."

Her composure wavered a bit. "I heard that she'd been killed and wondered if the police would come here."

"This was her last place of employment before her marriage."

"I know. I was at her wedding. Come on back."

Freddie followed her to a spacious office at the end of a long corridor. On the way, they passed numerous offices where staff members were hunched over computers or on the phone. Whenever he saw people working in offices, he was grateful for a job he loved. While at times unbearably stressful and dangerous and sad, it was also exhilarating and deeply satisfying—and it kept him on the streets and out of offices that looked like this one. "Busy place," he said.

"Yes, especially since the auto industry bailouts. We've got a lot on our plates ensuring that Congress continues to support the American autoworkers."

"A worthwhile task, it would seem."

"We think so," she said, seeming pleased by his comment.

Susan gestured for him to take a seat in one of her visitor chairs. "Because I thought we might hear from the police, I pulled Victoria's personnel record." She handed him a thin manila folder.

A quick perusal showed a printout of an online application, a recommendation from an Ohio congressman, a commendation from Ford for her participation on a project and Victoria's letter of resignation.

"There isn't much," Susan said, "but she was a good worker. Dedicated and professional. We were grooming her for bigger and better things when she met Derek Kavanaugh. Naturally, we understood that she couldn't continue her employment here when her husband's boss was running for president."

"What did you know of her personal life, beyond her relationship with Mr. Kavanaugh?"

"Not much, to be honest. I worked with her for almost a year, but it occurred to me only today, after I heard about what'd happened, that I didn't know her all that well. You know how some people have one persona for work and another outside of work?"

Freddie nodded, even though the people he worked with tended to be more or less the same whether at work or not.

"She didn't talk much about her life away from the office until she met Derek. It was obvious to all of us that she was quite taken with him."

"So she never said anything about her personal life, and then suddenly she's a sharer?"

"It wasn't so much that she was sharing the details as it was hard for her to hide that she was falling in love with him. Whenever one of us mentioned his name, her face turned bright red. That kind of thing."

"So it seemed to be a genuine love match?"

"Oh, yes, definitely. Anyone who attended that wedding left with no doubt they'd make a go of it."

"Would you mind making a copy of her file for me?"

"Of course not." Susan buzzed for an assistant and asked her to make the copies. While they waited, she said, "You're Sam Holland's partner, aren't you?"

"That's right."

"What's she like in person?"

"Much like she is in the media," Freddie said hesitantly. Sam's notoriety had skyrocketed after her marriage to Nick, and Freddie went out of his way to guard her privacy. "She's a great boss and friend."

"Seems like she would be. I admire them both very much."

"So do I."

The assistant returned with the copies, and Freddie rose to leave. "I appreciate your help." He handed her his card. "If you think of anything else that might be relevant to the investigation, my number is on there."

"I'll let you know," she said with a warm smile that melted her cool façade. "I hope you find the person who did this to Victoria, and find her sweet baby too."

It dawned on Freddie all at once that she was looking at him with what might've been interest. "We're doing everything we can."

"I'll walk you out."

"That's all right," he said, hoping to discourage whatever she might be thinking. "I can find my way. Thanks again."

He had an uneasy feeling she was watching him as he headed for the exit.

FELICITY RIDER WORKED as a legislative aide in the Capitol Hill offices of Senate Minority Leader William Stenhouse.

"Why do I know this guy's name?" Arnold asked Gonzo.

"Other than the fact that he's the number two guy in the Senate, you mean?" Gonzo asked his young partner, who was often a bit of a dunderhead.

"Well, duh. I know that much."

"He was on Sam's short list of suspects when Senator O'Connor was murdered," Gonzo said as they entered the Hart Senate Office Building. "He and the first Senator O'Connor were bitter enemies for decades. So when John O'Connor turned up dead the night before his first big bill was up for a vote, Graham O'Connor suspected Stenhouse. Graham said Stenhouse would rather see Graham's son dead than have any success in the Senate."

"It's all coming back to me now."

In Stenhouse's vast office suite, they flashed their badges and asked for Felicity at the reception desk. They were shown to a conference room where pictures, plaques and mementos from the Missouri senator's illustrious career decorated every inch of wall space.

"Guy's got a big opinion of himself," Arnold muttered.

"Don't they all?"

"Nick doesn't."

"True." Their boss's husband had come from humble roots, and Gonzo couldn't imagine Nick's prestigious job ever going to his head the way it clearly had with Stenhouse.

Felicity came into the room several minutes later. Tall and attractive with brown hair and eyes, she seemed frazzled and unnerved to be meeting with cops.

After they produced their badges and introduced themselves, Gonzo asked her to have a seat at the table.

"This is about Victoria," Felicity said in a dull, flat-sounding tone.

Gonzo nodded. "You were a close friend?"

"At one time, yes. I can't believe she's dead. I'm still absorbing the shock."

"We're sorry for your loss," Gonzo said. "It would help to hear how the two of you met and anything you can tell us that might be pertinent to the investigation."

"I haven't seen her in a couple of years. How did you even know about me?"

"You were listed as the maid of honor at her wedding. We assumed you were close friends."

"*Were* is the key word. Once she married Derek, we didn't see much of each other."

A glance at her left hand showed it lacked wedding rings. "And that upset you?"

She shrugged. "Sure it did at first, but it happens. A lot of women forget about their single friends once they're happily married. Wasn't the first time it's happened to me, or the last."

"When was the last time you saw her?" Gonzo asked.

"At the baby shower Derek's mother had for her about a year and a half ago."

"What can you tell us about her life before she lived in Washington?" Arnold asked.

"Not much. She was from Ohio, but her parents were dead. No siblings. I remember feeling sorry for her when we first met because she didn't have any family. She spent a couple of Christmases with my family, but then she met Derek, and that was that."

"The real thing?" Gonzo asked.

"Oh, for sure. She was mad over him from day one. It took weeks for him to ask her out. I thought she'd go crazy waiting on him. She was about to ask him when he finally worked up the nerve. He was very handsome and sweet. I could see why she was so into him. She was also attracted to the fact that he was successful, which was important to her."

"How so?"

"She always said she wanted to be a stay-at-home mom when she had her family. While a lot of women these days go out of their way to maintain a career and a family, she had old-fashioned values about being home with her kids. Marriage to him would ensure she'd be able to do that."

"Can you tell us who some of her other friends were at that time and where we might find them?"

"Caroline Horan was one. I believe she works at a PR firm on Mass Ave. Leslie Newman was another. Last I knew, she was an event planner at the Willard. Victoria met them both at the yoga studio she frequented."

"Do you happen to know if they were still in touch with her?"

"I really don't. They were her friends, not mine."

"You've been very helpful." Gonzo handed her his card. "If you think of anything else, please get in touch."

She took the card from him. "Do you think you'll find the baby before…"

"We're doing everything we can," Gonzo said.

Nodding, Felicity preceded them out of the conference room.

AFTER THIS CASE was closed, Agent Avery Hill decided as he drove from Herndon to the District, he was requesting a transfer out of the D.C. area. Some time in Phoenix or San Diego would be the thing to get him back on level ground and return his focus to what he cared about most in life—his career.

He'd been off track and out of whack for months, ever since he'd come face-to-face with Lt. Sam Holland and had the kind of instantaneous reaction to a woman he'd heard about but never before experienced. After pursuing petite, perky blondes for most of his adult life, it had been jarring to suddenly discover at thirty-eight that he actually preferred a tall, mouthy, ballsy, brave, irritating, flat-out gorgeous woman with honey-colored hair that spilled down her back in a riot of curls when she released it from the clip she used to contain it at work.

He'd learned he preferred pale blue eyes that ran the gamut from shrewd to suspicious to frigid when she looked at him—the dreaded interloper on her precious turf—to fiery hot when she looked at her beloved husband.

Any time he was near her, Avery found it nearly impossible to take his eyes off her, something her new and famously devoted husband had tuned into awfully fast last night.

Avery had spent a distressing amount of time over the last few months thinking about her, reading about her and basically acting like a besotted middle school boy in the throes of a first crush. When he'd received the call about Victoria Kavanaugh's murder and been asked to consult with Sam on the case, Avery had wanted to whimper and cheer at the same time. First, he'd thought, *Oh God, I have to see her again,* which quickly morphed into, *Thank God, I get to see her again!*

On his way from Quantico to the District late on Sunday afternoon, he'd tried to prepare himself to see her. Maybe what'd happened before had been a weird one-time reaction that would've passed in the ensuing months. He was a rational guy who prided himself on an abundance of self-control. He'd made a career out of being cool and logical and patient and all the things that made for an effective agent.

Nothing about his reaction to the brassy lieutenant had been cool or logical. And then to realize she was the one who'd famously—and recently—married the senator… He blew out a deep breath as he recalled the moment he'd put two and two together to get that she was permanently off-limits. That had thrown him for a loop, and he hadn't quite recovered his legendary mojo since then.

A quick glance at her face the night before had cemented his doom. It hadn't been a random one-time thing. It had been a life-altering reaction that wouldn't change no matter how many times he saw her. And now to be thrown back into a case with her right when he'd reached the point where he didn't think about her every minute of every day anymore... Well, that was damned unfair.

The cosmic joke of it all wasn't lost on him. He, who'd never had any trouble getting any woman he wanted, was gone over one he could not only never have but who couldn't stand the sight of him. It would've been laughable if it hadn't been so bloody pathetic.

Thus his desire to transfer out of the area to ensure he'd never have to see her again when they closed the Kavanaugh case.

After spending the morning with a ragged-looking Derek Kavanaugh at his parents' Herndon home, Hill had nothing much to add to the ongoing investigation. They'd gone over everything Kavanaugh had worked on in the last year, touching on issues that might be controversial or polarizing, but nothing stood out as a motive for murder or kidnapping.

As he drove to HQ and mulled over the interview with Kavanaugh, he caught the news at the top of the hour, which was the first he'd heard about Sam's heroics that morning.

"Jesus," he whispered when he realized how close she'd come to being shot or worse. The radio announcer mentioned a video of the incident from the store that had "already gone viral" and wondered what Sam would think of that. "What does it matter what she thinks?" he said out loud. "She's nothing to you, and she never will be. Time to get real, buddy."

But even as he said the words, he knew he wouldn't rest until he saw with his own eyes that she was truly okay.

THE FIRST THING Sam noticed when Celia pulled into the parking lot at HQ was the horde of reporters gathered outside the main entrance. "Would you mind taking me around the corner to the morgue entrance?" Sam hated to ask because Celia had left Skip at home alone for the twenty minutes it would take to drive Sam to work and return home. Neither of them wanted him alone any longer than necessary.

"No problem."

"Thanks. Anything to avoid the vultures."

Celia laughed at that. "So what was going on between you and your father earlier?"

"Nothing. Why?"

"Don't bullshit me, Sam Cappuano. Spill it."

Stunned by her stepmother's rare curse, Sam said, "He's mad because I didn't tell him about an old investigation of his that I reopened when he was in the hospital earlier this year."

"The Fitzgerald case?"

"Yeah," Sam said, surprised again. "You know about that?"

"Of course I do. He used to talk about it a lot when he was still working. Before…"

Their lives were divided evenly in half—before the shooting and after. "I always forget you two were secretly dating before he was shot."

Celia's pretty round face flamed with color as it always did when this topic came up. "We were going to tell you girls. Eventually."

"I don't blame you for keeping it to yourselves for as long as you could," Sam said, thinking of the bombs her ex-husband had attached to her car and Nick's, which had blown the lid off their secret relationship. "Once everyone knows, it changes things."

"Yes, it does. Your dad was still very raw over what'd happened with your mother, even though that was years before we met. It'd left him bitter."

Sam thought of something her sister Tracy had said a few months ago about there being two sides to the story of what'd happened with their parents. They hadn't discussed it since. While Sam was fine with not knowing her mother's side of the story, Tracy's comment rankled nonetheless. She didn't want to be curious, but she was, and at some point she needed to ask her sister what she'd meant.

Sam hadn't seen or talked to her mother in more than five years. After her wedding, she'd received a card indicating her mother would like to see her and meet Nick. The overture had been on Sam's mind in recent months, but she'd yet to act on it. "Anyway, Dad is mad I didn't tell him we took another look at Fitzgerald."

"I take it Joe told him?"

"Yes," Sam said, feeling guilty all over again. "We didn't uncover anything new, so I didn't think to mention it to him."

"Especially since he'd already told you once to leave it alone."

Shocked, Sam looked over at her stepmother. "You know about that too?"

"I know that on the day he was shot, you two had a rare disagreement, and it was about the Fitzgerald case. The last time I talked to him before he was shot he told me he'd had words with you over it."

For days afterward, when they'd been uncertain he would survive the shooting, Sam had been convinced her last words to her father would be angry ones. "Why do you suppose he's so adamant about me leaving it alone?"

"Maybe you should ask him that, huh?"

"Do you know why?"

"Nope. But something about that case nags at him. He's never said what it is."

"Failing to find the killer of a little boy would nag at any detective, long after he was out of uniform."

"True, but I've always suspected it's something more than the failure to close the case." Celia pulled up to the morgue entrance. "There you are, my dear. If you give me the prescription for the pain meds, I'll drop it off on the way home. You can pick it up later."

Even though Sam had no intention of picking up medication that would make her groggy and useless, she didn't have time to argue. She handed the paper to her stepmother. "Thanks. For everything. I don't know what I ever did without you."

"Aw, honey." Celia leaned over the console to give Sam a quick hug. "Be careful, will you please? Your father suffers whenever you get hurt. And so do I."

Touched, Sam gave her a kiss on the cheek. "Will do. See you later."

EIGHT

Sam hustled inside and jogged through the hallways and passageways that led to the pit where her detectives were gathered around a computer.

"Play it again," she heard Gonzo say. "Whoa, right there, look at that!"

"Totally awesome," Cruz said. "The guy has no idea what hit him."

"Badass," Arnold said.

On tiptoes, Sam looked over her partner's shoulder. The convenience-store encounter played on the screen. As the gun made contact with her face, she winced along with the others. "All right, everyone. Show's over."

They nearly jumped out of their collective skins when they realized she'd joined them, which of course gave her a thrill. She liked to keep them jumping. "In the conference room. Five minutes."

"Holy crap," Freddie said when he saw her face. "It's even more colorful than it was before."

McBride recoiled and turned away, as if she couldn't bear to look.

Once again, Sam thought of her plans for the evening. Disappointing her husband was never high on her to-do list, which was why she was determined to attend that fundraiser even if she looked like something out of a horror movie.

As she headed for her office to check her e-mail before

the meeting, Agent Hill came into the pit and zeroed in on her. His heated stare burned a hole right through her. What was that all about? The guy's quiet intensity made her uncomfortable.

"You're all right?" he asked as he came up to her, his sharp eyes taking a full inventory that only added to the discomfort.

"Perfectly fine and itching to get back to work. We're meeting in five minutes in the conference room." She went into her office and shut the door to discourage him from following her, since her better judgment was telling her to stay far, far away from the sexy agent.

Shaking off the encounter, she fired up her computer and did a quick scan of her e-mail, which included a response from Bryn Mawr that said, "Lt. Holland, We were unable to find a match for the student you inquired about. Perhaps she was here under a different name during that period? If you can provide additional information, we'd be happy to assist in your investigation." The message was hardly a surprise after what Lindsey had uncovered, but it was further confirmation that everything from Victoria's name to her fingerprints to her college degree had been fabricated. Why? That was the question of the day.

Also included in her e-mails was one from Nick. "Hey, babe. How's my favorite pretty face? Not too banged up, I hope." Sam cringed, imaging what he'd say when he saw the mess on her formerly pretty face. They hadn't yet invented the makeup that could cover the disaster she'd seen with a quick glance in the mirror at home. Despite her determination to attend, he'd probably beg her to sit out the fundraiser so she wouldn't scare away his supporters.

"Anyway," he'd continued, "you asked about my impressions of Derek and Victoria, so here you go." Sam did a quick scan of the message, printed it out and took it with her to the meeting. He'd ended with, "Can't wait to see you later and kiss it better. Love you."

Buoyed by his sweet love, she sent him a quick text to let him know she was fine and back to work. She ended it with, "See you at 6," so he'd know she hadn't forgotten their plans. She'd let him decide when he saw the carnage whether or not he wanted her with him.

Sam was the last one to step into the conference room. As she was about to start the meeting, Chief Farnsworth walked in with Captain Malone in tow.

Farnsworth took an up-close look at her battered face. "That was some fine work this morning, Lieutenant."

"Thank you, sir. Right place, right time."

"I'm sure your face would disagree."

"I told you it was gruesome, Chief," Malone added.

"Shit happens," Sam said, anxious to get on with it. She hated being the center of attention.

"I see a commendation in your future," Farnsworth said.

"Oh, well, um, thanks?" One of these days, she'd learn how to take a compliment.

Farnsworth rolled his eyes and headed to his usual post in the back of the room.

Relieved to be off the hot seat, Sam said, "Cruz, you're up first, then Gonzo, Hill and McBride. Let's hear what you've got."

The others reported in, and Sam listened intently to each detail while she stewed over the biggest detail of all—that Victoria Taft Kavanaugh's entire life up to the point where she met and married Derek Kavanaugh had been a lie. She hated that she'd soon have to share that tidbit with the federal agent who kept his gaze set on her while the others reported.

Why did he do that? Hadn't his mother taught her smooth Southern gentleman that it was rude to stare at other people?

"Hill," she said brusquely, "it's to you. What've you got that you can share with us lowly detectives who lack top-secret security clearances?"

"Not much of anything," he said in that honeyed accent that once might've set her heart to pitter-pattering, before another man had taken ownership of her heart and soul, leaving no room for anyone else. Hill gave a brief rundown of his morning with Derek Kavanaugh, detailing the legislation Kavanaugh had worked on as well as the congressional members and staff he'd clashed with on the president's behalf.

"How many people are we talking about?"

"Five," Hill said.

"Give us a list," Sam said. "Bears looking into."

"You read my mind." Hill handed over the page he'd prepared in advance.

"Thanks," Sam muttered, gesturing for Freddie to take possession of Hill's list. "I asked Nick to share anything he could think of that might tell us more about Derek and Victoria, their wedding, etcetera. But I don't see anything in his message that we don't already know."

Sam stood and used a dry-erase marker to establish a timeline of Victoria's life, beginning with her start date at Calahan Rice, one of the few things Sam knew for sure about her.

"She met Kavanaugh thirty days later," Hill said, consulting his notes. "At the gym he'd frequented for many

years by then. They began a friendly flirtation but he
didn't ask her out for another month."

Sam used a magnet to place a photo of Victoria alive
next to the image from the morgue contained in Lindsey's report.

"What we also know is the woman in these photo-
graphs is not Victoria Taft Kavanaugh."

Hill, Farnsworth and Malone all spoke at once.

"What do you mean?" Farnsworth said.

"Who is she, then?" Malone asked.

Hill's amiable expression turned furious in the blink of
an eye. At least he wasn't staring at her with that heated
look anymore. "When were you going to tell me this?"

"I was getting to it."

"Explain," Farnsworth said.

Sam filled them in on what Lindsey had discovered as
well as the e-mail from Bryn Mawr, indicating that they'd
had no student named Victoria Taft in the years leading
up to the date on the degree that hung in Victoria's home.

"We found no record of a Greg or Betty Taft in Defiance, Ohio," Jeannie said. "I also ran a check on the
Social Security number that was on record at the Department of Motor Vehicles."

"Good thinking," Sam said, thrilled to see her friend
and detective engrossed again in her work after surviv-
ing an egregious abduction and sexual assault earlier in
the year. "What'd you find out?"

"The number was registered to a William Eldridge,"
Jeannie said. "Records show he died about eight years
ago at the age of fifty-six. I found an obituary in the *Post*
that confirms the date of death."

"So not only did someone screw with AFIS, but we've

got Social Security fraud going on here too?" Hill asked, rising and resting his hands on lean hips.

"What I want to know is why the goddamned DMV requires Social Security numbers for people to get licenses but never bothers to check them," Sam said.

"That's honestly your most pressing question?" Hill asked.

Unused to being questioned by any member of her team, Sam immediately began to seethe. "What I mean, Agent Hill, is that if the DMV had bothered to check, we might've uncovered this scheme or whatever it is years before a woman was murdered and her baby kidnapped."

"There's no way we can ignore the fact that this has to be connected in some way to her husband's work," Hill said.

"If you're so sure about that, find the connection," Sam shot back.

They engaged in a stare down that was broken only when Gonzo cleared his throat.

Sam looked away from the aggravating agent, unnerved by the confrontation. "I don't disagree that his work is the obvious tie-in," she conceded, anxious to get back on track.

"Because he has a security clearance, his wife would've been investigated at some point," Hill said.

"If the investigation was handled properly, all of this would've come out then."

The statement hung in the air for a charged moment of silence as everyone in the room pondered the consequences.

"So you're saying the investigator was probably in on whatever scheme they were running," Sam said, trying to wrap her mind around the potential magnitude of the fraud.

Hill shrugged. "I suppose we'll find that out when we dig a little deeper."

"Who handles the background-check investigations?" Gonzo asked.

"The Defense Security Service oversees them, but they often use investigators from NCIS, the FBI and other federal agencies."

"Can you get the name of the investigator who did Victoria's background check?"

"I'll work on that," Hill said. "But in the meantime, someone has to tell Mr. Kavanaugh what we've learned about his wife."

All eyes turned to Sam. Her heart literally ached at the thought of having to tell Derek that the woman he'd loved had lied to him about everything—even who she was.

"Cruz and I will do it," she said.

"Great," her partner said under his breath, earning him a glare from her.

Lt. Archelotta from the IT division stepped into the room. As the only fellow officer Sam had ever been romantically involved with, his presence always caused her a moment of anxiety. This time was no different, and she noticed that Hill picked up on the vibe. Of course he did.

"I heard you were meeting on the Kavanaugh case," Archie said, handing her a sheaf of papers. Tall and handsome with dark hair, he'd been exactly what she needed after her split from Peter. "Here're the reports on the last thirty days of calls into and out of the vic's phone."

"Thanks for the quick work," Sam said, handing the reports to Gonzo.

"I'll let you get back to it," Archie said with a jaunty wave on the way out the door.

"Before we adjourn, no one is to breathe a word of what we know about Victoria Kavanaugh," Sam said. "Until we have a better handle on what exactly we're dealing with, we need to keep a tight lid on this investigation. Do I make myself clear?"

The other detectives in the room acknowledged her with nods and murmurs in the affirmative.

"I'll tolerate no leaks," Farnsworth added. "Keep your mouths shut."

"Gonzo, Arnold, McBride and Tyrone, divide up the phone logs and get to work," Sam said. "Cruz, you're with me."

"And where am I?" Hill asked with the condescending edge to his voice that grated on Sam's nerves.

"I don't know, Agent Hill. Where are you?"

"He's with you too," Farnsworth said. "Take him with you to tell Kavanaugh what you've uncovered about his wife."

"Three's a crowd," Sam said.

"Then leave Cruz here to help with the phone logs," the chief said sternly. "The quicker we wade through that data, the faster we might find out who this woman really was. Maybe then we'll find her killer—and her daughter." With a devilish twinkle in his eye, the chief added, "And before you go to Herndon, you need to update the press. They're clamoring for information about the foiled robbery and your condition. They missed their promised seven a.m. briefing, so they're extra ravenous, not to mention hot and bothered after waiting all day for you."

Sam bit back a moan at the idea of facing off with the reporters.

The others filed out of the room, leaving her alone with the agent who stared at her. This day kept getting better.

"Since I know where we're going and have two working eyes, I'll drive," Hill said.

"Both my eyes work fine."

He tilted his head for a better look at her face. "Um, okay, whatever you say. I'm still driving."

"Fine! Drive! Ask me if I care! I need to get some food, and then we can go."

"I need some fuel too, so we'll eat on the way. Let's go."

Sam had a sneaking suspicion her husband would be extremely unhappy to know she'd be spending the next few hours alone with Agent Hill. It would probably be best for everyone if she "forgot" to mention that to Nick. As she walked into her office to retrieve her wallet and keys, the numbness in her face began to wear off.

Rooting around in her top desk drawer, she found a bottle of ibuprofen and downed three of them using one of the half-filled bottles of water her husband had aligned like tin soldiers on the left side of her desk. He was such a freak show, but she loved him anyway.

"Ready?" Hill said from the door.

"As ready as I'll ever be to truly ruin the life of someone who thought his life was already ruined."

THE FIRST NICK heard about the video of Sam's altercation was from Graham O'Connor when he called to check in about the evening's fundraiser.

"It's all over the news," Graham said.

Holding the phone to his ear, Nick strolled out of his office toward the bank of televisions in the conference room that were tuned to the cable news shows. Graham wasn't kidding when he said the video was all over the airwaves. It played on every screen. Riveted, he watched Sam approach the guy from behind right as the gunman's arm swung back, catching her square in the face with the gun.

Thankfully, she never missed a beat. A shudder rippled through Nick as he realized what a freakishly close call it had been. Often he was left to his own imagination to picture how these things went down. This time, he got to see it for himself. He preferred his imagination.

"Nick? Are you still there?"

With a shake of his head, he forced his gaze off the televisions and returned to his office, but the sick feeling remained. She'd taken one hell of a hit that she'd played down in her retelling of the incident. "Yeah," he said to Graham. "I'm here."

"Is Sam okay?"

"She says she's fine." It had taken all the fortitude he could muster to stay away from the emergency room when everything in him pulled him toward her—as always. "A plastic surgeon stitched up her face, and she's back to work now."

"We'd totally understand if she can't make it tonight."

While Nick knew he was being completely irrational, the thought of going without her irritated him. He never asked her to support his work. Everything in their lives was about her work, her cases, her investigations. As soon as he had the thoughts, he regretted them. She was hurt, for crying out loud. She'd saved numerous lives, including her own. What right did he have to be angry that her injuries might mess up his big night? But was he wrong to want his wife with him for an important event in his career? "I guess that'll be up to her," he said to Graham. "If she feels up to it. I'll let you know as soon as I hear."

"No need. If she's there, she's there. If not, everyone will understand."

"I feel bad. We set this up months in advance."

"Don't apologize. We certainly know better than most people how unpredictable her job can be."

"That's good of you. Thanks for understanding."

"No thanks needed. So, there's something I need to talk to you about. I was hoping to do it tonight, but it'll probably be too crazy."

"What's going on?"

"I got a call from Halliwell," Graham said of the new Democratic National Committee chair. Halliwell had replaced Mitchell Sanborn after Sanborn's arrest earlier in the year. "He wanted my take on what you'd think about doing the keynote at the convention."

Nick was rendered speechless. By putting him front and center at the convention, they'd be setting him up for a White House run in the next election. The DNC had expressed their interest in the past, but this would make his heir-apparent status official. "What did you tell him?"

"I suggested he speak to you directly," Graham said with a laugh. "You certainly don't need me behind the scenes pulling the strings anymore. Back in the day, I would've killed for your approval ratings. They're grooming you, Nick. You get that, don't you?"

"I've never won an election in my life, and they're grooming me for the top job," Nick said, amused and honored and astounded. And saddened. This should've been John's moment. Nick never lost sight of that.

After a long pause, Graham said, "You're thinking about John, aren't you?"

"Always."

"Me too. Last week, I started to pick up the phone to call him, and then I remembered… Whenever that happens, it takes me right back to that first awful day."

While Nick tried hard to never think about finding his best friend and boss murdered, it was also the day he'd reconnected with Sam years after a memorable one-night stand. That something so great could've come from such a heartbreaking event still astounded him. Nick set his gaze on the photo of John that he kept on the credenza. "I do the same thing. I find myself wanting to tell him something, to ask his opinion. Far more often than I care to confess."

Graham cleared the emotion from his throat.

"What'll you say to Halliwell?"

"I suppose that depends on when and if he asks."

"He will. You're their top choice. Apparently, Derek Kavanaugh was going to speak with you about it, but then his poor wife… Is there any sign of the baby?"

"Not that I've heard. Not yet anyway."

"Lord, what he must be going through."

"It's not pretty." Nick had heard from Harry at lunchtime that Derek was in worse shape today. As the hours dragged on with no word about Maeve, Derek's composure was shattering.

"It's a nightmare," Graham said, speaking from experience. "Anyway, about the convention…"

"If they ask me, I'll do it. Of course I will, but I want you and Laine to know that it never leaves my mind that all this should've been John's." This wasn't the first time Nick had worried that his adopted parents would think he was capitalizing on the opportunities their son's death had afforded him.

"We know, son. Of course we do. But we're so very proud of you too. I hope you know that."

"Thank you," Nick said in a hushed tone. It never got old to hear that the senator who meant so much to him, who'd taken an ambitious young man under his wing and given him a life he never could've imagined, was proud of him. "You don't know what that means to me."

"I can't wait to see you up there front and center at the convention. You'll blow them away. Even the Republicans will be lining up to vote for you."

The notion was so preposterous that Nick couldn't help but laugh. "Sure they will."

"Some kind of dogfight heating up for the general election, huh?"

"Sure is. The caucus is worried about Arnie," Nick said of the fabulously wealthy businessman, Arnold "Arnie" Patterson, who was running for president as an independent candidate. "The closer we get to the election, the more his support grows, and unlike Nelson and Rafael," Nick said of the incumbent president and his GOP rival, "Arnie is in no danger of running out of money in the home stretch."

"I can't imagine this country is ready for the likes of him," Graham said, his tone rife with distaste. "No one even knows how he really came by his money. Everything about him is shady."

"But he's giving the people what they want—promises of lower taxes, less government, a renewed focus on family values, a Christian with liberal leanings. He's an amalgamation of the best of both worlds, and that's attractive to a lot of voters."

"My fear is he's going to take enough of the support

away from Nelson that Rafael will get a cheap win," Graham said. "Halliwell said Nelson's camp is worried."

"A lot can happen between now and November," Nick said. "I've seen him on the stump, and I've noticed the loose-cannon element that worries his advisors. Look at how many staffers he's gone through since Memorial Day. I hear he has his sons running the show, so that provides some continuity."

"Word is if they don't agree with him, he replaces them. I bet he'd fire his own kids if they disagreed with him."

Nick laughed. "I ought to adopt that strategy. It would make for much quicker staff meetings, that's for sure."

"No kidding," Graham said, chuckling. "So Scotty will be in town soon, huh?"

"We're going to get him Sunday. Three whole weeks together. We can't wait."

"Bring him down to the farm to ride."

"I will.

"I'll see you tonight."

"Looking forward to it."

Nick hung up the phone and stared for a long time at the photo of John, thinking of their years together at Harvard, weekends with the O'Connors in Leesburg and working side by side during John's five years in office. For the first time in a while, he allowed in the grief and longing. Nick would happily give up his office and all the notoriety that went with it for one more day with his best friend.

SAM STEPPED OUT the main door of HQ and into madness. The questions flew at her in one big roar as cameras flashed. Her gruesome mug would be all over the front pages in the morning.

"What can you tell us about the robbery?"

"How many stitches did you get?"

"Is there any sign of Maeve Kavanaugh?"

"Will you interview the president?"

"Is Derek Kavanaugh a suspect?"

Sam held up her hands to quiet the crowd. When the questions continued to fly at her, she zeroed in on a light post in the parking lot behind them until they got the hint that she wouldn't say a word until they shut the hell up. It took a few more minutes, but they finally got the message.

"I'll give you a statement and then take some questions," she said. "The investigation into the murder of Victoria Kavanaugh and the apparent abduction of Maeve Kavanaugh is ongoing. Mr. Kavanaugh is not a suspect. I repeat, Derek Kavanaugh is not a suspect in the death of his wife or the abduction of his daughter." Even though she reemphasized the point, Derek's innocence would probably be buried under lurid sensationalism about a murder that touched the highest levels of the Nelson administration.

"We have no plans to speak to the president at this time, but he did confirm Mr. Kavanaugh's alibi for the time of the murder and kidnapping. He was with the president's senior team and campaign officials at a strategy session held at Camp David over the weekend." She paused, made eye contact with several of the more familiar reporters. "One more time for the hearing impaired— Mr. Kavanaugh is not a suspect."

Before they could shout more questions at her, Sam took a deep breath, praying the painkillers would kick in soon, because her face was starting to seriously hurt. "We ask your assistance in continuing to publish and broadcast the photos of Maeve Kavanaugh. SVU detectives are following up on every lead in the investigation into her disappearance."

"Do you have any persons of interest yet?" one of the Barbie-doll TV reporters asked. Sam could never remember their names. They all looked alike.

"We're following a number of leads."

"What can you tell us about the robbery this morning?" Darren Tabor asked.

"I'm sure you've seen the video." Sam shrugged, figuring the quicker she gave them what they wanted, the sooner she could get back to work. "I was buying a bagel, noticed the guy waving the gun around, texted my officers for backup and made my way to the front of the store, where I was able to neutralize the gunman. That's all there was to it."

"You left out the part where he pistol-whipped you in the face," someone shouted.

She gestured to the mess on her face. "I figured that part was pretty obvious."

A wave of laughter went through the crowd.

"How many stitches?"

"I wasn't counting."

"Has the senator seen your face?"

"Not yet," she said, and then immediately wanted to take back the words. She probably shouldn't have said that, because he'd come across as unfeeling for not rushing to the hospital. While the old Sam wouldn't have given a shit less what they thought, the new Sam had a politician husband who was in the midst of his first-ever campaign to protect.

"He was in hearings this morning," she said through gritted teeth. "Anything else?" Not giving them even half a second to respond, she said, "That's it for now," and nodded at Hill to follow her through the horde to the parking lot.

"I don't know how you can stand the constant scrutiny," Hill said when they were clear of the reporters.

"Part of my job," Sam said, uninterested in making small talk with the agent.

"I mean about your personal life."

She sent a glare his way that probably wasn't as effective as usual since half her face wasn't working properly at the moment. "I knew what I was getting into."

As they approached his nondescript sedan, he clicked the remote unlock button. "Hmm."

Sam slid into the passenger seat. "What's that supposed to mean?"

"All I said was 'hmm.'"

"People say that instead of what they really mean."

"Is that right?" he said in that drawl that'd probably left a trail of wet panties in his wake.

A minute later he pulled into a sub shop and they picked up sandwiches and sodas.

"What is your problem anyway?" Sam asked once they were under way again.

"I wasn't aware that I had a problem," he said, devouring a turkey sub as he drove them northwest through downtown traffic, on the way to Route 66 West.

Sam had gotten tuna thinking it would be easier to eat, but her face hurt too much to chew. "Didn't your mother ever tell you it's rude to stare?"

"What's that supposed to mean?"

"You stare. At me. All the time." Out of the corner of

her eye, she noticed a flush of color settle in his cheeks and wanted to laugh. The oh-so-cool agent blushed like a schoolgirl.

"I've heard about your considerable ego, Lieutenant, but trust me when I tell you I'm thinking about the case— and not you—when I'm supposedly staring at you."

For some reason, Sam didn't believe him. It was something more than that—something she would do well to leave alone despite her usual inclination to pick apart such things. "So you've heard my ego is considerable, huh?"

Hill laughed. "Figures you'd take that as a compliment."

"Why wouldn't I? I've had good reason to be cocky. Have you read about my case closure rate?"

Rolling his eyes, he said, "Who hasn't? Your face is in the paper more often than the president's these days."

"Now that is not true."

"Whatever you say. Let's talk about Derek Kavanaugh and how we're going to handle this meeting."

"Ugh, do we have to?"

"I suppose we do. You said last night that you know him socially?"

"He and Nick are friends. Have been for years. I've only known him since last Christmas, but we got together with them once in a while."

"What did you think of her?"

"There was nothing not to like about Victoria," Sam said. "Gorgeous and vivacious and stylish and quick to laugh. Very much in love with her husband and child, or so it seemed to us." Thinking about what they'd learned about the murdered woman had Sam questioning her every impression. "But who knows if she was an award-winning actress playing the part of the devoted wife when really she was part of a nefarious plot of epic proportions."

"People suck," Hill said, surprising her with his bluntness.

"Very often they do." Sam rested her head against the seat, suddenly exhausted. "Where do we even start with this one?"

Hill turned to her, agape. "Are you honestly asking my opinion?"

"Keep your eyes on the road and call it a momentary lapse in judgment brought on by intense pain."

"Is it bad?" he asked, sounding like he actually cared.

"It doesn't feel great. That's for sure." She reached for the visor and pulled it down for a look in the mirror. "Holy shit," she whispered. The entire right side of her face was purple and swollen with a strip of white bandage slashing horizontally across her cheek. Her right eye had been completely eclipsed by the swelling. "Wow, even more spectacular than the last time I looked." Once again she thought of the evening's fundraiser with a sinking feeling in the pit of her stomach and was sorry she'd looked.

"It does make a statement."

Sam couldn't help the gurgle of laughter that escaped despite her intention to remain aloof where he was concerned.

"Since you asked my humble opinion, I'd suggest we start with the people whose identities were ripped off. Hopefully Cruz and the others can get us some leads from the phone logs. And then there's the investigator who handled the background check. We've actually got quite a lot to go on."

"Yes, I guess we do." Watching the world whiz by through the passenger-side window, she said, "This is going to turn out to be a big deal, isn't it?"

"I fear you may be right, but it won't be your first time with big-deal investigations. In the last year alone, you've investigated murdered senators and Supreme Court nominees, brought down the speaker of the House, the chair of the DNC and a long-standing senator. I'd think this stuff would be old hat for you by now."

"How is it that you know everything about me, but I don't know the first thing about you?"

His smile was sexy and suggestive at the same time, making Sam instantly regret the question.

"What do you want to know?"

"Nothing. Forget I asked." Exchanging confidences with this particular man felt like cheating for some reason.

"I grew up in Charleston, South Carolina. Attended the Citadel. Did a stint as an Army Ranger and later in special ops. Got out after ten years and have been with the FBI ever since. That's pretty much the extent of the Special Agent Avery Hill story."

Something about the way he said that told Sam there was much more to the story, not that she'd ever take the time to dig deeper. That would bring her perilously close to a line she wouldn't cross with a gun to her head.

After a long period of silence, Hill navigated the exit for Herndon. "What's the plan with Kavanaugh?"

"I guess I'll tell it to him straight. In my experience, that's always the best way to handle these things."

"Agreed." Clearing his throat, he said, "So you'll be the one to tell it to him straight, correct?"

Sam snickered. "I got it, Hill. Don't worry yourself."

"I was thinking it might go down easier coming from a friend."

"I can't imagine there's any way this goes down easy."

"Yeah, I guess not. I feel sorry for the guy."

"So do I."

NINE

A SHORT TIME LATER, they pulled into a subdivision of neatly kept colonials, the kind of place where regular people raised their kids and grew old sitting on the front porch with their spouses. After a couple of turns, Hill parked behind a black BMW that Sam would recognize anywhere as her husband's car. "Perfect," she muttered to herself.

In addition to a predictable reaction to her injured face, Sam could only imagine what Nick would have to say about her showing up there with Hill. Bracing herself for the fireworks as well as the grim task she had ahead of her with Derek, Sam got out of the car and preceded Hill up the sidewalk.

Nick answered the door. "Fancy meeting you here." His expression softened at the sight of her battered face and then hardened when he got a look at her companion.

"Chief's orders," she said under her breath as he stepped aside to admit them. "What're you doing here anyway? I thought you had a town hall meeting."

"Not until four. Let me see your face." He took her by the hand and led her into a formal living room.

"I'll give you a minute," Hill said before he disappeared into the kitchen.

Nick brought her closer to the picture window and took a long, hard look at her face. "Nothing major, huh?"

"It looks worse than it feels," she said, playing it down as she always did.

"Somehow I doubt that." He pressed a gentle kiss to her forehead. "Did they give you something for the pain?"

"I haven't picked it up yet."

"Of course you haven't."

"I took some other pills. I'm fine. Really."

"Come here." He held out his arms to her, and she pressed her uninjured cheek to her favorite chest. She was determined to take one minute of the comfort only he could provide before she went in the other room and crushed Derek Kavanaugh into a thousand tiny pieces.

"Did you see the video?" she asked.

"What do you think?"

Sam would've cringed, but her face fought back. "Sorry. I hate that you had to see it."

"You were quite something, babe. Very impressive." In her ear, he added, "Very sexy."

Sam laughed out loud. "Only you."

"It'd better be only me."

"Oh, come on, Nick. Farnsworth made me bring him here. You know I don't want him around."

"I wish you could see the way he looks at you."

She had seen it but would never admit as much to her husband, because it would only upset him. "That's his problem. Let's not make it ours. Please? We've got enough on our plates without looking for trouble where there is none, okay?"

Grudgingly, or so it seemed to her, he nodded.

"I've got to go in there and talk to Derek. What I have to tell him is going to upset him greatly."

"More so than having his wife murdered and his daughter kidnapped?"

"Yes."

"Jesus."

"It's way, way out of regs for me to let you be in there for this, but if Hill agrees, I want you to hear it, because Derek will need the support of someone who knows what's going on."

"Okay," Nick said hesitantly.

Sam didn't blame him for the hesitance. She'd rather be anywhere but in the midst of Derek Kavanaugh's worst nightmare. "Give me a second to talk to Hill, and quit looking like you want to kill someone whenever his name is mentioned."

"If he steps one foot out of line with you, I want to know about it. Do you understand me?"

"Oh for God's sake, Nick! We're colleagues. Professionals."

"I don't care. I want your word, Samantha."

She took a deep, shuddering breath, a tiny bit ashamed that his jealousy was a huge turn-on. "I promise. There. Are you satisfied?"

"I'll be satisfied when this case is closed and we're looking at his taillights as he heads out of town."

She poked him in the belly. "You're a pain in my ass, you know that?"

"You're a much bigger pain in mine."

"True," Sam said. Why deny it? She went up on tiptoes to kiss him, which proved difficult and painful. "Stay here and behave. I mean it. I won't appreciate you acting like an alpha man in front of him. You got me?"

"Yes! Go. Talk to your *colleague*."

Sam stalked into the kitchen, where Hill was speaking with an older woman who Sam assumed was Derek's mother.

"Lieutenant Holland, this is Mrs. Kavanaugh," Hill said.

She was trim with short gray hair. Her eyes were ringed with red, and an aura of exhaustion and sadness clung to her. Sam could see the resemblance to her son. "You're Nick's Samantha," she said as she rose to hug Sam.

"Yes," Sam said, awkwardly returning the embrace. Affection from strangers was another on the long list of things that made her uncomfortable. "I'm so sorry for your loss."

"Thank you, honey. I assume you need to speak to Agent Hill, so I'll leave you."

"We're doing everything we can," Sam assured her.

"I have no doubt," Mrs. Kavanaugh said, patting Sam on the arm on her way out of the room.

"Nice lady," Hill said when they were alone. "They so don't deserve any of this."

"None of them ever do." She stopped, considered. "Well, some of them probably do, but not these people."

Hill replied with a small smile that made his striking face more so. "Ready to talk to Derek?"

"Before we do, I wanted to ask you what you'd think of letting Nick sit in. He has a clearance, and I was thinking it would be good for Derek to have someone close to him hear—"

"Sam," he said, using her given name for the first time. "Stop. It's fine. I agree with you."

Rattled by the familiarity and easy capitulation, Sam nodded and went into the next room. She gestured for Nick to follow them into the family room, where Derek was asleep on the sofa. Wearing a Cherry Blossom Festival 5-K T-shirt and ratty sweat pants that might've dated back to when he lived in this house, he hardly resembled the polished professional he'd been only two days ago.

As much as she hated to disturb what was probably the first sleep he'd had since his world imploded the day before, she turned to Nick, knowing he would understand what she needed him to do.

Sure enough, her husband went over to the sofa and gently shook Derek awake. "Derek, wake up. Sam is here, and she needs to talk to you."

Sam watched Derek's eyes open and bore witness to the moment when the awful reality came rushing back to remind him that life as he knew it was over. When his eyes locked on her, he sat right up. "Is it Maeve? Did you find her?"

Sam ached as she shook her head and dashed his hopes. What would it be like, she wondered, not to know where her child was? Unimaginable.

Out of wild-looking eyes, Derek glanced from Sam to Nick to Hill and then back to her. "What? What's happened?"

Sam sat next to him on the sofa, wishing she could spare him what he was about to hear. "In the course of our investigation, we've discovered some…inconsistencies…regarding Victoria."

"What kind of inconsistencies?"

"For one thing, we couldn't find any record of her online before she worked at Calahan Rice."

"So what? That doesn't mean anything."

"There's more." Sam took a deep, fortifying breath. "As a routine part of the autopsy, the medical examiner ran Victoria's fingerprints through the Automated Fingerprint Identification System. Her prints were registered to a thirty-six-year-old woman named Denise Desposito, who died in a prison fight six years ago."

Looking totally stunned by what he was hearing, Nick stared at her without blinking.

Derek stood and rested his hands on his hips. "Wait a minute... So what you're saying..."

"She wasn't who you thought she was." Sam tore off the bandage as quickly as she could.

That didn't stop the pain from registering on Derek's face. "What do you mean?"

"The Social Security number on file at the DMV was registered to a William Eldridge, who died eight years ago at the age of fifty-six."

Derek began to pace the small room. All at once, he stopped and turned to them. "I don't understand."

"Neither do we," Hill said.

"There was a background check done, after we were married," Derek said. "If she was lying about who she was, wouldn't they have discovered it then?"

"If the investigation was done by someone who wasn't involved in whatever this was," Hill said.

"What does that mean? 'Involved in whatever this was'?"

"Exactly what I said," Hill replied. "We suspect she was part of some sort of scheme. Whether she was a willing or unwilling participant remains to be seen."

"Are you implying that she...that we... It was all a lie?"

"We don't know that for sure, Derek," Sam said, touched by the agony she heard in his voice. "You shouldn't jump to any conclusions until we know more. It's clear that someone has gone to a lot of trouble to set her up with a false identity that seems to have begun the day she arrived in Washington, which was about thirty days before she met you."

"So you're trying to tell me that someone orchestrated our meeting? Our entire relationship, our marriage, our family… It's all a lie? How could it be a lie? She loves me. Nick! Come on, you know that. You saw it!"

"Yes, I did," Nick said.

"Tell them! It wasn't a lie! She couldn't have faked that kind of love!" Derek's voice broke on the last word. He covered his mouth with a shaking hand. "It can't be true," he whispered. "She loved me. I know she did."

Sam stood and went to him, resting a hand on his arm. "We're working really hard to figure this out. I promise you, we'll get to the bottom of it."

"It wasn't all a lie. You'll never convince me of that."

"We need to know anything you can tell us about her past. Anything she might've mentioned about people from home, memories of school or friends or cousins, places she lived or worked."

He ran his fingers through his hair, leaving it standing on end. "She didn't talk about the past a lot. I got the sense that her childhood was painful, so I left it alone."

"When you say you got the sense it was painful, what do you mean?" Hill asked.

Derek returned to the sofa and dropped down to the cushions, expelling a weary sigh. "From time to time, she'd get an almost haunted look to her, as if it was unbearable to go back in time. I didn't push her. I never wanted to cause her that kind of pain. And besides, it didn't matter to me. All I cared about was who she was now. That was who I loved." He stopped himself, thought for a moment and then looked up at them beseechingly. "Was I a total fool?"

"I don't believe it's ever foolish to care about someone," Sam said.

"Sometimes it is," Hill muttered.

Sam turned to him. "What did you say?"

"Nothing." He waved his hand at her. "Proceed."

Sam studied the agent for a moment before she turned back to Derek. "What about when you were planning your wedding? Did it strike you as odd that she had no one to invite?"

"She had friends here in D.C. by then, so she had people to invite. Besides, it was a small wedding."

"If you could think about it and let us know if you remember anyone she spoke of from her past, that would help."

"Was she really from Ohio?" Derek asked.

"We don't know," Sam said.

"I'll think about it," Derek said.

Sam wondered how he'd think about anything else. "Thank you. We need to get back to the city, but you have my number."

Derek nodded.

"I'm so sorry to have had to tell you this."

He shrugged helplessly. "I'm sorry that everything about my life with her was built on lies."

Nick went to sit next to Derek. "It wasn't all lies, Derek. I saw you two together. She loved you. No one will ever convince me otherwise."

"Thanks. That helps."

"Unfortunately, I have to get back to the Hill for a town hall meeting," Nick said. "I'll check on you later, and Harry will be back shortly."

"Thanks for coming out," Derek said flatly. "I know how busy you are."

"It's no problem."

"Um, Derek," Sam said, "it's really important that you not tell anyone—even your parents—what we've uncovered about Victoria. If this is part of a larger scheme, we don't want to tip our hand that we're on to them."

"I understand."

"I'll call you later," Nick said. "And you know how to reach me if you need to. Any time. Day or night."

"Thanks, Nick." Derek stretched out on the sofa and covered his face with his hands.

Nick tipped his head toward the door, indicating they should go.

"I feel bad leaving him like that," Sam said.

"I do too," Nick said.

"I'm sure he wants us to go figure out what the hell is going on," Hill said.

"I'll give you a lift back to the city," Nick said to Sam.

She glanced at Hill, torn between what she should do and what she wanted to do. "Oh, um, well…"

"Go on ahead," Hill said. "I'm going to look into who did the security clearance update when Derek married Victoria. I'll meet you back at HQ."

"Sounds good," Sam said. When they were ensconced in Nick's cozy BMW, she said, "You might've asked rather than told me I was going with you."

"What's that supposed to mean?"

"I don't need you acting all…husbandly…in front of my colleagues."

Nick snorted out a laugh. "I am your husband, and I shall act accordingly for the rest of my life."

"Not in front of the people I work with!"

"I hate to point out that you don't actually work with Hill, thank God."

"Nick! That's not the point!"

Chuckling, he reached over to cover her hand with his and resisted her attempts to push him away. "I'm sorry if I went about it the wrong way, but I won't apologize for wanting to spend whatever time I can with you, especially when you're injured, in pain and trying to hide it from me."

Oh, she hated when he said stuff like that right when she was working up a good mad! "Don't try to charm your way out of this."

"Why not? It usually works."

Because she could no more resist his charm than she could a box of chocolates when it was put right in front of her, she linked her fingers with his, tipped her head back and closed her eyes. The pain was making its presence known, giving her a sick, queasy feeling that dulled her usually sharp senses. "I hated having to do that to Derek."

"I know, babe."

"Whenever he thinks about the moment he learned she wasn't who he thought, he's going to remember it was me who told him."

"He knows you're doing your job."

"Sometimes I hate my job."

"I always hate your job."

That made her laugh, which helped. Being with him always helped.

"But you're so good at it," he added. "What you did today in that store was nothing short of amazing. You saved a lot of lives—your own included."

As always, receiving compliments, even from him, made her twitchy. "I was glad I was there. It worked out well."

"For everyone but the gunman and your face."

"I'm sorry this happened today of all days, but don't worry. I'll be there tonight with bells on."

"You don't have to go if you don't feel up to it. I'd totally understand."

"I'm going, and that's the end of it."

When Nick's cell phone rang, Sam released his hand so he could retrieve it from his coat pocket. He handed it to her. "See who it is."

She glanced at the caller ID and smiled. "Scotty." They'd bought him a phone so he could call them any time he wanted. "Hi, buddy," she said.

"Sam! Oh my God! I saw the video! Are you okay?" She hated the worry she heard in his voice. It hadn't occurred to her to call him, but with hindsight, she realized she should have. "I'm totally fine. Where did you hear about the video?"

"I heard people talking about it at swimming camp, and when I got home, Mrs. L and I watched it on the computer. You were so awesome. Mrs. L thought so too. She said you were like Wonder Woman."

"Aww, thanks. It was kind of crazy, but all's well that ends well."

"Did it hurt when he hit you with the gun? Duh, that's a dumb question, huh?"

Sam laughed. "It didn't feel great, but they stitched me up, and I'm back to work."

"Are you with Nick?"

"Yep, he's giving me a lift. You want to talk to him?"

"In a second. Can you keep a really big secret?"

"Dude, are seriously asking me that?"

Scotty snorted out a laugh that sounded an awful lot like the way Nick often laughed at her. "Sorry. Of course you can. That's kinda your job, right?"

"Duh."

Nick flashed her a grin, as he was no doubt enjoying her side of the conversation with the boy they both adored.

"So what's the big—"

"Don't say it! I don't want him to hear!"

"All right already. Sheesh!"

"Senator O'Connor invited me to the fundraiser tonight. Mrs. L is going to drive me up to Ashburn. We're leaving in a little while. I wasn't going to tell you guys, but I figured since you were hurt and stuff, you might not go."

"I am for sure," she said, more determined than ever now that she knew he would be there. "That's a good one. He'll be thrilled."

"Don't make him wonder what we're talking about."

"Yes, sir," she said, thoroughly charmed. "We're looking forward to this weekend—and the next three weeks."

"I am too. Counting down the days!"

Sam smiled and rested a hand on Nick's leg. "Do you want to talk to Nick?"

"Sure, if he can."

"He's always got time for you. We both do. I hope you know that."

"I do. That's cool, Sam. Seriously."

"Can't wait to see you."

"You too."

She handed the phone to her husband and leaned over to rest her head on his shoulder while he conducted an animated conversation with Scotty, more than half of it centered on Red Sox stats as well as talk of the D.C. Federals and their incredible season.

"Do you mean Willie Vasquez?" Nick asked.

Sam recognized the name of the Federals' star center fielder.

"He's coming to your camp? Wow, that's great. I might have to call in sick to work that day and go to camp with you." Nick paused and laughed at whatever Scotty said in response. "All right, pal. I'll see you Sunday. Can't wait."

Sam took the phone from him and returned it to his suit pocket before resuming her position on his shoulder, breathing in the familiar scent of his cologne.

"He's so excited about the camp and spending three weeks with us," Nick said. "I hope he decides to stay forever."

"I think he'll get there eventually, babe," Sam said. "You can't blame him for being afraid to make such a huge change."

"I don't blame him for that. Not one bit. We're asking him to change his whole life."

"We'll make him feel so at home with us that he'll never want to leave."

"That's the goal. Now tell me, what'll I be thrilled about?"

"I'm not at liberty to disclose that information."

"I don't like you two ganging up on me."

"Now you know how I feel when you guys do it to me."

As they encountered bumper-to-bumper traffic on Route 66, he raised his arm and put it around her. "Close your eyes for a few minutes. I can tell you're running on fumes."

"Don't act like you know me so well."

"It's not an act."

Laughing, she nudged him with her elbow.

"Behave yourself while I'm driving and take a snooze. We're going to be here awhile."

As her eyes burned closed, Sam's mind raced with the details of the case, the fundraiser, Scotty's impending visit, the conversation she needed to have with McBride and Tyrone about the Fitzgerald case, and then the conversation they all needed to have with her dad about that situation. Her brain was as tired as the rest of her by the time she gave in and let the darkness take her away from it all.

TEN

"Babe, wake up. We're at HQ."

"Not yet," she muttered, snuggling closer to him. He tightened his arm around her and let out a tortured groan. "You know I'd much rather be with you, but I've got to get to the Hill. I'm running late thanks to the hideous traffic."

Reluctantly, Sam sat up and rubbed the sleep from her eyes, gasping when she connected with her injured face. How had she managed to forget about that? She shook off the cobwebs and turned to him. "Thanks for the lift."

He studied her with those sharp hazel eyes that never missed a thing where she was concerned. "Feel any better after the nap?"

"I'm sure I will when I wake up." She took a look around and noticed they were at the morgue entrance. "Was the main entrance crawling with reporters?"

"Crawling is the right word. Hundreds of them. I knew you wouldn't be up for that."

"I've already had my encounter with them for today." She leaned in to kiss him and gasped when her face throbbed with pain. "Thanks for thinking of that and delivering me to safety."

"Any time. Take it easy on yourself this afternoon. You took quite a hit this morning, even if you're trying to play it down."

"I'd tell you not to worry—"

"But that would be a waste of time."

"I'll see you in a couple of hours."

"Yes, you will."

Sam braved the pain and treated herself to one last lingering kiss.

"That was mean."

She grinned at him as best she could with only half her face working. "See ya, Senator." Now fully awake and firing on all cylinders, she got out of the car and jogged through the sizzling heat into the cool dankness of the morgue.

Lindsey McNamara was coming down the hallway toward Sam. "Hey," she said, grimacing when she caught sight of Sam's injured face. "Double ouch."

"No biggie. Looks worse than it is. Anything new for me?"

Lindsey shook her head, making her ponytail swing back and forth. "Not yet. I'm leaning on the lab to get me something on the DNA we found under Victoria's nails."

"Good. Thanks." Sam started off down the corridor.

"So I'll see you tonight? At the fundraiser?"

Sam turned back to her. "You're going?"

Lindsey's face turned bright red. "Terry asked me to go with him. I hope that's okay."

"Sure it is," Sam said, annoyed as always when her world collided with her husband's. With two of her people dating two of his people, it happened far too often. "Why wouldn't it be?"

"No reason. I wanted to make sure you were okay with it."

"It's a free country," Sam said, immediately regretting the snotty comment. "I'm sorry. I'm still trying to figure out how all this works."

"All what?"

"My job, his job, how they connect, how you connect with Terry and how Gonzo connects with Christina. It's all kinda...messy."

Lindsey laughed. "I hate to break it to you, Sam, but life is messy."

"Tell me about it. Gotta get back to it. See you later on."

In the lobby, she ran into Chief Farnsworth and Captain Malone. The god of productivity had totally abandoned her today.

"How'd it go with Kavanaugh?" the chief asked.

"About how you'd expect. He's in total denial that she lied about everything. You can't convince him that she didn't love him and their life. Nick confirms that nothing about them ever seemed fake or contrived." Sam paused as a thought came to her. "Perhaps she was hired to infiltrate Nelson's campaign and administration, but maybe she fell in love for real. Maybe that's what got her killed."

"That's as good a motive as any I've heard so far," Farnsworth said.

"We'll look into it."

"How's the face?" Malone asked.

"As gorgeous as ever," Sam said, sticking her chin out for emphasis. "Wouldn't you say?"

"Absolutely," Malone deadpanned. "The recent work you've had done is a huge improvement."

Farnsworth choked back a laugh.

"Very funny."

"On the not-so-funny side of the house," the chief said, sobering, "Melissa Woodmansee has filed suit against the department alleging police brutality."

Shock radiated through Sam. That the murdering bitch would have the gall to sue them was infuriating. "It was a clean shot," Sam said. "If Cruz hadn't blown the detonator out of her hand, she would've killed us all."

"No one is quibbling with that part of it. The suit is focused on your actions to use her injury to get her to confess to the murders."

"I kept her from bleeding to death until the EMTs got there!"

Farnsworth raised an eyebrow. "And maybe you enjoyed stepping on her bloody stump and extracting information in exchange for pain meds?"

"Hell, yes, I did! I'd do it again. Why would we have put her out of her misery when she had information we needed to close the case?"

"Tell it to the judge," a new voice said.

Sam spun around to find her nemesis, Lt. Stahl, smiling sweetly at her. The sight of him made her want to barf. "In trouble again, Lieutenant? Tsk, tsk, tsk. It sure seems to follow you around."

"Screw you, Stahl."

His face turned the murderous shade of purple that usually accompanied one of their conversations. He turned to Farnsworth and Malone. "You're going to let her talk to a superior officer that way?" Stahl never missed a chance to remind Sam he had more time in rank than she did.

"Get back to work," the chief barked.

With a hateful look for Sam, he waddled off to find the rock he lived under.

"I thought you were trying to get rid of him?" Sam asked the chief.

"Trying is the key word. He's refusing to take early retirement."

"Because he's got nothing better to do than bother me."

"Forget about him. The general counsel will be in touch about the lawsuit and will want to depose you and your team."

"Fine. Whatever. See if you can postpone that until after we close the Kavanaugh case."

"I'll do what I can."

"What've you done with Agent Hill?" Malone asked.

"He had to do some FBI thing. Nick was at Kavanaugh's parents' house, so he gave me a ride back to town."

"Good," Farnsworth said. "I was afraid you were going to tell me you buried the body and hid the shovel."

"Don't put ideas in my head. Can I get back to work now?"

"By all means."

As she stormed into the pit, she wondered if this day could get any more frustrating. "Someone had better have something," she announced. Every head in the place whipped up at the sound of her voice. That pleased her—a bright spot in an otherwise crappy day. "Conference room. Five minutes. Cruz, see if you can get Ramsey down here to report on where we are with the search for the baby."

"On it."

In her office, Sam pulled out the bottle of pain medicine and took three more, which left one in the bottle, so she took that one too.

Gonzo appeared in the doorway and zeroed in on her face. "It's even more spectacular than it was earlier."

"So I'm told. What's up?"

"Um, well, I was wondering…"

Surprised by his unusual stammer, Sam said, "Spit it out, man."

"Christina asked me to go to the fundraiser tonight."

"Of course she did." Gonzo was engaged to Nick's chief of staff, Christina Billings.

Her unflappable colleague actually seemed embarrassed, which Sam found fascinating. "We got a babysitter, and I rented a tux. But with the case and everything…"

"You can leave at six. Turn everything over to second shift."

"Are you sure, L.T.? If you need me to stay—"

"Are you trying to talk me out of it because you don't want to go?"

Damn if he didn't get all embarrassed again. "I kinda want to go. With Alex living with us, we never get a night out together." He shrugged. "As long as it's okay with you."

This was why she hated her world and Nick's colliding. She was giving Gonzo permission to leave work earlier than he normally would to go to her husband's fundraiser. What a freaking mess. "It's okay. Let's get to it."

"Thanks," he said as he turned and headed for the conference room.

Sam stepped in after him and was pleased to see Sgt. Ramsey and his partner in the room. "How are we making out with the search for Maeve?" Even though she hoped her investigation would lead them to the missing child before Ramsey's did, she still needed to keep in touch with the SVU detectives.

"Since we issued the Amber Alert, we've been inundated with reported sightings," Ramsey said. "We're following up on every one of them."

To his credit, the sergeant looked like he hadn't slept in more than a day.

"Cruz, Gonzales, what'd we get from the phone logs?" Sam asked.

"A lot of numbers," Cruz said. "We were able to tie many of the local ones to women who have children around the same age as Maeve Kavanaugh." He handed her a printed list of five names, addresses and phone numbers. "We're working on the out-of-state numbers."

Sam checked her watch. "I've got ninety minutes until I have to be home. Cruz, let's get to one of Victoria's mom friends."

"Sure."

The single word was uttered without any of his usual enthusiasm. What was that all about? "McBride and Tyrone, a word before you go? Everyone else get back to work." To her partner, Sam said, "I'll be right with you."

McBride and Tyrone exchanged uneasy glances as they waited for the others to file out.

"What's up, L.T.?" Jeannie asked when the three of them were alone.

"My dad heard through the grapevine that we re-opened Fitzgerald while he was in the hospital earlier this year."

The discomfort emanating from the two detectives ratcheted up at the mention of the name Fitzgerald.

McBride swallowed. Hard.

Sam's every sense was suddenly on full alert. "He wants to know about your investigation."

"We told you, L.T.," Tyrone said, casting a nervous glance at his partner. "We didn't uncover anything new."

"All right," Sam said, playing along. Had she been so embroiled in her own case at the time that she'd failed to notice an odd vibe coming from two of her best detectives?

Jeannie kept her eyes trained on the floor.

"My dad wants to talk to you both about your investigation. Would you mind—"

"It's not true," Jeannie said so softly Sam almost didn't hear her.

"Excuse me?" Sam had a feeling this day was about to go from bad to worse.

"It's not true that we didn't uncover anything new," Jeannie said.

Tyrone's eyes nearly bugged out of his head. "Jeannie!"

"Shut up, Will. I'm not going to stand here and lie to her. Again."

The partners engaged in a visual battle of wills that served to further fray Sam's already battered nerves. "Somebody had better start talking," Sam said. "Right now."

Neither of them said a word for a long, charged moment until Jeannie finally looked up at Sam and made eye contact. The torment Sam saw in her detective's pretty brown eyes made her blood run cold. Sam decided that whatever this was about, she probably didn't want to know.

"You need to remember what was happening then," Jeannie said. "Your dad was in the hospital, and you weren't sure if he would make it. We had someone killing perfectly nice people, and you were receiving threatening mail."

"I remember," Sam said tightly. "Get on with it."

"We, ah, we started from scratch, as if the case were new," Jeannie said.

Sam nodded. She would've done the same.

"It became clear to us…"

"What?"

"Your dad. He, ah, well… He failed to follow up on some rather obvious leads."

The blow hit Sam like a gun to the face. Of all the things she'd thought they might say, that one had never crossed her mind. As if the wind had been knocked out of her, she had to force air to her lungs. "What kind of leads?"

"For one thing," Will said, "he never interviewed Cameron Fitzgerald's girlfriend. We think it's possible Cameron might've had something to do with his brother's murder, but they let him go into the military a couple of days after his brother went missing. We thought that was odd, among other things."

"What other things?" Sam's heart was beating so hard that she wondered if it would burst through her chest. Was this why her father had forbidden her to reopen the case? A thousand thoughts cycled through her mind with each heartbeat. And why in the world had two of her most trusted detectives lied to her?

"There were all kinds of inconsistencies," Jeannie said. "The medical examiner said your dad was 'off' around that time, but he refused to elaborate. He thinks fondly of your father and didn't want to sully his reputation. Neither did we."

Sam recalled the conversation with her sister Tracy, something about their parents that had happened during the original investigation. The idea of digging into that hornet's nest had Sam breaking into a cold sweat.

The two detectives stood before her, vibrating with discomfort.

"I would like to know," Sam said in a low, quiet tone,

"why you felt the need to lie to me when you said you'd found nothing new."

"We did it to protect your dad, Sam," Jeannie said imploringly. "If we blew the lid off this case and then he died, that would've been all they'd say about him. We couldn't let that happen."

"While I appreciate your concern for me and my dad, that was not up to you to decide."

"We thought that's what you'd want us to do," Will said.

"I wanted the truth."

"We're sorry, Sam," Jeannie said. "We thought we were doing the right thing."

"My father recovered, and still you didn't come to me. You didn't tell me that you'd lied to me."

"We considered that," Will said.

Sam held out her hand. "I'll take your weapons and shields."

They gasped.

"Why?" Jeannie asked, her face slack with shock.

"You lied to your superior officer. You're suspended for one week without pay." Sam kept her gaze unwavering even as she died on the inside. Not to mention that this was the worst possible time to lose two of her best officers.

"Lieutenant," Jeannie said.

"Your shields and weapons," Sam said again.

Will looked at Jeannie, his eyes bright with unshed tears.

Jeannie nodded to her partner and tugged the handgun from her shoulder holster. She put the gun and gold detective's shield in Sam's hand.

Will followed suit.

"I'm extremely disappointed in both of you. Go home. Report back next Tuesday at zero seven hundred."

"Yes, ma'am," they said.

Sam watched them leave the room.

Will turned back to her. "Lieutenant—"

"Go."

Jeannie grabbed her partner's arm and dragged him along with her.

Sam took a couple of minutes to gather herself and rein in her emotions before she emerged from the conference room carrying their weapons, which drew the immediate attention of everyone in the pit. A quiver of shock and dismay rippled through her ranks as the other detectives watched McBride and Tyrone retrieve their personal belongings from their cubicles and leave without a word to anyone.

With her heart still pounding and feeling clammy from the cold sweat, Sam headed to her own office and ran smack into Lt. Stahl. As she bounced off his protruding belly, Sam fought back a vicious wave of nausea.

Naturally, he zeroed right in on the weapons and badges in her hands. "Problem, Lieutenant?"

"Nope."

"Why do you have those weapons and shields?"

"None of your business."

"You know damned well that if you've suspended any of your officers, that's a matter for IAB," he said, referring to the Internal Affairs Bureau where he was moved after Sam was given his former command over the Homicide detectives. He'd set out to make her life miserable ever since.

He knew as well as she did that the only way this incident reached IAB level was if McBride or Tyrone fought the suspension, but Sam was fairly confident they wouldn't. They'd be foolish to fight it.

"I don't know what you're talking about," Sam said. "Get out of my way. I've got work to do."

His face turned the predictable shade of purple Sam usually relished. At the moment, she couldn't care less. "You won't get away with this," Stahl said.

"Talk to the hand," she said, flashing him the bird. She went into her office and locked the weapons in her top desk drawer. With a wistful glance at the gold shields McBride and Tyrone had more than earned in their careers, Sam tossed them in with the weapons and locked the drawer.

That was when her hands began to shake. Had she done the right thing? "Of course you did," she muttered. "They fucking lied to you. You can't condone that. The minute you do, you lose control of everything."

"Lieutenant?"

Sam spun around to find Cruz in the doorway, looking at her with big eyes full of shock and dismay.

"I'll be right with you," Sam said. She took another moment to get it together before she stepped into the pit. All eyes landed on her. The weight of their expectations sat heavy upon her shoulders. She stood up a little straighter, in full command.

Since Stahl was already sniffing around, she made a decision right in that moment to keep her mouth shut about what had transpired with McBride and Tyrone.

"Let's go, Cruz." The weight of their disappointment was even heavier than their expectations had been.

Freddie jogged to catch up with her, and they walked out of HQ in silence. When they were clear of the building, she said, "Don't ask me, because I'm not going to talk about it."

"I wasn't going to ask." He pulled her car keys from his pocket and held them up.

She gestured for him to go ahead and drive. "Where to?" she asked.

"Judging from the phone logs and what Derek told us, Victoria's closest friend seemed to be Ginger Dickenson. She has a son the same age as Maeve Kavanaugh. She's also a stay-at-home mom and lives a few blocks from the Kavanaughs in your neighborhood."

"What does the husband do?"

"He's a muckety-muck at Homeland Security. Senior executive, answers directly to the secretary."

"Good work."

"Thanks."

Sam noted the unusually clipped tone and was tempted to ignore it. "Are you pissed about something?"

Startled by the blunt question, he looked over at her and then back at the road. "No."

Sam was ready for this day to be over. "Just tell me, will you?"

"I'm not pissed."

"You're something."

"Annoyed maybe."

"Are you going to make me pull it out of you?"

"Hill. He shows up, and suddenly I'm relegated to second string."

Ah, she thought, her sensitive partner's feelings had been hurt. "I don't want him around any more than you do. I'm following orders."

"I know that," he said sullenly. "I don't like him. Something about him bugs me."

"You and Nick both."

Freddie brightened at that news. "So he doesn't like him either?"

"He barely knows him, but like you, he's bugged by him. Hill's not a bad guy once you get to know him. Like us, he's following orders, doing his job. We can use all the help we can get on this one."

"Getting to be a long time on the kid."

"Yeah." Sam watched the city whiz by out the window. It was better if she didn't think about what Maeve might be going through—if she were even still alive. "So I need to tell you something that's going to be upsetting to hear, but before I say it, you need to know it's totally bogus."

He glanced over at her. "What?"

"Melissa Woodmansee is suing the department, claiming police brutality."

Staring at her, he said, "You're kidding."

"Eyes on the road!"

"Tell me you're kidding."

"I'm not kidding, but it's totally bogus. Everyone thinks so. Well, except Stahl, but I expect him to take perverse pleasure in anything that might make us look bad."

"It was a clean shot. If I hadn't taken her hand off, she would've killed us all."

"That's never been in question."

"Then how the hell can she sue us?"

The fact that he was swearing—and "hell" was as close as he ever came to actually swearing—told Sam how upset he was. "Oddly enough, your part isn't in question. It's what I did after that she's focused on."

"What do you mean?"

"I took advantage of her pain to extract a confession."

"You took a murderer off the streets."

"Apparently, she takes issue with how I did it."

"It won't go anywhere," he said fiercely. "Hell, we both got commendations for what we did that day. That's got to count for something."

"I guess we'll see."

He looked over at her again. "Are you worried about it?"

"Hell, no. I did my job. I'd do it the same way if I had it to do over."

"Me too," he said firmly.

Sam knew it had taken him weeks of sleepless nights and many mandated appointments with the department shrink to come around to that hard-won conclusion, and it pissed her off that Melissa was making him question himself—again. "Don't let it get to you. We both know we did the right thing, so there's nothing to worry about."

A long period of silence ensued while he seemed to be absorbing her advice. "Can I ask you something that has nothing to do with work?"

"Sure," Sam said, relieved that he had taken the news about the lawsuit better than she'd expected. All at once, the sleepless night, the injury, the strain of the bizarre case and the situation with McBride and Tyrone caught up to her in the form of bone-deep exhaustion.

"What does it mean that Elin is sneaking around behind my back?"

"Define 'sneaking around.'"

"Texting in the bathroom when she thinks I'm asleep. That kind of thing."

"Freddie…"

"She's not cheating on me."

"How can you know that for sure?"

"I know," he said tightly. "Things are really good between us. Better than ever since we moved in together. She wouldn't do that to me."

"What else would it be?"

"I have no idea. That's what I'm asking you."

Sam thought about it for a few minutes before the answer dawned on her, sending her into a fit of laughter that made her face burn. That she hadn't thought of it immediately was a testament to the fog that had taken over her brain since she was pistol whipped earlier in the day.

"What the hell is so funny?"

"What's coming up next week?"

"I don't know. What're you talking about?"

"Think about it."

"Oh my God. My birthday?"

"It's not every day a guy turns thirty."

"Is she having a party?"

"I'm not telling you that."

"Come on, Sam."

"No way. You're not getting that out of me."

"Huh," he said. "It certainly beats some of the other things that've crossed my mind lately."

"It's concerning to me that you don't entirely trust her."

"I trust her."

"Do you?"

Freddie gripped the steering wheel so tightly his knuckles turned white. "Sometimes I wonder…"

"About?"

"What the hell she's doing with me."

"Oh, for crying out loud, Freddie! She's lucky to be with you, and she knows it."

"And you're not at all biased," he said with a chuckle.

"Not at all," she said, thinking of Jeannie and Will.

"Let me ask you something."

"Whatever you want."

"Am I too cozy with my detectives?"

That set him off into a fit of laughter. "Cozy? You?"

Sam bit back a sharp retort, annoyed that he would laugh at her when she was being totally serious.

"Friendly. You know what I mean."

"We all think of you as a friend and a mentor, but we never forget that you're our boss first. Never."

"I don't know how to be just your boss. You're all important to me."

"We know that, Sam."

"Hypothetically speaking, if you learned something during an investigation that would cause me or my family serious heartburn, would you tell me or would you bury it to protect me?" It was as close as she'd ever come to telling him what'd happened with McBride and Tyrone.

"Is the info critical to the investigation?"

"Yes."

Freddie thought about that for a moment. "I'd tell you."

Sam nodded, comforted by his reply. "Good answer."

He pulled the car up to the curb on Ginger Dickenson's block and killed the engine. "Whatever happened with McBride and Tyrone, I'm sure you felt you had no choice."

"I didn't."

"Okay, then."

As always, she appreciated his unwavering support. She pulled open the passenger side door. "Let's get this done. I've got a fundraiser to get to."

"Looking like you went ten rounds with Mike Tyson?"

Sam shrugged. "Nick knew what he was getting when he said 'I do.'"

That sent Freddie into a new fit of laughter. "Sure he did."

Sam followed him up the sidewalk to a brick-front town house with wrought-iron accents. He rang the bell, and they waited for at least a minute before they heard footsteps inside.

"Who is it?" a female voice said.

"MPD," Freddie said. "Lieutenant Holland. Detective Cruz." They held up their shields so she could see them through the peephole.

A series of locks disengaged, and the door swung open. Ginger Dickenson was petite with long, light brown hair that she had tacked up in a messy bun. She wore yoga pants and a T-shirt that showed off a trim figure. A chubby toddler appeared between her legs. She bent to scoop him up. "What can I do for you?"

"May we have a few minutes of your time, Mrs. Dickenson?" Sam asked.

"You're the one who married the senator."

"Yes," Sam said through gritted teeth. She'd never get used to the notoriety her marriage had generated in the capital city.

Ginger stepped out of the doorway to admit them. "Come in."

They followed her into a living room that was scattered with the toys of a busy little boy. She'd been in the midst of folding a basket of laundry. Ginger reached for the remote and turned off the TV.

Sam couldn't help but wonder what it might be like to have nothing more to think about in a day than taking care of her child, folding some laundry and watching TV. She decided she'd probably be bored out of her skull without the work that had defined her adult life, but wouldn't it be nice to get the chance to find out? As her gaze landed on the toddler who was cruising around the coffee table, Sam was filled with the familiar sense of longing. She shook it off before the sadness could take hold.

"This is about Victoria," Ginger said with a wary glance at first Sam and then Freddie.

"Yes," Sam said.

"Is there any word on Maeve?"

"Not yet."

Ginger sat on the sofa and gestured for them to take the loveseat. "God. I can't think about anything else but where she might be, what she might be going through."

"We're having the same thoughts," Sam said. "We're doing everything we can think of to find her. How long had you known Victoria?"

"Since we had the kids. We were roommates in the hospital. My Trevor was born the same day as Maeve, so we had an instant bond. We became very close. I can't believe what's happened. Who would want to hurt Victoria? She was the nicest person. And Derek... What he must be going through."

"He's understandably distraught," Sam said.

"He's not a suspect, is he?" Ginger asked.

"No."

"That's good," Ginger said, visibly relieved. "He was so devoted to her. I told my husband that if it turned out to be him, I was giving up on people."

"What did Victoria tell you about her family?" Sam asked.

"Other than Derek and Maeve, she didn't have any family. Her parents were dead, and she was an only child. I remember when she first told me that, how sad I was for her. But there was nothing sad about her. She was a very positive, upbeat person to say she'd been through so much."

"Did you ever meet other friends of hers?" Cruz asked.

Ginger shook her head. "It was quite the other way around. The only people she knew in the city were her former colleagues from Calahan Rice. I introduced her to my girlfriends, and they loved her. She fit right into our group like she'd always been there. We had a girls' night out once a month, playgroups with the kids. That kind of thing."

"You said Derek was devoted to her," Sam said.

"Extremely. You only had to be around them to know what I mean. They put out that stupidly in love vibe." To Sam, she said, "You spent time with them. You must know what I mean."

"They seemed very happy."

"Yes," Ginger said.

"Was she equally devoted to him?"

"Oh absolutely! He was all she talked about—well, him and Maeve. She was madly in love with him."

"And you never heard her say anything negative about him or their marriage?" Freddie asked.

Ginger shook her head. "We used to poke fun at how she never joined in the husband bashing that we occasionally indulged in. I suspect she was more reserved in how she talked about him because of his job, but I also think it was because she didn't have a bad word to say about him. It was admirable."

"Did you notice any changes in her over the last few weeks?" Sam asked.

Ginger thought about that for a moment. "She might've been a little off, but she'd had the flu, and it lingered. Before she got sick, she told me she and Derek were talking about having another baby." Ginger's eyes sparkled with tears. "I can't understand how this could've happened."

"We're working to get to the bottom of it," Sam assured her. "Were any of your other friends closer to her than you were?"

"No, I was the closest to her."

"Would you mind writing down the names of the other women in your group and their phone numbers for us?"

Ginger took the notepad that Freddie handed her. When she was done, she handed it back to him and turned to Sam. "The day of your wedding, the other girls and I got together to watch the coverage. Victoria was so excited that she got to be there. She and Derek thought you were so perfect for their friend." Ginger brushed at a stray tear that slid down her cheek. "I thought you might like to know that."

Sam stood riveted in place, astounded by the rush of sadness that caught her off guard.

"Lieutenant?" Freddie said, raising a brow in question.

Sam met Ginger's tearful gaze. "Thank you for telling me. I thought she was a lovely person."

"Thank you for your time," Freddie added.

"I hope you find whoever did this to her, and please find Maeve."

"We're doing everything we can," Freddie assured her.

ELEVEN

Jeannie McBride was in shock as Will drove her home to the Foggy Bottom neighborhood where she lived with her boyfriend Michael.

"I can't believe this has happened," she said for the tenth time since they left HQ.

"It's our own damned fault," Will said. "We should've told her the truth back in April."

"We couldn't have told her then. Her dad was in the hospital. No one was sure if he was going to make it. Did you want to be responsible for possibly destroying his reputation when he might've died?"

"We shouldn't have lied."

"Well, we did, and now we're screwed."

"Will this end our careers?" he asked.

"How the hell do I know? I've never been suspended before." A knot of anxiety settled in her chest, reminding her of the awful days and weeks that followed her attack. "I don't think it will. She's pissed—and rightfully so. I guess we can hope it'll blow over after we serve out the suspension."

"Should we fight it?"

Incredulous, Jeannie spun around in the seat to stare at him. "Are you out of your freaking mind? On what grounds would we fight the fact that we lied to our lieutenant? And would you really want the whole department knowing why we were suspended?"

"Won't they find out anyway?"

"Not if the three people involved keep their mouths shut. The worst that'll happen is people will know we were suspended but not why."

"So she can send us home like that? With no due process?"

"Of course she can! The due process comes in if we choose to fight it, which we will not. You got me?"

"Yeah," he grumbled. "I got you. Shit, a week without pay... That's gonna kill me."

"I can spot you some money if you need it. This is all my fault anyway. It was my call to tell her we'd found nothing new—and I came clean with her today without talking to you about it first."

"The hell with that. This is on both of us."

As they sat at the curb in front of Michael's house, Jeannie tried to bring herself to open the door, to go inside, to figure out how to get through the next week without the job that kept her so busy the demons couldn't find her.

"Did we do the right thing, Jeannie?" Will asked in a small voice that made him sound more like a frightened boy than a seasoned detective.

"Yes, we did," she said without hesitation. "When she has time to think about it, she'll see why we did it." Even as she said that, Jeannie suspected she'd dream about Sam telling her she was disappointed with her. She'd never forget that. After what they'd endured together following Jeannie's assault, when Sam had stood by her through the rape examination and investigation, she thought of Sam as much more than a boss. She was also a close friend. That she had disappointed her boss and close friend was a bitter blow to absorb.

"What she said, about how we disappointed her..." Will's voice wavered. They were on the same wavelength. "That hurt."

"Yeah, it did. I'm sorry I dragged you into this and took you down with me."

"I was well aware of what we were doing and why, so don't go there."

Jeannie appreciated that he wanted to share in the blame, but he'd done what she'd told him to. As his superior, the blame fell squarely on her shoulders. "You get why we can't tell anyone why we were suspended, right?"

"Don't worry. No one will hear it from me. Will you tell Michael?"

Jeannie glanced at the house that had been her haven since the attack. She'd finally given up her own apartment and officially moved in with him a month ago. Things had been going so well, and now this. "I suppose I'll have to explain why I'm not going to work. He knows what happened anyway. He didn't approve of me lying to her. He told me it would come back to bite me in the ass."

"Looks like he was right."

"He certainly won't take any pleasure in that." She met Will's gaze. "Come over in the morning, and we'll write up the report we should've given her at the time."

Will's boyishly handsome face brightened at that idea. "I'll be here."

"Try not to worry. She knows we're good at our jobs. That's going to count for something."

"I hope you're right."

Jeannie got out of the car and waved as he drove off. Trudging up the stairs, she felt as if she had twenty-pound weights attached to her legs. She used her key in the door and stopped short when she realized the alarm wasn't set.

That alarm had kept her sane by making her feel safe after she was viciously raped and beaten. "Michael?"

He came bounding down the stairs and was surprised to see her. "Hey, baby. What're you doing home?"

At the sight of him, Jeannie's composure crumpled. Rushing over to her, he put his arms around her.

"What, honey? What is it?"

She burrowed her face into his chest, absorbing the comfort he offered without hesitation. "I got suspended."

"What? Why?"

"Fitzgerald." Ironic that the cold case Sam had used to lure her back to work after the attack had led to the first disciplinary action of her career.

"She found out that you held back on the report."

Jeannie nodded. "I should've listened to you."

"You thought you were doing the right thing at the time. No one can fault you for that."

"She certainly didn't want to hear that today."

"She thinks the world of you, Jeannie, personally and professionally. Everyone knows that."

Hearing him say that broke what was left of her composure. "She said I disappointed her."

He tightened his hold on her. "Aww, baby."

"I'm going to fix this," she vowed. "No matter what I have to do, I will fix it."

Since it was already five thirty when they left Ginger's house, Sam had Freddie drop her at her Ninth Street home. "Pick me up at seven?"

"I'll be here."

"Take good care of my car tonight. I know you're not used to cars that don't backfire and belch." She never got tired of cracking on the vintage Mustang he was so proud of.

He rolled his eyes at her. "Tell me about the party Elin is having for me."

"Get the hell out of here," she said as she got out of the car. "There's no party."

"I'm going to tell her you told me," he called through the open window.

"I didn't tell you anything! Jesus! Will you go already?"

He scowled at her. "Don't use the Lord's name in vain."

"Don't give me reason to!" She headed toward her father's house, fueled by the annoyance her partner had caused, but with every step she took toward the ramp that led to her dad's front door, she wanted to turn and run away.

A haze of humid heat hung over the city, sucking the life out of her. Sweat that she couldn't blame entirely on the heat coated her back as she scaled the ramp. She could count on one hand the number of times she and her dad had truly been at odds with each other. After today, she'd probably need the fingers on her second hand.

She rapped on the door and stepped inside. The blinds were drawn to keep the heat out and the cool air from the air conditioner in.

"Hi, Sam," Celia said, coming from the kitchen to take a close look at Sam's face. "Well, I suppose it could be worse."

"How could it be worse?"

"Um, I'm not sure."

"Nick's fundraiser is tonight, and I have to go looking like this."

"Tracy was here. She said she found just the thing to cover up the bruises."

"Does it come with a rolling pan?" Sam asked.

Celia laughed. "She never mentioned a roller, but she said it works miracles, and they use it on movie sets. Apparently, she did some research after she heard what happened earlier."

"I have the best sisters in the whole world." They were always there for her when she needed them. "Have you talked to Ang today?" The younger of Sam's two older sisters was due to deliver her second child any day now.

"I was over there earlier. She's absolutely miserable. The heat isn't helping anything."

"It'll be over soon." And then her sister would have a second beautiful child while Sam was still hoping to have her first someday. "Could I ask you something?"

"Of course, honey. Anything."

"So you know how I thought I couldn't get pregnant…"

She nodded. "I know the last miscarriage was a terrible blow, but at least you know now that you can get pregnant."

"That's sort of the problem. How do I risk that happening again? It was almost more bearable when I thought I couldn't get pregnant."

"I can see how knowing you can conceive would torment you after all you've been through."

"The three-month birth-control shot I had before the wedding is wearing off."

"I didn't realize you'd done that. I have to admit that's a bit of a relief to know you were using birth control. I kept hoping you'd conceive again."

"I needed some time to decide if I want to go down that road again."

"What does Nick say?"

"That it's up to me. Whatever I want is what he wants."

Celia rested a hand on Sam's arm. "Why am I not surprised? He's such a sweetheart."

"Yes, he really is, and he's been terrific about this situation from the beginning." Sam took a deep, shuddering breath. With everything else she had going on today, she had no business wandering down this fraught path, but the impending birth of her new niece had stirred up all the old feelings. "They're so good to me, and I love them more than almost anyone, but I'm so jealous of Tracy and Ang," she said softly. "Isn't that an awful thing to say?"

"No, honey. It's totally understandable. They have the one thing you've been denied. Of course you're jealous." Celia wrapped her up in a tight hug. "Want to know what I'd do if I were you?"

Sam nodded. At some point in the last few months, her new stepmother had become one of her closest friends.

"Give it one more try. Go in knowing it could go either way, and be prepared to accept any and all consequences. If it doesn't work, be done with it and examine other options. If you don't try once more, you're apt to spend the rest of your life regretting it and wondering what might've been."

"It all sounds so simple when you put it that way." Sam swiped at the tears that suddenly dampened her face. So predictable. She couldn't speak of this issue without tears.

"I don't mean to make light of what you've been through. Four miscarriages would be enough to break anyone's spirit."

"You make a good point," Sam said. "I'd always wonder what might've happened if I tried one more time."

"Tried what?" Skip asked as he wheeled his chair into the room.

"To have a baby," Sam said, brushing away the last of the tears, because she knew they'd upset him. She gasped when her hand connected with her injured face.

"Are you, uh, you know…"

"Pregnant?" Sam asked, amused by his reaction. He still liked to think his three little girls were untouched despite evidence to the contrary. "Not at the moment."

"Oh, um. Okay."

"But I might be before much longer," she said, realizing her stepmother's wise words had pushed her to a decision. She'd try one more time.

"Are you sure that's a good idea?" he asked haltingly.

"Hell, no, I'm not sure of anything. It's probably a terrible idea. But Celia is right when she says I'll always wonder what might've been if I don't try once more."

"I don't know if I could stand to watch you go through that again, baby girl."

"I don't know if I could stand it, either, but how do I not try now that I know it's possible?" Goddamned tears. She fucking *hated* that she couldn't get through a single conversation on this issue without them.

Celia handed Sam a tissue.

She wiped the tears from her sore face. "This isn't even what I came here to talk to you about."

"What's up?" her dad asked.

"Work stuff."

"I'll be in the kitchen if you need me," Celia said. She kissed Sam's forehead. "Hang in there, honey. I know it's a tough decision, and we're here for you no matter what."

"Thank you. That helps."

Celia left the room, and Skip turned his gaze on Sam. She made an effort to clear her mind and get her emotions under control. "I talked to McBride and Tyrone."

"And?"

Sam dropped onto the sofa and forced herself to make eye contact with him when she'd rather be looking anywhere but into his intense gaze. "They lied."

"About?"

"They said they hadn't uncovered anything new, but they discovered several leads that should've been followed up on. They were surprised you hadn't done that."

He didn't blink when he said, "Why did they lie? Did they say?"

"You were in the hospital. We weren't sure you were going to make it. They were concerned about your reputation and wanted to spare me the added worry when I was already so wound up about you."

"So what now?"

"I'm not entirely sure, to be honest. I only found this out a short time ago. I suspended both of them for a week without pay."

"Because they lied to you."

"Yes."

"I suppose you had no choice."

Sam wanted to scream at him to tell her why he'd left loose ends in a murder investigation. "No, I didn't, but I don't plan to tell anyone else why I suspended them, so I'd appreciate if you didn't either."

"If they contest it, you'll have to tell IAB."

"They won't contest it." She paused, waited, hoped he'd say something more, but he didn't. "You're not going to tell me why?"

"No, I'm not."

Astounded, Sam stared at him. "Seriously? You're going to blow me off?"

"I'm going to tell you the same thing I told you the first time we talked about this case. Remember?"

"How could I forget? It was the day you were shot."

"And what did I say then?"

"You said to leave it alone."

"I say the same thing now."

"How do you expect me to leave it alone?" She got up from the sofa so she could pace off some of the energy zipping through her veins. "I've got two detectives who know there was more to the story than what you reported. What do you expect me to do about that?"

"I suppose that's up to you, isn't it? If you'd done what I'd told you and stayed out of it, we wouldn't be having this conversation, would we?"

"You're putting me in an impossible situation."

"You put yourself there."

"I did this for you! To clear up your last open case! It got Jeannie back to work after the attack. I thought I was doing a good thing."

"You did a good thing giving her a cold case. That was a smart move. It's too bad you gave her this one."

"I'm sure she'd agree, since the detective in charge of the case is stonewalling us. And the investigation got her suspended." Sam released her long hair from the clip she'd worn to work and ran her fingers through it. "What am I supposed to do now?"

"Let. It. Go. That's what you do."

"What aren't you telling me?"

His fierce stare answered for him. Whatever he was hiding, he had no plans to share it with her.

"Great," Sam said. "Thanks a lot for your help. I really appreciate this. I can't tell you how much. Tell Celia I'll see her tomorrow." She'd reached the door before another thought hit her, so big and so overwhelming it took her breath away. Turning back to her father, she said, "Does this have something to do with why you were shot? Have you known all along who shot you and you've let me chase my tail?"

"No! Absolutely not. I have no idea who shot me. I swear to you."

Sam wanted to sag under the weight of the relief but refused to give him the satisfaction of knowing how undone she was. Without another word, she walked out of his house and down the ramp to the sidewalk. Other than the day they'd had words about the Fitzgerald case and his dismay over her choice to marry Peter Gibson, Sam couldn't remember a time when she'd been so angry with him—or so disappointed in him. It was their job to get justice for those who couldn't get it for themselves. He'd owed Tyler Fitzgerald more than to let obvious leads go uninvestigated.

A glance at her cell phone told her the visit to her dad's house had taken far longer than the few minutes she'd intended. It was now five after six. She rushed up the ramp and into her own house.

Only the sight of her sexy husband in a tuxedo could wipe the last twenty minutes from her mind. Seeing him in formal attire took her right back to the best day of her life. "Sorry. I know I'm late, but I'll be quick."

He stopped her from rushing past him to the stairs.

"Have you been crying?"

Leave it to him to notice. "Maybe a little."

"Over what?"

"Celia and I were talking about the issue." Sam knew she didn't need to say anything more. He would know.

His brows knitted with concern. "And?"

She went up on tiptoes to kiss him and realized she was going to have to give up kissing until her face healed. "Let's talk about it in the car, okay?"

"Sure. Tracy's upstairs with her magic makeup."

"She's always thinking, that one."

"Good thing, huh?" he asked with barely concealed humor.

"Shut up and let me go. My husband will be pissed if I'm not ready on time."

"By all means. Go on ahead. We don't want him pissed with you."

"No, we don't." Sam scurried up the stairs. "He's far too fond of make-up sex."

That got a chuckle out of him. "Sam," he called after her.

She turned to him. "Yeah?"

"Don't bother with the paint if it hurts to put it on."

Only half her face cooperated when she tried to smile. "I'm sure it'll be fine. I'll be quick." In her bedroom, she called for Tracy, who came out of the adjoining bathroom and flinched when she caught a first glimpse of Sam's face.

"Holy shit," she whispered. "Does it hurt like a mofo?"

"Sure does. I've been popping pills all afternoon."

"Should you stay home tonight?"

"Probably, but I can't do that to him, Trace. We're all about my work all the time around here. It's his turn. Plus, Scotty will be there, but Nick doesn't know that."

"You'll surely make a stir, not that you don't always."

"I heard you have some magic cover-up that'll make me as good as new."

Tracy snorted with laughter. "You'd need actual paint to cover that mess."

"Aw, now you're hurting my feelings."

"Let's see what we can do." Tracy led her into the bathroom where she'd laid out her makeup case.

"Any word on Ang?" Sam asked as she took a seat in the chair that Tracy had dragged in from the bedroom.

"Nothing but a whole lot of bitching. She's in the beyond-uncomfortable stage of pregnancy. Sucks."

The words "I wouldn't know" were on the tip of Sam's tongue, but she held them back, not wanting to make Tracy feel bad. As she settled into the chair, exhaustion seized her, and she wondered how she would possibly get through the long night of schmoozing.

Tracy produced a huge foam cup of coffee and handed it to her sister.

"Jesus, Trace, do you think of everything?"

"I try."

"You're so good to me."

"That's what big sisters are for."

"I'm nowhere near as good to you as you are to me."

"Seriously? What about all the years I was a single mom and you took Brooke on the weekends? I'll never be able to repay you for that."

"That's true." Sam took a big drink of coffee. "I don't feel so bad anymore."

"Ha! You got over that pretty quick."

"How're things with Brooke?"

"Awful. She's so damned willful and mouthy."

"Can't imagine where she gets that from."

"I know! I tell Mike every day that she's just like her Auntie Sam."

Sam laughed. "How'd that go so wrong on me?"

Tracy smiled as she worked with intense concentration. "That was a softball."

"You're okay, though, right?"

"I'm told it gets better, but I hate to say I'm counting the days until she graduates next June and goes away to college. We could all use a break from the war zone."

Sam met her sister's gaze in the mirror. "I know you've already got enough going on, but I need to talk to you about something else."

Tracy paused in her application of makeup to the un-injured side of Sam's face. "Okay."

"Remember when Dad was in the hospital in April and I told you I'd reopened Fitzgerald?"

"What about it?"

"You said something then about what was going on between Mom and Dad at that time and how I was too young to remember. What were you talking about?"

"It's all ancient history, Sam. Why do you care now?"

"Humor me, will you?"

"I don't know anything for sure. I only have my own suspicions."

"About?"

"Right around the time that Dad caught the Fitzgerald case, Mom accused him of having an affair. That was the first time she moved out."

Sam tried frantically to process the idea of her father being unfaithful to her mother. It was her mother's in-fidelity that ultimately ended their parents' marriage, the day after Sam, their youngest child, graduated from high school. Sam, who'd always been closer to her dad, hadn't seen much of her mother since then—and not at all after her mother caused a big scene at Sam's first wedding. "Do you know if it was true?" Sam asked. "Did he cheat?"

"I don't know for sure, but I suspect there was something going on based on the way he was acting. He was hardly ever home, but when he was, he was distracted as all hell. I vividly remember that."

Sam wished she could recall, but she'd been so young.

Tracy handed Sam the makeup sponge. "Why don't you do the bad side yourself? I don't want to hurt you." Sam stood up to get closer to the mirror and dabbed the liquid foundation on the bruises above and below the white strip of bandage. "Damn, this stuff is amazing."

"I had it left over from my theater days. It covers a world of sin."

"Not much I can do about the eye that's swollen shut, but the rest looks a little less evil than it did. Thanks."

"Any time. Let's get you into this gorgeous dress."

"Knock, knock," a familiar voice called from the bedroom.

"Come in," Sam said.

Shelby Faircloth came around the corner into the spacious bathroom and stopped short at the sight of the gorgeous silk dress. "Oh. My. God. I think I just passed out for a second. Is that pink?"

"Absolutely not," Sam said. "It's champagne."

"It's pink."

"She's queer for pink," Sam said to Tracy.

Tracy eyed Shelby's pink suit and the matching sky-high pink heels that brought her almost to Sam's shoulder. "I can see that."

"She's seeing pink in places where there is no pink," Sam said.

"If there's one thing I know, it's pink. And that dress is *pink*."

Sam assessed the dress more critically, still not seeing any sign of the dreaded color. "What're you doing here, Tinker Bell?" Sam asked, reverting to the nickname she'd given Shelby during the planning of her wedding.

"I had to drop off some paperwork to Nick for my new job." Shelby clapped her hands and let out a squeak. "I can't wait until Monday."

"What's Monday?" Tracy asked.

"They've hired me to run their lives," Shelby said with barely contained glee. "I'm so excited!"

"What a great idea," Tracy said. "I could use some help bailing her out of one scrape after another." Tracy gestured to the carnage on Sam's face.

The three women shared a laugh.

"I'll take all the help I can get," Sam said.

"Nick said you were up here primping, and then I discover the dress is pink," Shelby said with an exaggerated sigh. "Put it on. I need to see that gorgeous thing in action."

"Hang on." Sam gave up trying to convince Shelby she was seeing things. "There's torture-chamber underwear that goes on first."

"Oh," Shelby said with a shiver. "Underwear."

"She's not right in the head," Tracy called after Sam as she crossed the hallway to her super-deluxe closet. "I've been saying that since before the wedding," Sam said as she rolled on thigh-high hose and wrestled her way into a corset contraption that the designer had provided. "No one listens to me."

"Be quiet and put your panties on," Shelby said. Sam slid on the thong that matched the corset. When she turned to go back to the bedroom, she found her husband blocking the doorway.

His eyes blazed a path down the front of her as he took in the getup.

"Don't give me that look," she said, holding out a hand to stop him from coming in. "We so don't have time for that look."

Nick stepped into the room and closed the door behind him. "I need one quick feel to tide me over until later, when I'll spend a lot more time examining every delicious detail."

Sam released a nervous laugh and pressed her hand to his chest to keep him from getting too close. "It won't be my fault if you make me late."

"So noted," he said, taking her hand from his chest and pulling her in. He put his arms around her and ran his hands from her shoulders to her waist and below to cup her buttocks. When he drew her tight against him, his arousal pulsed between them. His lips found her neck, and Sam tipped her head to give him better access. "How am I supposed to function tonight knowing what's under your dress?"

Sam bit her lip to keep from crying out when he hit the spot on her neck that made her crazy. She slid her hands into his tuxedo jacket and took a good long feel of her favorite chest and rock-hard belly. "Why did you come back upstairs?"

"Forgot my phone in the bedroom."

A knock on the door startled them.

"Are you fooling around in there?" Tracy asked. "If you mess up my makeup job, Nick, I'll shoot you."

"Go away," Nick growled.

"The car will be here in fifteen minutes," Tracy reminded him.

"She'll be ready."

"Nick…" Sam laughed and shuddered as his industrious hands set her nerve endings on fire. "Come on. We really don't have time for this."

"I hate that there's always something demanding our time."

She placed her hands on his smooth face and compelled him to look at her. "It makes the anticipation that much sweeter." On tiptoes, she pressed her lips lightly to his, gasping when even that slight contact sent pain radiating through her injured face. "You'll have hours to anticipate what happens when we get home and you have me all to yourself." She let her hand drop below his belt to squeeze his erection.

He groaned. "You're not helping anything." Grabbing her hand, he brought it up to his lips. "Besides, you're injured. I shouldn't be pawing at you like a crazed beast."

"I love the way you want me so much," she assured him. "Don't ever stop."

"No worries there, babe." He stepped back from her and made a visible effort to gather himself. "The longer we're together, the more I want you. It's like a fever."

She did her best to smile at him. "I can get your phone for you."

"Probably a good idea. I can't show my face in the hornet's nest with such a visible 'problem.'"

The doorbell chimed through the house, making Nick groan. "Who the hell is that now?"

"Could it be the car service?"

"Probably. Jeez, you've got my whole brain scrambled."

"I told you not to touch me. This is what you get." Sam laughed at his tortured expression and scooted out the door ahead of him.

Shelby and Tracy were gabbing up a storm when Sam stepped into the bedroom.

"Ah," Tracy said, jumping up from her perch on the bed. "Finally! Is the grope session over?"

"For now," Sam said, blushing despite her iron will not to. She never had been able to dodge her older sister's penetrating stare. She hoped the makeup would cover her blush.

"I suppose I'd better get used to this kind of thing," Shelby said.

Sam detected a hint of wistfulness in her tone.

"They're all over each other every chance they get," Tracy said.

"Hello," Sam said as she stepped into the dress Tracy held for her. "I'm in the room."

"I only speak the truth."

Shelby giggled at their sisterly banter.

After Tracy zipped Sam into the dress, she turned her to face the full-length mirror.

"You look gorgeous, Sam," Shelby said. "Pink is definitely your color."

"It's not pink." Sam had to admit that she looked pretty damned good, despite the puffiness on her face.

"One thing is for certain, they'll notice the dress and your killer bod before they see your face," Tracy said.

"That's comforting," Sam said. She went into the bathroom to brush her teeth—carefully—and comb her hair one last time. Since they so rarely got to spend an evening together during campaign season, Sam had left her hair down the way her husband liked it best. Emerging from the bathroom, she gave her sister a quick hug. "Thanks a million, Trace. As always, you came through for me big-time."

"My pleasure, hon. You're stunning. Go knock 'em dead."

In deference to the special occasion, Sam slid her sparkling engagement ring on over the wedding band she wore all the time and fastened the diamond key necklace Nick had given her as a wedding gift.

She grabbed Nick's phone off his dresser and led the other women downstairs, stopping short when she found Agent Hill standing in her living room. He and Nick were eyeing one another like wary dogs about to tear each other's throats out.

And then Nick noticed her, and his full focus was on her.

Later, when she was alone and had time to process it, she would pick over the moment of unguarded awe Hill sent her way when he first laid eyes on her in the slinky dress. Luckily, his usual flat mask was back in place before anyone else noticed. But Sam had noticed, and the observation left her reeling as she tried to figure out what it meant.

TWELVE

Nick walked over, put his arm around her and kissed the top of her head. "You look amazing."

"Thanks." In a low tone that only he could hear, she said, "Don't you dare lift your leg and pee on me."

He drew back from her and looked down at her, puzzlement marking his face. "Huh?"

Sam decided she'd deal with him in the car. "What's up, Hill?"

"I'm sorry to bother you at home, but I've come from the Kavanaughs' house, and since I was close by, I wanted to let you know we've had a rather significant break in the kidnapping case."

Sam was instantly on alert and right back in cop mode. "Speak. Quickly."

"Crime Scene detectives found records of a GPS locating device Victoria had implanted in the baby the day after her birth."

"Are you serious?" Sam asked. "Who does that?"

"Perhaps a mother who's concerned about the very scenario that later unfolded."

"Did Derek know about it?"

Hill shook his head. "The IT division has traced the signal to a house in Bellevue," he said, referring to a rough neighborhood in the city's southeastern corner.

"I'll let Cruz know," Sam said. "He can oversee our team."

"Already done. He's notified SWAT, and we're mobilizing in fifteen minutes."

Sam stood perfectly still as she fought the overwhelming desire to be part of the team that would hopefully recover Maeve Kavanaugh. The weight of her husband's hand on her shoulder reminded her that she had somewhere else to be tonight. "Good. Keep me posted."

Hill seemed almost surprised that she didn't want to be part of the mission.

Sam watched his eyes shift to her right and realized he'd noticed Shelby and Tracy. "My sister, Tracy, and our, um, new assistant, Shelby Faircloth. Agent Avery Hill."

Hill nodded to the women. "Ladies." To Sam, he said, "You have an assistant, huh?" The touch of amusement in his honey drawl irritated her.

Sam wished her usual scowl was available. "Don't you have a raid to get to?"

"On my way. I'll let you know how it goes." To Nick, he nodded and said, "Senator."

Nick said nothing as Hill let himself out. Then Nick turned to his wife. "So he had to come to our house to tell you that? Is your phone not working?"

She handed him his phone. "It was down here in my purse, and I'm glad he came to tell me they might've found Maeve. Aren't you glad too?"

His expression was positively thunderous. "Of course I am."

Wow, Sam thought. When she thought he couldn't get any sexier, jealous Nick proved otherwise.

"Oh. My. God." Shelby fanned herself with her hand. "Who the hell was that?"

"I told you," Sam said, annoyed. "Agent Hill."

"What kind of agent?" Shelby asked, looking a bit flushed and doe-eyed.

"FBI."

"That accent," Tracy said. "Listening to him talk was almost as good as sex."

"I know!" Shelby said. "I was thinking sex-on-a-stick, baby. I call dibs."

Tracy dissolved into laughter. "Sadly, I'm already married. He's all yours."

"I'm so going to like working here," Shelby said. "All the guys I get to meet in my current line of work are already spoken for. Will we be seeing more of the very yummy Agent Hill?"

"God, I hope not," Nick said.

"Is he single?" Shelby asked.

"Hell if I know," Sam said. "If you're done drooling over my colleague, we've got a fundraiser to get to."

"The car will be here in five minutes," Nick said.

"Tell me again why we aren't driving ourselves?" Sam asked.

Nick slipped an arm around her bare shoulders and drew her in close to him. "I don't get much time alone with my wife. Why would I spend two hours driving there and back when I could use that time with her so much more...productively?"

"Y'all are too damned cute," Shelby said.

"*He* is cute," Sam said with a pointed look for her new assistant. "I am most definitely not cute. Got me?"

"Absolutely." Shelby made a poor attempt to hide her smile. "Gotcha, boss."

"ARE YOU GOING to tell me why you were crying before?" Nick asked the minute they were settled in the backseat of the black sedan. A privacy screen sealed them off from the driver as they headed south toward Leesburg.

Sam reached for his hand. "I talked to Celia about the birth-control shot wearing off and the big decision."

He seemed to stop breathing. "And?"

"She pointed out that if we don't try at least once more, I'll always wonder what might've been."

"How do you feel about that?"

"She's right. I would always wonder. For so long, I didn't think it was possible, and now..."

"Now that you know it's possible, it's all you can think about."

"Yes." She forced herself to look directly into his eyes. "I want to try again. One more time. If it doesn't work, we'll adopt or hire a surrogate or do whatever people do when they can't have kids of their own."

"You're sure?"

Not trusting herself to speak, she nodded.

"If you were to get pregnant, how would you handle work and everything?"

"That's something I've thought a lot about. There's no way I could roll up into a ball for ten months and do nothing. I'd want to keep my routine as regular as possible for as long as I could."

"And then you'd roll up into a ball?"

Smiling, she nodded. "I wouldn't take any foolish chances, but I can't roll myself in bubble wrap, either."

"Trust me, if that was possible, I would've done it a long time ago." He raised his arm, inviting her closer.

Sam rested the uninjured side of her face on his chest, using her hair to protect his suit from her makeup.

"We're really going to do this?"

She nodded.

"And you're really going to be all right if it doesn't go our way?"

"Will you be there to put the pieces back together?"

"Always."

"Then I'll be all right."

"I love you so much, Sam. You have no idea how much."

"If it's anywhere near as much as I love you, it's an awful lot."

He squeezed her shoulder and ran his lips over her forehead. "I have a good feeling about this."

"I'm glad." She closed her eyes tight against the rush of emotion, mindful of the mascara Tracy had applied. "Other than the last five minutes, this has been such a shitty day."

"Does your face hurt bad?"

"It's bearable, but that's the least of my problems." She told him about what'd happened with McBride and Tyrone as well as the unsatisfying confrontation with her father.

"Jeez," Nick said. "As if getting pistol whipped in the face wasn't enough for one day."

That made Sam laugh and then moan when the wound protested the movement. "Don't make me laugh."

"What do you think your dad is keeping from you?"

Sam was still trying to get her head around the awful certainty that he was hiding something that would blow his life—and maybe hers, too—to smithereens if it was ever revealed. "I think he was having an affair, and some-how it's tied to the Fitzgerald case."

"Really? I so don't see him as the cheating type."

"Well, to be fair, you've only known him as a quad-riplegic."

"Still, I know him, and I don't see it."

"Tracy has alluded to something big going on between my parents around the same time as the Fitzgerald case, but even she doesn't know what exactly. Apparently, that was the first time my mother moved out. I don't remember it, though."

"How old were you?"

"Ten."

"And you don't remember your mother moving out?"

"She was always going off somewhere with her girl-friends or her sisters, so I wouldn't have thought anything of her being gone. She eventually came back."

"I hate to say this…"

"I'm already thinking it," Sam said.

"If your father won't talk about it, maybe she will."

The thought of calling her mother after so many years of silence filled Sam with anxiety.

Nick rubbed a soothing hand up and down her arm. "You don't have to do anything about it until you feel ready."

"I'm afraid my father will never speak to me again if I pursue this, but how can I not now that I know there were leads that weren't fully investigated?"

"As the lieutenant in charge of the Homicide division, you have an obligation to do your job. Wouldn't he do the same in your position?"

"Probably, but it's hard to remember it's my job when my dad is telling me to leave it alone."

"He's put you in an untenable position."

"That's putting it mildly. Not that you ever would, but you can't say anything about this to anyone. I had no choice but to suspend McBride and Tyrone, but if I have my way, no one will ever know why. Of course Stahl is already sniffing around."

"Don't worry, babe. I won't say a word."

"I wish I'd hear something from Freddie about the raid."

"You will. As soon as they have something to tell you, you'll hear."

FREDDIE KNEW THE goal was the safe recovery of Maeve Kavanaugh, and every cell in his body was focused on the baby. That didn't mean, however, he wasn't rankled to be taking orders from the Fed who'd put himself in charge of this operation in Sam's absence.

Ramsey and his partner were stuck in traffic in Maryland, where they'd gone to check out a couple of leads that'd been called in after the Amber Alert was issued.

While they waited for the SWAT team to move into place, Freddie held his position, awaiting Hill's order to go in. Sweating like a pig from the combination of the Kevlar vest he wore over his clothes and the oppressive heat, he had his weapon drawn and kept his gaze fixed on the small, shingled house. From the outside, it appeared the place had seen better days, which meant it fit right in with the other houses in the tired neighborhood.

With SWAT in position, Hill ran through a roll call, checking to make sure everyone was in position. When he was finished, Freddie waited to hear the word in his earpiece.

"Go," Hill said, signaling SWAT to take control of the house. Using a battering ram, they took down the front door as if it were made of paper. A woman's shrill shriek greeted them.

"Secure," the SWAT team commander reported less than thirty seconds later.

"Cruz, Arnold," Hill said. "Go."

Freddie ran for the open door with Detective Arnold right behind him, providing cover. Inside, they found an older black woman crying hysterically. Her hands were up in deference to the two-dozen semiautomatic weapons trained on her.

The house appeared clean and well kept on the surface. Sitting in a high chair in the kitchen that adjoined the living room, Maeve Kavanaugh watched the goings on warily, as if she didn't know what to make of all the commotion.

"Hi, Maeve," Freddie said gently, trying not to scare the poor kid any more than necessary. "My name is Freddie, and your daddy sent me to get you."

A quick assessment showed the child to be clean and apparently well cared for. There were no outward signs of trauma, which didn't mean the kid hadn't been traumatized.

"Dada."

"Yes, Dada sent me." As Arnold arrested the hysterical woman and recited her rights, Freddie fumbled with the tray, trying to figure out how to get it off the chair.

One of the SWAT officers took mercy on him and reached beneath the tray to release it.

"Thanks," Freddie said. "No kids."

"No kidding," the officer said with a grin. The relief in the room was palpable now that they'd found Maeve unharmed.

When Freddie lifted the blond-haired toddler from the chair, she stiffened and let out a shriek of protest. Her tiny body went rigid in his arms. She was probably tired of being handled by strangers.

"Mama! Mama!" Maeve began to cry in earnest as Freddie carried her out of the house to the paramedics, who whisked her away.

"I'll ride with her," Freddie said to Hill as the agent met him outside. "Have you notified Mr. Kavanaugh?"

"Already done. He'll meet you at GW."

As a Homicide detective, Freddie didn't get to see many happy endings. Reuniting Maeve Kavanaugh with her father was something he was truly looking forward to.

"What do we know about the woman?" Freddie asked. There hadn't been much time for questions before the raid.

"Only her name. Bertha Ray. Apparently, she's known around the neighborhood as a grandmotherly type, always taking in strays."

"That doesn't jibe with the profile of a kidnapping murderer."

"No, it doesn't," Hill said, seeming as frustrated as Freddie felt. "I'm going to HQ to question Mrs. Ray. Keep me posted on Maeve's condition."

"I will, and I'll let the lieutenant know that—"

"I'll take care of notifying her," Hill said.

What the hell was that all about? "Yes, sir, Agent Hill." Freddie made no effort to keep the sarcasm out of his tone. "Whatever you say."

With a curt nod, Hill went to talk to the SWAT commander.

"SO FUCKING STUPID," Hill muttered to himself as he walked away from Cruz. He was doing a piss-poor job of hiding his feelings for the outrageously sexy lieutenant.

When he thought about how she'd looked floating down the stairs in that shimmering evening gown...

Her husband had noticed her at the same instant Hill did, which was the only reason Hill was still alive. If the senator had seen the reaction Hill had to the sight of his gorgeous wife, Hill wouldn't have blamed the senator for resorting to violence.

He'd stooped to an all-time low by lusting after another man's wife. Now Cruz was wondering why he was so insistent on calling the lieutenant himself rather than the far more logical scenario of her partner taking care of it.

Hill stormed over to talk to the SWAT commander, who viewed him suspiciously.

"Everything all right, Agent Hill?"

"Yeah," Hill said. "We're good. Pass along my thanks to your team."

"Will do. Glad we found the kid."

Hill nodded in agreement. His every emotion was simmering on the surface of his skin, reminding him of the time he'd stumbled upon a nest of fire ants as a kid. He waited for the Crime Scene unit to arrive and got them started processing the scene before he got in the car and turned the air conditioning to blast.

For a long time he sat there, letting the cool air pummel him. He wasn't thinking about the interrogation he needed to oversee or the child he'd helped to rescue or the confusing case that promised to expose a scheme of epic proportions. No, his every thought was still focused on the image of Sam coming down the stairs in that amazing dress. If he lived to be a hundred years old, he'd never forget how gorgeous she'd looked in that moment.

Burying his fingers in his hair, he took a series of deep

breaths, hoping to calm his fast-beating heart. He needed to call her and tell her the raid had been a success. Even though he could more than handle the interrogation on his own, he wanted her thoughts on how best to proceed.

When the hell had her voice become the one in his head? At this very moment, she was snuggled up to her dashing husband in the back of a limo on the way to the fundraiser. She probably hadn't given him a thought since he left her house. Whereas she was all he could think about.

Why had he gone to the house in the first place? He couldn't really say, except he'd assumed she'd be suffering more than most over the missing child. He knew about her history of miscarriage—hell, everyone knew after the *Reporter* printed the salacious story about her earlier in the year. He'd wanted her to know as soon as he did that they'd had a break. When she didn't answer her phone, he'd acted without thinking, and now he had an image burned into his brain that would stay with him forever.

"That's what you get, asshole. Poking your nose into places you don't belong. Get it together, for crying out loud." He could lecture himself all night, but it wouldn't change anything. Reaching for his cell phone, he found her number in his contacts—why her number was in his contacts was another cause for concern—and pressed Send.

While he waited for her to answer, he pinched the bridge of his nose, where a headache had formed in the last hour.

"Holland." Her voice sounded husky and sexy, as if she'd been sleeping or… No. Don't think about that. Do. Not. Think. About. That.

"Hill? Are you there?"

"Sorry, someone was talking to me. We got the kid."

"Is she…"

"She seems fine. The paramedics are taking her to the ER where her father is meeting her. Cruz went with her."

"That's good. What a relief."

"For sure."

"Who had her?"

"An older woman named Bertha Ray. My gut is telling me she's got nothing to do with the kidnapping. Word on the street is she's the neighborhood babysitter. A real grandmotherly type. The goal will be to figure out who hired her."

"Sounds like a plan. Keep me posted."

"Tomorrow we need to start over and dig into this thing big-time." Another thought occurred to him. "Are you working tomorrow?"

"Of course I am. Why wouldn't I be?"

"I thought with the injury—"

"I'm fine. I'll see you in the morning. Make sure someone gets word to me about what you get from the interview with Ray."

"I will."

The line went dead. She was gone. Off to spend a glamorous evening with her glamorous husband.

Avery drove through the congested city to HQ. He was halfway there when Detective Arnold called to find out if he was coming to do the interrogation or if he expected them to handle it.

"I'll be there in ten minutes."

He had to get his head back in the game. There'd be plenty of time later to think about what he couldn't have.

OUTSIDE THE EXAMINATION room where Dr. Harry Flynn
was checking a very vocal Maeve Kavanaugh, Freddie
was thinking about calling Sam. Who cared what Hill
said? She was his partner, and he'd damned well call
her if he wanted to. His phone rang, startling him out
of his snit. He didn't recognize the local number on his
caller ID.

"Cruz."

"Malone."

Freddie stood up a little straighter at the sound of the
captain's voice. "Sir."

"You have the Kavanaugh child?"

"Yes, sir."

"And she's in good health?"

"Apparently so, sir. The doctor is with her now."

"The media has caught wind of the fact that we've
found her. I'm told there's a mob outside the emergency
room. I want you to handle them."

"Um, handle them, sir? In what way?"

"The usual way. Give them a statement of what went
down earlier. Don't mention the GPS locating device or
Mrs. Ray's involvement."

Freddie broke out in a cold sweat. "You want me to
talk to the media?"

"That's what I said. Can you handle it?"

"Yes, sir. Of course." He spoke with far more confidence than he felt.

"When you're done there, go home. We'll be recon-
vening at zero seven hundred at HQ."

"Yes, sir."

"Did the lieutenant mention that Melissa Woodmansee
has filed suit against the department?"

"Yes, sir. She did."

"They're apt to ask you about it. If they do, you have no comment. Understood?"

"Yes, sir."

"Thanks, Cruz."

For a long time after the line went dead, Freddie stood there like a stooge, holding his phone away from his body as if it contained explosives. Sam always took care of the media. That was never his thing.

Until now.

Deciding to put off the encounter for as long as he could, Freddie waited in the hallway, hoping for a report from the doctors.

The double doors burst open a short time later, and Derek Kavanaugh came running down the corridor, followed by two older people who Freddie assumed were his parents. Kavanaugh looked quite a bit worse for the wear since Freddie had last seen him. His hair was standing on end, his eyes were wild-looking and he hadn't seen a razor in days.

"Where is she? Where's my daughter?"

"Dr. Harry is with her now," Freddie said, gesturing to the cubicle.

Kavanaugh rushed by him and let out an agonized moan at the sight of his child sitting on the big bed.

"Dada."

"Yes, baby, it's me." Derek broke down into ragged sobs. "It's Dada." He pushed past Harry and the nurses and scooped up the blond-haired girl, hugging her tightly enough that she squawked in protest. "Is she okay?" he asked Harry.

"Seems to be fine," Harry replied. "We found no injuries or obvious signs of trauma. She was apparently well fed and cared for."

"Thank God," Derek's mother said as she wiped tears from her face.

"Can I take her home?" Derek asked.

"We're waiting on some blood work, and then she'll be good to go."

"Thank you, Harry," Derek said, burying his face in blond ringlets as his shoulders shook with sobs. "Thank you so much."

Harry rested a hand on his friend's back as Derek's parents pulled their son and granddaughter into a hug.

Feeling like an intruder in an intensely personal reunion, Freddie left the room.

Harry came out a minute later, discreetly wiping tears from his face. "Such a relief," he said.

"For sure. I hear there're reporters outside. Is there any way to get the family out of here without Mr. Kavanaugh having to carry his daughter past them?"

"We'll arrange to have them escorted through the main doors. I'll call security."

"Thank you."

Still trying to prepare himself to deal with the media, Freddie decided to wait around until Maeve was released.

Derek stepped into the hallway a few minutes later. His eyes had lost some of their wildness, but his face was now streaked with dampness. From inside the cubicle, Freddie could hear Maeve's grandparents talking to her.

"Where did you find her?" Derek asked.

"At a house in Bellevue."

"And this GPS device, the one my wife had implanted in my child without my knowledge, that's what led you to her?"

"Yes." Freddie couldn't blame the guy for the bitterness in his tone when he spoke of his late wife.

Derek's jaw shifted, and his eyes fixed on the far wall. "Why would she do that? Why would she have a locator device put in our child?"

"I imagine for the same reason anyone would—a fear of one day needing it." The desolation Freddie saw in Derek's eyes broke his fragile heart.

"It would seem, from what you've uncovered so far about my wife, that she had a greater-than-average reason to be afraid of such a scenario."

Freddie had no idea what he was supposed to say to that. "I wouldn't know that for certain, sir. Does the name Bertha Ray mean anything to you?"

Derek shook his head. "Is that who had her?"

"Yes."

"Why would someone I've never heard of kill my wife and take my child?"

"We don't know yet that she did either of those things."

"But she had Maeve!"

"Someone could've hired her to care for your daughter. Agent Hill and Detective Arnold have her in custody and will be interviewing her shortly."

"So even though you found Maeve, you may not have found the person who killed Victoria."

"That's correct." Derek's probing questions were good practice for the upcoming encounter with the press.

"If only Maeve were a little older. She could tell us who did this."

"It's a blessing that she won't remember it."

"That's true." Derek ran a hand through his hair, which only added to the disorder. "I'd like to be kept informed."

"Of course."

"And I'd like to be able to bury my wife."

"As soon as the medical examiner completes her work,

you'll be notified." Freddie paused for a moment to see if he had other questions. "Hospital security will help you get your daughter out of here without a media circus."

"I appreciate that."

"I've been asked to brief the media. May I tell them your daughter is in good condition?"

Derek pondered that for a moment. "People have been so worried about her. We should tell them she's fine, or as fine as she can be after what she's been through."

"I'll take care of it."

Derek's mother peeked through the curtain. "She's asking for you, honey."

With a nod for Freddie, Derek went back to his daughter.

Freddie released a long, deep breath and let his head fall back against the wall. Closing his eyes, he tried to imagine the hell Derek Kavanaugh was going through after learning his wife wasn't who he'd thought she was. Even though they'd found his daughter unharmed, his life was still permanently changed. Nothing they could do would bring back his wife. And while Freddie was certain they'd eventually find her murderer, Derek may never know for sure if her feelings for him had been genuine.

Sometimes this job truly sucked, Freddie decided as he opened his eyes and summoned the fortitude he'd need to square off with the rabid reporters. Before he headed for the door, he pulled out his cell phone and called Elin.

"Hey," she said, sounding rushed. "Where are you?"

"At the GW ER."

"Did Sam get hurt again?"

"Earlier today. Did you see the video?"

"I did. It was amazing. She was amazing. Why are you still at the ER?"

"We found Maeve Kavanaugh."

"Oh God, is she…"

"She's fine. Back with her dad and grandparents."

"Oh, Freddie. That's such good news. People have been talking about it at the gym nonstop. How did you find her?"

"I'll tell you about it when I get home." He loved their new apartment in the Woodley Park neighborhood where he'd grown up and looked forward to their evenings together. "Where are you?"

"Leaving the gym."

"Why so late?"

"Last client was running behind, so I waited."

Freddie refused to think about the studly dudes she trained and called friends. He'd learned that was a fast track to Crazyville. "So, um, you might see me on the news."

"How come?"

"Malone asked me to brief the media that are gathered outside the hospital."

"That's so cool! Are you nervous?"

"Hell, yes. I've never done it before."

"You'll be great. Be yourself. They'll love you."

"You have to say that because you love me," he grumbled.

Laughing, she said, "Yes, I do. Now hurry up and do your press thing and get home. I'm horny."

Freddie released a tortured groan. "You had to say that right now?"

She laughed harder. "Hurry!"

Freddie ended the call and returned the phone to his pocket, his entire body filled with tension. Like he hadn't been nervous enough. Now he had visions of his lover's pierced nipples in his mind too. Determined to get the press conference over with and get home to her, he headed for the double doors.

The minute he stepped into the damp humidity, questions flew at him. There had to be at least thirty reporters and four or five TV cameras. The parking lot was lined with satellite trucks, ready to broadcast the latest news.

"Where was Maeve Kavanaugh?"

"Who had her?"

"How did you find her?"

"Did you find the murderer?"

"Is the lieutenant attending her husband's fundraiser?"

Freddie suppressed a laugh over that last one. As if he would tell them anything about Sam's personal business. Taking a page from Sam's book, he held up his hands to quiet them. "If you give me a second, I'll tell you what I can." They surprised him when they fell quiet, giving him their full attention.

"At approximately eighteen forty-five, accompanied by the MPD's SWAT unit and acting in partnership with the FBI, we entered a house in the Bellevue neighborhood, where we found Maeve Kavanaugh physically unharmed. She was transported here, and doctors have found her to be in good condition. Her father and grandparents are with her, but we ask that you respect their privacy at this difficult time."

"How did you find her?" Darren Tabor asked.

As much as Freddie would like to tell the reporter who'd been decent to Sam and to him, Freddie said, "We're not able to disclose that information at this time."

"Was the person with Maeve the same person who killed her mother?"

"We're still sorting out the details."

"Did the lieutenant's injuries keep her home from the fundraiser?" This from a blonde who worked for the *Reporter*, the tabloid that published regular stories about Sam and Nick with little regard for whether or not they were true. Their relentless focus on the couple had been a source of endless aggravation for his partner and her husband.

Freddie ignored the question.

"Is it true that Melissa Woodmansee is charging the MPD with police brutality?"

"No comment. That's all." He pushed his way through the crowd to Sam's car, feeling as if he'd done a decent job handling the questions the way Malone had asked him to.

He started the car and tore out of the parking lot. He needed to get home. His girlfriend was horny.

THIRTEEN

As THEY DROVE through the gates to the Belmont Country Club in Ashburn, Sam experienced a flutter of nerves. Being on display as the wife of an up-and-coming politician was so wildly out of her comfort zone it wasn't even funny. Since they'd been married, Sam had attended a couple of rallies for his campaign and several small fundraising dinners. That she'd been able to handle, but this, she decided as the car rolled up the hill to the stately brick mansion, was going to leave her comfort zone in the dust.

Nick squeezed her hand. "Don't freak out."

"Who's freaking out?"

Laughing, he brought her hand to his lips. "You are."

"It's irritating when you act like you know me so well."

"It's not an act. I do know you. Better than anyone, and that's why I know you're freaking out."

"There will be lot of people here."

"Yes."

"How many?"

"Graham said they expect about a thousand."

"Come on… Seriously?"

"Uh-huh."

"And they each paid how much to be here?"

"Ten thousand a head."

"Jesus. Why are you calm and cool when I'm freaking out?"

"I'm freaking out on the inside."

"You are not."

"Yes, I am. I still feel like an imposter, you know? I'm always waiting for John to tap me on the shoulder and tell me the show's over. He's back, and he's got this covered."

"Nick…" She caressed his face. "You're not an imposter. All these people are here tonight because of you. They believe in you. I believe in you. And I'm so proud of you. So very, very proud, even if I'm a little freaked out."

He flashed the grin that made her—and every other woman in the capital region—swoon. "That means a lot to me, babe. Thanks." Leaning in, he gave her a very careful kiss on her lips and then her forehead. "Ready?"

"As ready as I'll ever be." She gripped his hand.

"Don't let go, okay?"

"Never."

Their arrival had been timed to occur thirty minutes after the guests arrived, which was why the ballroom and terrace erupted into applause when they walked in hand in hand.

Graham and Laine were waiting right inside the elegant room and greeted them with hugs and concern about Sam's latest injury.

"You look gorgeous, honey," Laine whispered in Sam's ear. "Only you could take a pistol to the face in the morning and turn out in high style in the evening."

Taken aback by the compliment, Sam hugged Nick's adopted mother. "That's very sweet of you to say."

The whirlwind of greetings included Nick's deputy chief of staff, Terry O'Connor, and his girlfriend Lindsey McNamara.

"Looking good, Sam," Lindsey said.

"You too. Wow, look at you."

The medical examiner wore a pale green strapless gown that perfectly complemented her red hair and green eyes. Standing beside her in a tux, Terry looked relaxed and happy.

"Nice to see you, Sam," Terry said, kissing her cheek. They'd come a long way from Sam suspecting him of his brother's murder to being cordial acquaintances, both recognizing their accord was in Nick's best interest.

"You too, Terry. Nice to see some friendly faces in the mob."

"Gonzo and Christina are here somewhere," Lindsey said.

"So I heard."

Judson Knott and Richard Manning, chair and vice chair of the Virginia Democratic Party, swooped in on Nick. Right behind them was Virginia Governor Mike Zorn and his wife Judy.

Nick released her hand only long enough to shake hands with the other men, and then he reached for her again.

Sam gave his hand a squeeze to show her appreciation.

He didn't miss a beat in the conversation when he squeezed back, making her smile.

"I thought you guys would never get here!" a young voice said.

As if the governor and party leadership were no one special, Nick turned away from them when he heard Scotty's voice.

Wearing the suit they'd gotten him for their wedding, the boy beamed at them and moved in for hugs.

"Oh my God!" Nick said. "This is the best surprise ever!"

"So good to see you, buddy," Sam said, kissing the top of his silky head.

"Is this what you guys were talking about in the car earlier?" Nick asked.

Scotty flashed the grin so much like Nick's he could've been his biological son. It was one of many mannerisms he'd picked up from Nick. "Maybe."

"I'm so happy you're here." Nick hugged Scotty once more. "Thank you for inviting him and for doing all of this," he said to Graham.

"Our pleasure." Graham's pride in Nick shone through his gruff exterior. "Now you and your wife have got some serious mingling to do, young man."

Sam watched Nick take in the enormous crowd, his gaze circling the room before it came back to her and Scotty, leaving little doubt about where her husband would prefer to spend this evening. "So I see."

She linked her arm with his, earning a grateful smile from her husband. "Let's get to work, Senator."

"We'll see you in a bit, buddy," Nick said to Scotty. "No problem. Mrs. L said we don't have to leave to go back to Richmond until nine thirty."

"We'll work fast so we get plenty of time with you," Nick assured him.

From behind him, Laine looped her arms around Scotty's shoulders. "I'll make sure Scotty finds the ice cream bar."

Scotty looked up at her. "Is it as good as the ice cream we made at the farm?"

"Nowhere near as good, but it'll do in a pinch."

"Awesome," Scotty said, letting her lead him away.

AFTER TWO HOURS of working the room, Nick could tell that Sam was starting to fade. If his hand ached from all the vigorous shaking, he could only imagine what hers must feel like. Leaning in close to her, he whispered, "Why don't you take a break, babe?"

"I'm fine."

Over her shoulder, Nick made eye contact with a tall blonde, who waggled her fingers at him. When he recovered somewhat from the shock, he said, "Oh shit."

"What?"

"Um, babe…" Before he could prepare his wife, the blonde pounced, engulfing Nick in a tight, perfume-laced hug.

"Nicky! It's so good to see you! What's it been? Four or five years?"

Not long enough, Nick wanted to say. "At least four."

Sam cleared her throat and squeezed his hand.

He glanced down to find her looking amused—and confused. "Patrice, this is my wife, Samantha."

Before Patrice could pounce on Sam, she stuck out her hand. "Nice to meet you."

Seeming disappointed to be denied a hug, Patrice shook Sam's hand. "You too. I've heard so much about you."

"I wish I could say the same."

If the situation hadn't been so dreadfully uncomfortable, Nick would've laughed at his wife's chilly comment.

"Don't worry," Patrice said in what she considered a whisper. Everyone around them had tuned in to some sort of drama unfolding. "It's been over between me and Nicky for a while. He's all yours."

"That's so good to know," Sam said.

Nick couldn't help the snort of laughter that erupted from his chest. Oh, he would hear about this later! "What're you doing here, Patrice?"

"I came with Bryce, but I wanted to support your campaign. And I was hoping to see you and meet your lovely wife. It's been far too long. We should all get together sometime."

Perhaps when pigs flew in hell. "It was nice to see you," Nick said, seeking an exit strategy, "but we've got to keep moving."

"Don't be such a stranger, Nicky," she said with a pout that probably worked on most men. It'd never done it for him. "We had some good times. So nice to finally meet you, Samantha."

Double shit! He was the only one allowed to call her that. This was going from bad to worse.

"Likewise," Sam said through gritted teeth. "Graham is looking for you, Nick."

"Back to work. See you, Patrice."

"Bye, Nicky."

As they walked away, Nick said, "Am I going to pay for that later?"

"What do you think?"

"Oh, I can't wait." With his arm around her, he tugged her close and pressed a kiss to her temple. "Go find Scotty and Laine and take a load off for a bit. I can tell you're running on fumes."

"I'm afraid Patrice will steal you away if I let you out of my sight, Nicky."

"No worries there. I'm all yours, babe. Go on ahead. I'll find you in a bit."

"If you insist, but I'll be watching you, Nicky."

"I wouldn't have it any other way." Sending her off with a smile and a discreet pat on the bum, he watched her work her way through the crowd to the table Laine, Scotty and his guardian, Mrs. Littlefield, had claimed.

"That was quite a show your lovely wife put on this morning," Governor Zorn said.

"She is so brave," his wife, Judy, added.

With his eyes still fixed on Sam, Nick said, "Yes, she is."

"Don't you worry?" Judy asked sotto voce. "Her job is horribly dangerous."

"It's a concern," Nick said lightly as he finally took his eyes off Sam to focus on the governor and his wife. He wasn't about to share his deepest fears with people he barely knew.

"Well, you should be very proud of her," the governor said.

"I am."

Nick was saved from further discourse about his wife's job when Graham joined them with Brandon Halliwell in tow. The new chairman of the Democratic National Committee was a few years older than Nick and full of fiery passion for his role.

He extended a hand to Nick. "Great to see you again, Senator."

"You too, Brandon," Nick said, shaking the other man's hand.

"I wonder if I might have a word in a private?"

Nick glanced at Graham, whose eyes danced with barely restrained glee that made Nick smile. Despite retiring from the Senate nearly seven years ago, Graham was still very much in the game and loving every minute of it. "As long as Senator O'Connor can join us," Nick said. This moment was as much Graham's as it was his. After all, none of it would be happening without Graham's support and backing.

"Not a problem," Halliwell said.

The three men ventured outside to a quiet corner on the patio.

"I take it Senator O'Connor has mentioned our keynote offer," Halliwell said without preamble.

"He did."

"And?"

"I'm honored to be asked, and I appreciate the opportunity."

"I hope you understand that the party is prepared to put our full support behind whatever future aspirations you may have."

Which, Nick knew, was political speak for: If you want to run for president in four years, we'd be all for it.

"The vice president has indicated he has no interest in running again," Halliwell continued. "That means we're in need of an heir apparent. All eyes are on you, Senator, as the great hope of the party."

Nick could almost feel Graham's buttons busting as the DNC chair continued to gush.

"How do you feel about that?" Halliwell asked.

"Astounded, to be honest," Nick said. "You have to understand. Eight months ago, I was sworn in to complete my friend's term. It was supposed to be a year and out, and now you're talking about things so far beyond my wildest imagination. It's somewhat overwhelming, especially since I've never won an election in my own right."

"The outcome of your campaign is all but assured. I wish the same were true for our incumbent president," Halliwell said with a grimace. "The latest poll numbers show that Arnie Patterson is making inroads into traditionally Democratic strongholds. The guy is determined, ruthlessly ambitious and extremely well funded. He's a worry. Nelson is vulnerable. He's been an effective president but hardly the lightning rod we'd hoped he'd be. And then, of course, the mess with Sanborn didn't help anything."

Nick still saw red whenever anyone mentioned the man Sam had tangled with while newly pregnant, resulting in the miscarriage they were both still recovering from. But assaulting a police officer was the least of Sanborn's crimes. The former DNC chairman had murdered two immigrant women in an effort to hide the prostitution ring he and other high-placed government officials had been running for years.

"The party needs you, Senator," Halliwell said, "and the keynote is only the start of our plans. But before we go any further, I need to know you're in it all the way."

As always, Nick wanted to glance over his shoulder, certain he'd find John standing right behind him waiting for Nick to give him his cues.

Graham rested a hand on Nick's back in a silent show of support and understanding.

"I'll tell you what," Nick said. "I'll do the keynote, and we'll see what happens in November. After that, we can talk again about next steps."

"Fair enough," Halliwell said, shaking hands with Nick and Graham. "If there's anything I can do for you between now and then, my door's always open."

"I appreciate the support."

After Halliwell walked away, Nick turned to Graham. "Is this for real?"

"You bet your ass it is."

"How can they be grooming me for the top spot when I haven't even won an election yet?"

"You have everything they want. You're young, movie-star handsome, personable, charismatic, effective, without a scandal in sight and madly in love with your gorgeous new wife, who's a hero in her own right. You're the perfect candidate. They'd be fools not to be grooming you for big things."

"Movie-star handsome, huh?" Nick made a joke to hide the surge of emotion he'd experienced as Graham ticked off the compliments.

Graham barked out a laugh. "Oh, shut up. As if I'm telling you something your wife doesn't tell you every day."

"I don't like it when she says it, either."

Smiling, Graham rested his hands on Nick's shoulders and looked up at him with fatherly pride all over his weathered face. "This was a big moment, son. I hope you get that. You've been anointed." Graham punctuated his words by squeezing Nick's shoulders.

"I'm not sure I deserve it, but I do get it."

"I have something I want to say to you."

"Okay." Nick's heart hammered, and his breathing slowed as he waited to hear what Graham had to say.

Graham took a long moment to gather his thoughts. "I loved my son."

"I know that. He knew it too."

"I really hope so." Graham took a fortifying breath and looked up at Nick. "I loved him, but I also recognized his limitations. He ran for the Senate because I wanted him to, not because he wanted to. Terry was the one who wanted it, not John." Terry had ruined his chances with a DUI charge weeks before he was due to announce a candidacy long in the making.

"John grew into the job," Nick said, compelled to defend his late friend.

"That he did, and he made me proud every single day

that he served the people of Virginia, but you... You have the fire in your belly that John didn't have. I know you often think you're living out what should've been his, but I don't think Halliwell ever would've had that conversation with John."

"You don't know that for sure."

"'Course I don't. We'll never know for sure, but I feel pretty confident saying it never would've happened for John, mostly because he wouldn't have wanted it. So I want you to embrace every single bit of this as yours and yours alone. You with me, Senator?"

Jesus Christ, the old guy was going to have him weeping in about two seconds if Nick didn't put a stop to this immediately. "Graham, really..."

"This is your moment, Nick," he said gruffly. "No one else's. Not mine. And not John's. It's yours. There's absolutely no question in my mind that you could go all the way to 1600 Pennsylvania Avenue in four short years. If that's what you want, there's nothing I won't do to make sure you get it."

"I'm humbled, as always, by your faith in me. Anything I have today is because of you."

"Aw, hell. I could argue that one 'til the cows come home, but enough with the sappy shit. Let's go find our wives. I'm in the mood to celebrate."

Relieved that he'd gotten through the conversation without losing his composure, Nick said, "Sounds good to me."

AVERY HILL STOOD outside the interrogation room at HQ and studied the woman inside. She was heavyset, mid-to-late sixties, with gray hair and dark brown skin. Her arms were crossed over an ample bosom in a defiant pose that set his nerves on edge. He'd been more optimistic about extracting information from her when she'd been terrified. Defiant wasn't good.

Detective Arnold joined him.

"Are you ready?" he asked the young detective.

"Whenever you are."

"Follow my lead."

"Yes, sir."

They stepped into the room, and Bertha Ray greeted them with a piercing glare. "I want a lawyer."

Ugh, Hill thought. *That's that. "I'd be happy to call your attorney for you, Mrs. Ray, but if you cooperate with our investigation, you shouldn't need one." Every fiber of Hill's being told him this woman had nothing to do with Victoria Kavanaugh's murder or the kidnapping of her daughter.*

"I want one anyway." Despite the defiant tone, Hill noted that her hands were shaking and her face was streaked with drying tears.

"Who would you like for us to call?"

"How should I know? I've never needed a lawyer before! Don't you have to provide one for me if I can't afford one of my own?" She gestured to Arnold. "That's what he said when he dragged me away from my home in handcuffs."

"We'll be happy to call the public defender for you," Hill said. "However, you should know that we might not be able to get anyone here at this hour. You'll most likely have to spend the night in jail before we can sort this out."

At that news, she appeared to crumble a bit. "I want to go home."

"We'll call the public defender's office and see what

we can do to get an attorney here." He nodded for Arnold to precede him out the door.

"Wait."

Hill turned. "Yes?"

"What do you want to know?" she asked warily.

"I'm afraid I can't ask you anything unless you're willing to waive your previous request for counsel."

Her mouth shifted, first to the left and then the right, as she considered that. "I'll waive the request."

"Detective Arnold, could you please record this interview?"

"Yes, sir." Arnold produced a tape recorder and brought it to the table. "Interview with Mrs. Bertha Ray." He cited the time and date. "Parties present are FBI Special Agent Avery Hill and MPD Detective Arnold Arnold."

Hill shot the detective a quizzical look.

Arnold shrugged. "My dad had a sense of humor." He resumed his position at the door.

"Mrs. Ray, have you waived your earlier request for counsel?" Hill asked.

"I have."

"And did you do that under duress?"

She gave him a blank look.

"Is it your choice to waive your earlier request for counsel?"

"Yes, it is."

"Thank you. Now, could you please tell us how you came to be in possession of Maeve Kavanaugh, the juvenile who was kidnapped from her home after her mother was murdered?"

She blanched, her eyes bugged and her mouth fell open, confirming Hill's suspicion that Mrs. Ray had no idea who the child in her custody really was. "She was what?"

Hill planted the palms of his hand on the table and leaned in. "Kidnapped from the scene of her mother's murder."

"He didn't say nothing about no kidnapping or murder!"

"Who didn't, Mrs. Ray?"

She hesitated before she shook her head. "I can't say."

"Do you watch the news, Mrs. Ray?"

She shook her head. "I've never had a television in my house, and I never will."

"Newspaper?"

Once again she shook her head. "Nothing but bad news in there. What do I want to be bothered with that for?"

Realizing he was dealing with the one person in the District who hadn't heard about the murder of the White House deputy chief of staff's wife and the kidnapping of his daughter, Avery pulled out the chair on his side of the table and sat. He propped his left foot on his right knee in a pose intended to show how relaxed he was. As if he had all the time in the world to wait her out.

He let a full minute of silence pass. "Did the person who asked you to watch her tell you she is the daughter of the White House deputy chief of staff?"

Again her eyes bugged and her mouth fell open. She pondered her predicament for another long moment. "If I tell you who asked me to watch her, will that person get in trouble?"

"Depends on whether the person was responsible for murder and kidnapping."

"Oh." Her hands were shaking much more noticeably now.

"Mrs. Ray?"

"I'm sure he had nothing to do with a murder or kidnapping."

"Okay."

"He's a good boy with some friends who aren't so good."

"Uh-huh." He let her twist in the wind awhile longer. "What did this good boy with the lousy friends tell you when he asked you to watch the child?"

"He said her parents got called out of town in an emergency and could I watch her for a few days."

"And you never thought to wonder why her parents didn't arrange for her care themselves?"

She shrugged. "People bring their kids to me all the time. I don't ask questions. I take care of the babies. That's how I make my living—how I've always made my living. Everyone knows they can come to me when they're in a pinch."

"Did he tell you the baby's name?"

"He said her name was Susie."

"Who said that, Mrs. Ray? Who brought her to you?"

Tears filled her eyes and spilled down her lined cheeks. "I can't." Weeping openly now, she looked him in the eye. "If I tell you, will you arrest him?"

"We'll detain him for questioning. If he was an innocent party in these crimes, he'll have nothing to worry about."

Judging from Mrs. Ray's expression, she had reason to doubt that the man in question was an innocent party.

"My son," she said softly. "Bobby."

"Is his last name Ray too?"

She nodded.

He passed his notebook across the table to her. "Write down his address and phone number."

Her hands were shaking so badly Hill wondered if they'd be able to read her handwriting.

She pushed the notebook back to him.

Hill tore off the page and handed it to Arnold, who left the room.

"Does Bobby have a record?"

Nodding, she said, "Mostly petty stuff and one felony."

"For?"

"Breaking and entering." Seeming ashamed, she lowered her eyes. "I did what I could with him, but I was a single mother, and he fell into a bad crowd. I tried to tell him… He wouldn't listen to me."

Hill could see he surprised her when he put his hand on top of hers. "Let me give you a ride home."

"Oh, I can go? I can go home?"

"Yes, ma'am."

While Arnold saw to the all-points bulletin for Bobby Ray, Hill drove Bertha home. He walked her up the crumbling sidewalk, past the MPD officer who'd been positioned outside the house, and held her arm as she climbed the stairs. She stopped short at the sight of her front door hanging open.

"Oh Lord," she whispered. "What'll I do about that?"

"Do you have a hammer and some nails?"

"I think so. In the basement."

"Let me see what I can find."

"The basement door is in the kitchen."

Avery found the door, flipped on the light and took the stairs to a dank space, letting his eyes adjust to the murky glow of a single bulb. On a table positioned against the far wall, he found a variety of tools and a tin can with some nails. He noticed a pile of discarded wood and picked through it for a piece big enough to cover the hole the battering ram had put in the door.

He took his findings upstairs, removed his suit coat and got to work on repairing the door.

"This is mighty kind of you, Agent Hill," Bertha said.

"It's no problem. I wouldn't want my mother's door hanging open all night."

"Your mother must be proud of you. Imagine having an FBI agent for a son."

As opposed to a career criminal, Avery thought. "She's a little too proud sometimes. She likes to embarrass me in front of her friends."

"That's a mother's job."

Chuckling, he said, "I suppose it is." He pounded in a few more nails to ensure the patch was firmly in place and turned his attention to the latch, which had been bent in the raid. Using muscles he didn't know he had, he was able to bend it back into position so the door would lock. "That'll hold for now, but you'll need a new door."

"I suppose you're right." She wrung her hands nervously. "Do I need to be afraid that whoever gave that baby to my Bobby might come after me?"

Avery considered the question and decided honesty was the best policy. "If you have any friends or family out of town, this might be a good time for a visit."

"My sister lives in Philadelphia. I could go there."

"Do you want to pack a bag while I wait? I could drop you at Union Station."

"Now? I can't wait until the morning?"

"I'll give it to you straight, okay?"

Trembling again, she said, "Okay."

"I wish I could tell you we know who killed Mrs. Kavanaugh and took her baby, but we have no idea. We've uncovered some things in the course of our investigation that are extremely disturbing. I don't know what role your son played in all this, but somehow that baby ended up in his possession. I can promise you we're going to find out how he came to have her, and when we do, there's apt to be trouble. So my best advice to you—the advice I'd give my own mother—would be to get as far away from this house and this city as you can. Now."

"Give me a minute to pack." She scurried off to a back room.

Avery lowered himself into a chair and tipped his head back, exhausted and frustrated. His ringing cell phone had him getting up to retrieve it from his suit coat pocket. "Hill."

"Arnold. Patrol went to Bobby Ray's address, but he was nowhere to be found. None of the neighbors have seen him in a few days. Phone is off, and calls are going to voice mail. I've asked the IT division to get us a GPS location if the phone has that capability."

"Good thinking." Hill rubbed his tired eyes. "Naturally, he's in the wind. It would've been too easy to find him at home watching the game and drinking a beer."

"We never get that lucky."

"Tell Patrol to keep looking."

"Already done, and I put some of our second-and third-shift people on it too."

"Good work, thank you. I'll brief the lieutenant and see you in the morning."

He ended the call with Arnold, and without giving himself too much time to think about it, he called Sam.

"Holland."

His heart positively raced at the sound of her voice. "Sorry to disturb you, Lieutenant. I wanted to give you an update." He went through the finer points of the conversation with Bertha Ray and what they'd learned about her son. "Arnold's got second and third shift working on locating him and IT tracing the phone. I've convinced Mrs. Ray this might be a good time for a visit to her sister in Philly. I'm waiting for her to pack now."

"Good call to get her out of town."

"Does the son's name ring any bells?"

"Nope."

"By the way, Arnold did good work tonight. Thought you should know."

"He's coming along."

"How's the fundraiser?" he asked and then winced. What business was it of his?

"Fine. Lots of schmoozing." She paused, as if thinking about something. "Do me a favor, Hill. Pick me up at my house at zero six thirty. Wait for me outside. I need to talk to you about something."

"Um, sure," he said, wondering what she wanted to talk to him about. "No problem. See you then."

The phone line went dead. She really needed to learn the fine art of saying goodbye at the end of a conversation.

"No, dickhead," he said out loud, as if that might make it actually sink in. "You do. You need to say goodbye to the insane notion that she thinks of you as anything other than an annoying colleague."

Bertha Ray appeared a minute later, suitcase in hand. "Can I tell my neighbor next door where I'm going? She'll worry if I disappear."

"If you tell her, you'd be potentially endangering her—

as well as yourself and your sister if she tells someone where you are."

She deflated a little more as that thought registered. "You're right."

"Do you have everything?"

Taking a glance around her small, neat home, she nodded.

"Let's go, then."

FOURTEEN

As she listened to Graham introduce Nick to the crowded ballroom, Sam's heart was full of love for her handsome husband. To see how important and influential he'd become was a powerful reminder of how much both their lives had changed in the last year. She'd offered to go up to the stage with him, but he'd wanted her to stay off her feet. He said he could tell by looking at her that the pain was getting worse, and she couldn't argue.

The injury made it hard to chew without excruciating agony, so she'd been unable to eat much of anything, which had left her feeling woozy and a little nauseated.

As Graham was winding up his glowing introduction, someone tapped her on the shoulder. "Mrs. Cappuano?" he whispered.

Startled to hear her married name, she turned to find one of the white-jacketed waiters. On a tray, he held a frosty-looking pink concoction in a tall glass. It was topped with a dollop of whipped cream. "A fruit smoothie compliments of the senator, ma'am."

Her hungry stomach rumbled in anticipation as her heart melted at his thoughtfulness. "Oh, thank you."

He placed the drink and a straw on the table and left with a quick bow.

"Nick is so sweet," Laine said.

"He's the best," Sam agreed, touched beyond belief that in the midst of his big night, he'd thought of her.

Scotty smiled his approval of Nick's gesture and went back to listening intently to Graham, who was turning the podium over to Nick.

The senator was greeted with uproarious applause that went on for several minutes.

"Thank you so much," Nick said when the applause finally died down. "Thank you, Senator O'Connor, for that wonderful introduction. I can't imagine walking this path without you by my side. It's been an honor and a privilege to call you friend for more than half my life, and now to hold the seat that was yours for nearly four decades and your son's for five wonderful years."

The crowd responded with a warm round of applause for Graham and John.

Standing behind Nick, Graham smiled broadly and nodded in appreciation of the compliment.

"I can't thank you all enough for coming tonight, for your generous donations to my campaign and for your warm welcome. I'd be remiss if I failed to mention the late Senator O'Connor, whose hard work and dedication to the commonwealth and its people I aim to emulate every day."

After another round of generous applause in John's honor, Nick talked about his efforts in the Senate on behalf of Virginia and his desire to continue the work he and both Senators O'Connor had begun. "I must also thank my wife, Sam, for her support of my campaign. She and I agreed to a year in office, and somehow we're now looking at the possibility of six more. Not sure how that happened," he said to laughter. "As you know, she was hurt today in the line of duty, and there are seven citizens in the District of Columbia who are alive tonight because of her courageous action."

The eruption of applause astounded Sam as she briefly stood to acknowledge the crowd. By the time she returned to her seat, her face was burning with mortification. She would kill him for that!

"Sam and I are delighted to be here tonight, and we look forward to a successful outcome in November. With your support, the victory line is within reach. Thanks again." His remarks were met with more enthusiastic applause.

Nick had finished speaking when Dr. Harry fought his way through the standing-room-only crowd to the table where Gonzo, Christina, Terry and Lindsey had joined Sam, Scotty and Laine. Sam stood to greet Harry with a hug. "How's Derek?"

"Much better now that he's with Maeve."

"And she's really all right?"

"Right as rain. I examined her myself. You'd never know she'd been through such an ordeal to look at her."

"That's wonderful news. She must've been thrilled to see her daddy."

Harry nodded. "And vice versa. It was a very emotional reunion. How'd you all know where she was?"

"I'm afraid I can't talk about that yet." Sam reached up to straighten Harry's crooked bow tie and patted his shoulders affectionately. He had dark hair and eyes and adorable dimples. Though a sea of people surrounded them, no one was paying attention to them at the moment. "You clean up nicely, Doc."

"I could say the same for you. How's the boo-boo?"

"Hurts like a mo-fo," Sam said, borrowing her sister's term.

Harry's brows furrowed with concern. "Didn't they give you pain meds?"

"Forgot to pick them up," Sam said with a sheepish grin that she instantly regretted when pain ricocheted through her face.

"What're we going to do with you?"

"I get that question a lot," Sam said. "Is Maggie with you?"

Harry's smile faded a bit. "No. We've, well… Apparently, we make for better colleagues than lovers." His small sad shrug conveyed a world of hurt.

"I'm so sorry to hear that! Are you okay?"

"Happened a while ago, actually. I'm better now."

"Jeez. I'm a sucky friend. I had no idea."

Harry laughed. "Don't feel bad. I haven't even told Nick yet."

"Good, because I was going to have to shoot him for not telling me." She squeezed Harry's arm. "You know we're here for you, right?"

"Sure I do."

"Sometimes we make for lousy friends because it seems like everything is always about us, but we know who matters to us—and you matter."

"That's nice of you to say, and I appreciate it." He kissed her forehead and lowered his voice. "Since it truly is all about you, have you made any decisions?"

Sam took a deep, calming breath. "No more shots."

Raising a brow, he said, "Is that right?"

She nodded. "One more try. If it doesn't work, we're done."

"And you're okay with the possibility of it not working?"

"I say I am, but…"

"I know. For what it's worth, I think you're doing the right thing. You'd always wonder."

"That's what Celia, my stepmother, said too."

"Even though things didn't work out between Maggie and me romantically, she's a great OB/GYN. You should think about seeing her to make sure everything's working properly before you get busy trying to conceive."

"Who's getting busy with my wife?" Nick asked as he joined them.

"No one but you, my friend," Harry said, shaking hands with Nick. "Wonderful turnout. Congratulations."

"It was all Graham's doing," Nick said as he slipped an arm around Sam and drew her in close to him.

"Sure it was," Harry said. "You're far too modest, Senator."

"Maeve?" Nick asked.

"Safely back in the arms of her father," Harry said.

"Oh thank goodness," Nick said. "Derek must be thrilled."

"He is, but still… You know."

"Yes," Nick said.

"Can you join us yet?" Sam asked her husband.

"I think so. I need some time with my buddy." Nick reached down to ruffle Scotty's hair, startling the boy who was deep in conversation with Gonzo. "Are you talking baseball without me?" He took a seat next to Scotty and tugged Sam's hand to encourage her to sit next to him.

"Come on, Harry," Sam said. "They can't talk baseball without you."

"What does he know?" Nick asked. "He's widely regarded as a fair-weather sailor. He's not a hard-core fan like us." Nick gestured to Scotty to include him in the "us."

"I'm willing to wager the Feds will be in the World Series this season," Harry said confidently.

Nick glanced at Scotty. "What do you think? Should we take that bet?"

"Definitely," Scotty said. "We'll win. Everyone's saying the Feds will crash and burn by August."

"You heard the young man," Nick said, reaching his hand out to Harry. "You've got yourself a bet."

Harry shook his hand. "You're on."

Sam smiled at her husband and reached for his free hand under the table.

"Are you feeling okay?" he asked.

"I'm fine. Thank you for the smoothie. That was incredibly sweet of you."

"No problem, babe. I knew you had to be hungry."

"I was." She reached up to smooth a lock of his hair. "This was actually more fun than I expected it to be."

"That's because you're surrounded by friends." He glanced at the foursome across the table who were talking politics. "I told you it was a good thing that your people got involved with my people."

Sam rolled her eyes at him. As he well knew, she found the cross-pollination of their people to be equal parts baffling and irritating.

"Sam," Scotty said. "What do you think? Will the Feds make it to the World Series?"

Sam pretended to give that some considerable thought. "Not only will they make it to the World Series," she said, "I predict they'll face off against the Red Sox."

Scotty's eyes went wide with amazement. "That'd be totally righteous! Can we can get tickets if that happens, Nick?"

"I'll tell you what," Nick said. "If that happens, I'll get tickets to all the games in Washington. How's that?"

"Holy cow. Wait 'til I tell the kids at home about this!"

Sam squeezed Nick's hand, knowing he felt the same way she did about wanting Scotty to think of their home as his home. He fit right in with them, holding his own at the table full of adults as the talk turned from baseball to politics to Scotty's upcoming stay at their house.

"I told Nick to bring you down to the farm to ride," Graham said. He stood behind his wife with his hands on Laine's shoulders.

"That'd be so cool," Scotty said. "I love it there. Can we make ice cream again, Mrs. O'Connor?"

"I told you to call me Laine," she said with mock sternness that made Scotty smile.

He glanced at Mrs. Littlefield. "Mrs. L says it's bad manners to call adults by their first names."

"Except when they give you permission," Mrs. Littlefield chimed in.

"See?" Laine clapped her hands victoriously. "That's what I tried to tell you."

"We've already had this argument," he said to Mrs. Littlefield, making the other adults at the table laugh.

"You've raised a very polite young man," Graham said to Mrs. Littlefield.

"Indeed," Nick added. "We hear about the gospel according to Mrs. Littlefield quite often."

"Like the time he said I could go to the baseball camp without even asking how much it cost," Scotty said, clucking and shaking his head with disapproval.

"I heard about that one for a few days," Nick said. "I believe his exact words were, 'Mrs. Littlefield says it's not responsible to agree to buy something before you know how much it costs.'"

The older woman blushed and laughed at the same time. "I'm glad to hear some of my words of wisdom have stuck." She gazed at the handsome boy wistfully, as if she knew what was coming even if he hadn't quite figured it out yet.

Sam caught Mrs. Littlefield's gaze and sent her a reassuring smile. As far as she and Nick were concerned, the woman who'd served as Scotty's surrogate mother for the last six years would always be welcome with them, if they were lucky enough to bring Scotty home for good someday. So much was riding on the next three weeks.

A short while later, Mrs. Littlefield told Scotty it was time to head back to Richmond. The boy offered a bit of protest before Nick reminded him that they'd be down to pick him up for the three-week stay on Sunday. "I'm counting the days," Scotty said as he hugged Nick and then Sam.

"So are we," she said.

"We're going to call it a night too," Nick said to Graham and Laine. "Sam is beat, and we both have to work tomorrow."

"Thanks so much for being here, Sam," Graham said, gently kissing the uninjured side of her face. "I know you probably had better things to do tonight."

Glancing up at Nick, she said, "There was nowhere else I'd rather be."

Nick shook hands with Graham. "Thanks again."

"Our pleasure. Keep making us proud."

"I'll do my best." Nick hugged and kissed Laine and said his good-byes to the staffers in attendance. "See you all bright and early."

Christina replied with a good-natured groan.

"My boss gave me the day off tomorrow," Gonzo joked.

"Dream on," Sam said. "Briefing at zero seven hundred."

"That's inhuman," Gonzo said, making Lindsey and Terry laugh.

Sam and Nick walked Scotty and Mrs. Littlefield to her car and saw them off while the valets retrieved their hired car. The minute they were settled in the backseat, Sam kicked off her heels and crawled into her husband's outstretched arms. He'd removed his tuxedo jacket, so Sam went to work on the diamond studs that served as buttons.

"Um, excuse me, what're you doing?"

"I need skin." She pushed his shirt open and rested her cheek against his beautiful chest.

His hand slid from her ankle to her knee to her inner thigh.

"And what are you doing?"

"Same as you—seeking skin."

Sam sighed with contentment. "I'm so happy I get to go home with you tonight."

"Just tonight?"

"Every night, but particularly tonight. Every woman in that room wanted you for herself, and none of them can have you, because you're all mine."

"Yes, I am."

"I love that, you know? No matter what shitty crap happens during the day—and a lot of shitty crap happened today—when it's over, I get to go home to you. It's the best thing in...well...ever."

He tightened the arm he had around her and nuzzled

her hair. "It is the best thing ever. You're the best thing ever."

She closed her eyes and breathed in his endlessly appealing scent, the scent of home.

"And here I thought I was in the biggest trouble ever."

"Oh, you are, Nicky." Sam thought her imitation of Patrice's breathy voice was spot-on, if she said so herself. "And making a big deal out of me in front of all those people. You're in so much trouble."

"I love your brand of trouble." His fingers moved in a seductive pattern over her thigh, moving higher with each stroke but never quite reaching the place that ached for him.

"Nick," she gasped. "Quit teasing me!"

"Shhh. Relax, baby."

As he well knew, she melted like butter whenever he spoke to her in that sexy, gravely tone he usually reserved for their bedroom. Relax? Right… How was she supposed to relax when he was making her crazy with the slide of his fingers over her sensitive flesh?

Excruciating minutes passed in a sensual haze before he finally pressed his fingertips against the silky satin of her thong.

Sam squirmed on his lap, trying to give him better access.

He let out a grunt and then a groan when her bottom came into contact with his erection. "Careful, babe. I'm quite fond of my boy parts."

"So am I. You have the best boy parts in the whole world."

He chuckled softly against her ear, sending a torrent of sensations spiraling through her, awaking every one of her girl parts. "No one gives a compliment quite like my wife."

"Nick." She pushed her hips against his hand, hoping to encourage him to pay closer attention to what he was doing.

"What?"

Placing her hand over his, she directed him to exactly where she wanted him. "Yes. There. Right there."

He kept his fingers on the outside of her underwear, sliding back and forth over the place that pulsed and throbbed for him. "Is that what you want?"

"Yes!" She was so focused on the heat building between her legs that she didn't notice his other hand move to the front of her dress until his talented fingers were inside the bodice and tweaking her nipple. The combination had her gasping and panting and exploding. She bit her lip to keep from crying out, and the intense pain of her wound took nothing away from the equally intense release.

He brought her down slowly, keeping pressure on her clit and nipple until the aftershocks subsided.

"Mmm," he said against her neck. "Do you see now why I hired the car?"

Still breathing hard, Sam shifted off his lap and went to work on his pants. "Not only are you a sexy devil, you're smart—and you plan ahead. How lucky am I to have such a husband?"

While she freed him from his pants, he twirled a lock of long hair around his finger. The instant he burst free, she wrapped her hand around his thick cock and stroked him until the tip gleamed with moisture.

His head fell back against the seat, and his eyes went heavy with desire. "What're you up to, Samantha?"

"This." Gathering up her long skirt, she straddled him, pushed the scrap of useless underwear aside and took him into her still-pulsating channel. "Oh God, that's good," she whispered.

Under her skirt, his hands found her buttocks and squeezed. "There's nothing better."

"Are you sure the driver can't see anything back here?"

"Maybe you should've asked me that before you had your wicked way with me."

She stopped moving and stared down at him. "He can't see, can he?"

"No," Nick said, laughing at her. "At least I hope not."

"At this point, I don't even care. A dozen photographers could pop out of the ashtray, and I wouldn't stop."

"Awfully brazen talk for a potential first lady of the United States."

That stopped her again. "What did you say?"

"You heard me." Anchoring her hips, he surged into her and succeeded in making her forget everything but the feel of him hard and hot inside her. "I need breasts."

Sam squiggled and squirmed and tried to forget what he'd said about her being first lady long enough to come again. Somehow she managed to free her breasts from the dress.

With his hands still gripping her bottom, he said, "Feed them to me."

She cupped her full breasts and brought them to his mouth.

He made her whimper with the pull and tug of his lips, the sweep of his tongue and the suction he knew she loved.

"I wish you could see how hot you look right now,

holding your breasts with your skirts all bunched up around your waist. Very sexy."

"You forgot my swollen face."

"Every inch of you is sexy to me." He made his point by letting his fingers wander deep between her buttocks, setting off a fiery finish that left them both panting and sweating.

"I haven't done it in a car since high school," she said when she recovered the ability to speak. "I've been missing out."

"I thought you'd be too tired and sore tonight to take full advantage of the car."

"Haven't you learned to never underestimate me?"

"Apparently, I'm still learning."

Sam braved the pain to press a light kiss to his lips. "I missed the kissing. That's usually one of my favorite parts."

"Mine too. I hope you heal quickly so we can make out like teenagers the way we usually do."

As the throbbing wound made its presence known, she let her head drop to his shoulder. "Can we pick up the pain pills on the way home?"

"Sure, baby." He wrapped his arms around her. "Whatever you need."

That was the last thing Sam remembered until he was shaking her awake near their Capitol Hill neighborhood so they could disentangle and fix their clothes before they arrived at home.

"I'll go pick up your prescription."

"Are you sure you don't mind?"

"Of course I don't." He kissed her forehead and then her lips, gently, mindful of her injury. "I want you to go draw a hot bath and fill it with lots of bubbles and soak for a good long time. When I get back, I'll tuck you in."

"You're on. Hurry back."

He saw her inside, cleaned up in the half bath downstairs, retrieved his car keys and kissed her once more before he jogged down the ramp he'd installed for her father.

Sam was halfway upstairs when the doorbell rang. Wondering why he didn't use his key, she went back down and threw open the door. "What did you forget?" The words died on her lips when she saw the two police officers standing on her front stairs. She recognized one of them, but not the other. Her first thought was of Nick, but he hadn't been gone long enough to encounter trouble.

The older of the two, the one she recognized, seemed surprised to find her in formal attire. "We're sorry to bother you at home, Lieutenant. I'm Officer Wilkins. This is my partner Officer Ramirez."

"What's up?" Sam feared this crazy day was about to get worse. She told herself that if something were wrong with a member of her family, someone would've called her.

"We were contacted by the emergency room at the Washington Hospital Center. You're listed as the next of kin for a Peter Gibson."

Sam tightened her grip on the doorknob. "What about him?"

"He was brought in tonight unresponsive. Several empty bottles of sleeping pills were found in his apartment along with a note addressed to you as his next of kin." The officer held out a folded piece of paper to her.

Sam looked at it but made no move to take it from him. "I'm not his next of kin. We've been divorced for years."

"He had your name in his wallet and in his medical records, so we assumed…"

"I'm sorry, but you assumed wrong. His mother lives in Wilmington, Delaware. You could call her."

"You don't happen to have her number, do you?"

"I'm sorry, but I don't. Her first name is Irma, though."

"That's helpful, thank you. Um, do you want the note?"

Sam glanced down at it and then up at the earnest young officer. "No." Nothing Peter Gibson had to say was of interest to Sam.

"Sorry again to bother you, ma'am. Thank you for your assistance."

"Officer Wilkins?"

"Ma'am?"

"Is he expected to live?"

"I'm sorry, but I don't know that."

Sam nodded and was about to close the door when Nick pulled up to the curb, back from the nearby pharmacy. She waited at the door for him.

With his eyes on the Patrol car as it drove off, he came up the ramp. "What's going on?"

"Peter," Sam said, suddenly chilled even though the night air was thick with humidity.

Nick shepherded her inside. "What about him?"

"He apparently tried to kill himself and left a note for me. I was listed as his next of kin, so they came to find me. I refused to take the note, though. I don't care what it says."

Nick's expression conveyed his displeasure that her ex-husband had once again upset her. "I wouldn't put it past him to pull something like this to get your attention."

"I wouldn't, either. Passive aggression is his forte."

Nick put his hands on her shoulders and dipped his knees to meet her gaze. "This has nothing to do with you, Sam. You know that, right?"

"Yes."

"Do you want to go there? To the hospital?"

Surprised he would ask that, she said, "No."

"Are you sure?"

She nodded. He was right—Peter's problems were no longer hers. There was nothing she could do for him. And if he'd done this to get her attention, showing up at the hospital would play right into his hand.

"Are you okay?"

"Yeah, it's kind of shocking."

His arms slid around her, drawing her in close. "I know, babe. But it's not your fault. I'm glad you didn't read the note, because he's probably blaming you for everything that's gone wrong with his life, and none of it is your fault. He made his own bed."

Nick held her for a long time before he let her go and nudged her toward the stairs. "Enough for one day. Go on up. I'll shut off the lights and be right behind you."

"Thanks," she said with a small smile that made her face hurt.

"Any time."

Sam took the bag from the pharmacy and trudged up the stairs, fortified by Nick's assurances. It wasn't her fault. Whatever Peter did had nothing to do with her anymore. It was because of him, after all, that she and Nick had lost six years they should've spent together when Peter, her platonic roommate at the time, failed to deliver Nick's messages after the night they met.

That and the miserable four years she'd spent married to Peter would've been enough to make her hate him. But he'd given her plenty of cause since then, including trying to bomb her car and Nick's and then later walking away from criminal charges after her officers entered his apartment without a warrant. Not to mention threatening her on the sidewalk outside her home the night before she married Nick.

Shuddering at the memory, Sam took one of the horse-sized pain pills, ran the bath and sent Freddie a text to let him know she was all set for a ride in the morning. She needed to deal with the odd vibe coming from Hill and put an end to it once and for all before it caused trouble with Nick. She was stepping out of her dress when Nick joined her in the bathroom.

"Damn, that's such an incredible visual," he said, as he took in the sight of her in the corset.

Watching him tug his bow tie free, she was reminded of how very different her second marriage was from her first. She turned off the water. "I don't need a bath." She walked over to him, pulled his shirt free of his pants and flattened her palms against his belly. "I need you. Only you."

"You have me, my love. I'm all yours." Sam took his hand and led him to bed.

MUCH LATER, NICK held her in his arms as their bodies cooled after a frantic coupling left him astounded, as always, by the power of his love for her—and hers for him.

"Nick?"

"Hmm?"

"What were you doing with her?"

Confused, he said, "Who?"

"That awful woman Patrice."

Laughing, he kissed Sam's forehead. "Is she awful? I hadn't noticed."

She raised her head off his chest to look him in the eye. "Seriously?"

"I noticed." He ran his fingers through his hair, which was damp with perspiration after the strenuous lovemaking. "After I met you and you didn't call me back, I was kind of a mess for a while. She was…there. You know?"

"Hell, yes, I know. How do you think I ended up with Peter?"

"I can't tell you how often I think about what might've been different for both of us if I'd gone after you, rather than accepting your silence as a verdict."

"I wish the same thing. I couldn't believe you didn't call after that night. I simply couldn't believe it. I should've called you. That I didn't is my single greatest regret in life."

"No sense having regrets, babe. Maybe we would've made an awful mess of it back then and not had what we have now."

"We wouldn't have made a mess of it. We were always meant to be together. I believe that."

"So do I." Her skin was warm and smooth under his hand as he caressed her back. "I knew it the first second I ever saw you. Ah, I thought. There she is."

Sam propped her chin on her hand so she could see his face. "Did you really?"

Looking at her with his heart in his eyes, he nodded. "I recognized you in the crowd of people on that deck. I recognized you as mine."

She turned her head, rested her cheek on his chest and was quiet for a long time. "What did you mean before about me being first lady?"

"I wondered if you'd remember that."

"Kinda hard to forget that one."

"Halliwell talked to me tonight about doing the keynote at the convention. He said the party is in need of an heir apparent because Gooding isn't interested in running again." The current vice president had run twice before and was now in his mid-seventies.

"How do you feel about that?"

"I'm blown away. A year ago, I was John's chief of staff, and now he's dead, I'm running for his seat and the DNC is talking about me running for president in a few short years. It's beyond comprehension."

"Do you want that? To be president?"

"Shit, I don't know," he said, laughing at the lunacy of it. "I can't believe my name is being used in the same sentence as the word president."

"You could do it. I know you could. I bet you'd win." Continuing to play with her hair, he brought a hank of it to his nose to inhale the scent that would remind him always of her. "You're very good for my ego, babe."

"What did you tell Halliwell?"

"I said I'd do the keynote, but I want to wait until after November to talk about anything else. I need to win this election before we start contemplating my future."

"You're going to win."

The nervous tenor of her tone wasn't lost on him. "I've already won, Samantha." He tightened his hold on her. "I have everything any man could ever want. We'll decide together what the future holds, whatever that may be. If it's not something we both want, end of conversation."

"You can't walk away from an opportunity like this because it might not be something I want you to do."

"Sure I can. One of these days, I hope to succeed in

convincing you that you are what really matters to me. Everything else is secondary."

"You're crazy."

"About you. Now go to sleep. You're so far beyond exhausted it's not even funny." He continued to comb his fingers through her hair and caress her back until he was almost certain she was asleep.

"Nick?"

"I thought you were asleep."

"Almost."

"What, baby?"

"I forgot to tell you I love you."

"I love you too."

She released a long, deep breath, and this time he was certain she'd fallen asleep.

FIFTEEN

RUNNING ON CAFFEINE and adrenaline and fear and shame, Jeannie McBride threw herself into work to take her mind off what had happened earlier. Every time she thought about Sam saying she was disappointed, her heart broke all over again. That was the last thing in the world she ever wanted to hear from her beloved lieutenant.

Though she'd asked Will to come over to work on the report in the morning, Jeannie had finished it two hours ago. She'd detailed every step they'd taken in their new investigation of the Fitzgerald case and had included a list of people who should've been interviewed the first time around and hadn't been for reasons known only to Skip Holland.

In the morning, she planned to wait for Will to arrive and then venture to the Annapolis home of Dr. Norman Morganthau, the retired medical examiner she'd called about the Fitzgerald case. Jeannie had sensed back in April that the older man had wanted to tell her something about Skip Holland but had held back in deference to his old friend. Maybe if they went to see him in person, he'd be more forthcoming.

She needed to do something to avoid sitting around for the next week rehashing what'd happened. Since Michael was long asleep and she'd done everything she could for the night on the Fitzgerald case, she turned next to one of the leads she'd wanted to look into further with the Kavanaugh case.

It had occurred to her that there might be some connections between the two names used to fake Victoria Kavanaugh's identity. Jeannie took to the Internet to read everything she could find about Denise Desposito and William Eldridge.

An hour later, she had tied Desposito to a Medicare scheme the Feds had busted almost ten years earlier in Ohio.

Typing frantically, Jeannie recorded the details of the phony doctor's office, documenting how the scheme had worked and the role Desposito had played in defrauding the government of millions. What they hadn't known was that the government was on to them from almost the beginning and had built a solid case against the perpetrators before their arrests.

Jeannie made a list of the other people arrested and spent another hour tracking down where they were incarcerated. Maybe one of them would have an idea of how Desposito had come to be tied to Victoria Kavanaugh.

The only William Eldridge she could find was a former officer in the Patterson Financial Group in Ohio, but there was nothing more about him on file. It wasn't much, Jeannie decided, but it was something—and she hoped it would help to restore her standing with the lieutenant.

"What're you doing up, baby?"

Even all these months later, Jeannie's first impulse was to jump and move away when his hands landed on her shoulders to knead her tight muscles. Breathing in and letting it out, she reminded herself that this man loved her. This man would never hurt her. This man was nothing like the man who'd beaten and raped her.

"I'm sorry I startled you," Michael said, attuned as always to her fears.

"That's okay. What time is it?"

"Almost three. Why are you down here and not in bed with me?"

"Couldn't sleep. Too much on my mind. I did some work, and that helped."

"Do you think you might be able to sleep for a bit now?"

Jeannie didn't think so, but she said what he wanted to hear. "I could try."

Michael held out a hand, helped her up and shut off the desk light. He linked their fingers and led her through the dark house to their bedroom upstairs. Standing by the bed, he turned to face her. He drew the T-shirt over her head and helped her out of the shorts.

Then she returned the favor, pushing the boxers he'd put on to go find her over his hips. He was tall and muscular, his dark brown skin smooth and soft. Everything about him appealed to her.

It had taken a long time after the attack for her to feel comfortable with his touch, to slide naked into bed with him the way she had before, as if it were no big deal. Now they were nearly back to where they'd been. At times, though, she was still skittish, and the memories returned occasionally in dreams that were so real and vivid that for days afterward, she was forced to relive the nightmare all over again.

Soon she'd be forced to face Mitchell Sanborn in a courtroom and recount publicly what he'd done to her. Jeannie shuddered at the thought of it.

"What're you thinking about?"

"The trial."

"Aw, Jeannie." He pulled her into his embrace. "Why're you thinking about that now?"

"Because it won't really be over until that's behind me. The thought of having to see him again, to have to look at his face… I don't know if I can do it, Michael."

"Of course you can. If it means he gets put away for life for what he did to you, then you can do it."

"I hope you're right."

"My poor baby has so much on her mind."

She looped her arms around his neck and kissed him. "I'm sorry to dump all my troubles on you."

"Where else would you dump them?" He arranged her so she was resting on top of him and continued to knead the tension from her shoulders. "I was thinking about this situation with Sam."

"What about it?"

"I know you're very upset because you think you disappointed her."

"I did disappoint her. I lied to her."

"You did it with her best interest at heart. When she has time to think about it some more, she'll see that as your friend. As your lieutenant, she had no choice but to suspend you. Sam is wise enough to be able to separate the two parts of this equation."

"Maybe."

"I want you to remember you've survived so much worse than this, and you'll survive this too. It's a momentary setback in the grand scheme of things."

"You're right."

"I am?"

Smiling, Jeannie leaned in to kiss him. "Don't sound so surprised. I don't mind letting you be right once in a while. As long as it doesn't happen too often."

"Is that so?" In one smooth move, he turned them so he was on top of her.

Jeannie didn't want to recoil from the sensation of being surrounded, but the instinct was involuntary.

"Just me, baby. Just me."

His voice calmed and soothed her as did his lips when he claimed her mouth.

She clutched his shoulders and worked her legs apart, letting him know what she wanted. Only he could make it all go away. Only he could make her forget that another man had once hurt her. "Love me, Michael."

"I do, baby. You know I do." He entered her in slow thrusts that made her blood boil and her breath catch in her throat. Lowering his head, he laved her nipple and rolled it between his teeth, making her cry out from the overwhelming need.

Arching her back, she sought to take him deeper, but he wouldn't be rushed.

"Slow and easy," he said. "Nice and slow."

Jeannie thought she'd go mad waiting for him to pick up the pace, but he took his own sweet time, making her come twice with his fingers before he thrust fully inside her, taking her over a third time and letting himself go too.

She held him for a long time afterward, his body so alive and vital on top of her. Only he could've made her forget her litany of troubles, even for a short time. "Michael?"

"Hmm?"

"Do you still have that ring you showed me a while ago?"

He stiffened and raised his head to meet her gaze. "Yes."

She knew he'd waited months to hear her say she was ready to wear the ring he'd planned to give her the weekend after she was attacked. "Where is it?"

"In a safe place."

"Could you possibly get it?"

"Any particular reason?"

"Maybe."

He studied her face and then kissed her, withdrew from her and got up.

Jeannie got an excellent view of his ass as he stalked out of the room on long legs, a man on a mission.

He returned a minute later, ring box in hand.

"Could I see it again? I've forgotten what it looks like."

"Now that's a bald-faced lie. You memorized every detail the first time I showed it to you."

"Okay, so I lie. I still want to see it again."

Michael sat next to her on the bed and opened the box. The bedside table lamp sent a warm glow over the room as the ring sparkled, a fiery presence in the dark velvet nest.

As it had the first time, the sight of the ring he'd chosen with her mother's input took her breath away. She looked up to find him watching her intently, as if trying to gauge the import of this moment. To his credit, he didn't say anything. He didn't push or prod her. He'd been the picture of patience and fortitude during the bleakest days of her life. And she loved him. She would always love him. Of that much she was certain.

"Would it be possible for me to wear it now?" she asked tentatively.

"If that's what you want."

Jeannie bit her bottom lip and nodded, determined not to cry.

He surprised her when he slid off the bed and knelt on the floor, taking her hand and bending his head to kiss the back of it. For a long moment, he stayed like that, bent over her hand, until Jeannie realized he was weeping.

She curled her hand around his head. "Michael."

"I'm sorry, baby. I wondered for so long if we'd ever get back to where we were. Before. And now... I'm sorry," he said, releasing a deep, shuddering breath, and wiped his face with his free hand. "You took me by surprise. That's all."

"You've been so patient and so wonderful, and I love you so much for that—more than you could ever know. You've been exactly what I needed, what I'll always need." She reached out to him.

He pushed up from the floor and into her arms, holding her so tightly she could barely breathe. He'd done that so rarely since the attack, always fearful of a setback.

"Jeannie, my sweet Jeannie. I love you so much. I love your courage and your strength and your determination. I love your beauty and your sweetness. Will you make me so happy and marry me? Will you spend forever with me?"

"Yes, Michael, I'd be honored to marry you."

And then he was kissing her and crying with her and making love with her all over again, and for the first time since the attack, he didn't hold back. He gave her everything he had, all the love and passion that had driven them from the beginning, with no thoughts of the horrors or pain of the past.

Jeannie gave back to him in equal measure until they were straining toward a release that left her shattered and sobbing out her love for him. Their bodies were still trembling and rippling with aftereffects when he slipped the ring on the third finger of her left hand, curling his hand around hers as if to cement their bond.

"I'm sorry I made you wait so long for me," she said.

"It was certainly no sacrifice. Being with you is the best thing to ever happen to me."

Jeannie held up her hand so they could see how the ring looked.

"Exactly as I pictured it," he said.

"Better than I could've imagined. Thank you, Michael. Thank you."

He pulled her closer to him, pillowing her head on his chest and running his hands over her back, letting her know she was safe and she was loved. She had everything she needed. The situation with Sam would right itself. Eventually. And she would face Mitchell Sanborn in the courtroom and ensure he never had the chance to do to another woman what he'd done to her.

Surrounded by Michael's love, Jeannie felt like there was nothing she couldn't handle. He was right. She'd already been through the fire and survived. She would continue to survive because she refused to consider the alternative.

Breathing in Michael's familiar, comforting scent, she was able to sleep.

SAM WOULD'VE SLEPT through the alarm—again—if Nick hadn't kissed her awake—again. "Why do you hear it, but I don't?" she muttered, keeping her eyes closed to enjoy the slide of his lips over her back. Her face throbbed like a bastard, making her yearn for another pain pill that she wouldn't take with a full day of work ahead of her and no more time to waste in finding a killer.

"Because you know I'll hear it and wake you up, so you're not listening for it."

"I used to get myself out of bed without anyone's assistance." That came out grumpier than she'd intended, but it seemed like she never got enough sleep these days.

"Isn't it nice that now you don't have to?" He was endlessly cheerful in the morning, which she found endlessly annoying.

"It's very nice. Too nice. It makes me forget all about the fact that I need to get to work."

"We'll have another day off together soon," he assured her.

"When?"

"If you can catch Victoria's killer by Sunday, I'm off. I have a rally on Saturday, but I told them to leave me free on Sunday—in case."

"In case of what?"

"In case I could score a day off with my wife before we pick up Scotty Sunday night. I think we need a full day to loll about in bed to get it out of our systems before he gets here."

She raised a brow and opened her eyes to look at him. "You think one day will get it out of our systems?"

"Not a chance, but it sure will be fun trying."

"Yes, it will."

"Now you have a goal—catch a killer by Saturday and spend Sunday in bed with your husband. Time to get up and get to it." He emphasized his instructions with a sharp slap to her rear that startled and stirred her.

"Did you just seriously spank me?"

"No, not seriously. If you want me to seriously spank you, I can do better than that."

A blast of heat traveled through her body, converging in a throb between her legs.

"Oh, well," he said, studying her closely. "Who knew my lovely wife got turned on by the idea of a good spanking?"

"I'm not turned on."

He barked out a laugh. "Samantha, please don't insult my intelligence. I'm not an expert on many things, but knowing when my wife is turned on? Come on."

When she attempted to get up in a huff, he pulled her back in with one strong arm around her waist.

She struggled against his tight hold, embarrassed and undone by the odd exchange.

"Stop." He arranged her so she was under him and stared down at her with those eyes that saw right through her. "Don't ever be ashamed to tell me what you want, do you hear me?"

She averted her gaze. "I don't want that." Her face felt like it was on fire, which infuriated her.

His finger traced the blaze on her uninjured cheek. "I think maybe you do. Are there other things you want that I don't know about?"

"I don't have time for this right now. I have to get to work."

Moving his finger to her chin, he urged her to look at him. "Don't hide from me, Sam. If you want something, ask for it."

Her heart beat madly. "I didn't know I wanted it until you did it."

His eyes widened and his breath caught, while his cock throbbed against her belly. "Sam…"

"I have to go." She reached up to frame his face and

brought him down for a kiss that caused her tremendous pain.

When she released him, he uttered a tortured groan. "Call in sick. We both will."

That made her laugh. She poked him in the ribs and took advantage of his surprise to scoot out from under him. She was halfway to the shower when he again stopped her by hooking an arm around her waist.

"To be continued," he whispered gruffly in her ear, the words making her shudder nearly as much as the hint of promise in his tone.

They showered together but kept an unusual distance, both seeming to get that the merest touch would make them very late for work.

"I can drop you at HQ on my way," Nick said as he knotted a maroon tie.

"I've got a ride." Sam hoped and prayed Nick would be gone before Hill arrived to pick her up. She hadn't counted on Nick being up so early when she made the arrangements.

"With whom?"

She started to say Freddie but stopped herself. The lie would make things worse when—not if—he discovered it. "Hill. We've got some stuff to go over this morning about the raid last night, and I wanted to hash it out with him before we meet with the team."

Nick's expression darkened, but he held his tongue.

Sam pushed her weapon into her hip holster, grabbed her cuffs, notebook and badge and crossed the room to him. "I've said it before, and I'll say it again, you have nothing to worry about. You are, however, very sexy when you're jealous."

"Jealous? Of *him*?"

"Uh-huh."

"I am not jealous of him. What reason would I have to be jealous of him?"

"None whatsoever, but that doesn't seem to be stopping you."

"He's got a big, bad thing for you. You'll never convince me otherwise."

"Okay, then I won't try. All you need to know—and you need to hear me on this." She waited until she was sure she had his full attention. "The only guy I have a big, bad thing for is the one I'm married to. You got me?"

"Yeah," he said, more contrite now as his hands landed on her hips and his fingers dug in. "So it's a big, bad thing, huh?"

"So big and so bad."

"In this case, bad is good, right?"

Sam laughed, even though it made her face hurt something awful. "Bad is so very, very good. I love you, you big oaf. Now stop acting like a Neanderthal and let me go to work."

"Tell him to keep his eyes off my wife. I love her too damned much for my own good."

"No, you love her just enough. Perfectly, in fact." She left him with one last kiss and a pat to his freshly shaven face, loving that the scent of his cologne would cling to her skin long after they parted. "Have a good day."

"You too, babe. Be careful out there."

"Always am." Breathing easier since the conversation about Hill hadn't escalated into a fight, she bounded down the stairs. Her cell phone chimed with a text from Jeannie.

"I have news I want to share with you—as my friend—and a thought on the Kavanaugh investigation I want to share with you as my boss. Call me when you have a minute."

Sam smiled as she read the message, grateful and relieved that Jeannie was making an effort. Suspending her and Tyrone had been her lowest moment yet as the lieutenant in charge of the Homicide division. Wait. That wasn't entirely true. Jeannie's egregious attack had been the ultimate low moment.

She found Jeannie's number in her list of contacts and pressed Send while she waited for a slice of bread to toast. She'd learned her lesson about grabbing something to eat on the way into work.

"Good morning, Lieutenant."

Jeannie sounded far more chipper than Sam had expected after what had transpired yesterday. "Good morning, Detective. What's the word?"

"Well, I wanted you to be one of the first to know that Michael and I are officially engaged."

"Congratulations, Jeannie. That's awesome news. I'm very happy for you both. Especially after what you guys have been through."

"He's been amazing, and I figured he'd waited long enough."

"He's a good guy."

"Yes, he is." Jeannie paused, took a breath and released it. "Lieutenant... Sam... I want you to know I deeply regret that I lied to you, but I also want you to know if I had it to do over again, I would've done the same thing. I know what your dad means to you, what he means to the department, and the thought of him possibly dying with a hint of scandal hanging over him was simply unbearable to me. I made the call, and Tyrone went along with it because I told him it was the right thing to do. What I do regret is not setting things straight with you after your dad recovered. That I should've done, and you had every right to suspend me."

"I didn't want to suspend you, but you didn't give me much choice."

"I know that. I have the full report ready for you. I'll send it to you this morning."

"Thank you."

"And I want you to know that Will and I are going to see Dr. Morganthau this morning."

"The old medical examiner? Why?"

"Because he knows something. I could hear it in his voice when I spoke with him on the phone in April. He knew your dad and implied he was 'off' during that case, but he refused to say any more out of respect for your dad. I'm hoping he'll be more forthcoming in person."

"My dad is furious with me. He all but ordered me to leave it alone."

"Is that what you want us to do? If so, say the word. Only Tyrone and I know there's more to the story than what we told you initially. Oh, and Michael knows too. For the record, he told me back in April that I was making a huge mistake lying to you about what we uncovered. I only told him because I was so torn. So very torn."

Sam took a moment and chose her words carefully. "I want you to know… I understand why you lied, and I appreciate that you were trying to protect my dad and my family. Your friendship means a lot to me."

"And yours means a lot to me. Especially after everything that's happened."

"Our friendship has to come second to the job, Jeannie. The job has to come first for as long as we're both on active duty."

"I understand."

"I can't lift the suspension. I won't lift it."

"I understand that too."

"Anything you do on your own time is without the backup of the department, so proceed with caution and keep me apprised of what you're doing."

"We will. Do you want me to see Morganthau, or should we let it go?"

Sam thought about what her father had told her to do and what her own conscience was telling her to do. Massaging the back of her neck where a headache had taken root, she felt pulled in multiple directions. "Four people know there's more to the story."

"None of us would ever breathe a word of it."

"Still," Sam said. "Four people know."

"Five, counting your dad."

"That's five too many," Sam decided. "Go see Morganthau. Keep it under the radar, and report to me verbally afterward. I'll decide what we do next."

"Yes, ma'am."

"You said you had some thoughts on the Kavanaugh case?"

"Yes." Jeannie reported on what she'd uncovered about Desposito and Eldridge and her connection to a Medicare scheme years ago.

"That's good work, Detective."

"I'll shoot you the details in an e-mail."

"Thank you," Sam said, relieved to know that there'd been no permanent damage done to a relationship she valued personally and professionally.

"Have a good day, Lieutenant."

"Let's hope it's less eventful than yesterday."

"Yes," Jeannie said, laughing. "Let's hope so."

"Congratulations again. I'm so happy for you both."

"Thanks, Sam."

Sam jammed her phone in her pocket, rehashing the conversation and hoping she was doing the right thing allowing McBride and Tyrone to dig even deeper into a case her father had told her to leave alone. As much as she respected and loved her dad, she had a job to do, and she would do it to the best of her ability.

The day she no longer did that was the day she no longer belonged in command of her squad. That would also be the day she no longer deserved the gold shield she proudly carried. Resigned to deal with the fallout with her father, she put peanut butter on her toast, told Nick she was leaving and ran out the front door, as Hill pulled up to the curb.

Sam ventured a glance at the second floor and found Nick staring at her from the bedroom window, looking none too pleased. She gave him the best possible smile she could in light of her injuries and waved as she got in the car.

"You didn't tell me you were bringing breakfast," Hill said, eyeing her toast and taking a good long look at her too. The clean scent of his cologne and the thick humidity filled her senses. "I already ate. Thanks, though."

"Listen, Hill, I don't know what it is you're up to—"

"Whoa! Wait a minute. I was making a joke about your toast. How did that turn into me being up to something?"

"You know full well what I'm talking about." Sam took a bite of the toast that she no longer wanted, especially since it still hurt to chew. The lump of bread got stuck in her throat. Mindful of Nick watching them, she said, "Drive, will you?"

Hill shifted the car into gear and pulled away from the curb.

"Aren't you going to say anything?" Sam asked when a full minute passed in silence.

"What is it that you'd have me say?"

Sam became more uncomfortable by the moment as confronting him on the weirdness between them suddenly didn't seem like such a good idea. "Why are you doing this?"

"What exactly is it that I'm doing?"

She crumpled the remnants of the toast into the paper towel she'd brought with her. "Do you think I didn't see how you reacted to me last night? Do you think I haven't seen it other times? I'm a trained observer of people, Hill, and I'm a woman. I know when a guy is looking at me with interest that has nothing to do with the job we're supposed to be doing together."

His only reaction, other than a pulse of tension in his cheek, was the tightening of his hand on the wheel.

"That's it?" she said. "You're not going to say anything?"

"Again I ask—what would you have me say?"

That, she realized, was as close as he'd come to confirming her suspicions. "It's got to stop."

"I agree."

"I have no intention of being unfaithful to my husband."

"I'd never ask you to be. Jeez, Sam, give me a little credit, will you? I've never treated you with anything other than decorum or respect."

When he was rattled, she discovered, his Southern accent became more pronounced.

"As long as we understand each other," she said.

"Tell me one thing…" He shook his head. "Never mind."

She didn't want to ask, but her curious nature couldn't let it go. "What?"

"Nothing. Doesn't matter now."

"You're pissing me off. If you want to ask something, ask it. And then we're never talking about this again."

Stopped at a light, he ventured a glance at her and then returned his gaze to the road. "If we'd met before you were married, do you think…?"

Sam shook her head, wishing she'd left well enough alone. "There's no way I can answer that. Nick is it for me. He always was, and he always will be. There's no room for anyone else in that equation, so rhetorical questions are pointless."

"I had a feeling you might say that." He drove in silence until they reached the HQ parking lot. "I hope he knows he's a lucky guy."

"He does. He's very good to me." She paused before she said, "If I did or said anything to encourage—" she waved a hand between them "—this…"

"You didn't. It's all on me, and I'll deal with it. Don't sweat it."

Since this excruciating conversation had gone on long enough, Sam nodded and got out of the car right as Cruz pulled her car into the lot. When he saw her alighting from Hill's car, he looked furious. Jesus H. Christ, the men in her life and their issues with Hill! Not only was she now extremely motivated to close this case so she could have Sunday in bed with her husband, she needed to get Hill out of her hair once and for all. He was causing her far too much trouble—at home and at work.

"It's not what you think," she said as she caught up to her partner, leaving Hill behind.

"What do I think?" Freddie popped a powdered donut in his mouth and chased it with an energy drink.

"You think I blew you off so I could ride with Hill, but I needed to talk to him about the raid, so I killed two birds. That's it."

"Fine by me. You're the one with the guilty conscience."

Sam would very much like to take his head and crack it against Nick's. Since that wasn't an option at the moment, she walked with him through the crowd of reporters who were clamoring for more information on the recovery of Maeve Kavanaugh. Sam ignored them. For now.

"Malone e-mailed me about you handling the media last night," she said to Freddie when they were safely inside.

"Yep."

"Were you freaking out?"

He scowled at her. "Give me some credit, will you?"

"You were freaking out."

Freddie stopped her from pushing through the double doors to the pit. "You need to know… People are speculating about what's going on with McBride and Tyrone."

"It's none of their business."

"Maybe so, but they're speculating just the same."

"Good to know. Thanks for the heads-up."

"After the meeting, we need to talk to the Ohio congressman who gave Victoria a recommendation for the job at Calahan Rice."

"I'll go with you. Now that Maeve is safely back with her father, we can focus on the homicide investigation."

"Barring any pistol-whipping robbers, of course," he teased.

"Of course."

They pushed through the doors together, and Gonzo rushed over to her. "L.T., third shift caught a homicide late in their tour. They've identified the victim—it's Bertha Ray's son, Bobby. They found him down by the Naval Yard, and whoever offed him sent a message—they gouged out his eyes and cut out his tongue while he was still alive."

"Jesus," Sam muttered.

In deference to the situation, Freddie said nothing about her use of the Lord's name.

"What happened?" Hill asked as he joined them.

Sam updated him.

"Shit," he muttered when he heard Bobby Ray was dead. "I'll take care of notifying his mother. I formed a bit of a bond with her last night."

"That'd help," Sam said, thankful she didn't have to deliver the bad news for once.

Detective Arnold joined them. "We're getting word that Mrs. Ray's house was firebombed. Fire department is on the scene." Arnold turned to Hill. "Was she staying there?"

Hill shook his head. "I was afraid of something like this, so I got her out of town last night. She's staying in Philly with her sister."

"Oh, good," Arnold said, visibly relieved. "She was a nice lady caught in the middle of something that has nothing to do with her."

"Wise move," Sam said to Hill, respecting his judgment more all the time. "Conference room in five minutes, everyone. Let's regroup and dig in deep." Sam went into her office and retrieved Jeannie's report on Denise Desposito and William Eldridge.

Scanning the report, Sam decided to send Gonzo and Arnold to Harper's Ferry, West Virginia, to interview Eldridge's widow. Jeannie had included the address and directions to the woman's apartment in an assisted living complex.

As she got up to head for the conference room, her phone dinged with a text message from Nick: "Every time I think about spanking your ass, I get hard."

Sam's entire body heated at the reminder of their earlier conversation. And here she was all heated up at work. This called for an emergency intervention.

She texted back: "It's not, Sam, Senator. It's Darren Tabor." Laughing as she imagined him receiving that text, she gathered up her files.

The phone dinged again. "Very funny. Are you trying to give me a heart attack?"

She replied, "A reminder that X-rated texting can be dangerous to your political career, Senator. Now leave me alone. I have work to do."

"You're going to pay for this. Be ready."

SIXTEEN

SAM CARRIED NICK'S playful threat with her into the conference room, where Gonzo was updating the murder board to include an old mug shot of Bobby Ray.

"Here's the 'after' shot," Lindsey said when she joined them. She handed the autopsy photo to Gonzo, who went pale when he glanced at it.

They saw a lot of gruesome shit in this job, but this was more gruesome than most. When Gonzo posted the photo to the board and secured it with a magnet, Sam took a good look at what had been done to Bobby. Bloody black holes occupied the spots where his eyes once resided, and his lips were grotesquely swollen.

"Choked on his own blood," Lindsey said matter-of-factly, though Sam knew she suffered on behalf of the victims. They all did.

"Someone wanted to send a message," Sam said. "This is what'll happen if anyone talks."

"Exactly," Hill said.

"Who caught the call?" Sam asked.

"Dominguez and Carlucci," Gonzo said. "They're on their way in with a report."

"There went our best lead," Sam said. "So let's get busy finding another one. Cruz, do you want to report on our next step?"

"We're going to talk to Ohio congressman Roy Tornquist, who wrote a letter of recommendation for Victoria Taft when she applied to Calahan Rice."

"Gonzo, I want you and Arnold to go to Harper's Ferry, West Virginia, to speak to William Eldridge's widow, Myrna. I want anything and everything you can get that would link him to Denise Desposito. Both their names were used to falsify Victoria's identity, so let's see how they're connected."

"Got it."

"How close are we to figuring out who did Victoria's background check?" Sam asked Hill.

"Getting closer. My contact at the Defense Security Service promised to get back to me today."

"Lindsey, any word on the lab report on the skin found under Victoria's nails?"

"Nothing yet. I'll put some pressure on them to get back to us."

"Let me know if you need me to get involved," Chief Farnsworth said from the back of the room.

Where had he come from? Sam wondered.

"Couldn't hurt," Lindsey said.

"I'll make a call," Farnsworth said.

"I was also thinking we should go back to the gym where Derek and Victoria met and have them pull her record," Sam said. "We might get some insight into her life before she met him. Cruz and I will do that after we leave the Capitol."

Sam also wanted to talk to the friends who'd known Victoria before she met Derek, and wished McBride and Tyrone were available to take care of that.

A knock on the door preceded Detectives Dani Carlucci and Giselle "Gigi" Dominguez into the conference room.

"Morning," Sam said to the third-shift detectives, both

of whom looked a little tenser than usual. "What've you got on Bobby Ray?"

"A worker arriving at the Naval Yard spotted him lying on the median on the MLK Parkway," Dominguez reported. She was short and compact with dark hair and eyes and an olive-toned complexion. Although she kept to herself, Sam found her to be sharply competent and good at her job. "The body was still warm when we arrived right after six, so Dr. McNamara placed the time of death between five and six a.m."

"They'd done a number on him," Carlucci said. Known for being proud of her Italian heritage, she resembled her Norwegian mother and was tall, blonde and stacked. The other detectives called her "Barbie," a name she claimed to hate, but sometimes Sam suspected she secretly embraced the moniker. Carlucci gestured to the photo of Ray on the murder board. "As you can see."

"Agent Hill will notify the next of kin," Sam said.

"Oh, good," Dominguez said, visibly relieved. "I wasn't looking forward to making that call."

"We'll stay to write up the report and interview his known associates, if that would help," Carlucci said.

"That'd be a big help," Sam said, pleased by the initiative. "Thanks. Okay, everyone, you've got your marching orders. Report back at sixteen thirty. Gonzo, if you're not back by then, call in."

"Will do. Let's go, Arnold."

Sam asked Carlucci and Dominguez to stay for a minute as the others filed out of the room. "This was a tough one. Are you okay?"

"Yeah," Carlucci said. "I'm not particularly interested in breakfast today, but I'm okay."

"Ditto," Dominguez said. "Gruesome."

"You held up well," Sam said. "Thanks for sticking around. I appreciate it. I'll authorize the overtime."

"Thanks, L.T.," Carlucci said. "We'll let you know if we find anything else that's relevant."

"Great." Sam emerged from the conference room and headed for her office to collect her keys and radio before heading out with Cruz. She stopped short when she found a woman sitting in the visitor's chair, scrolling through messages on a smart phone. She wore a business suit, heels and her light brown hair in one of those funky twist thingies that Sam could never pull off with her own unruly curls. "Um, can I help you?"

"Lieutenant Holland?"

"Who wants to know?"

She rose and extended a hand. "Jessica Townsend, department counsel."

Reluctantly, Sam shook her hand. "What happened to old Leonard?"

"Retired."

"Huh, I didn't hear. What can I do for you?"

"I believe you're aware that Melissa Woodmansee has filed suit against the department, alleging police brutality?"

As if the mention of lawsuits and thoughts of depositions didn't make her heart beat a little faster, Sam picked up her keys, radio, sunglasses and cell phone. "I heard a rumor to that effect."

"Your actions at the time of the arrest are at the heart of the suit. I'm going to need a statement from you."

"You have a statement from me. It's called a police report. Have you read it?"

Jessica's blue eyes got awfully frosty. "Yes, I've read the report. I have additional questions."

"Well, I can't do it now. Got somewhere to be. You can make an appointment."

"I have the authority to retain you at my convenience for questioning."

"And I have the authority to track down the killer of a young mother who also stole a kid from the scene. Sorry to be blunt, but my stuff trumps your stuff any day. Now, if you want to make an appointment, I'd be happy to tell you all about how entirely justified I was in the tactics I employed to take a killer off the street, but I'm not doing it now." Sam stepped around Jessica. "Cruz! Let's go!"

Freddie came bounding out of the cubicles and followed Sam as she left the pit. She half expected Jessica to come after her, but she didn't. "Shit," she muttered.

"What now?" Freddie asked.

"I was a total hag to the department counsel about the Woodmansee thing. She wanted to talk to me, and I blew her off."

"I don't blame you for being pissed. I'm pissed that she's suing us."

"No kidding. I'd like to see what other people would do if some crazy chick came strolling into their house with a bomb strapped to her chest."

"They'd do what we did and not apologize for it."

"Exactly." Sam rolled her shoulders and stepped into the maelstrom of reporters. Didn't they ever go home? Or give up? Or get hot in the blazing sun? Apparently not. Their appetite for sensational tidbits took precedence over every other thing. "Unfortunately, however, it's not the department counsel's fault that we're being sued."

"No, it isn't, but she has to know you're busy."

"What've you got on the body found by the Naval Yard today?" one of the reporters shouted.

"Not much," Sam replied.

"Was it a murder?"

"Yep."

"When will you release a name?"

"Later."

She and Freddie pushed through the crowd and continued toward her car in the lot. "Does that count as a press conference?" she asked.

"It does in my book. You conferred with the press."

"I like how you think." She opened the car door and recoiled from the blast of heat that greeted her. "It's hotter than a billy goat with a blowtorch."

"Where in the heck did you hear that?"

"Doesn't everyone say that?" Sam asked, genuinely surprised.

"Um, no."

"Huh. My dad has always said it." Her heart ached a bit at the reminder of the father who was currently furious with her. "I thought it was something everyone said."

Freddie laughed. "Not that I've ever heard, but I continue to learn and grow in your presence, Lieutenant."

"Quit your sucking up and tell me what we've got on Tornquist," Sam said as she drove out of the parking lot and headed for the Hill, wondering if she might run into her handsome husband while she was there. Wouldn't that be nice?

"He's an independent from Dayton, Ohio," Freddie said of Tornquist. "Apparently he was a Democrat, but he left the party after he was already in office. I read that his reelection hopes are nearly nil, but he's a big supporter of Arnie Patterson. Word is he'd be a shoo-in for a cabinet post in a Patterson administration."

"Isn't Patterson from Ohio too?"

"I think so."

"Interesting," Sam said. "Run with me here for a minute…"

"I am your faithful servant, as always."

"For Christ's sake, Cruz."

"I've asked you not to take the Lord's name in vain."

"And I've asked you to quit being such a suck up."

"As it seems we're at an impasse, please…proceed with your speculating."

He could be a pain in the ass, but her partner was always entertaining. "I have all this stuff floating around in my head, parts and pieces that don't add up, but it keeps going back to Ohio. Victoria's fake identity leads back there—the recommendation from the congressman, Desposito was involved in a Medicare scheme there, Eldridge worked for Patterson, Patterson is from there, the congressman and Patterson are in tight. And then I go back to who would have a motive to plant someone high up in the Nelson administration?"

"You think it's Patterson? That this was all part of some ruthless attempt to secure the presidency?"

"I know it sounds way out there. It would've taken years of planning and a shit ton of money to target a member of Nelson's team who'd be high enough to be worth the trouble, to create a whole new identity for Victoria, to fake the background check after she marries Derek, to fake her Social Security number and her fingerprint profile and to pay her God knows how much dough to take the gig in the first place. Who has those kinds of resources and a motive to go with it?" Sam glanced over at Freddie to find him staring straight ahead, pondering the magnitude. "I know it's far-fetched…"

"This whole case is far-fetched. From the minute we

found out Victoria wasn't who we thought she was, it's been one bizarre thing after another." Freddie paused, pondered some more. "You're right about one thing."

Sam raised an eyebrow, which made her face burn like a motherfucker. She kept forgetting her face was unavailable for her many expressions. "Just one?"

"You really need to do something about your lack of self-confidence. It'll hold you back in life if you don't grow a backbone."

"As much as I hate to admit this, your sarcasm has come a long way under my tutelage, and I'm very proud of you."

"Aw, shucks… Thanks."

"Now tell me what I'm right about. I live for these moments."

Laughing, Freddie said, "Patterson certainly has the money to back something like this—and the ambition."

"Nick told me the Democratic Party is worried about him. Nelson is vulnerable, and Patterson could take enough of the middle to deny Nelson a second term."

"Listen to you talking like the political wife."

"Bite me."

"That's not very diplomatic, Mrs. Cappuano."

"Bite me harder." Sam's cell phone rang, denying his opportunity for a comeback. "Holland."

"Sam, hey."

"Hi, Trace," Sam said to her sister. "What's up?"

"I thought you'd want to know—Ang is in labor."

The news hit Sam square in the solar plexus, knocking the wind right out of her for a second. Her mind went totally blank.

"Sam!" Freddie said, pointing to the yellow light at the upcoming intersection.

She slammed on the brakes.

"Are you there?" Tracy asked.

"Yeah, sorry."

"Sam…"

"Don't say it, Tracy. Please."

"Angela told me not to call you. We never know what to say to you at these moments."

"God, I'm such an ass. My sister is in labor, and all I'm thinking about is myself."

"Honey, come on. This is tough on you. We all get that."

Sam forced a deep breath into her lungs and hit the gas when the light turned green. "I'm fine. It's not about me. It's about Ang and Spence and Jack. Who's got him?" she asked of her six-year-old nephew.

"Dad and Celia have him for the duration. Her water broke at eight, and Spence took her in. They said it'll probably be later today before our niece makes her appearance."

"Keep me posted?"

"I will."

"I'll be there after my tour."

"You're sure you're okay?"

"Positive. Thanks for calling, Trace." Sam ended the call and stashed the phone in her pocket.

"Angela is having the baby?" Freddie asked.

"Uh-huh." Sam appreciated that he didn't say anything more. Her fertility struggles were no secret to him or anyone who knew her well. What else was there to say?

She pulled into the parking lot at the Longworth House Office Building and killed the engine. On the way inside, she stopped Freddie. "Let's keep this possibility about

Patterson between us until we have a chance to dig in a little further."

"Will you ask Tornquist about his connection to Patterson?"

"Let's see where our conversation leads. I'll play that one by ear."

"Got it."

"Hang on one sec." Sam reached for her phone and scrolled through the recent calls to get Hill's number. When she had him on the line, she said, "You know what else we need to look into?"

"What's that?" he asked.

"The doctor who implanted the GPS device in Maeve Kavanaugh. Where the hell has he been since word broke of the kidnapping?"

"Good thought. I'll take care of that."

"Great, see you later." Before Sam jammed the phone back in her pocket, she dashed off a text to Nick to let him know Angela was in labor. "Let's go," she said to Freddie.

They found Tornquist's office at the end of a long corridor on the third floor. Inside was a beehive of activity, with staffers on the phones, at computers and walking between cubicles and the congressman's office.

Sam flashed her badge to the congressman's assistant. "Lieutenant Holland, Metro P.D. My partner, Detective Cruz. We'd like to speak to the congressman."

"Do you have an appointment?" the perky blonde asked.

"You know we don't."

"He's tied up all afternoon, but I could get you in tomorrow morning around eight thirty? Would that work?"

Freddie grunted out a laugh as Sam leaned forward, placing her palms on the desk and her face two inches from Blondie's upturned nose. "We're cops. We want to talk to your boss. Now. Got me?"

Blondie's eyes bugged, and her head bobbed. She bolted from her seat and disappeared into the congressman's office.

"I love when they say stuff like that," Freddie muttered. "In my head, I count down. Five, four, three... You never make it past three, incidentally."

"I'm pleased to be predictable."

Blondie returned, looking red-faced and distressed. A group of men and women in suits followed her from the room, each of them eyeing Sam and Freddie with nervous interest. When they were clear of the doorway, Blondie said, "He'll see you now."

"I love that kind of cooperation," Sam said. "Don't you agree, Detective Cruz?"

"You know I do, Lieutenant."

Sam enjoyed watching Blondie swallow hard as they brushed past her on their way into the congressman's office. He was short and round with dark hair and horned-rimmed glasses. Not the fashionable kind of horned-rims, but the old-fashioned kind that made him look like the class nerd.

Sam handled the introductions. "We appreciate you clearing your schedule for us," she said in a sweet tone that was so not her, almost daring Cruz to laugh again.

Tornquist gestured for them to take a seat on a sofa and lowered his corpulent body into an armchair that groaned when he landed. "Of course. I'm always happy to accommodate the Metropolitan Police Department. Now, what can I do for you today?" He folded his hands over his beer belly as if he were settling in for a pleasant chat over iced tea and cucumber sandwiches.

"We're investigating the murder of Victoria Kava-naugh."

"Ah." Tornquist clucked with dismay. "Such a sad thing. I know Derek Kavanaugh, and I can't imagine his terrible grief."

Sam held out a sheet of paper. "You wrote this letter of recommendation for Victoria, when she was known as Victoria Taft, when she applied for a position at the lobby firm Calahan Rice."

Tornquist took the page, scanned it and returned it to her with a sanctimonious smile. "That's my electronic signature. Do you know how many of these my office handles every year for ambitious young Ohioans who come to the Capitol looking to begin a career?"

"Then you didn't know Ms. Taft?"

"I did not."

"So you write these letters for your constituents re-gardless of whether or not they're qualified for the posi-tions they're applying for?"

"It's not my job to determine whether or not they're qualified. I assume the employer takes care of vetting potential employees. I merely vouch to their character."

"How could you do that when you'd never met Ms. Taft? How do you know you're vouching for a worth-while character?"

"Lieutenant, I'd think that in light of your marriage, you'd have a better-than-average understanding of how these things work."

Freddie cleared his throat, a sure sign he was trying not to laugh. She'd bet her life he was counting down in his head again.

"Congressman, let me tell you how things work in my world. People vouch for people they know. They don't vouch for people because they had the good sense to be born in the great state of Ohio."

"Surely your husband—"

"We're not talking about my husband! We're talking about you! Did you or did you not know Victoria Taft when she requested a recommendation from you?"

A bead of sweat suddenly appeared on the crown of the congressman's head as his face twisted with discomfort. "Do I need a lawyer?"

Sam loved when they asked that question. Nothing screamed of something to hide quite like a request for a lawyer. "You tell me. Do you need one?"

"I didn't know her," Tornquist said hesitantly.

"But?"

"I know someone who did," he said, "and he asked me to write the letter."

"I find it very interesting that you remember a letter you wrote years ago for a woman you say you didn't know. Don't you find that interesting, Detective Cruz?"

"Absolutely, Lieutenant. I mean you gotta figure he writes a lot of letters. Why is it that he remembers anything about this one?"

As they held their private conversation, Tornquist continued to sweat and fidget.

"So," Sam said, returning her attention to Tornquist, "are you going to tell us who asked you to write the letter for Victoria Taft?"

His face turned that unappealing shade of purple that Sam usually associated with Lieutenant Stahl. Releasing the top button of his shirt, he pulled his tie free and seemed to be struggling to breathe.

Sam and Freddie exchanged glances.

"Congressman," she said, "are you all right?"

"I-I don't know. My chest hurts, and I'm having trouble breathing all of a sudden."

Oh, for fuck's sake, Sam thought. Just when we were getting somewhere. She reached for her radio and called for an ambulance. Then she helped the congressman onto the floor, tugged his tie off and released two more buttons on his shirt. "Cruz, let the staff know to be on the lookout for the bus."

"On it."

"Am I having a heart attack?" Tornquist asked as he gasped for breath.

"Let's hope not."

Since he was conscious and breathing, Sam didn't have to get up close and personal with rescue breathing or anything else that would force her to put lips or hands on his sweaty body.

"What did you do to him?" Blondie asked as she came running into the room.

Freddie was right behind her.

"We didn't do anything," Sam said. "One minute we were talking to him, and the next he was turning purple. How's that our fault?" She was getting sick and tired of being blamed for doing her damned job.

"Congressman, are you all right?" Blondie asked, squatting next to him.

"I'm sure I'll be fine, Melody. Don't worry."

Melody, Sam thought. How fitting.

Ten minutes passed in uncomfortable silence as Tornquist fought for every breath. When the paramedics came rushing in, Sam and Freddie stood and stepped back to make room for them.

After taking a minute to assess the congressman's

condition, the paramedics strapped him onto a gurney. On his way past, Tornquist reached out to Sam.

"Talk to Christian Patterson. He asked me to write the letter."

And that, Sam realized as the paramedics whisked the congressman from the room, was the first major break in the Kavanaugh case.

SAM AND FREDDIE followed the paramedics from the building and watched them load Tornquist into the ambulance.

"Do you think he's in on it?" Freddie asked.

"He knows something. That cardiac event came on awfully suddenly."

"That's what I was thinking too. It was almost convenient."

"What do we do about what he told us?"

"We dig into Christian Patterson." She took off toward the car. "Can we talk about how I called this one?"

Freddie groaned. "Do we have to?"

"Yes, we have to. Not even thirty minutes ago, I said, 'Gee, I wonder if Arnie Patterson had anything to do with this,' and not five minutes ago, Tornquist hands us the man's son on a platter."

"Do you know what my first thought was when he said the name Patterson?"

Sam was practically skipping on the way to the car. She gave a little shake of her hips for emphasis. There was nothing more thrilling than a big lead in a confounding case. "I haven't a clue. Why don't you tell me?"

"I thought, 'Oh my God, she's going to talk about this *forever*.'"

That made Sam laugh—hard. "How well you know

me, my friend." In the car, she pulled out her phone and called HQ. "Put me through to the pit."

"The what?" the dispatcher asked.

Sam sputtered with exasperation. "Are you new?"

"Who is this?"

"Lieutenant Holland. Connect me with the Homicide unit, please." She rolled her eyes at Freddie. "Don't they tell them these things in orientation?"

"Apparently not."

The phone rang and rang. "Carlucci."

"Oh, good, you're still there. I need an address for Arnie Patterson's local office."

"The Arnie Patterson? The bazillionaire candidate?"

"One and the same."

"I'm looking it up."

Sam could hear the clicking of computer keys in the background.

"Looks like New Hampshire at R Street, near Dupont Circle."

"Got it, thanks Carlucci. Do me one more favor—do a run on Christian Patterson, Arnie's son."

"Hang on."

After some more clicking of keys, Carlucci said, "Let's see, Google has him listed as a top adviser to the campaign, a vice president in his father's investment firm. He was an all-American football player at Ohio State. He's married to a former Miss Ohio, and they have two sons, ten and twelve. Looks like his father—tall and blond with the toothy smile."

"That's what I needed. Are you guys almost done?"

"Getting there."

"I won't keep you. Thanks for the help."

"No problem, Lieutenant."

Sam ended the call and shared what she'd learned with Freddie.

"I take it we're heading to New Hampshire Avenue, then?"

"Let's stop by the gym on the way. I want to cover all the bases."

"What gym was it?"

"Fitness Emporium on Mass Ave."

"Hey, Elin used to work there! Years ago."

"Did she know Victoria?"

He shook his head. "She would've said so. At least I think she would've."

"Call her. Ask."

"Um, okay."

Freddie withdrew his cell phone from his pocket and placed the call. "Hey, hon. Yeah, everything's fine. Sam and I were wondering if you remember a client named Victoria Taft when you were at the Emporium."

Sam listened intently, trying to hear what Elin was saying.

"They sign an agreement when they start that they can't talk about the clients of the gym. Ever. She can get sued."

"Are you kidding me?"

Freddie held the phone to the side. "She's not kidding." To Elin, he added, "Will they talk to us if we go there?" He paused. "I was afraid of that. Okay, thanks. Appreciate the info." Glancing at Sam, he said, "Yeah, me too."

"Aww, does she love you?" Sam asked, making smooching noises.

"Bite me."

"You're not allowed to say that to me. I'm only allowed to say it to you."

"Bite me hard."

Sam snorted with laughter. "What'd she say about the gym?"

"We'd need a warrant."

"Well, then, let's get one." As she drove to New Hampshire Avenue, she placed a call to Captain Malone.

"Are you back in the ER again?" Malone asked when he answered.

"You crack yourself up, don't you?"

"Indeed, I do," he said, chuckling. "What can I do for you, Lieutenant?"

"First of all, you need to tell your new dispatcher what the pit is."

"I'll get right on that."

"And when you're done with that, I need a warrant for Victoria Taft's records at the Fitness Emporium on Massachusetts Avenue. Cruz's girlfriend used to work there, and they've got a strict confidentiality policy."

"I'll take care of it."

"Any word from the lab on the DNA taken from Victoria Kavanaugh?"

"Not yet, but the chief put in another call an hour ago."

"That's good," Sam said. "We need that info. I'm working a promising angle. If it pops, and I think it might, it's going to be huge."

"Isn't it always huge with you, Holland?"

"How is that my fault?"

"Never said it was your fault. I'm only making an observation. Tell me this—what's going on with Tyrone and McBride?"

"Um, I, uh… I decline to comment except to say that I'm handling my squad the way I see fit."

"If they contest it—"

"They won't."

"Stahl is sniffing around like a dog on the path of a juicy bone."

"Let him sniff. He won't get anything."

"Be careful, Lieutenant," he said in a tone that was far more stern than she was used to hearing from him.

"Always am, Captain. Let me know when you get that warrant."

"Will do."

Sam slapped the phone closed. "That motherfucker."

"I assume you're referring to our old pal Lieutenant Stahl."

"Who else? Why doesn't he get a life and a real job and leave me alone to do mine?"

"Because that would be absolutely no fun."

"Speaking of the men I love to hate, Gibson tried to off himself last night. Left a note for me, apparently."

"Oh my God, Sam. Really?"

"Yeah. Patrol showed up at my door. Can you believe he still had me listed as his next of kin after all this time?"

"The guy doesn't give up. You've gotta give him credit for that."

"Do I?"

"Rhetorically speaking. Is he going to be all right?"

"I don't know, and I tell myself I don't care."

"No one would blame you if you didn't care."

"Yeah."

"We could find out, you know. Wouldn't take much more than a phone call. All you have to do is say the word."

Sam thought about it as she pulled into the lot at the building that housed the Patterson campaign headquarters and parked. Turning to Freddie, she said, "I want to know if he survived or not. That's it. No other details."

"I'll take care of it."

"Thanks. I appreciate it."

"It's no problem."

"Let's go have a chat with Christian Patterson."

SEVENTEEN

INSIDE THE STOREFRONT that served as Patterson's Washington office, they encountered a young man working the reception desk. Otherwise, the place was quiet. The windows and walls were plastered with Patterson signs, slogans, stickers and other campaign paraphernalia.

"May I help you?"

They flashed their badges. "Lieutenant Holland, Detective Cruz, MPD. We're looking for Christian Patterson."

He took a long, measuring look at the badges as his Adam's apple bobbed in his throat. "May I ask what this is in reference to?"

"Nope. Is he here?"

"Not at the moment."

"Where is he?"

"He, I... I'm not at liberty to disclose that information."

"We love that answer, don't we, Cruz?"

"One of our favorites."

"Here's the thing," Sam said, leaning on the raised counter that hid his cubicle from prying eyes. "You can either tell us where we might find Mr. Patterson, or we can arrest you for interfering with our investigation. What's your pleasure?"

She enjoyed watching his eyes bug out of his head as she said the word "arrest."

"You can't arrest me for not telling you where someone is."

Leaning on one elbow, Sam turned to face Freddie. "Can I arrest him for not telling me where someone is?"

"Yes, ma'am, you absolutely can. If the person you're seeking has information material to a homicide investigation, you can arrest anyone who impairs your efforts to seek that person."

"Thank you, Detective." She pivoted her gaze to the ashen-faced young man. "So you see, I can arrest you, and I will arrest you. But all that unpleasantness and paperwork can be avoided if you simply tell me where he is."

"I'll get fired if I do that."

Sam raised her hands as if weighing her options. "Fired or arrested. Hmm, which would you prefer, Cruz?"

"I think I'd take option A, as a firing wouldn't be attached to my name forever. Whereas an arrest... Well, that can make for some rather nasty business when it comes to getting another job."

"I'd imagine," Sam said, "if you get arrested, you'll probably get fired too. Tell me what I need to know, and you'll only get fired."

"I've heard about you," he said as his fear turned to anger.

"Ohhh, is this when you tell me you've heard I'm a nasty bitch? I so love when they tell me that, don't I, Cruz?"

"Yes, ma'am. That's one of your favorite parts of the job."

Sam propped the uninjured side of her face on her upturned hand and gave the young staffer the best smile she could with only half her face working properly. "Now, what's it going to be?"

"He's at home." He fairly spat the words at her.

"Which is where?"

"Gaithersburg."

"Write down the address."

With a shake of his head and another glare that fell far short of intimidating, he scrawled the address on a sticky note and handed it to her.

"There, now was that so difficult?"

She could tell that the words go to hell were burning on his lips, but he wisely held his tongue. "Cruz, let's go to Gaithersburg." She headed for the door but turned back to find the young man holding the phone to his ear. "If you tell him we're coming, I'll be back to arrest you."

He froze and quickly dropped the phone.

Satisfied that he'd gotten the message, she pushed open the door. "Oh my God, that was so much fun. Wasn't that fun, Cruz?"

"For sure," he said, laughing.

"Do we have the best jobs ever?"

"Most of the time, no. Our jobs suck the big, fat one. That, though... That was fun."

"I gotta tell you, you're the best partner I've ever had." The words were out before Sam could take a second to filter herself. She glanced over to find him staring at her, mouth agape. Oh shit.

"I am? Really?"

"I can already feel this going to your head."

"I'll live off the high for weeks."

"Jesus. Me and my big mouth."

Scowling darkly, he said, "You know I don't appreciate it when you use the Lord's name in vain."

She unlocked the car. "Bite me. Phew. Back on track. Crisis averted."

"I haven't forgotten what you said."

"What did I say?"

"That I'm the best partner you've ever had."

"I have no memory of that."

"You're a piece of work, Lieutenant."

"I hear that a lot. So Christian Patterson runs a tight ship. If that kid tells where the boss is, he gets fired?"

"I thought that was weird too."

"I'm getting the buzz on this one. Every fiber of my being is pointing me in the direction of Patterson and his campaign. We gotta keep a lid on this until we can prove it. We have to nail them every which way to Tuesday before we tell anyone."

"Anyone?"

Sam was thinking it through as she drove. "Anyone."

"So, we're not telling Malone or Farnsworth or Hill?"

"Not yet. We can't afford the slightest leak on this, and the more people who know the more risky it becomes that it gets out. For right now, it's you and me on the trail. We'll bring the others in when we know for sure that we've got them."

"You could get in big trouble for this."

"Let me worry about that. If we close the case, they'll be too caught up in the success to worry about the methodology."

On the way to Gaithersburg, Sam's phone rang. She glanced at the caller ID, saw it was Nick and took the call, her heart doing a little happy dance that still took her by surprise all these months later. "Hey, babe."

"How's it going?"

"Pretty good, actually. We're finally catching a few breaks on this one."

"Anything you can tell me?"

Sam thought of what she'd told Freddie. Anyone.

"Not yet. Have you talked to Derek today?"

"A few minutes ago."

"How's Maeve?"

"Asking for Mommy, but otherwise, she seems fine. She slept well last night. Apparently, he had her in bed with him, and she clung to him all night."

"God, that's so sweet and so sad. How do you tell a baby her mom is gone forever?"

"I have no idea. It's awful. Derek was saying he'd like to get into the house to get some of Maeve's stuff and more clothes for both of them. Could you make that happen?"

"Sure." To Freddie, Sam said, "Make a call to Crime Scene about letting Derek Kavanaugh into his house to retrieve some belongings. Have them reach out to him to set up a time."

"On it."

"Freddie's taking care of it," she said to Nick.

"Thanks. Speaking of babies…"

Sam's belly ached at the reminder that her sister was in labor. "You got the text about Ang."

"Uh-huh. How are you, babe?"

Touched that he knew—he always knew—that this would hit her hard, she said, "Fine, good, you know. Excited to meet my niece."

Freddie had gotten busy with his own phone, but Sam was still mindful that he could hear every word she was saying.

"You'll get your turn. I really believe that."

Sam took a deep breath, trying to combat the swell of emotion as his softly spoken words went straight to her heart. She couldn't talk about this anymore without losing it. "How's your day going?"

"It's been surreal. I'm actually thinking about the speech we need to write for the Democratic National Convention."

"Oh wow. No pressure, huh?"

"Right," he said with a laugh.

"It'll be so awesome. They're going to love you."

"You might be a tad bit biased."

"Nah."

"Samantha."

Her entire body tingled whenever he said her full name in that particular tone. "Yeah?"

"Don't go to the hospital to see Ang without me, okay?"

"Okay."

"I'll be home as soon as I can. We'll go then."

"It's a date."

"Love you, babe. Be careful out there."

"Love you too," she said, because she damned well didn't care if Cruz heard her say it. "And I'm always careful."

"Oh, and I haven't forgot your punishment. See ya." He ended the call before she could respond, but the reminder sent a bolt of heat straight to her most sensitive areas. Damn him!

It took nearly forty minutes to get to Gaithersburg in midday traffic. Christian Patterson lived in a gated community on the outskirts of town. At the gate, Sam showed her badge. The rent-a-cop examined it closely before returning it to her.

"You the one married to the senator?"

As Freddie snickered in the passenger seat, Sam said, "Yep." God, she fucking hated when people she encountered through her job asked about her private life.

"Hmm."

"What's that mean?"

"Nothing. Go on through."

"If you give him a heads-up that I'm coming, I'll be back to arrest you. Got me?"

"Yeah, yeah. You're a real charmer, aren't you?"

"That is so nice of you to say." She rolled up the window to seal off the oppressive heat. "I'm getting all kinds of compliments today."

"It's a banner day for you." Freddie glanced over at her and then straight ahead.

"Something on your mind?"

"I'm wondering…"

"About?"

"Nick will go to the hospital with you to see Angela and the baby, right?"

She'd expected him to say something about the case. Touched that he was concerned about her, she said, "Yes, he's going with me later. Don't worry about me. I'll be okay."

"As long as he'll be with you, I won't worry."

"You're very sweet to think of that."

"It's been a banner day for me with the compliments too."

She appreciated his effort to diffuse the emotionally charged topic with humor. "Sheesh. Me and my big mouth."

"I'll live off this for months and months."

Christian Patterson lived in a brick-fronted mansion.

There was no other word for it. The colonial-style home had black shutters and tall white columns with a beautifully manicured yard.

"Check this place out," Sam said.

"Nice digs. If this is temporary, imagine what the regular place looks like."

She turned the car into the half-circle driveway and parked next to a silver Mercedes sedan and a white Mercedes SUV, both with Ohio plates. "My poor little car is feeling intimidated."

Chuckling, Freddie followed her up the stone walk to the fancy stained-glass entryway.

She rang the doorbell and listened to the chimes echo through the big house. "That would scare the shit out of me if I lived here."

"You'd never live here. Too pretentious."

"True." Sam leaned on the bell again. "It's like a freaking church or something."

"Do you have to use the words 'freaking' and 'church' in the same sentence?"

"Do you have to be so freaking sensitive all the time?"

Before he could fire back, the door swung open, and Christian Patterson stood before them, tall, blond, all-American handsome and wearing nothing but a silk robe. His hair was mussed, and his jaw was covered in stubble. He looked like he'd just rolled out of bed. "Can I help you?"

They held up their badges, and Sam handled the introductions. "We'd like a few minutes of your time."

"What's this about?"

"We're investigating the murder of Victoria Kavanaugh." Sam watched him closely but he gave nothing away at the mention of Victoria's name.

"What's that got to do with me?"

"May we come in to discuss it further?"

He glanced over his shoulder and then back at them. "Um, sure, I guess."

"Are you home alone, Mr. Patterson?"

"My wife is here, but she's upstairs."

"And your children?"

"They're at camp."

Ah, Sam thought, so Mom and Dad were taking some time for themselves while the kids are out of the house.

He stepped aside to admit them.

"Nice place," she said in what had to be the understatement of the century.

Showing them to a formal living room, he said, "Oh, thanks. It's temporary. We're only here until the election, and then it's back home to Ohio."

Sam and Freddie sat on a sofa while he took the love seat across from them. She said a silent prayer of thanks that his robe stayed closed as he sat, because she suspected he was naked under there.

"What's your role in your father's campaign?"

"I'm a senior adviser."

"And what does that mean?"

"Basically, I'm one of the campaign managers—one of two with direct access at all times to the candidate."

"With such an important job in the campaign, I'm surprised to find you at home in the middle of a work day."

"We've been on the road for the last week. I got back late last night."

Sam noted that the travel put him conveniently out of town at the time of Victoria's murder. "And where were you?"

"Houston, Dallas, Austin, San Antonio, Oklahoma

City, Little Rock, Nashville, Chattanooga and Atlanta. I think that was all the stops. It's a blur of airports and cities and hotels."

Sam produced the letter of recommendation Tornquist had written for Victoria and handed it to Patterson. "Have you ever seen this before?"

He scanned it and handed it back to her. "Um, no. Should I have?"

"According to Congressman Tornquist, you asked him to write the letter for Victoria."

For the first time, Christian's cool composure seemed to rattle a bit. "He said I did what?"

Sam made an effort to speak more slowly to ensure he'd understand this time. "He said you asked him to provide a letter of recommendation for Victoria Taft, later Victoria Kavanaugh, when she applied for a position at Calahan Rice."

"I have no idea who Victoria Taft or Victoria Kavanaugh is. I've never heard of her or Calahan Rice. What is that? A law firm?"

"It's a lobby firm representing the auto industry."

"I've never heard of it. Or her."

"So you didn't hear this week that the wife of White House deputy chief of staff Derek Kavanaugh was murdered and his young daughter kidnapped? It was kind of a big story. I'd imagine the media in Austin and Oklahoma City and Chattanooga covered it."

He held up a hand to stop her. "Of course I heard about her this week. I meant that I'd never heard of her before this week."

"Oh, well, I'm glad you clarified that. So can you explain why the congressman would've told us that you asked him to write the letter?"

"I have no idea why he would've told you that. I barely know him."

"Christian!" a woman called from upstairs. "Are you coming back to bed?"

His face heated with color. "I'll be right there, honey." Returning his attention to Sam and Freddie, he said, "Sorry about that. We don't get many days together during the campaign."

"We're so sorry to interrupt," Sam said, making sure to inflict her tone with a hint of sarcasm. "How long has your father been planning to run for president?"

The question seemed to take him by surprise. "Ah, I'm not sure when he first started making plans. He's been talking about it for a long time."

"Define 'long time.' Are we talking a year, two years, five years, ten?"

"Probably more like ten. It's always been a goal of his. He's gotten serious about it in the last decade or so."

"Would you describe him as an ambitious man?"

That drew a laugh from Christian. "Yeah, you could say that. He's a self-made billionaire. What does that tell you? He grew up in total poverty in Appalachia."

"In West Virginia?" she asked, thinking of William Eldridge.

"Yes, why?"

"No reason. Just wondering."

"He's extremely ambitious and driven to succeed. He's instilled those same qualities in me and my siblings."

"How many siblings do you have?"

"Two brothers and a sister."

"Do any of them work for your father's campaign?"

"My brother Colton does."

"And what does he do?"

"Same as me. Senior adviser."

"Where can we find him?"

"He lives in the guesthouse out back, but I don't think he's home."

"Where else would he be?"

"I wouldn't know. I don't keep tabs on him."

"Was he on the trip with you?"

"Not this one."

"What do your other siblings do?"

"My brother Billy is a firefighter in Ohio, and my sister Tanya is married and lives there with her family."

"Whereabouts in Ohio?"

"Defiance."

Same town the fictional Victoria Taft was from. Bells and whistles sounded in Sam's head as the planets slipped into alignment. It was all she could do to hide her reaction. *Play it cool*, she thought. *We still haven't proven anything.*

"I'm afraid I have to ask if there's a point to all these questions that you might be getting to sometime today? My wife is waiting for me—"

"I know, I know," Sam said, "and you don't get much time alone with her."

"Yes," he said, flushing again.

"One last question," Sam said. "How driven are you to ensure your father is elected?"

"What do you mean?" he asked, clearly taken aback by the question.

"How far would you or your brother go to make sure he gets what he's always wanted?"

"We wouldn't break any laws, if that's what you're implying."

"I'm not implying anything. I'm merely asking how far you'd go to help him reach his goal."

"Well, I've put my own life on hold for the last year to help run his campaign. I've moved my wife and school-aged kids halfway across the country, away from their friends and activities, so I could be better situated. I'd say I've already shown how far I'd go to help him get where he wants to be."

"What's in it for you?"

"What do you mean?"

"Why do all that? Why uproot the family and put your own life on hold to help your father?"

He looked at her as if she'd asked the most ludicrous question he'd ever heard. "Because he asked me to."

"And all he has to do is ask?"

"He's my father, Lieutenant."

"Your brother feels the same way?"

"Of course he does. Our father did everything for us. There's nothing we wouldn't do for him."

Bingo, Sam thought. He'd said exactly what she'd wanted to hear. She stood, and Freddie scampered to his feet, no doubt surprised by her sudden retreat. "Thank you for your time, Mr. Patterson."

"You're not going to tell me what this was about?"

"I'm not really sure what it's about," she said, eyeing him. She wished her more intimidating look was available, but the damned injury was impairing her. "But you can bet I'm going to find out."

"What does that mean?"

"Exactly what I said." She handed her card to Christian. "Have your brother give me a call."

Leaving Christian Patterson holding her card and staring at her with puzzlement on his handsome face, Sam headed for the door with Freddie hot on her heels.

"Holy shit, holy shit, *holy shit*," Freddie whispered as they went down the walk to the car.

"You're swearing," she said, making an effort to sound scandalized.

"I thought the occasion warranted it."

"You're damned right it does." She got in the car and started it, relieved by the immediate flow of air conditioning. Today was even hotter than yesterday had been, if that was possible. As she shifted the car into reverse, she noticed Christian Patterson watching them leave from a downstairs window.

"What do we do now?" Freddie asked as they drove away.

"Now we rip apart the Patterson family and figure out which one of them—or how many of them—set this whole thing in motion."

AFTER LUNCH, NICK called his top three advisers to his office, intending to share the news about the keynote and start work on the speech. Christina Billings, his chief of staff, who'd arrived late that morning due to a babysitting crisis with her fiancé's son, was the first to come into the office.

The petite blonde looked uncharacteristically flustered. "I'm so sorry about this morning, Nick. Angela wasn't due for another week, so Tommy's mother isn't here yet to help us with Alex while Ang is on maternity leave." Sam's sister Angela watched Gonzo's son while he was working.

Nick had never seen Christina so undone. She was

usually the picture of cool competence. "It's no problem. You worked late last night."

"Still, I feel bad being out without prior notice. Tommy couldn't miss the morning meeting at HQ, so I stayed home until Celia called and offered to take Alex. She saved our lives."

"She's pretty awesome," Nick said. "Take a deep breath, Chris. Everything's fine." He was shocked when Christina's chin began to wobble. *Oh shit*, he thought. "What is it?"

"I don't know if I can do this," she said softly. As chief and deputy chief of staff to John O'Connor they'd formed a tight bond that had only deepened since John died. When Nick took office, he'd promoted her to the top spot on his staff.

"Do what?" he asked, sitting next to her.

"Something's got to give. I can't have this job and a family too."

"Why not?"

"Because, I constantly feel pulled in a thousand different directions. I never feel like anything gets enough of my attention. I feel like I'm staying one step ahead of disaster at all times." She stopped herself and looked up at him, seeming horrified. "God, what am I thinking? You're my boss, for God's sake. You're the last person I should be having this conversation with."

"I sort of thought we were friends too. We've been through an awful lot together, you and me."

"Yes, we have," she said as tears spilled down her cheeks.

Terry O'Connor knocked and stuck his head in. "You wanted to see me, Senator?"

"Give me ten minutes. Tell Trevor too."

"Okay."

Terry closed the door when he left.

"Talk to me as your friend—not your boss," Nick said.

"Kinda hard to separate the two," she said with a wan smile.

"Try."

"Well, if you insist… I love Tommy and Alex. I love them both so much, and we're so happy together. But no matter where I am, I feel like I need to be somewhere else."

"Have you talked to Tommy about it?"

She shook her head. "How can I when he certainly feels the same way? Ever since Alex came into our lives, we've both been going a mile a minute. We never get to take a breath."

"A year ago, I might've told you you're crazy to be talking this way. I would've reminded you how lucky we are to have such kickass jobs, and said you'd be crazy to even think about giving that all up to stay home with a baby who isn't even technically yours."

"And now?"

"Now everything is different, and I get it. Some things are more important than work. I'd hate to lose you on my team, especially right when things are starting to get interesting, but you have to do what's best for you and your family."

"What does that mean, 'when thing are starting to get interesting'?"

Nick told her about the conversation he and Graham had had with Brandon Halliwell the night before.

"Oh, Nick…" Her eyes widened. "I mean, Senator. I'm sorry. I still forget sometimes."

Nick laughed. "So do I, and you're talking to me as

my friend, remember? I'm Nick to you. I'll always be Nick to you."

New tears spilled down her cheeks. "I hate myself right now. I hate women who cry at work. I've spent my entire adult life thinking less of women who make fools of themselves over men and consider giving up amazing careers to take care of babies, and would you look at me now? Crying all over my boss, who's a freaking United States senator, and considering doing all the things I disdain?"

He knew he shouldn't laugh, because she was dead serious, so he curbed the impulse. "Things change, Chris. Shit happens. Who knows that better than I do? I really do get it." Resting his elbows on his knees, he leaned forward and took her hands. "Look at me."

Her watery gaze met his. "You said something has to go, right?"

She bit her lip and nodded.

"Is giving up Tommy and Alex an option?"

"No."

"I'd venture to say giving you up isn't an option for him either, so if you're torn and stretched so thin and it's not working, one of you has to give up your job. If it has to be you, I'll understand. I'll miss you like hell, but I'll certainly understand."

"Do you think Sam would say the same to Tommy?"

"Absolutely not," he said without hesitation. "In fact, I'd guess that she'd be somewhere beyond furious, and in the end, it would turn out to be all my fault for having the audacity to invite you to the New Year's Eve party where you met him."

Christina laughed, as he'd hoped she would. "I can so see her pinning that on you."

"It might be better for both of us if you were the one to give up your job."

"I make more money than he does."

"You *have* more money than all of us put together," he reminded her.

She grimaced. "I never should've told you my family has money."

Smiling at the face she made, he said, "You've made your own way your entire adult life and had a successful career doing something you love. If you use some of those resources now so you can focus on your family for a while, that doesn't make you less successful. It means you've got your priorities straight."

Christina squeezed his hands and released them. "Your wife is a lucky woman. I hope she knows that."

"Um, thanks... I think she knows."

"You might run for president," she said fretfully. "I want to be part of that."

"So go home for a few years, get your family launched and come back when and if that pipe dream ever comes to pass. Unless the voters have a huge change of heart between now and November, I'm not going anywhere, and there'll always be a place for you on my team."

Christina stood and leaned in to hug him. "Thank you for being an amazing friend. I'm sorry for the meltdown."

"No apologies needed. Take a few minutes, and when you're ready, get Terry and Trevor in here. We've got a speech to write."

After she left, Nick went around his desk and dropped into his chair. While he really did understand Christina's dilemma, he couldn't imagine this place without her guiding his team. The thought of starting over with someone new was nearly unbearable.

He glanced at the photo of him with John that sat on the credenza. Nick scooted forward and picked up the picture, which had been taken shortly after John took office. Studying the two young men, Nick wondered what they might've done differently in life if they'd known what awaited them. Nick wouldn't have accepted silence from Sam as an answer, and John would've been more considerate of the son who'd killed him in a fit of rage. Things could've been so different for both of them.

Returning the photo to the credenza, he picked up the other one he kept close by—of him with Sam on their wedding day. She was so stunningly beautiful, he thought as he ran a finger over the glass. That he got to go home to her every night was the single best thing about his new life. All the rest of it was noise when stacked up against their marriage.

Nick wished he had more time to spend with her, and more than anything, he wanted to give her the baby she wanted so badly. He wanted it pretty badly too, not that he'd ever admit that to her. She was under enough pressure on that subject as it was. He refused to add to her burden by sharing his own desire to be a father. They'd get there. One way or the other. And they were already pretty darned lucky to have Scotty in their lives. Hopefully, he'd come to visit this summer and decide to never leave.

A knock on the door preceded Christina, Terry and Trevor into the room.

Nick put down the photo and turned to them. "Christina said you have some news," Trevor asked.

"What's going on, Senator?"

"The Democratic National Committee has asked me to deliver the keynote speech at the convention."

Terry's face slackened with shock. "Wow, that's amazing. Congratulations."

"Thank you. I was surprised, to say the least."

"It makes perfect sense," Terry said, nodding. "Of course they've got their eye on you. No one in either party has numbers like yours."

"I'm still not convinced those numbers are all mine."

"How do you mean?" Christina asked.

"I got the sympathy nod after John was killed, and all the craziness surrounding the wedding helped too."

"You're selling yourself short if you think you're still benefitting from that stuff," Terry said. "It doesn't hurt that you're half of what's become somewhat of a celebrity couple, but that's not the only reason you're so popular. You've done a damned good job on behalf of the Commonwealth. You've earned those numbers, Senator."

Unaccustomed to such praise from Terry, Nick said, "Thank you."

"I'd like to take the first cut on the speech," Terry said. "If that's okay with you, of course."

"Sure it is," Nick said, pleased by Terry's enthusiasm. They'd come a long way from when Nick insisted Terry spend thirty days in rehab before he joined his staff.

Trevor, who normally worked with Nick on the speeches, nodded in agreement. "I'll take all the help I can get on this one."

"What do you have in mind, Terry?" Nick asked.

Terry leaned forward, five months sober, sharp-eyed and fully engaged once again. "Here's what I think we ought to do."

EIGHTEEN

AVERY WAITED FAR longer than he should have to place the call to Bertha Ray. Visions of her various expressions—fear, outrage, dignity, resignation, acceptance—from the night before marched through his mind, torturing him with the knowledge that he had to break what was left of her heart. He had no doubt whatsoever that she'd given her son everything she had to give, but it hadn't been enough to keep him straight.

At times like this, Avery wished he'd gone into construction or some other field in which telling people news that would shatter their lives wasn't a part of his job description.

Knowing he couldn't—and shouldn't—put it off any longer, he picked up the phone and placed the call to the number Bertha had given him. Since Sam was out, he'd commandeered her office and was forced to stare at a picture of her and her adoring husband on their recent wedding day. He diverted his gaze but, like a magnet, it was drawn right back to her as he listened to the phone ring. The office smelled of her, adding to the torture. What was he even doing in here?

"Hello," a breathless woman finally said, as if she'd run for the phone.

"This is Special Agent Avery Hill with the FBI. May I speak with Mrs. Ray, please?"

"Yes, one minute, please."

While Avery waited, he took advantage of the opportunity to stare at Sam without having to worry about
looking like a deviant fool in her eyes and those of their
colleagues. For that's what he'd become since he met her,
and she'd called him out on it earlier. Reliving that awkward conversation had him wincing with mortification.

He released the top button of his dress shirt and tugged
at his tie, needing to get more oxygen to his lungs. God,
she'd made him feel like such an ass! And the worst part
was that he'd deserved every derisive comment she'd
directed his way. He couldn't even pretend to plead ig-
norance of what she was talking about, because he *had*
been staring at her. He had been wearing his heart on
his sleeve like an unseasoned boy rather than the mature
man he'd thought himself to be. It had to stop, he thought
as he studied her gorgeous face. Right now.

Well, one more minute of staring wouldn't make anything worse, would it?

"Agent Hill?" Bertha said when she came on the line.

He put the picture of Sam facedown on the desk, unable to look without wanting. "Yes, I'm here."

"Has something happened?"

What was it they said about a mother's intuition?

"I'm afraid so."

She let out a whimper that tugged at his overly involved heart. "Is it Bobby?"

"Yes." He closed his eyes and pinched the bridge of
his nose, hating that he had to do this to her. "I'm sorry
to have to tell you he's been killed." For as long as he
lived, Avery would never forget the sound she let out as
his words registered. He heard someone speaking to her
in the background, and then the phone was dropped. It
landed on the floor with a loud thud.

"Agent Hill? This is Bertha's sister Delores. What's happened?"

"I'm sorry to tell you that your nephew has been murdered."

"Oh, Lord. Oh, no, no, no. Poor Bertha. That boy has done nothing but break her heart for so many years." She sniffled and took a moment to collect herself.

Avery thought about the shack on the beach he'd stayed in during a vacation to Jamaica a few winters back. After this case was closed, he was going back there for a few weeks to clear his badly muddled mind.

"Can you tell me what happened?" Dolores asked.

"He…they… It was bad."

"Lord," she whispered. "What do we do?"

"The medical examiner, Dr. Lindsey McNamara, will be in touch with you once they release the body. You'll need to make arrangements with a funeral home, preferably there in Philly. I don't want Bertha back in Washington until we close this case."

"I understand."

"There's more…"

"God, what else could there be?"

"They firebombed her house."

"Oh… Her home… Why would anyone do that to her?"

"We believe they're sending a message to anyone else who might be involved in whatever it is they're doing. Until we get to the bottom of this, I need you to be strong for Bertha and keep her there with you."

"Yes, of course. She told me you were kind to her, Agent Hill. Thank you for that."

"She's a sweet lady who doesn't deserve any of this."

"No, she doesn't. Is there anything left of her home?"

"I'm not sure. I haven't seen it yet, but I'm heading over there now. I'll get back to you afterward." He paused, choosing his words carefully. "I know this is a difficult time for her, but is there any way you could ask Bertha about who his friends were? We need to talk to them about what he might've said to them."

"Hold on a minute."

Avery could hear the buzz of them talking in the background. Bertha's sobs were also audible.

"Agent Hill?"

"I'm here."

"She said to talk to Sonny Jordan. He was Bobby's best friend."

"That helps. Tell her I appreciate the info."

"Thank you for calling."

"Tell Bertha I'm thinking of her."

"I will."

Avery hung up the phone and headed out of the office. He needed to get out of there and do something productive before he lost what was left of his mind. On the way to the parking lot, he took a call from the Defense Security Service contact who'd been helping him track down the agent who'd handled Derek Kavanaugh's security clearance update after he married Victoria.

"Hill."

"I might have something for you."

"Lay it on me."

"The guy who did Kavanaugh's security clearance update? Delman Jones with NCIS? He's dead. Killed about a month after he turned in the update paperwork."

"Of course he's dead," Avery said as his headache took a turn for the worse. "Give me everything you've got."

Retired Medical Examiner Dr. Norman Morganthau lived at the end of a long dirt road outside of Annapolis, Maryland. "Pretty out here," Jeannie said as she navigated the rutted road.

"Uh-huh," Will replied. He hadn't said much on the long, tense ride from the city.

"Are you pissed at me, Will?"

He turned to her. "No, I'm not pissed with you. I'm pissed at myself. I'm pissed at the situation."

"I want you to know what I told Sam earlier."

"You talked to her?"

Jeannie nodded. "I called to tell her about the engagement and to let her know I'd done the new version of the report."

"I wanted to help with that," he said sullenly.

"I didn't mind doing it. I feel responsible for dragging you into this in the first place."

"You didn't drag me into anything. We agreed that not telling her was the right thing to do at the time."

"I still believe it was, and I told her so. The idea of Skip dying with a possible scandal hanging over him was unbearable."

"What did she say when you told her that?"

"She said she understood why we did it and appreciated the sentiment behind it, but we were wrong to lie. I told her the only thing I truly regret was not setting the record straight after Skip recovered."

"Yeah, I was thinking about that too. That's where we really screwed up."

"Agreed. Maybe we can get to the bottom of it with Dr. Morganthau."

"Let's hope so."

The sprawling ranch house was tucked way back in a

wooded lot. Jeannie knocked on the front door. Since the doctor was expecting them, she wasn't surprised when he came around the side of the house.

"There you are," he said with a smile. He was of average height with a wiry build and kind blue eyes. A big straw hat sat on his head, and he tucked dirty gloves in his pocket when he reached out to shake hands with them. "You found it okay?"

"Your directions were great," Jeannie said. "I'm Detective McBride, and this is my partner, Detective Tyrone."

"It's a great pleasure to meet you both. As I mentioned to you the first time we chatted, I'm a big admirer of yours, Detective McBride."

He'd told her then how much he admired the way she'd handled herself after Mitch Sanborn attacked her. "Thank you, sir. We appreciate you seeing us."

"Come on back. I never miss a chance to show off my garden."

Jeannie and Will followed him around the house to a fragrant garden that was in full bloom.

"Wow, this is amazing," Jeannie said.

"It's my retirement passion."

"I can see that." She pointed to tall stalks with bright yellow blooms clustered at the top. "What are these?"

"Snapdragons. Over here are my prize roses."

The roses were white and yellow and red and three shades of pink.

"You've got quite the green thumb," Will said.

"Never used to," Dr. Morganthau said. "Back in the day, I had a reputation for killing everything I touched. My friends and family called me Dr. Death, and not because of what I did for a living."

"That's funny," Will said, chuckling.

"It's all about having the time to devote to your passions," Dr. Morganthau said, "but of course you're not here to talk about my garden. My wife Amy set out a pitcher of iced tea and some cookies on the deck before she left to go shopping with our daughter. Can I tempt you with a cold drink?"

"That sounds wonderful," Jeannie said. "This heat is oppressive."

"Wait until you have a few more years on you, young lady. When you're always cold, it feels pretty damned good."

"I'll have to take your word for that."

Jeannie and Will followed him along a stone pathway that led to a deck filled with potted plants and inviting outdoor furniture.

"Have a seat," he said, pouring three tall glasses of tea. "It's already sweetened. Hope that's okay."

"Fine by me," Will said as Jeannie nodded in agreement.

Dr. Morganthau took a seat at the table. "Now, what can I do for you?"

"As I mentioned when I called earlier," Jeannie said, "we're continuing our investigation into the Fitzgerald murder. When we spoke in the spring, you mentioned something that's stayed with me about Skip Holland being 'off' during that investigation. I wondered if you might consider elaborating further on that."

"I believe I told you then that Skip was a friend, a good colleague who I was honored to work with."

"Yes," Jeannie said, "you did. I don't mean to put you in an awkward position, but if there's anything you could tell us that might help us to put this case to bed once and for all, we'd really appreciate it."

Morganthau removed the straw hat and smoothed his hand over thinning white hair. He suddenly seemed a million miles away. "It was a tough case from the get-go. Any time a kid goes missing, it's gut wrenching. I'm sure I don't have to tell you after what you've been dealing with this week in the Kavanaugh case."

He took a drink of tea and seemed to be choosing his words carefully. "The department was going through a tough time with budget cuts. We were shorthanded, stretched too thin. Everyone was working insane hours and fighting to keep their heads above water.

"And in the midst of all that craziness, Alice Fitzgerald's kid goes missing." He shook his head. "It was too much, you know?"

"You say that as if you knew her," Will said. "Mrs. Fitzgerald."

Morganthau seemed surprised by the question. "Of course, we knew her. She was Steven Coyne's widow."

Jeannie and Will exchanged glances.

"Who was Steven Coyne?" Jeannie asked, having the sneaking suspicion that she ought to know.

"How fast people forget," Morganthau said, shaking his head again. "He was Skip's first partner when they were still in Patrol. He was gunned down in a drive-by shooting that was never solved."

Jeannie wondered if Will was having the same earth-tilting-on-its-axis reaction that she was to discovering Tyler's mother had a connection to Skip and the department. Suddenly, a lot of things made sense.

"There was no mention of her connection to the department in the reports or in the papers," Jeannie said.

"We kept it quiet. Steven had been gone almost twenty years at that time. After a very difficult mourning period, she'd gotten on with her life. We saw no need to resurrect those painful memories when she was dealing with the disappearance and later the murder of her son." He looked from Jeannie to Will and then back to Jeannie. "You didn't know about Alice?"

Jeannie's heart beat erratically. "No, sir."

"I can imagine how it must look to you with hindsight, but try to imagine the spot Skip was in with his murdered ex-partner's wife back in the middle of another murder investigation."

"He did what he could to protect her and her family," Jeannie said, trying to process it all.

"He did what any of us would've done."

"Could I ask," Will said hesitantly, "why he was assigned a case that struck so close to home for him? Wouldn't it have been a conflict of interest?"

"It would've been a conflict for any member of the department. We take care of our own, as you surely know, so everyone knew her. As I recall, Skip insisted on handling it, and because the department was so shorthanded, no one objected to him taking a case that promised to be thankless, to say the least."

No wonder Skip had gone to great lengths to keep the heat off Alice's broken family. He'd allowed Cameron Fitzgerald to go into the military days after his brother went missing, which now made far more sense than it had before.

"Did Skip have a personal relationship with Mrs. Fitzgerald?" Will asked. "Beyond looking out for her?"

"I can't answer that. I have no idea."

"Did anyone ever imply there was more to their relationship than friendship or concern?" Jeannie asked.

"There were rumors, but you know how people gossip."

"Was there any truth to the rumors?" Jeannie asked.

"I wouldn't know."

"What do you think?" Will asked.

Morganthau took a moment to consider his reply. "I think Skip Holland was a good guy who was torn in a lot of competing directions, and he did the best he could in a difficult situation."

And that, Jeannie thought, was as much as the good doctor was going to say about the situation. Only Skip Holland could attest to the true nature of his relationship with Alice Fitzgerald, and Jeannie doubted he'd be inclined to discuss it. How to handle that would be entirely up to Sam.

Jeannie stood and extended a hand to the doctor. "Thank you for your time and hospitality. We very much appreciate your insight."

"You're very welcome. I hope it was helpful."

"More than you know," Jeannie said.

Will shook the doctor's hand. "Thanks, Doc."

"Give everyone my regards," Morganthau said when he walked them to their car. "I miss the people but not the bodies. All that senseless death. It got to me after a while, you know?"

Did she know? Hell, yes, she knew. "Yes, sir. Enjoy your retirement. You've certainly earned it."

"Thank you. Be safe, you hear?"

"We will."

They drove down the driveway in silence and were

on Route 50 on the way back to Washington before Will broke the silence.

"That certainly explains a lot."

"Sure does."

"Now what?"

"Now we tell Sam and let her figure out what to do about it."

"I don't envy her this one."

"I don't envy her most of them."

"But this…"

"Yeah," Jeannie said. This would suck worse than most.

"WHAT DO WE know about Colton Patterson?" Sam asked Freddie. They had commandeered the conference room and put a keep-out sign on the door. Luckily, the pit was empty, so no one was paying attention to them. She was still mulling over why she'd found her wedding picture facedown in her office and the scent of Agent Hill's aftershave clinging to her phone. It worried her that he hadn't gotten the message earlier. But she shook off those unpleasant thoughts so she could stay focused on the case.

Freddie scanned his laptop screen as Sam paced and squeezed a stress ball. "He's forty, also graduated from Ohio State, never been married, known as a bit of a playboy. He used to date Tenley James," Freddie said, referring to the famous actress. "Whereas Christian went the home-and-hearth route, his brother seems to have taken the opposite path—a new girl every week."

"What's he look like?"

"Here, see for yourself." Freddie spun the laptop around to display a photo of a handsome, rugged-looking man who was as dark as his brother was blond. "He must look like the mother."

"I can see why the ladies dig him. Let's run them both through the system and see if anything pops in the way of a criminal record."

"Doing it now."

"We also need to dig into Defiance and see if the town holds any dirty secrets."

"What kind of dirty secrets?"

"Missing young women, for one."

"Ah, I see."

"Do a search for the names Greg, Betty and Defiance, Ohio."

Freddie typed frantically, trying to keep up with her rapidly moving thoughts.

Energy coursed through Sam's veins like lightning. She lived for the buzz that came with knowing she was on to something.

"There's nothing for a Greg and Betty Taftof Defiance." His brows knitted with concentration as he scrolled through the information. "Oh wow. Oh man. Check this out. A George and Barbara Tate were killed in a house fire twelve years ago. Their teenage daughter Valerie was taken in by the Patterson family." Freddie spun the computer around to reveal a photo of a much younger Victoria Kavanaugh.

"Holy shit!" Sam thrust a fist in the sky. "We've got 'em!"

"I hate to point out that all we've got is a connection between Victoria and the Patterson family. That doesn't prove they murdered her."

"It's a start," Sam said. "We've also got motive. Who else would have a motive to insinuate a plant close to the

Nelson administration but someone who was gunning for Nelson's job?"

"Still gotta prove it," Freddie said.

"You're a buzzkill, you know that?"

"So you tell me."

Sam continued to pace in front of the murder board. "Do a search for Valerie Tate of Defiance, Ohio."

Freddie's fingers flew over the keyboard. "Lots of stuff about the fire, about the Patterson family taking her in. Couple of pictures. In every one of them, Colton has his arm around her."

"I wonder if they dated."

Freddie was reading, his lips moving as his eyes darted back and forth over the screen. "So this one article talks about how Colton got really sick in first grade, so he repeated and ended up in the same class as Christian and Valerie. There's a picture of the three of them in caps and gowns, graduating from high school. Apparently, everything the Patterson family does is news in Defiance."

"Where did Valerie go to college?"

"Bryn Mawr," Freddie said, glancing at her.

"I knew it! How can this not be related to the Patterson family in some way or another?"

"Not denying that it's related to them. Pointing out—again—that even though there's a connection doesn't mean we've caught a murderer."

Sam scowled at him and took another lap of the conference room, nervous energy coursing through her as she tried to put the puzzle pieces together.

"Check it out—Valerie's online presence ends right around the time she graduated from Bryn Mawr. There's not a single other mention of her anywhere."

"Very interesting. So someone in her rich pseudo-family set her up to infiltrate the Nelson campaign. I want to know who, and I want to know why. Rich people like them have flunkies. They have people who take care of situations such as a plant who stops cooperating. We need to figure out who the Patterson's flunkies are and have a talk with them."

"Great. How do we do that?"

"Um, ask them?"

Freddie considered that for a minute. "We call Christian Patterson and say, 'Who are your flunkies?'"

"Sure," Sam said with a shrug. "Why not?"

A knock on the door interrupted them. Sam waited until Freddie closed the screen on the laptop. "Enter."

Agent Hill stepped into the room. "What's going on?"

"Nothing much," Sam said. "You?"

"I got the name of the NCIS agent who handled Derek's security clearance update after he married Victoria."

"And?"

"He's dead."

"Of course he is," Sam said. The Patterson family was nothing if not thorough. "How?"

"His death was ruled a suicide. He went off a bridge in Alabama."

"Did anyone dig beneath the surface?"

"Nope. Apparently, he was a bit of a loner, so no one even reported him missing for a week. By the time they found him, there wasn't much left to investigate." Avery pushed his fingers through his hair, a gesture Sam had come to recognize as one of frustration. "Speaking of not much left to investigate, Bertha's house was incinerated, along with the houses on either side of hers."

"Anyone hurt?"

He shook his head. "Luckily, everyone got out in

time." Gesturing to the computer on the table, he said, "Did you find out anything more from the congressman?"

"Not too much," Sam said. "He had a heart attack before we could question him."

"Jeez, we can't catch a break, huh?"

"We will. We have to keep at it."

"I'm going to talk to the doctor who implanted the tracking device in Maeve Kavanaugh. I'll be back for the meeting at sixteen thirty."

"We'll be here."

He eyed them suspiciously before he stalked from the room.

"He knows something's up," Freddie said.

"Good for him."

"When do you plan to let the others in on what we've uncovered?"

"Soon. We need a little more, and I know right where to get it." She waved her arm, indicating that he should follow her.

He grabbed the laptop and scrambled after her.

"Where're we going?"

"Back to see our friend at Patterson's campaign headquarters."

SHE'S HIDING SOMETHING, Avery thought as he drove to the Washington Hospital Center on Irving Street, Northwest. He had the worst time figuring out all the Northwest, Northeast, Southeast, Southwest business in Washington. Why didn't they use street names without the directions? Any time he'd asked that question of a D.C. native, they looked at him like he had two heads and said that's the way they'd always done it. Still, didn't they get that it was confusing to out-of-towners?

His thoughts naturally returned to Sam, who'd been a little too nice and a little too accommodating. He knew her well enough by now to get that was usually a sign she was up to something. Hopefully, she'd come clean with him soon, and they could close this damned case. The minute they did, he was heading for Jamaica.

Derek Kavanaugh had told him that Dr. Bernard Saltzman had attended Victoria when Maeve was born. Saltzman's office was housed within the Washington Hospital Center where he also had labor, delivery and surgical privileges.

Avery parked and walked what seemed like a mile to the main door, where he asked for directions to Saltzman's third-floor office. The waiting room was full of expectant women. At reception, he flashed his badge. "FBI Special Agent Hill to see Dr. Saltzman."

The older woman eyed the badge and then looked up at him. "He's with a patient at the moment." She gestured to the waiting room. "With many others waiting to see him."

While he normally would demand to see the doctor immediately, he had no desire to interrupt what went on in this place. "I'll see him between patients." Avery scanned the available chairs and found one next to an extremely pregnant woman. Several of the women in the room were holding hands with terrified-looking men.

Avery sat, hoping he wouldn't be kept waiting for long.

Being around pregnant women always made him feel twitchy. He never knew what to say or how to behave. His sisters had been pumping out kids for years now. Avery stayed far, far away from that business. Once they were born, he was happy to be a doting uncle, but he left the pregnant, hormonal and emotional stage to his brothers-in-law to manage.

The office door opened, and in walked the blonde sprite he'd met the night before at Sam's house. What was her name? He racked his brain trying to remember and strained to hear as she checked in. Shelby! That was it. The new personal assistant to the senator and his wife. Maybe she wouldn't notice him sitting there, trying to blend in among the sea of preggos.

She turned to find a seat and zeroed right in on him, her eyes widening with surprise. "Agent Hill? Are you expecting?" She glanced at the woman to his right.

Horrified by the assumption, he shook his head. "I'm here to speak with the doctor about a case I'm working on."

Shelby took the chair on the other side of him. Judging by her slim figure, she either wasn't yet pregnant or was newly pregnant.

"Is he in trouble?" she whispered.

"No. Nothing like that." He glanced at her, wondering how well she knew Sam. "When are you due?"

Her smile faded, and he instantly regretted the question. "I'm not pregnant yet. Still trying."

Trying to be sly, he glanced at her left hand.

"I'm not married, either."

Clearly, he wasn't sly enough. He held up both hands. "No judgment."

Her blue eyes filled with tears, and Avery yearned for a high roof to jump from.

"I'm sorry," she said, dabbing at her eyes with a tissue she produced from the largest pink purse he'd ever seen. Come to think of it, everything on her was pink. "I'm all hopped up on hormones, and everything makes me cry. The other day, the car in front of me hit a bunny on a side street, and I cried for an hour!" As she spoke, tears rolled down her face, and she wiped frantically at them, trying to stem the tide. "God, I'm a mess."

Since Avery didn't disagree, he kept quiet.

"So you can't tell me what the doctor did," she said in what she considered a whisper.

"No."

"Sorry, I shouldn't have asked that."

"Sam won't want you asking that stuff when you're working for her." The words came out more harshly than he'd intended.

Her eyes flooded once again.

"Oh, come on. I didn't say that to make you cry."

"I'm sorry," she said, looking wounded. "I can't help it."

Trying to make conversation, he said, "What does your boyfriend think of the waterworks?"

"I don't have one of those either." Again, Avery was sorry he'd asked.

"Your accent is lovely," she said wistfully. "Is it Charleston?"

"Yes," he said, surprised by how she'd figured out where he was from. "How'd you know that?"

"Spent some time there once. Long time ago."

"Don't," he said, filling his tone with warning when her chin wobbled and her eyes went shiny.

"Sorry." She pulled out a fresh tissue. "Painful memories."

"I'm almost afraid to ask how you plan to have a baby with no husband or no boyfriend."

She gave him a wan smile. "Science."

"Huh."

"What does that mean?"

"What does what mean?"

"Huh?"

"Nothing. It's surprising."

"What is?"

God, how do I get myself into these situations? "I'd think you'd have men standing in line wanting to father your child."

A sob hiccupped from her chest. "You really think that?"

"Don't make me sorry," he warned her.

The receptionist stepped into the waiting room.

"Agent Hill? The doctor will see you now."

"Thank God," Hill muttered. "Ah, it was nice to see you. Good luck with your, ah, project."

"Thank you," Shelby said, reaching for another tissue.

Avery followed the stout older woman down a series of hallways that led to the doctor's office.

Saltzman was dictating into a handheld recorder but waved him in and gestured to a seat.

The receptionist closed the door when she left the room.

Saltzman was tall and thin, with salt-and-pepper hair and wire-framed glasses. When he was finished dictating, he clicked off the recorder. "Sorry to keep you waiting. I'm Bernie Saltzman."

Avery shook his outstretched hand. "Special Agent Avery Hill, FBI."

"You're here about Maeve Kavanaugh and the tracking device."

"Yes—"

"Before you ask why you didn't hear from me right away when she went missing, I just returned yesterday from an African safari with my wife and children. I only heard about the Kavanaugh case this morning after the baby had been found."

"That answers some of my more pressing questions."

Saltzman dropped into his chair and stretched out his long legs. "It's awful. Victoria was a lovely person. She and her husband were so excited about the baby."

"Do you remember all your patients so clearly?"

"I wish I did, but there are a lot of them. They stood out because of his connection to the president."

"After the baby was born, Victoria had a GPS locating device implanted in Maeve's arm. Is that a common practice?"

"Becoming more common all the time."

"Did Victoria tell you why she wanted the device implanted in the baby?"

"She was concerned that someone would take the child because of the nature of her husband's job."

"Did you find that odd?"

"Not really. She had some issues with anxiety that she was quite open about, so it didn't surprise me."

"Was she on medication for the anxiety?"

"Not while she was pregnant."

"Were you aware that her husband didn't know about the GPS device?"

That seemed to surprise him. "No, I didn't know that, but it's not uncommon for me to deal solely with the mothers after their babies are born. The fathers are in and out."

Avery stood to leave and handed Saltzman a card. "Thank you for your time, Doctor. If you think of anything else, please give me a call."

"Agent Hill?"

He turned back.

"I reread her file last night to refresh my memory. You might like to know that Victoria had more than the average amount of interest in hospital security before she delivered."

"How do you mean?"

"She wanted information about who could come into the ward, what kind of measures were in place to record the comings and goings of visitors. That kind of thing."

"Did it seem to you that she was worried about someone taking the baby?"

"Yes, with hindsight, I'd say she did seem concerned about that."

"Thanks again."

Avery followed the exit signs to the waiting room, where he nodded to Shelby.

She gave a small wave.

He was glad to see she'd stopped crying. Halfway to the elevator, he heard his name. Turning, he found Shelby chasing after him.

"Sorry," she said, flushed.

"Is there something I can help you with?"

She was so tiny that even wearing spike heels, the top of her head only reached his chest. Bending her head back, she looked up at him. "I was wondering if you might like to have coffee sometime."

Was she asking him out? "Ah, well, I'd love to, but I won't be sticking around after we close this case. I've got somewhere I need to be." *Far, far away from here*, he thought.

Her expressive face fell with disappointment. "Oh, okay. I won't keep you."

"Good luck," he said, glancing at the doctor's office door, "with…everything."

"Same to you."

In the elevator, he replayed the odd encounter and experienced a twinge of regret that he hadn't met someone like Shelby years ago, back when he was still interested in the kinds of things she wanted. Back before he knew Sam Holland was in the world. Yeah, things were a lot simpler then.

NINETEEN

SAM PUSHED OPEN the door to Patterson's campaign head-quarters and strolled in like she owned the place.

The young man behind the counter blanched when he saw her and leaped to his feet, the color leaching from his face. "I didn't tell him you were coming! You can't arrest me!"

"Relax," Sam said. "No one is being arrested. Yet."

"What does that mean?"

"I need some more information. If you help me out, we're square. If you don't…" She glanced at Freddie. "We might have a problem."

His gaze darted from her to Freddie and then back to her. "What kind of information?"

Sam leaned on the counter as if settling in for a chat with an old friend. "Let's start with your name."

"Sam."

"Hey!" Sam said. "What a coincidence. That's my name too. Isn't that cool?"

"I guess," he said with a shrug. He clearly didn't think it was as cool as she did. Running a trembling hand through wavy dark hair, he vibrated with nerves.

"I imagine it takes a lot of people to run this organization."

"Yeah, so?"

"About how many?"

"A couple hundred, give or take, work here and a thousand or more working across the country."

"Where's everyone today?" Sam asked, even though she already knew.

"Everyone is off today after the big Southern swing."

"Why aren't you off?" Freddie asked.

"Someone had to answer the phones."

"How many of the thousand or more people working on the campaign are paid?"

"More than five hundred. The rest are volunteers. Arnie has attracted a heck of a following. We have more volunteers than we can accommodate."

Spoken like the proud disciple, Sam thought. "Who works closest with the candidate?"

"His sons, Christian and Colton."

"And who works closely with them?"

He crossed his arms and seemed unnerved. "I've probably said enough."

"Who instilled the gag order on the staff?"

"Christian. He's more or less the boss of the staff. He's particular about leaks."

"Particular in what way?"

"He makes it clear that anyone caught talking to outsiders about the campaign won't work here for long."

"Have there been instances of people being fired for telling tales out of school?"

"Yes."

"Who?"

"I'm... Y-you're going to have to get a warrant. I'm not going to talk about personnel issues. I'll be in enough trouble as it is."

Realizing that avenue was a dead end, Sam said, "Who are Christian and Colton's closest associates?"

"Porter Gillespie works for Colton and Jonathan Thayer is Christian's aide."

Freddie wrote down the names. "Can we get their local addresses?"

Young Sam collapsed into the desk chair. "I'm so going to get killed for this." On a yellow notepad, he wrote down the addresses.

"Go ahead and add the cell numbers while you're at it," Freddie said.

"So Christian and Colton go way back with these guys?" Sam asked.

"Yeah. I guess."

"How far back?"

"All the way back. The Patterson family has a lot of friends. People like them."

"Let me ask you this," Sam said.

The young man seemed to barely breathe as he waited to hear her next question.

"If one of the Patterson brothers had, say, a...dirty... job to be done, would they get Porter or Jonathan to do it for them?"

His Adam's apple bobbed frantically. "What kind of dirty job?"

"You know, the sort of thing that needs to be done in a heated campaign." Sam leaned in a little closer. "The sort of thing that the candidate and his family wouldn't want to do themselves."

"I don't know what kind of thing you're referring to."

Sam couldn't tell if he was being intentionally obtuse or if he was that naïve. "I suppose I mean things that skirt ethical or legal boundaries."

"We run a very clean campaign, Lieutenant," he said

indignantly, leading Sam to wonder if he actually believed that.

"Sure, you do. Don't they all, Detective Cruz?"

"I'm sure they do. There's nothing dirty or unethical about politics."

Sam settled into the conversation with Freddie, ignoring the nervous young man whose eyes darted between them as if he were watching a tennis match. "Except in some cases they're as squeaky clean as they appear. I don't think this is one of those cases. Do you?"

"Something about this one smells bad," Freddie said, following her lead perfectly as he did so often.

When had he become every bit as good at this as she was? *Huh*, Sam thought. *That snuck up on me.* "I can't quite get a handle on this particular odor," Sam said, returning her attention to young Sam. "But it's particularly stinky, isn't it, Detective Cruz?"

"Particularly. Yes. It has an aura of bad food, onions, maybe, with a hint of dirty diaper thrown in there."

Sam held back a laugh as she nodded in agreement.

"Talk to Jerry," young Sam said, seeming suddenly anxious to be rid of them.

"Excuse me?" Sam asked, as if she hadn't heard him perfectly.

"I said, talk to Jerry."

"Jerry's last name?"

"Smith."

"And what does he do?"

"He drives people and does odd jobs and...stuff."

"Ohhh," Sam said, clapping gleefully. "Stuff. Why do I suddenly suspect you knew all along what we meant by dirty jobs? Now where would we find this illustrious Jerry Smith?"

He wrote the address on a piece of paper and tore it off the pad, thrusting it at her. "If I end up dead, it's on you."

"No, my friend, it's on you for being stupid enough to work for people who'd kill you for telling the truth. You might want to reconsider your career choices." Sam started to leave but then turned back. "Write down your full name, address and phone number."

"Why?"

"Because we might need to talk to you again, and I'd hate for you to disappear on us."

His hand was visibly trembling as he wrote down the information and passed her the paper.

"Excellent. Stay local in case we need you."

They pushed through the door into a swampy blast of heat that seared her lungs. "This has been an extremely fun day," Sam said.

"While some people might question your idea of fun, I completely agree."

"The dirty diaper thing was a nice touch."

"Did you like that? I thought it was rather brilliant myself."

Sam rolled her eyes at him as she unlocked the car. "How much you want to bet that Jerry Smith's DNA is going to match what was found under Victoria Kavanaugh's nails?"

"I'd bet the farm on that one." Freddie gestured to the campaign office. "That poor kid is never going to be the same. You made him your bitch in there."

"I really did, didn't I?" Sam asked with a satisfied grin as she started the car. "He needs to get another job. He knows they're scumbags, but he was willing to put his own ass in a sling defending them. I don't get that kind of blind loyalty to people who don't deserve it."

"Patterson has a huge and loyal following in this country. People see what they want to see, you know?"

"Yeah. It's true."

Jerry Smith resided at an extended-stay hotel that featured efficiency apartments, located six blocks from campaign headquarters. Young Sam had even included his room number, which saved Sam and Freddie the trouble of dinking around with the front desk and having to threaten them with a warrant.

In the parking lot, Sam noticed a black Lincoln SUV with tinted windows and a Patterson for President bumper sticker and pointed it out to Freddie. "At least we know he's here."

They entered the lobby and went straight for the elevator, taking it to the fourth floor.

Sam rapped on the door of number 424 and held up her badge to the peephole when she heard rustling inside the room. "Metro Police, open up, Jerry." She rested a hand on her weapon, nudged Freddie and tossed her chin, indicating that he should move clear of the doorway in case this went bad. It suddenly occurred to her that they probably should've called for backup before coming here. "Jerry, you're testing my patience. I know you're in there. I saw your car out front."

"What do you want?"

"We need to talk to you. Open the door, or I'll send my partner to get the manager."

Another minute passed in which the only sound coming from the room was the blare of the TV. If they hadn't been on the fourth floor, Sam would've worried about him escaping out the window. As the security chain scraped and jangled, Freddie drew his weapon.

Since he had her covered, Sam kept hers holstered.

The dead bolt disengaged, and the door swung open. At more than six feet tall, Jerry was bald, muscled and tattooed. Sam's first thought was that petite Victoria wouldn't have stood a chance against this guy. He was a dirty-jobs guy sent straight from central casting, right down to the scruff on his jaw, the wife-beater T-shirt and the nasty scowl on his face. And was that a bruise on his chin? She wondered if that explained the bruises on Victoria's knuckles. Sam sure hoped so.

"What do you want?"

"Step inside," Sam said.

"Here is fine."

"Downtown would work better for us, wouldn't it, Detective Cruz?"

"We'd prefer that, actually. Although we'd have to cuff you for transport, and I'm thinking if I'm you, I'd rather let us in for a civilized conversation than be cuffed and hauled to HQ."

His scowl got nastier, if that was possible, as he stepped aside to let them into the messy space that stank of cigarettes and stale beer.

"Enjoying your day off, Jerry?" Sam asked.

"What do you want?"

"Let's start over, shall we? I'm Lieutenant Holland. This is my partner Detective Cruz. We're investigating the murder of Victoria Kavanaugh and the kidnapping of her daughter Maeve." Sam watched him closely for reactions to the Kavanaugh names, but his expression remained stubbornly nasty.

"What's that got to do with me?"

"That's what we'd like to know. Your name came up in our investigation."

That got a reaction as his nastiness turned to outrage.

"Who gave you my name?"

"Doesn't matter."

"It matters to me!"

"Why?"

As his lips curled into a snarl, Sam could see why young Sam had been so reluctant to tell them about Jerry.

"Because I'd like to have a conversation with the big-mouth."

"How we found you is irrelevant," Sam said. "We'd like to know where you were on Sunday."

"Why?"

"Um, because."

"I don't have to tell you that."

"Yes, you do, or I'll have no choice but to arrest you."

"On what charge?"

"Withholding information material to a murder investigation."

"I don't know nothing about no murder!"

"You got a record, Jerry?" With all the Jerry Smiths in the world, running him through the system before they came would've taken time Sam didn't have.

At that, some of his bluster fizzled. "Yeah, so what?"

"What kind of stuff?"

"Assault, larceny, theft."

"Lovely. Is your mother proud?"

That earned her another ferocious scowl. "Is there a point to this conversation?"

"Yeah, I want to know where you were on Sunday."

"I was here all day. Watched the ball game, had a pizza, took it easy."

"So while the rest of the campaign was swinging through the South, you stayed in town?"

"They didn't need me. They had local drivers lined up at each stop."

"Is that unusual?"

"Sometimes I go, sometimes I don't. Depends."

"On?"

"What else is going on. I go where I'm needed."

"Did you see anyone on Sunday? Talk to anyone?"

"I keep to myself when I'm not working, especially when it's hot as hell."

"Go anywhere?"

"Couple of errands. Dry cleaner, grocery store, that kind of thing."

"Did you make it over to Capitol Hill by any chance?"

"Not that I recall."

"Let me ask you about the Patterson family."

He was immediately on guard. "What about them?"

"You're in tight with them?"

"Yeah, I guess."

"All of them? Christian, Colton, Arnie?"

"Uh-huh."

"How tight is tight?"

"What're you implying?"

"I'm asking how tight you are with them. On a scale of casual acquaintance to there's nothing I wouldn't do for them, where do you fall?"

"They're family to me. Have been since I was a kid."

"In other words, there's nothing you wouldn't do for them?"

He shrugged as if that ought to be obvious.

"Would you kill for them?"

His eyes narrowed, and he looked like he wanted to kill her for asking that. "I want a lawyer."

Sometimes they made it so damned easy. While the

request for a lawyer could often be a pain in Sam's ass, other times it was exactly what she needed. "Cruz, place Mr. Smith under arrest."

"What for?" Smith yelled. "I didn't do nothing!"

"Since we can't question you any further without your attorney present, we're required to transport you to HQ where your attorney will be called. Once he or she is present, we can resume our conversation. Cruz?"

"Mr. Smith, you have the right to remain silent. Anything you say can and will be used against you in a court of law."

As Freddie recited the Miranda warning, Jerry fumed. The look he gave her should've made her wilt, but Sam wasn't known for being the wilting type. She turned off the TV and followed them from the room, closing the door behind them. As they escorted Jerry to the elevator, Sam hung back and placed a call to Captain Malone.

"I haven't heard from the judge yet," he said when he answered.

"I need another one."

"What now?"

She recited the name of the hotel, the address and the room number. "We have reason to suspect that the occupant of the room is the one who killed Victoria Kavanaugh."

"Tell me what you've got."

Despite her inclination to keep a tight lid on what they'd uncovered, Sam outlined what they'd learned about the Patterson campaign and Jerry's role as their henchman. "He doesn't seem like the kind of guy who does laundry on a regular basis, so we may get lucky with some bloody clothes or DNA that would tie him to Victoria. I also need a warrant for his DNA. If it matches what we found under her nails, which I think it will, we've got a slam dunk on the murder."

"Wow, good going, Holland. You never cease to amaze me."

"Smith is the tip of the iceberg," she said. "We've got bigger fish to fry before this one is wrapped up."

"Explain."

"One or all of the Pattersons gave the order to have Victoria eliminated."

Malone released a low whistle. "You'll take down the entire campaign with the accusation alone."

"That's why I'm going to be damned sure before a word of this hits the press."

"Holy shit. You weren't kidding when you said this was big."

"You gotta help me keep a tight lid on this until we we've got it all sewed up."

"Absolutely. What's your plan?"

She lowered her voice and dropped back as Cruz marched Jerry to the elevator. "I'm going to let Jerry cool his heels at HQ in the hope that some time in custody might make him more forthcoming. He's got a record, so he knows what he's in for if he gets sent back to prison."

"The Patterson organization will either swoop down en masse or abandon him completely."

"I'm banking on option B. I think the second we arrested Jerry Smith, he became persona non grata to the Patterson family. They're going to act like they've never met the guy, that anything he's done was all his idea of loyalty. They had nothing to do with it. Yada, yada."

"You're probably right about that."

"He's about to get a hard lesson on who his so-called

family will protect when the shit hits the fan. We'll be right in."

"I'll request the warrants."

"We need that DNA report on Victoria too."

"I'm on it."

"Tight lid, Captain."

"You got it, Lieutenant."

IN DEFERENCE TO the media camped out front and because she wasn't quite ready to tip her hand to the Patterson family, Sam and Freddie escorted Jerry Smith into HQ through the morgue entrance. "Take him up to processing," Sam said to Freddie. Smith would be strip-searched, fingerprinted and photographed, which ought to enhance his good mood. She lowered her voice so only Freddie could hear her. "I want to know if there are any scratches on him."

Freddie nodded in understanding.

"And then put him in interrogation."

"Got it."

Sam headed into the morgue to find Lindsey. "Hey, Doc?"

"In here," Lindsey called from her office.

"I need you."

"What can I do for you, Lieutenant?"

"I need you to take a DNA swab and rush through the results."

"Do you realize that every request we receive has the word 'rush' attached to it?"

Sam smiled at the saucy reply from her friend. "You're not going to get a rise out of me. I'm having a fantastic day. The best day I've had in longer than I can remember."

"Are you about to break into song?"

"I very well could before this day is over."

"I take it you've had a break in the Kavanaugh case."

"Oh yeah, and wait 'til you get a load of this one. That's all I can say."

"Bigger than the DNC chairman, the speaker of the House and a senior senator?"

"Maybe not quite that big, but it's big. We're waiting on the warrant for the DNA. I'll give you a call when it comes through."

"I'll be here. How's the face?"

"Still hurts like a mo-fo, but nothing's getting me down today, my friend." Sam turned to leave but stopped herself. She'd been trying to make an effort to be a better friend to the people who mattered to her, and Lindsey mattered. "How are things with Terry? You haven't said much lately."

Lindsey smiled, and a soft glow lit her green eyes. "Things are great. I'm so glad I took a chance on him. It was so totally worth it. He was worth it."

"I'm glad you're happy. You guys look great together."

"Thanks, and thank you for getting married and giving me the chance to meet him."

"Happy to oblige, even if the cross-pollination of my world and Nick's world continues to give me hives." Sam added a shudder for dramatic effect.

"They have medication for that," Lindsey said drolly.

"Ha-ha."

"I hear you'll be taking a trip to Charlotte later in the month."

For a brief second, Sam didn't know what she was talking about, and then she remembered. "Oh, right. The convention." It hadn't occurred to her until that very moment that she'd have to be there with Nick. *God, I really am a jerk*, she thought.

Lindsey raised a brow. "It's a pretty big deal, Sam."

"So I'm told."

"Are you freaking out?"

"Me? Freak out? Of course not."

"Whatever you say," Lindsey said with a snort of laughter. "I'm freaking out, and it's not my husband who's doing the keynote at the Democratic National Convention."

"Why are you freaking out?"

"Because my boyfriend is writing the speech, and he's freaking out. He said it has to be perfect. No pressure or anything."

Sam was almost ashamed to admit that she'd not given a thought to what would go into preparing Nick for his big moment. "I'm sure he'll do a great job."

"Yeah," Lindsey said, her smile fading.

"What?"

"I worry, you know? His recovery is still so new, and stress can be a trigger."

"He's doing great, and he seems to be loving his new life. Why would he risk all that?"

"I know you're right, but I still worry."

"I'm sure it'll all work out. He's the perfect person to write the speech. Nick is lucky to have him on his team, and he knows it."

Lindsey nodded in agreement. "Stay close to the phone."

"You got it."

As Sam traversed the winding corridors from the morgue to the pit, she thought about the conversation with Lindsey, which had served as somewhat of a wake-up call that she needed to be more tuned into what was going on with her husband in the next few weeks. Her work almost always took center stage in their relationship, but his was equally important—never more so than now with the convention and election looming.

She was anxious all of a sudden to see him.

Freddie met her in the pit. "He's in interrogation one. Officer DuPont is with him."

"Phone call?"

Freddie nodded. "He called Christian Patterson, told him he'd been arrested and he needed a lawyer. Patterson said they'd send someone right over."

"Excellent."

"What do we do now?"

"We wait. If I've called this one right, Patterson won't be sending anyone, and Smith has had his last contact with the Patterson family."

"And if you're wrong?"

"When does that ever happen?"

"You're insufferable, you know that?"

"I have been told that a time or two." Sam checked her watch. Four twenty-five. "Perfect timing. Everyone will be here for the four-thirty meeting in five minutes. Call the U.S. Attorney's office and get one of the AUSAs down here. I want them in on this going forward."

"Are you going to tell them what we've got?"

"I haven't decided yet."

"You'd better make up your mind. There's Hill now."

TWENTY

IGNORING THE INQUISITIVE look Hill sent her way as he stepped into the pit, Sam went into her office to give her e-mail a quick scan before the meeting. She also sent a text to Tracy to ask how Angela was doing.

"She's in transition," Tracy replied a minute later. "Lots of pain, but hanging in there. You should have a new niece in the next couple of hours."

"Tell her I love her," Sam replied. "And I'll be there soon."

"Will do."

Sam took a deep breath as a swell of emotions overtook her. She was excited to welcome a new niece and so happy for Angela and her husband, Spencer, who'd tried for four long years to have a second child after Jack was born and had nearly given up when Angela got pregnant. Still, Sam couldn't escape the fact that she was also jealous that her sisters were able to have children when she'd been so cursed with fertility issues.

"Maybe this time," she whispered.

"Everything okay, Lieutenant?" Hill asked from the doorway to her office.

Startled to see him, Sam said, "Sure. Yeah. What's up? Did you meet with the doctor who implanted the GPS device?"

"Yep. He was on safari with the family when it happened, which is why we didn't hear from him about the device."

"I'd wondered about that."

Checking his notes, Hill said, "According to the doctor, the GPS device is becoming more common. He said some parents are more paranoid than others. Victoria fell squarely into the paranoid department. When I asked him if she seemed to think she had good reason to be concerned, he said she was very thorough in vetting the safety and security measures at the hospital."

"So she was worried from the beginning about someone taking her kid."

"Seems that way."

"I want to ask Derek about that before the meeting. I'll be right in."

Hill started to turn away but stopped himself. "I saw your new assistant at the hospital."

"Shelby?"

"Yeah."

"What was she doing there?"

"Seeing Saltzman and crying—a lot. She told me she's trying to have a baby."

Sam nodded. "She's jazzed on hormones. They're making her crazy."

"Apparently. I'll let you make the call."

After he walked away, Sam picked up the phone and dialed the number for Derek's cell phone. He answered on the third ring.

"Hey, it's Sam."

"Oh, hi. How's it going? Do you know anything yet?"

"We're getting closer. I should have something for you in the next day or two."

"Good," he said in a dull, flat tone. "I know I should

be happy to hear that, but the reality is that catching the person who killed Victoria won't bring her back. It won't tell me what I really want to know."

Sam didn't have to ask him what that was. "How's Maeve?"

"She's great. Totally and blissfully clueless. She's giving us something else to focus on besides the grief."

"I'm so glad she's safe and sound. Speaking of her safety, I need to ask about whether Victoria was particularly concerned with her own safety or Maeve's."

"Yes," he said. "She was over the top when it came to safety. Maybe she always suspected someone might kill her and steal Maeve, or just steal Maeve. She was always checking the doors and windows at night. More than once, I caught her doing it in the middle of the night. I used to tease her for being OCD, but now I wonder if she didn't have good reason to be fearful."

"She may have." Sam wasn't yet willing to tip her hand on what they'd uncovered. "This really helps. Thank you."

"Sure, whatever I can do. Maeve is up from her nap, so I need to go to her. Keep me posted?"

"Absolutely."

"Thanks, Sam. I appreciate all you're doing."

"No problem."

His overwhelming sadness went a long way toward ruining her good mood. While it was a kick to be closing in on a killer, at the end of the day, Derek's wife would still be dead, and he'd still have questions that might never be answered to his satisfaction.

She was getting up to head to the conference room when her cell phone rang. Glancing at the caller ID, she saw Jeannie McBride's name and took the call.

"Hey, what's up?"

"I need to see you."

Sam's stomach and her good mood took another nose-dive. "I'm going into a meeting, and then I can meet you. My house in an hour?"

"I'll be there."

"If I'm late—"

"I'll wait for you."

"See you then." Sam was almost certain she didn't want to hear whatever Jeannie had to tell her. She wanted the truth, but that didn't mean she wasn't a tiny bit afraid of the truth. Anything to do with her dad was a weak spot for her, especially since he'd been so grievously injured by a shooter who remained at large in a case that had gone colder than the Alaskan wilderness.

She didn't want to hear that he'd acted less than heroically during the Fitzgerald investigation. She didn't want anything to ever besmirch his sterling reputation. And she certainly didn't want to be responsible for stirring up a hornet's nest that would cause heartburn for him or the department.

This is a fine spot you're in, she thought as she went to the conference room for the meeting. The expression "damned if you do, damned if you don't" came to mind. "Let's get this done, people," she said as she walked into the room where Freddie, Hill, Gonzo, Arnold, Malone and Farnsworth waited for her along with Assistant U.S. Attorney Charity Miller. "Cruz, anything from the strip search?"

"What strip search?" Hill asked in a testy tone.

"Hang on a sec. We'll get to that."

Cruz held up a photo of a hairy chest with three angry-looking scratches slashing from his collarbone to his ster-

num and a second photo that included Jerry's head along
with his chest. The bruise on his jaw was plainly evident.

"Excellent," Sam said, buzzing with excitement.

"Gonzo, what'd you get in West Virginia?"

"Interesting info from Mrs. Eldridge. Her husband,
Will, was Arnie Patterson's childhood friend."

"As in Arnie Patterson the presidential candidate?"
Hill asked.

"The one and only," Sam said. "We've established a
link to him too. I'll get to that in a minute. What else,
Gonzo?"

"Denise Desposito was Eldridge's daughter. From
what the wife said, Eldridge worked for Patterson Financial Group until Denise was arrested in a Medicare
scheme. After that, Will was fired, and Arnie refused
to take Will's phone calls. They never heard from him
again. She says Will died of a broken heart after they lost
Denise in a prison fight. Apparently, she was scuffling
with another prisoner and hit her head when she fell."

Sam's good mood came back with a vengeance. With
each thread they pulled, the net tightened around the
Patterson family.

"Agent Hill, what've you got?"

A visibly annoyed Hill recounted his visit with Dr.
Saltzman and what he'd learned about Victoria Kavanaugh's fixation on safety and security. "I also went by
Bertha Ray's house, or what's left of it, which wasn't
much. The fire marshal said it was definitely arson. The
fire took the houses on either side of hers too."

"You spoke with her about her son?"

"I did. I have the name of his closest friend, and I'm
planning to track him down after this meeting."

"Good work. So Cruz and I had an interesting day

too. What I'm about to tell you cannot leave this room. You can't mention it at home to your significant other or to any other member of the department or any other living human being. If you feel the need to tell someone, share it with your dog. We must keep a tight lid on this if we're going to make a case against the people behind Victoria's murder. Am I clear on that?"

Everyone in the room nodded in agreement.

Sam began with their visit to Congressman Tornquist and took them through the entire story, ending with the arrest of Jerry Smith. When she was done, she looked around the room at one stunned face after another.

"So you're saying," Hill began, "that the Patterson camp planted someone in the Nelson camp years ago in anticipation of Patterson's run for president and then killed her?"

"Had her killed," Sam said. "Big difference. Jerry Smith is the small fish in this case. He did the dirty deed, but someone above him set up this whole thing and ordered the hit on Victoria. That's the person—or people—I want."

"Why kill her now?" Hill asked.

"That I don't know yet," Sam said. "Perhaps she clammed up on them or threatened to expose them. Who knows? We need to go through the phone records again. If I can place even one phone call from a member of the Patterson family or staff on her phone, we've got them nailed."

"I'm almost certain none of the numbers matched anyone named Patterson," Gonzo said.

"How about a Jonathan Thayer or Porter Gillespie?" Sam asked.

"Gillespie rings a bell," Gonzo said. "Let me go get

the file on that. We've only gotten through the letter E on investigating the names that came up from the phone dump."

Sam nodded, and he rushed from the room. She positively buzzed with adrenaline zipping through her veins like cars on the Beltway at rush hour.

"What's your plan with Smith, Lieutenant?" Chief Farnsworth asked from his usual post in the back of the room.

"He's made his phone call to Christian Patterson, letting him know he needs an attorney. It's my belief that Patterson will ignore the request, so I'm going to let Smith stew in the interrogation room—under guard—until it sets in that he's been abandoned. Might take most of the night for him to catch a clue, seeing as how he referred to the Patterson as family."

"You really think they'll hang him out to dry?" Hill asked.

"I'm almost sure they will," Sam said.

"Why would they do that when he knows as much as he does?"

"They're counting on his loyalty to keep him quiet," Sam said, more certain by the moment that she was right about how this would play out. "I'll let him sit until he gets that they aren't coming, and then I'll try to break him. In the meantime, I'm waiting for a warrant to get Smith's DNA, and if it hits with what we found under Victoria's nails, at the very least we've got our killer. I want the big fish, though. I want Patterson and his sons, if they were behind this."

"What if you can't get them?" Farnsworth asked.

"Then we release everything we uncovered about Victoria and everything we've got on Smith to the media and let the public make their own conclusions. That ought to do enough to ruin his aspirations so we don't end up with a murderer in the White House."

Farnsworth nodded in agreement.

"But if he orchestrated this whole thing, I want to nail his ass to the wall," Sam said.

"Me too," Hill said.

The others nodded in agreement.

Gonzo returned to the room, holding up a piece of paper. "Bingo for Gillespie. Three calls to Victoria's phone from his the week before she was killed."

"That establishes a direct tie between the Patterson campaign and Victoria," Sam said. The pieces were falling into place one right after the other. "Go pick him up." Sam glanced at Charity, who nodded. "Cruz, pull up that picture of Colton Patterson so he'll recognize him if they cross paths."

Cruz typed on his computer and spun it around to show Gonzo the picture of Colton they'd found earlier.

"I'll issue the warrant for Gillespie's arrest," Charity said.

"Bring him in the front," Sam said. "I want the media wondering why a top aide from the Patterson campaign is in custody. Since I fully expect him to be as forthcoming as Jerry has been, we'll let him sit and stew overnight too. Maybe after a night in the city jail, they'll both feel talkative. Come to think of it, I want them kept in the same cell, and I want the cell monitored at all times. Video and audio."

"I'll set up the surveillance," Cruz said. "Here's the address of where he's staying in the city." Freddie handed the paper the campaign staffer had given them to Gonzo.

Gonzo gestured for his partner, Detective Arnold, to come with him.

"Charity?" Sam asked. "What do you think? Do we have enough to make a case?"

"With the DNA, you've got Smith for the murder and kidnapping," Charity said. "But you don't have Patterson—or his sons—yet."

"Cruz, let's go have a chat with our friend Mr. Smith," Sam said.

"Do you mind if I join you?" Hill asked.

"Not at all," Sam said. If she compartmentalized the odd personal dilemma between them, she couldn't deny he'd been an asset on this investigation. "Tossing around the FBI acronym might help our friend Mr. Smith get how big of a shit storm of misery he's in for."

"You do have a way with words, Lieutenant," Hill said, his lips quirking with amusement.

"So I'm told."

Inside interrogation room one, Smith was pacing from one end of the small space to the other. He reminded Sam of how a caged tiger might look as he radiated rage and fury that was instantly directed at her when she stepped into the room.

"This is Special Agent Avery Hill with the FBI."

The mention of the FBI had the desired effect, as Smith's eyes widened with surprise. "You can't keep me here! I haven't done anything."

"I can keep you here until the lawyer you requested arrives. Any idea when that might be?"

"My boss said he'd take care of sending someone over. He should be here any time now."

"Great. We'll bring him in as soon as he gets here. In

the meantime, is there anything I can get for you? Some water? Food?"

"I don't want anything from you," he said, glowering at her.

"Okay, then." Sam wondered if he'd be a little more contrite when ten or twelve hours had gone by without anything to eat or drink. "We'll see you when the lawyer arrives. If you need to use the restroom, let Officer DuPont know, and he'll escort you."

"Screw you."

"Aww," Sam said. "I'd love to, but I'm married, and my husband is the jealous sort."

As Jerry gave her the finger, they filed out of the room and closed the door.

"He's still certain they're coming," Sam said. "He's in for a long night. I've got some stuff to do elsewhere, but I'll come back later to check on him. We'll keep up the regular visits until he gets he's on his own."

"If he hadn't killed a woman in cold blood and stolen her child from the scene, I'd almost feel a little sorry for the guy," Freddie said. "Almost."

"I hear ya," Sam said. "You know what we still need is a connection between Smith and Bobby Ray. How'd they hook up?"

"I'll work on that," Hill said. "Bertha gave me the name of Bobby's best friend earlier. I'll see what he can tell me. Jerry Smith wasn't a name she mentioned."

"It wouldn't be," Sam said. "He's from Ohio, where the Pattersons are from. He's living here temporarily. He and Bobby will have met at a local bar or a gym or something like that. Find out where Bobby hung out and worked out. I bet that'll lead to Smith."

"I'm on it," Hill said.

"Thanks. I'm going to split for a bit. Cruz, why don't you call it a day? If I need you, I'll give you a call."

"Sounds good. See you in the morning, if not before."

"Good work today, Detective."

"Thank you, Lieutenant. Back at you."

To Hill, she said, "Let me know if you find a connection between Smith and Ray."

"I will. Have a good night."

"You too." Sam felt his eyes on her as she gathered her belongings and headed out of the pit, sending a text to Jeannie as she walked. "On my way home."

"See you in a few," Jeannie responded.

In the lobby, Sam ran into Captain Malone. "Got the warrant for the DNA," he said. "I let Dr. McNamara know, and she's going to take the swab now."

"Good," Sam said, "that'll give Jerry something else to worry about while he waits for the lawyer who isn't coming."

"No luck on the gym warrant, unfortunately. The judge said we hadn't given her good enough reason to issue it."

"That's okay," Sam said. "We probably won't need it after all. I'm going to head home for a bit, but I'll be back later to check on Jerry. I don't think he's going to realize until the morning that they aren't sending anyone."

"Probably not. I'll see you then."

"See you."

"Great job as always, Lieutenant," he called after her.

Sam stopped and turned to him. "As much as it pains me to admit it, Hill has been a resource on this case. His superiors ought to be made aware of the fact that he did very good work here."

"I'll make sure of it."

"Thanks, Cap."

Pushing through the media crowd gathered outside the main door to HQ, Sam almost hoped Smith refused to roll on the Patterson family. She'd love nothing more than to have the opportunity to stand before the media and single-handedly ruin years of planning and scheming—along with Arnie's campaign—through innuendo alone. She'd do it for Victoria. Even though she'd been in on the scheme to at least some extent, no one deserved to die the way she did.

Sam sent another text, this one to Nick. "On the way home. Got to meet with McBride, and then I want to get to the hospital to see Ang."

"Be there shortly," he responded. "Don't go without me."

"Wouldn't dream of it," Sam said as she started the car and headed for Capitol Hill. As she drove, she debated when and what she should tell Derek Kavanaugh about what they'd uncovered. While she trusted her colleagues implicitly, she still feared a leak. It could even come from the Patterson camp, not that she expected that, but still... Derek shouldn't hear the latest from the media.

With that in mind, she placed a call to him. "Hi, Derek," she said when he answered. "It's Sam again." She could hear Maeve crying in the background. "Do you have a minute?"

"Sure, let me get my mom to help with Maeve."

She listened to him speaking in the background as he settled the baby with her grandmother.

"I'm back."

"So, listen, I think we've got this thing figured out."

"Oh." The single word conveyed a world of emotion—hope, fear, grief, despair.

"I have to warn you, it'll be hard to hear."

He let out a bitter laugh. "Worse than what I've already heard?"

"I suppose not." Choosing her words carefully, Sam walked him through what they'd learned and the connection to the Patterson campaign.

"So they planted her with someone close to Nelson so they could spy on us?" he asked, incredulous. "It's right out of Watergate, for God's sake."

"That's our hypothesis at the moment. We're still trying to prove it. We believe we have the man who killed Victoria in custody."

"Who is he?" Derek asked in a small voice.

Sam told him about Jerry Smith, the Patterson family's go-to guy for unsavory matters such as murder.

"If they went to all that trouble to plant her, why kill her right before the election? Isn't this when she'd be most useful to them?"

"You would think. Maybe she clammed up, refused to provide damaging info or threatened to expose the entire scheme. Maybe she fell in love with her husband and didn't want to cause him harm."

"Yeah, sure," he said bitterly. "That's a likely scenario."

"It's as likely as any other, but we may never know for sure."

"You don't expect Smith to spill on the Patterson family, do you?"

"No. Even though they're going to abandon him, his sense of loyalty runs deep. He won't roll on them."

"So he'll walk for what he did to Vic?"

"I'm hoping we've got him nailed on the DNA, and we're searching his room for evidence that ties him to

Victoria. If we find a connection there, that'll be enough to put him away for life. We're still hoping to nail the people behind the scheme. We believe it's one or both of Patterson's sons and perhaps the man himself, but you need to prepare yourself for the possibility that we won't get them."

"So he'll go on his merry way and possibly be elected president in November?"

"Oh, no. We'll give the media enough to draw their own conclusions. There's no way he'll be president after we're through with them."

"Good. That's good." He paused, sighed. "All because of my goddamned job. From the minute I got home on Sunday and found her, I feared it would come back to my goddamned job in some way or another."

"It's not your fault, Derek. This was done to you. You didn't do anything wrong."

"Apparently, I fell for the wrong woman."

"I hope," Sam said, "when all the dust settles, you can remember the good times and try to forget the rest. There's no point second-guessing everything. You'll drive yourself crazy doing that."

"Too late."

"Derek, it's really important that you not breathe a word of this to anyone—not your parents or Harry or especially your colleagues at the White House. We're trying to build a case against the Patterson family, but if the word gets out, our job becomes a lot harder."

"I understand. I won't talk about the way my wife used me to pass political secrets to our rival." He released another bitter-sounding laugh. "They must've been disappointed with what she fed them. We hardly ever talked about the campaign or work, for that matter. Like I told you before, in the rare hours we got to spend together, especially lately, we didn't do much talking."

"Speaking as a woman here, Derek, let me assure you, she wouldn't have spent so much of her time that way if she didn't really want to. Hold on to that, okay?"

"I'll try."

"Take care. I'll be in touch as soon as I know more."

"Thanks, Sam, for everything. You and Nick have been great during all of this."

"We'll be here for you and Maeve for as long as you need us, Derek. I promise."

"I appreciate that," he said, his voice heavy with emotion as they ended the call.

Pulling onto Ninth Street, Sam saw Jeannie's car parked in front of her house. They met on the sidewalk by the ramp that led to Sam's front door. Sam noticed that Jeannie looked deeply troubled, which made Sam's stomach hurt. "Come in."

Jeannie followed her up the ramp and into the cool comfort of Sam's spacious home.

"Drink?" Sam asked.

"I wouldn't say no to some ice water. It's so freaking hot."

"I hear it's supposed to be for the foreseeable future. Thank God for AC."

"No kidding."

Sam filled two glasses and brought them to the kitchen table.

Jeannie pulled out a chair and sat, focused for a long time on the glass of water.

"Whatever it is, say it," Sam said.

Jeannie hesitated for a long moment, and when she

looked up at Sam, her eyes were tortured. "Does the name Steven Coyne mean anything to you?"

"Of course. He was my dad's first partner. Killed in the line by a drive-by shooter. The case is unsolved."

"Right." Jeannie took a drink of her water. "Alice Fitzgerald was his widow."

All the air left Sam's body in one big whoosh. She stared at Jeannie, almost as if she hadn't heard her right. "There's no mention of that anywhere in the case files."

"According to Dr. Morganthau, your dad and everyone else involved went to great lengths to keep Alice's connection to the department out of the media. They didn't want all the business about Steven's murder resurrected when she was dealing with the loss of her son."

Sam's mind whirled as she tried to process this new information. "This was why he allowed Cameron to go into the military rather than pressing forward with an investigation that pointed directly at him."

"Yes."

"And Alice... I didn't really know her, but my dad was close with a woman named Alice. Took care of her after her husband was killed." In the deep recesses of her mind, Sam somehow knew there'd been something more to it than that, but she couldn't remember what.

"That's what Dr. Morganthau said."

"Surely Chief Farnsworth knew about the connection to Coyne. And Captain Malone. Deputy Chief Conklin." Sam's heart beat fast as she thought back to the day her father was shot and the terrible argument they'd had over the Fitzgerald case. "This was why he told me to leave it alone. They all knew. They were taking care of one of their own. Jesus, Jeannie. If this got out, a lot of careers and reputations would've been ruined. No wonder he's so mad at me."

"It's possible," Jeannie ventured, "that the others didn't know who the mother was. How closely in touch would they have stayed with Alice after her husband was killed? Perhaps only your dad knew she'd remarried and that it was her son who was missing."

Sam pressed fingers to her suddenly aching temples. "It's becoming clear to me that I might've gotten very lucky when you and Tyrone lied to me. What if we had dug into what we'd learned? What if we'd pursued this further and it got out that my dad intentionally protected a murderer—if Cameron was in fact the murderer? My dad's reputation would be ruined. Hell, mine might've been too."

"I'm sorry to have to tell you this. I knew it would be upsetting to you."

"It's certainly not your fault. I'm rescinding the suspension. You and Tyrone are back on duty tomorrow. I'll make sure you're paid for today."

"You don't have to do that, Lieutenant. At the end of the day, we did lie to you."

"I'm going to forget that happened and count on the fact that it'll never happen again."

"It won't. I've learned my lesson, and so has Will."

"What do I say to my dad?" Sam asked as she heard the front door open and close.

"Babe?" Nick called. "Are you home?"

"In here," Sam said.

He was pulling off his tie as he came into the kitchen, stopping short when he saw she wasn't alone. "Oh, hey, Jeannie. How are you?"

"Fine, Senator. And you?"

"My name is Nick," he said with a smile, "and I'm great now that I'm home from an endless day of boring hearings." He took a closer look at Sam. "What's wrong?"

Jeannie stood and carried her glass to the sink. "I've got to get going, Lieutenant. Call me if there's anything I can do."

"I will, thanks. See you tomorrow." As Jeannie left the kitchen, Sam called after her. "Wait! I didn't see the ring."

Looking sheepish, she turned around and held out her left hand to show off the sparkler.

"Wow," Sam said. "It's gorgeous. Tell Michael I said he did good."

"I will."

"It's beautiful, Jeannie," Nick said, kissing her cheek. "Congratulations to you and Michael."

Jeannie nearly swooned from the kiss and the kind words from Nick. He had that effect on women, even those happily engaged to someone else.

"Thank you both so much. You've been such good friends to us. I hope you'll be able to dance at the wedding."

"We wouldn't miss it," Sam said. "I'll see you tomorrow."

When the front door clicked shut behind Jeannie, Nick sat down at the table and reached for Sam's hand. "Why is your hand freezing?"

Still in a state of shock over what Jeannie had told her, Sam struggled to find the words. "I… I heard something. About my dad. It was… Sort of upsetting."

"What is it?"

"If I tell you, you can't ever repeat it. Ever."

"Of course. That goes without saying. Tell me, baby."

In a halting recitation, she filled him in on what Jeannie and Will had gleaned from their visit with the retired medical examiner.

"Whoa," Nick said when she was finished.

"Yeah, exactly."

"What do you do with this info?"

"That's a very good question. Do I go to my dad and say, 'I know what you did, and I get why you did it, but Jesus, Dad. You took one hell of a risk with your career and your reputation'?" She kneaded the tension from her temples. "I suddenly have a splitting headache."

"Do you think there was more to his relationship with Alice than you know about?"

"Possibly. Remember what Tracy said about my mom moving out of the house during the Fitzgerald investigation. It doesn't take much imagination to figure it had something to do with Alice."

"Will you ask him about her?"

"I suppose I'll have to. He's been all up in my grill about the fact that we reopened the investigation in the first place. He's going to want to know what's going on." She expelled a deep, shuddering breath. "I can't imagine that conversation. Today was a really good day up until about twenty minutes ago. We got the guy who killed Victoria." She brought him up to date on the details.

"Holy shit," he whispered. "The Patterson campaign. Are you freaking kidding me?"

"Nope."

"Does Derek know?"

"Yeah, I talked to him earlier. He said it was right out of Watergate."

"No shit." Nick got up and moved behind her, pushing her hands away as he took over the massaging of her temples. "Something like that would've taken years of planning to pull off. Derek and Vic were married for four years. Add in another year of dating... Unreal. I knew Patterson was ruthlessly ambitious, but this... Wow. Why did they kill her?"

"Our hypothesis is that either she clammed up or wanted out of whatever agreement they made with her initially. If she spilled the beans on what they'd done before the election, that'd ruin everything. They probably decided they couldn't risk keeping her around."

"I can't believe the stuff some people will do to get what they want."

"You can't believe it because you'd rather win the old-fashioned way or go down fighting. This level of underhandedness goes against everything you believe in. You can't understand this because you don't think like they do."

"Thank God for that. Will you be able to pin this on Patterson or his sons?"

"That's the great unknown at the moment. We're hoping Smith will roll on them, but it's not likely."

"Even after it sinks in that he's being hung out to dry?"

"Loyalty runs deep. I suspect he'd rather take the fall for all of them than be responsible for derailing the campaign."

"He's a fool."

"Yep, but he's a loyal fool. Of course, I'm only speculating. Who knows? Maybe he'll sing like a canary and make it easy for us, but I don't expect him to. We've also got the assistant to Colton Patterson on the hook for making calls to Victoria, so we can tie her to the campaign. Whether or not he'll give up the ringleaders is also in question at the moment. We'll get Patterson one way or the other—either in actual court or the court of public opinion. We can do a lot of damage by implying he and his sons were behind this."

"His campaign will be over, that's for sure."

"As well it should be."

Sam's phone dinged with a text from Tracy: "Congrats Auntie Sam! Ella Holland Radcliffe arrived at five forty-two p.m. Weighing in at 8 lbs, 2 oz, 20 inches. She's gorgeous! Mom is doing great! Get on over here!"

"Ang had the baby," Sam said. "Ella Holland Radcliffe. They named her after my grandmother."

He rested his hands on her shoulders. "Congratulations, Aunt Sam."

"Same to you, Uncle Nick."

"Hey, that's right. I'm an uncle!"

"Yes, you are." Sam patted his hands. "Let me up."

He backed away, and she stood, turning to him. "Now, let's do this right." She stepped into his outstretched arms and let him surround her with his love. The press of his chest against her face, the strong beat of his heart and the arms he kept tight around her went a long way toward fixing what ailed her. "We should get to the hospital."

"In a minute," he said. "I need a little more of this first."

She wrapped her arms around him and held on tight to what mattered most.

TWENTY-ONE

As GONZO AND Arnold approached Porter Gillespie's brick-front townhouse in Adams Morgan, Gonzo stopped his partner and listened intently. "Sounds like a party."

They followed the music and noise to the back of the house where they found a group of about twenty well-dressed, good-looking young people gathered on a patio. Jimmy Buffet was singing about cheeseburgers in paradise, and several men stood around a grill, smoking cigars and holding glasses filled with amber liquid.

This is going to be fun, Gonzo thought, as he imagined hauling Gillespie out of his home in front of a captive audience. Gonzo's idea of fun had been skewed by ten years as a Homicide detective. Exchanging glances with Arnold, he noted the anticipatory gleam in his partner's eyes and realized he wasn't the only one looking forward to this arrest.

"Pardon me," Gonzo said, loudly enough to be heard over the music.

All eyes turned to them, and the chatter faded to complete silence other than Buffet and the cheeseburgers. Among the group gathered around the grill, Gonzo recognized Colton Patterson.

Gonzo held up his badge, and Arnold did the same.

"Detectives Gonzales and Arnold, Metro P.D. We're looking for Porter Gillespie."

Mouths fell open in shock as the group parted to reveal

Gillespie at the grill. He had immaculately groomed dark hair and wore wire-rimmed glasses, a light blue dress shirt and an apron that said Kiss the Chef.

"I'm Porter," he said.

"We'll need you to come with us, sir."

A buzz of dismay rippled through the group as Porter stared at them stone-faced. "Whatever for?" he asked in the cultured tone favored by rich people.

"We'll sort it out downtown."

"Sort what out?"

Since he didn't seem inclined to come to them, Gonzo and Arnold walked across the grass to the patio. Gonzo nodded to his partner to take the lead.

"Mr. Gillespie, you're under arrest on the charge of accessory to the murder of Victoria Kavanaugh and the kidnapping of Maeve Kavanaugh. You have the right to remain silent."

As Arnold slapped cuffs on his wrists and said the word "Murder," Gillespie's composure began to crumble. The group gasped and grumbled with outrage.

Gonzo watched Gillespie's gaze shift to Colton, who moved to the edge of the gathering, as if to separate himself from what was happening to his assistant.

"I don't know what you're talking about," Gillespie said. "I didn't have anything to do with any murder."

"Tell it to the judge," Gonzo said as he took Gillespie's arm to lead him from the yard.

"Colton, tell them! I couldn't murder anyone! I want a lawyer. Colton, get me a lawyer."

The word "lawyer" made Gonzo's day. Arnold flashed a small, satisfied smile. Gillespie had played right into their hands with that statement. Now they could hold him overnight—or until the lawyer who wasn't coming showed up.

"Don't worry, Porter," Colton said. "We'll figure this out."

Colton's assurances seemed to calm Porter.

A blonde woman came running out of the house.

"What's going on? Porter?"

"It's nothing, Cam." Porter attempted a calming smile that failed when his lips wobbled. "A misunderstanding. I'll be back in time for dinner."

"I wouldn't bank on that, sport," Gonzo said.

Cam grabbed hold of Porter's arm and held him back when Gonzo would've led him away. "You can't take him for no reason!"

"Oh, trust me, we have a good reason." Gonzo kept his gaze fixed on Colton, hoping to send the message that they knew a lot more than he thought they did. "And you can either release him or come with us. Your choice."

As if Porter had suddenly burst into flames, she released him and stepped back as tears rolled down her face. "I don't understand," she said softly. "What has he done to deserve this treatment?"

"Nothing, Cam," Porter said. "It's all a big mistake."

"Keep telling yourself that," Gonzo said. "Enjoy your dinner, folks," he said, still looking directly at Colton Patterson. "Sorry for the interruption."

He and Arnold walked Gillespie to the car.

"You people have no idea who you're messing with."

"Oh, we know, and shockingly, we're not the slightest bit intimidated," Gonzo said. This had been even more fun than he'd thought it would be. "Are we, Arnold?"

"Nope. Not scared."

"You will be when the full fury of Arnie Patterson

comes down on you and your department of Keystone Kops. You'll be intimidated then."

"Is that so?" Gonzo said, choosing to ignore the insult as Arnold drove them to HQ. "Well, your buddy Jerry Smith has been on ice in our cooler for what? About four hours now, Arnold?"

"Yeah, that's about right."

Gonzo turned so Gillespie could see his face. "He hasn't figured out yet that Arnie and the boys have cut him loose." Gonzo was gratified to watch the Adam's apple bob in Gillespie's skinny neck. "Wonder how long it'll take before he gets it? What do you think?"

"They won't cut him loose." Gillespie all but spit the words at them. "He practically grew up in their house. He's family to them."

"Is that so? Huh. Well, if I contacted my family and asked them to get me a lawyer because I'd been arrested, my sisters would've called out the cavalry within minutes of receiving the call. They certainly wouldn't have me waiting hours in jail. That's for sure."

"They probably couldn't get anyone this late in the day."

"You know, that's probably it," Gonzo said, enjoying this more by the minute. "I'm sure it's got nothing at all to do with blood being much thicker than water, not to mention what ambition does to people."

"You've got nothing on me, because I didn't do anything."

"So you've said, but I'm afraid we do have something on you, or we never would've gotten a warrant for your arrest from the assistant U.S. attorney."

The words "warrant" and "assistant U.S. attorney" caused more frantic bobbing of the Adam's apple.

"I suppose you consider yourself rather close to the Patterson family too?"

"I am close to them. Colton has been my best friend since we were in prep school."

"So he'll send someone to get you out of this jam?"

"Of course he will."

"Probably the same guy who's coming to take care of things for Jerry, right?"

Porter's eyes narrowed, and he began to seethe. "Are you going to tell me what you have on me?"

"Not yet," Gonzo said, turning to face the front. "Our lieutenant likes to do those honors herself. She's a real barracuda that way."

A minute later, the distinctive smell of urine filled the small space in the car.

As Arnold grimaced and rolled down the windows to let out the stink, Gonzo noticed his partner trembling with silent laughter.

Gonzo bit his bottom lip to hold back his own desire to laugh his ass off. As their jobs were so rarely as much fun as this had been, they had to get their kicks where they could.

Arriving at HQ a few minutes later, Gillespie recoiled when he saw the media gathered out front. "You're not taking me in that way."

"Oh yes, we are," Gonzo said, grabbing his arm and hauling him out of the backseat. The entire front of his dress pants was wet with piss.

"You can't do that! I haven't been charged with anything. You'll ruin my life, not to mention the damage you'll do to the campaign."

"You think we give a shit about any of that? You should've been thinking about your life and the campaign when you acted as an accessory to Victoria Kavanaugh's murder."

"I had nothing to do with that!"

"You can tell the judge all about it when you're arraigned."

"Arraigned?"

"What do you think happens after you've been arrested?"

"We're not going to even talk about this? I have rights!"

"You absolutely do, including a right to a lawyer, which you've invoked. As a result, there'll be no talking until he or she shows up."

The reporters had thinned from the usual brigade, but those still braving the evening heat tuned in to the fact that something was happening behind them.

Gonzo could hear them muttering, "Who is he?"

"Where have I seen him before?"

"Did he piss himself?"

"Doesn't he work for the Patterson campaign?"

"Detective, what're the charges?"

"Is this related to the Kavanaugh case?"

"Does Arnie Patterson know his aide has been arrested?"

Gonzo didn't respond to any of the questions as he hauled Gillespie through the gauntlet. Gillespie kept his head down the way arrestees often did when they were trying to avoid being photographed. Despite the effort, Gonzo fully expected to see Gillespie's face on the front page of the morning papers.

Once inside, they led him directly into processing, where he was strip-searched, fingerprinted and photographed. All the while, Gillespie was threatening to sue the department for police brutality and unnecessary search and seizure. The guy probably had a few law classes in college and thought he knew what he was talking about.

Gonzo had to admit that he took a certain bit of smug pleasure in watching as Gillespie was told to bend over and spread 'em. When the processing officers were done poking and prodding him, he was handed the same wet, smelly clothes he'd been wearing when he came in. As the indignities piled up, Gillespie became more rattled and shaky. His hands were trembling so hard that Gonzo wondered if he'd have to dress the guy. Finally, they deposited him in the interrogation room next to where Jerry Smith was being held.

"Have a seat," Gonzo said. "We'll let you know when your lawyer arrives."

"I need a change of clothes."

"We don't keep Brooks Brothers in inventory," Gonzo said. "All I've got handy is prison orange. Will that work for you?"

"Never mind," he muttered. "I can see you're enjoying the hell out of this."

"You bet I am. There's something extremely satisfying about closing a confounding case and getting the scumbags who murdered a young woman and stole her child."

Gillespie's complexion drained of all remaining color. "I didn't kill anyone or steal a child! I have no idea what you're talking about!"

"Then you shouldn't have anything to worry about," Gonzo said. "I'm off duty, so I'll see you in the morning. Officer Beckett here will be keeping an eye on you until your lawyer arrives. Good luck to you."

"Wait! You can't leave me here. I have rights!"

"Yes, you do, which is why we can't do a thing until your attorney arrives. The minute you said the words 'I want a lawyer,' it was out of my hands. You have a good night now."

"Wait! Stop! This is insanity! I demand to know what evidence you have that ties me to any of this!"

As Gonzo chuckled his way down the hallway that led to the pit, he heard Beckett telling Gillespie to sit down and shut up. And with that, a very good day came to a very satisfying end.

SAM'S CELL PHONE rang as Nick was driving them into the parking lot at the hospital. "Hey, Gonzo. How'd it go?"

"It'll go down in history as one of my favorite arrests ever," he said, sounding positively gleeful as he related the story of Gillespie's arrest. "And then he pissed himself in the car. It was awesome."

Sam couldn't help but laugh as he described the scene. "You're having way too much fun."

"I really am. I'm on my way home now. Beckett's with him as he waits for the lawyer Colton Patterson promised to send right over."

"Excellent. Thanks for the great work today."

"Let me know if you need anything tonight."

"I will."

"Hey, did Ang have the baby?"

"A little while ago. Ella Holland Radcliffe. We're heading in to see them now."

"Oh, great, tell her I said congrats. Alex will be excited. He loves her—and Jack."

"I'll pass that along. See you in the morning." She ended the call and stuffed the phone in her pocket, relaying the story of Gillespie's arrest to Nick, joining his laughter at the part about Gillespie wetting himself.

"The Patterson camp must be in total meltdown mode."

"I doubt they are. They think they've covered their asses every which way to Tuesday on this, and they may have. If their lackeys don't roll, we won't get them."

"So the worst that could happen to them for plotting this whole thing and ordering Victoria killed is that Arnie's campaign could be screwed?"

"Yep. I'm a hundred percent certain Jerry's DNA is going to match what was found under Victoria's nails, and we've got several phone calls from Gillespie to Victoria's phone in the weeks before she was killed. We know her father once worked for Patterson and that she spent time in their home after her parents died. But we've got nothing that directly ties any of the Pattersons to her murder."

He parked the car and turned off the engine, killing the lovely flow of AC. "You've got enough innuendo to bring down the campaign, though."

"Right." She eyed the hospital with trepidation.

He kept an arm draped over the wheel as he studied her. "What're you thinking?"

"A lot has happened to me since the last time one of my sisters had a baby. Jack is six, and Tracy had Abby seven years ago, which is hard to believe."

"You're worried about how you might react to this one."

"A little." Because she was afraid if she looked at him, she'd lose the tiny bit of composure she was still clinging to, she kept her gaze fixed on the hospital. "I'm so happy for Angela and Spencer and Jack. They've wanted another child for a long time."

"I know that, babe. And they will too. Of course they will." He reached for her hand. "If you don't feel up to this, they'd understand that too."

Sam shook her head. "Angela is my sister and one of my two best friends. Today is not about me. I can't make it about me." She closed her eyes and took a deep breath, let it out and opened her eyes, feeling calmer now that she'd talked it out with him. "Let's go."

"I'll be right there with you the whole time."

She squeezed his hand. "And that helps, believe me."

They were approaching the lobby elevator when Sam came face-to-face with someone she hadn't seen in five years. She released a startled gasp that drew Nick's attention to the woman who stared at Sam. "Sam," she said with a warm smile.

She hadn't changed much. Her shoulder-length dark hair was run through with more gray than black these days, but her brown eyes were exactly as Sam remembered, attractively lined at the corners from a lifetime of smiling and laughing.

"And you must be Nick."

"Yes," he said, sounding confused.

"I'm Brenda Ross, Sam's mother."

So she'd gone back to using her maiden name. Sam wondered if that meant she was no longer married to the man she'd left Sam's father for, but she didn't care enough to ask.

"Oh." Nick shook her hand. "It's nice to meet you."

"You too. I've heard so much about you. You're even more handsome in person than you are in pictures."

"Oh, um, thanks."

Sam watched and listened as if the conversation was happening on TV rather than right in front of her. She had no idea what to say. Thank goodness Nick had saved her the trouble of having to say anything.

"Are you going to see Angela?"

"Yes," he said.

"She's on the fifth floor. I'll ride up with you."

Nick eyed Sam with uncertainty as he shepherded her onto the elevator ahead of him.

No one said a word as they rode to the fifth floor. Nick waited for Brenda to step out before he put his arm around Sam, gave her a squeeze and followed Brenda down the hallway to Angela's room, keeping a bit of distance between them. "Are you okay, babe?" he asked softly.

Sam nodded.

"Say something."

"Something."

"Okay, good. You had me a little worried for a minute there."

"I was taken by surprise."

"I know, honey."

"I have to agree that you're far more handsome in person than you are in pictures. That's the first thing I've agreed with her about in nearly twenty years."

He laughed, as she'd hoped he would. "Yep, you're fine, and you can shut right up too."

Thank God for him, she thought for the millionth time. *Before he'd come back into her life, a random run-in with her mother would've thrown her off for weeks.*

This encounter had only taken minutes to get past because he was there to make everything better.

As they approached Angela's room, Skip and Celia emerged, stopping short when they saw Brenda coming with Sam and Nick behind her.

"Hello, Brenda," Skip said in the frosty tone he used to reserve for murder suspects.

"Skip." Sam realized her mother was seeing her ex-husband in a wheelchair for the first time. "Congratulations on your new granddaughter."

"Thank you."

"You must be Celia," Brenda said, extending a hand to Sam's stepmother. "So nice to finally meet you."

Because she was too polite not to, Celia shook Brenda's hand, but Sam wanted to cheer when Celia didn't say she was glad to meet Brenda.

"How's Angela?" Sam asked.

"She's wonderful," Celia said, brightening considerably when she turned her attention to Sam. "The baby is beautiful."

"Are you in a rush to get home?" Sam asked her dad.

"Not particularly."

"I could use a minute before you go."

"Then I'll wait for you."

"Thanks." Holding tight to Nick's hand, Sam led him around her mother, father and stepmother and went into Angela's room, feeling determined to get through the emotional battlefield with a minimal number of new scars.

TWENTY-TWO

"SAM!" HER NEPHEW Jack cried from his perch on the bed next to his mother. "Come see my new baby sister! She's so pretty!"

Sam smiled at the darling little dark-haired boy who looked like his father. "Let me see," Sam said, releasing Nick's hand and moving in for a closer look.

Angela positively glowed as she held the baby. Her husband Spencer hovered on the other side of the bed, looking exhausted but happy.

Sam wondered how Nick would look after coaching her through childbirth and hoped she had the chance to find out someday. "You're absolutely right, Jack. She's one of the prettiest baby sisters I've ever seen." Ella's face was red and scrunched, her lips pursed and her feathery eyebrows so faint Sam could barely see them, but she truly was one of the most beautiful things Sam had ever seen.

Tears filled her eyes as she studied each tiny detail.

"Do you want to hold her?" Angela asked softly, navigating a minefield of her own.

"Would it be okay?"

"Sure it would."

As she carefully took the sleeping baby from her sister, Sam marveled at how something that arrived in such a small package could be so hard to come by for some people. "Hi, Ella, I'm your crazy Auntie Sam, and this is your handsome Uncle Nick, but don't tell him I said that, because he doesn't like to be told he's handsome."

With his arm around her, Nick chuckled as he pressed a kiss to her temple.

"We can't wait to get to know you and have you and your brother over for sleepovers at our house."

"Can we schedule that now?" Angela asked, making everyone laugh and easing the tight grip of emotion that had seized Sam the second her sister placed the baby in her arms.

"Anytime," Nick said, speaking for both of them.

Tears rolled down her cheeks, but they were happy tears that she had yet another child in her life to love and spoil. She looked up at her husband. "Want a turn?"

He brushed the tears from her face. "I wouldn't say no to that."

Sam transferred the tiny bundle into his strong, capable embrace.

"Hey there, little one," he said, his expression a mix of awe and wonder. "Welcome to the world."

The sight of him holding the newborn did weird things to Sam's insides, which were already scrambled from running into her mother and meeting her new niece.

Jack came over to her and raised his arms. Sam hoisted him up the way she always did.

As if he knew exactly what she needed, he wrapped his pudgy arms around her neck and gave her a big hug.

"Oh, you give a good hug, buddy."

"How's your boo-boo?" Jack placed a very gentle kiss on Sam's cheek, below the bandage that covered her stitches.

"Much better," she said, it still hurt like the dickens.

Keeping a tight hold on her nephew, she moved over to Angela's bedside. "How was it?"

"I've had better days, but it's over now."

"She was a trouper," Spence said, squeezing his wife's shoulder.

"Mom is out there," Sam said.

"Oh, really? She said she might come up when the baby came, but I didn't think she was in town yet. Tracy must've called her. She left to go get Abby and Ethan to bring them to meet their new cousin. Apparently, Brooke had other plans."

"There's a shocker." Sam rolled her eyes. Their formerly lovely teenage niece had turned into a real pill in the last year. "You and Trace are in tight with Mom, huh?"

"I wouldn't call it tight, but we're in touch. You knew that."

Sam shrugged. "I guess."

"Did you talk to her?"

"Not really." Sam gave Jack one more big squeeze and then settled him on the bed with his mother. "Is there anything we can do for you guys?"

"Nope. We're good. Spencer's parents are coming tomorrow to help with Jack, and Dad and Celia are taking him tonight."

"I'm having a sleepover at Pop Pop's," Jack said. "Celia said we can make popcorn when we watch *Madagascar.*"

"Wow, that sounds like big fun." Sam leaned over to kiss Angela. "Congratulations, you guys. She's gorgeous."

Nick brought the baby back to her mother and gave Angela a kiss. "Ditto. What she said. Adorable." He reached out to shake hands with Jack and Spencer. "Good job, you guys."

"What'd they do?" Angela asked dryly.

"We can't talk about what I did in front of the boy," Spencer said with a shit-eating grin.

"Why not?" Jack asked. "I want to know!"

"On that note," Sam said, laughing at the mortified expression on Angela's face, "we're going so Mom can come in. We'll be back tomorrow."

"Hopefully, we'll be home tomorrow afternoon."

"We'll see you there with presents."

Jack lit up at that news.

Sam trailed a finger over the baby's downy soft cheek. "Love you, guys."

"You too," Ang said. "Thanks for coming by."

Sam preceded Nick out the door, where her mother leaned against a wall, apparently waiting for them to come out so she could have her turn. Sam's father and Celia were nowhere in sight. While Sam would never admit it to anyone, she appreciated the space her mother had given her to visit with her sister's family without their feud hanging over the proceedings.

She nodded to her mother and started down the long hallway, hoping she'd find her dad and Celia in the waiting room.

"Sam!"

Sam took a moment to gather herself before she turned back to face the woman who'd hurt them all so deeply. She'd left Skip the day after Sam graduated from high school for a man Brenda had been secretly sleeping with for quite some time. And now Sam had to wonder if she'd been wrong about everything she'd assumed about her parents' marriage.

"I'd like to see you," Brenda said haltingly. "To talk to you. There are things you should know, things I should've told you a long time ago." She glanced at Nick, who slid an arm around Sam's waist. "Hasn't this gone on long enough?"

"I don't have anything to say. Come on, Nick. Let's go."

Before she turned away, she saw her mother's face fall with disappointment. Sam didn't want to be moved by that, but damn, it bugged her. What right did she have to be disappointed about anything? She was the one who left! She was the one who put herself before everyone else! Maybe Tracy and Angela had been able to forgive her, but Sam never would.

"Take a breath, babe," Nick said as they moved as one down the hallway.

Sam took a series of deep breaths that helped to calm her rampaging nerves. "Will you entertain Celia for a minute while I talk to my dad?"

"Sure."

"Thanks. I only need a few minutes."

In the waiting room, which Skip and Celia had to themselves, Celia read to him from the latest issue of *Newsweek*.

"Celia," Nick said, extending his arm, "could I interest you in a drink? I hear this place has a great bar."

"I won't say no to an offer like that," Celia said as she stood and kissed her husband's cheek before taking Nick's outstretched arm.

"Don't go too far with my girl, Senator," Skip said.

"Wouldn't dream of it," Nick said with the charming grin that made Sam's heart race.

Celia giggled like a schoolgirl, which made Sam smile as she took the seat her stepmother had occupied.

"You okay, baby girl?"

Sam appreciated that he knew how tough it would be for her not only to meet her new niece but to see her mother for the first time in years.

"Sure, I'm good. You?"

"I'm great. I've got a brand-new baby granddaughter who's as pretty as her mama, her aunts and her cousins. Life is good."

"Yes, it is."

"I love that they named her after my mother," Skip said. "That pleases me."

"I knew it would." Ella Holland had been one of Sam's favorite people as a child, and she missed her. "Was it hard to see Mom?"

"Nah. She has no power over me anymore. Hasn't for a long time."

"It kind of bugs me that Tracy and Angela keep in touch with her."

"It's their prerogative. Regardless of what I think of her, she's their mother and your mother. Things went very bad between us in the end, but I'll always be grateful to her for the three beautiful daughters she gave me."

Even though he couldn't feel it, Sam wrapped her arms around his arm and rested her head on his shoulder, needing to be close to him.

"What's on your mind?"

She closed her eyes and imagined his strong arms around her, his big hand stroking her hair, the safety she'd always felt in his embrace. "I know about Alice."

He gasped.

"I know why you did what you did with the Fitzgerald case." She paused, giving him a chance to say something if he chose to.

He didn't choose to.

"I understand," she said after a long moment of silence.

"Who told you?"

"Jeannie talked to Morganthau. He connected the dots for us."

"What're you going to do about it?"

"Nothing," Sam said, deciding as she said the word. What good would it do now?

"For what it's worth, it was an accident. Cameron didn't intend to kill him, and when he realized he was dead, he panicked. He led us to the body, which never would've been recovered without what he told us. I didn't feel he was a danger to anyone but himself, which is why I let him leave as planned to go into the army. He's paid for that night every day of his life since then, and I've questioned my judgment almost as often."

Hearing confirmation that Cameron had been the killer brought a certain measure of closure for her. "Why didn't you tell me?"

"I didn't want to put you in a position of having to do something about it, of having to choose between me and justice for Tyler or me and your obligations to the job."

"Did you think I wouldn't understand about the murky gray area after all these years on the job?"

"I didn't want to say it out loud. It was bad enough that I knew, Alice and her husband knew, Cameron and her other son Caleb knew."

"Did Mom know?"

"Yeah."

"Is that why she left during the investigation?"

"How do you know about that? You were too young to remember."

"Tracy said something about it. I put two and two together."

"She was furious with me for risking my job and reputation for Alice. She never liked the time I spent with Alice. She was threatened by it."

"Did she have reason to be?"

He paused long enough for Sam to draw her own conclusions. "I had feelings for her, and she had them for me, but we never acted on it. Not once. I was dating your mother when Steven was killed, and we almost came undone over the time I spent with Alice after the shooting. We managed to hold it together and got married a few months later, but the fact that I took care of Alice was always an issue between your mother and me, especially after Alice got married again."

"Why then?"

"Jimmy's a good guy, but he hadn't been through what we had, you know? He wasn't part of her life with Steven, and I was, so she held on to me. Probably longer than she should have. Your mother grew to hate her, which I never understood but accepted as a fact of my life with her. Sometimes I think she felt that my relationship with Alice justified her behavior at the end."

"Thanks for telling me all this. It helps to fill in some blanks."

"Who else knows about this, besides McBride and Tyrone?"

"Nick."

"Is it too many people? Do you want me to come clean? I'd do it to save you the heartburn. Cameron has always known there might come a day when I couldn't protect him anymore."

"What about Alice?"

"I love Alice, and I always will, but I love you more. If you want to do something with what you found out, I won't stop you, and I won't hold it against you."

"None of the people who know would ever speak of it, so I don't see any reason to undo what was done years ago. But there is one thing I'd like to say, because I need to get it off my chest."

"I'm listening."

Sam was glad she was resting on his shoulder and not looking at him for this conversation. "You put me in a very difficult position by ordering me to leave this alone. I understand now why you did it, but that doesn't mean you can use our bond to bend me to your will. You're the one who taught me the job always comes first. You all but forced me to choose between you and my job on this one, and I didn't appreciate that."

"You're absolutely right, and I was absolutely wrong."

"Really?" Sam hadn't expected such easy capitulation. He snorted out a laugh. "Surprised you, huh?"

"Yeah, you could say that."

"I was scared of what would happen to Alice if it got out. I was also scared about what my sins might do to your career if people found out what I did."

"Your intentions were honorable."

"I'd like to think they always were, but sometimes life gets in the way."

"You don't have to tell me that." Sam raised her head and met the blue-eyed gaze that was exactly the same as hers. "So we're okay?"

"You bet we are."

"Good." Sam returned her head to his shoulder, flooded with relief. "I hate when we disagree. It makes me physically ill."

"Believe it or not, I hate it just as much."

Sam stiffened when she saw her mother coming down the hallway.

Brenda caught sight of Sam snuggled up to him and stopped in the doorway, propping her hands on slender hips. "Still two peas in a pod, huh?" When neither of them replied, she shook her head and continued on her way.

"You really ought to make peace with her, Sam. She's your mother—the only one you'll ever have. I'd hate for you to have regrets someday."

"I've been angry with her for so long I don't remember not being angry with her."

"Maybe it's time to let it go and move on. What happened between us was a long time ago. And you've spent enough time married by now to know it takes two people to make a marriage work, and it takes two people to mess it up. I wasn't entirely blameless."

Sam tried to imagine what it would be like to have Nick taking care of a murdered friend's wife for whom he had obvious tender feelings. For the first time, she could see that it hadn't always been easy for her mother to be married to Skip. "I'll think about it." Sam got up and kissed his forehead. "I've got to get back to HQ. I've got a couple of Arnie Patterson's flunkies sitting on ice waiting for the lawyers the Pattersons aren't sending."

Skip's mouth fell open in shock. "The Kavanaugh murder is tied to *Patterson*?"

"Yep, and I've got the lackeys screwed, glued and tattooed. Still hoping to nail Patterson and his sons too, but that's not a sure thing by any stretch. Either way, it'll fuck up his campaign. How do you like them apples?"

"Holy shit. This is gonna be huge!"

Sam smiled. "Malone said it's always huge when I'm involved."

"That's my kid." Skip's eyes danced with delight. "I'm so freaking proud of you, Samantha Holland Cappuano." In a whisper, he added, "So freaking proud."

Blinking back tears, she bent to kiss his forehead. "That means everything to me, Dad. Everything."

He grinned at her as best he could with one side of his face paralyzed from the stroke he'd suffered after he was shot.

"Let me go see what my husband has done with your wife." In the hallway, Sam saw Nick standing with Celia by the elevators. They were engaged in an animated conversation, and Sam's insides melted a little when Nick tossed his head back and laughed at something Celia said. God, she loved him so damned much.

He caught sight of her and smiled.

She signaled for him to bring Celia back.

When they strolled over to her, Sam hugged Celia. "Congrats, Granny."

"Thanks, Sam. I couldn't be more excited if little Ella were my own granddaughter."

"Of course she's your granddaughter. Don't be silly."

"That's sweet of you to say. Did you and your dad kiss and make up?"

"Yes, we did."

"Oh, good," she said. "He suffers so terribly when you two are at odds."

"I can hear you, Celia," Skip said as he rolled his chair into the hallway to join them.

Celia flashed him a saucy grin. "I only speak the truth, my dear."

"We've got to get going," Sam said. "We'll see you tomorrow."

"See you then," her dad said.

When Nick tossed an arm around her, Sam leaned into his embrace.

"Everything okay?" he asked.

As the familiar scent of him surrounded and comforted her, Sam realized she'd gotten through a difficult hour in large part because of the strength she drew from his love. "Everything is perfect."

"Good."

"I need to stop at HQ very briefly, and then I'm all yours until seven o'clock tomorrow morning."

"Oh, I like the sound of that. As I recall, we have an important conversation to finish."

"I have no idea what you're talking about."

As they stepped into the elevator, he slapped her lightly on the ass. "Liar."

Even as she tried to form a protest, every nerve ending in Sam's body was tuned in to the spot where his hand had connected to her flesh.

"Mmm," he said, nuzzling her neck. "This is gonna be *so* hot."

Sam reached for him at the same instant he reached for her, his hands seeming to touch her everywhere at once, inflaming her to the point of combustion. She wanted to kiss him so badly she burned with the need, but her face was still too sore.

"God, I miss kissing you," he whispered harshly as he cupped her breasts and pinched her nipples until they were hard and throbbing.

She squeezed his cock and made him groan. "Me too."

When the elevator dinged to indicate their arrival in the lobby, they broke apart. Breathing hard, they stared at each other, equally dazzled by the power of their desire. "We probably gave the hospital security guys one hell of a show." It appalled her that she hadn't considered that before the grope session.

He grabbed her hand and all but dragged her off the elevator. "The stop at HQ had better be very quick, you got me?"

"Yeah," Sam said, rattled and undone to realize she loved dominant Nick as much as she loved sweet, tender Nick. "I got you."

BECAUSE IT WAS too hot to wait outside, Nick came into HQ with her. As they made their way to the pit, Captain Malone waylaid them. "Lieutenant, the lab report is back with a match for Jerry Smith's DNA with the skin found under Victoria's nails."

"Yes," Sam said, pumping her fist. "Fan-fucking-tastic!"

Smiling at her choice of words, Malone said, "We'll be filing formal murder charges in the morning."

"You can add kidnapping to the charges against Smith," Hill said as he joined them. "I tracked down two associates of Bobby Ray's who'll testify that they met Smith in a bar, and when Smith said he had a kid who needed to be watched, Bobby mentioned his mother."

"Excellent," Sam said, feeling positively giddy as all their ducks lined up into a neat little row. "With that testimony, we won't even need forensics to tie Jerry to Bobby's murder."

"I was thinking the same thing," Hill said. "Why do you think they didn't kill Maeve too?"

"Maybe even scumbags like Jerry Smith have scruples when it comes to defenseless kids."

"Maybe so. Great work, Lieutenant. You called the Patterson connection, and you were spot on."

"Thanks," Sam said, unnerved by the praise coming from a man who admired her in more ways than one, especially with her husband standing right next to her. No doubt he'd have something to say about Hill handing out compliments, but she didn't have time to worry about that now.

"What do you say we move our guests to their accommodations for the evening?" Like Gonzo had been earlier, Sam was tuned in to how much fun her job could be at times like this when they had their suspects nailed from every possible direction, and everyone knew it—except for the suspects.

"What's your plan, Lieutenant?" Malone asked, looking a little gleeful himself.

"We're going to house Jerry and Porter together for the evening. Cruz set up manned surveillance. We're hoping one of them will be stupid enough to speak freely. My money is on Jerry."

"Remind them of their rights," Malone said.

"I'll do it when I get them in the cell, so it'll be recorded."

"Good," Malone said. "Try not to enjoy this too much."

"Why not?" Sam asked with a cheeky grin she instantly regretted. "How often do we get to have genuine fun on this job? Did you hear Porter pissed himself?"

Hill laughed at that news.

"Sure did," Malone said with a chuckle. "Beckett has been bitching about the stink all night."

"Let's go rescue him," Sam said, heading for the pit. She was dismayed to find Lieutenant Stahl skulking around the nearly deserted area. "What're you doing in here?"

"I was cutting through, not that it's any of your business. And speaking of your business, the department counsel tells me she can't get five minutes of your time."

"She'll get my time when I close the Kavanaugh case and not before. What business is it of yours, anyway?"

"Everything is my business, Lieutenant." His beady eyes narrowed as he spoke, making Sam's skin crawl.

"Step aside," she said. "I have work to do."

"What's he doing here?" Stahl asked, nodding to Nick. "He's not authorized to be back here."

"He's authorized to be anywhere that I say he's authorized to be, so fuck off and let me do my job."

His face turned the shade of purple that Sam had become accustomed to from him. "You need to watch yourself, young lady. That is no way to speak to a superior officer."

"So put me up on charges. You don't seem to have anything else to do with your free time."

"I might do that."

"Fine. Now move so I can get to work."

Stahl glowered at her for a good long time before he waddled off to bother someone else.

"Jesus," Nick said. "Is he always so pleasant?"

"That was actually one of our friendlier exchanges."

"I hate to think you have such formidable enemies here."

"It's only him, and he's hardly as formidable as he

thinks he is." She unlocked her office. "You can wait in here, but by all means please resist the urge to clean."

"I'm unable to resist that urge." He patted her bum. "And a few others, so you'd better hurry up before my urges get the better of me."

"Stop it," she growled, giving him a little shove. "Don't get my motor running here, for Christ's sake."

"Urges. I have them. I need you to control them."

"Stay," she said. "Don't clean. I'll be right back."

"Hurry."

She told herself she was hurrying because she wanted to, not because he'd all but ordered her to. She didn't take orders from anyone, except her higher-ups in the department, and only when absolutely necessary. Why, then, did the thought of Nick bossing her around in bed make her so hot her skin felt like it was on fire? She shook her head to rid it of salacious thoughts. No time for that now.

Stepping into interrogation room two, she nearly gagged at the stench that greeted her. Porter was pacing back and forth like a caged animal. When she entered, he stopped and turned to her. "I hope you're prepared for one hell of a lawsuit, madam."

"You can call me Lieutenant, Mr. Gillespie, and on what grounds do you plan to sue the department?"

"Police brutality! I was hauled out of my home, humiliated in front of the media, strip-searched and held here like a common criminal for hours!"

"And what part of that was brutal? I'm not seeing it."

He stared at her as if she was insane, and the wild look in his eyes had her wondering if he was having some sort of breakdown. *"All of it!"*

"Mr. Gillespie," Sam said in her best condescending tone, "I realize that being a criminal is all new to you, but everything you've experienced is common procedure. If the first words out a suspect's mouth are 'I want a lawyer,' then our hands are tied until the lawyer shows up. Suspects being charged with felonies are strip-searched as a matter of procedure, and we can't control where the media chooses to camp out on public premises. So I'm afraid your lawyer, if he or she ever gets here, will agree that you have no case against us. I'm sure he or she will be far more concerned about the accessory to murder and kidnapping charges, and you should be too."

"I will tell you the same thing I told that other officer who dragged me in here—I had nothing to do with any murder or kidnapping."

"We'll be happy to discuss that with you when your lawyer arrives. Any idea when that might be?"

Porter glowered at her. "No."

"Were you permitted to make a phone call?"

"I was offered it, but I chose to wait."

"Would you care to make that call now?"

"Yeah, I guess. I can't imagine what's taking so long."

Sam nodded to Beckett, who left the room and returned a minute later with a phone that he plugged into a wall jack. He pushed the speaker button and got an outside line before he gestured for Gillespie to make his call.

He glanced at Sam. "I have a right to privacy."

"Of course you do. We'll wait right outside. Make it snappy."

Sam and Beckett joined Hill and Malone in the observation room where they watched the fury and indignation roll off Porter in waves as he punched out the number from memory. The phone rang and rang until voice mail picked up. "This is Colton Patterson. I can't take your call right now. Please leave a message, and I'll get back to you as soon as I can. Thanks, and have a great day."

"Colton," Porter said with a hysterical edge to his voice, "where the hell is the lawyer? I've been here for hours! Send him over here, and tell him to bring me a change of clothes. Cam can get them. Hurry up, will you?" He punched the off button.

Beckett unplugged the phone and removed it from the room.

"Unfortunately, we need this room for other matters, so we'll be moving you to a cell in the city jail shortly."

"I have to stay here? Overnight?"

"Until your lawyer arrives, everything is on hold." She checked her watch. "Since it's now eight p.m. with no sign of the lawyer, I'm guessing this'll be going into tomorrow."

"When will I get to leave?"

"Depends on when the lawyer shows up and whether the judge approves bail, but I'll warn you that's highly unlikely in light of the charges." Sam watched as it settled on him that he might be in jail for quite some time. "Officer Beckett will escort you to your cell."

"You won't get away with this," Gillespie spat at her as she turned to leave.

"Neither will you," Sam said, leaving him with her most charming smile, even though the pain nearly made her faint. The agony was well worth the blatant fear that replaced the arrogance on his smug face.

"God, that was fun," she said to Malone and Hill as they stepped out of the observation room.

"Nothing quite like taking a pompous ass down a few pegs," Hill said.

"Exactly," Sam said. To Beckett, she said, "Get Gillespie and Smith settled in the cell that Cruz designated for surveillance earlier and let me know when they're there."

"Yes, ma'am, Lieutenant."

Since she had a few minutes, she wandered back to her office, checking the voice mail on her cell phone as she went. One of them was from Cruz. "Sam, I have the info you wanted me to get on Gibson. Give me a call when you get this message." Sam exited out of voice mail and returned the call. "Hey," she said when he answered. "What've you got?"

"Hi." He sounded sleepy and dopey, the way he often did since he'd been living with Elin. Sam rolled her eyes to high heaven. "I did a little digging into the Gibson situation. It was tough to find out anything because of the privacy laws, but I went over to see if one of the nurses could be charmed."

"And of course she swooned at the sight of you."

"Naturally."

Sam laughed. "And?"

"And he's going to be fine. He didn't take enough of whatever he took to kill himself. She said it seemed more like an attention-getting scheme. So I'd say you did the right thing to stay away. You would've been giving him exactly what he wanted if you'd gone over there."

As she listened, she went into her office where Nick had his feet on the desk, his hands crossed on his belly and his eyes closed. She wondered if he was asleep, but the second she crossed the threshold, he opened his eyes. Her gaze met his in a flashpoint of awareness that arced between them like an electrical charge. They'd always had a crazy attraction to each other, from the first night they met, but this was something all new and even crazier than what she was used to.

Apparently, he felt the charge too, because he sat up a little straighter in the chair and dropped his feet to the floor. "Done?" he asked.

She shook her head. "Thanks for the info, Freddie. I really appreciate you doing that."

"No problem. How's Angela?"

"She's great. She's got a gorgeous new daughter named Ella."

"That's awesome. How are you?"

"I'm good," she said, touched by his concern. "I'll see you in the morning." Putting the phone in her pocket, she went around the desk and rested against it, facing her husband. "Cruz found out that Gibson survived the fake suicide attempt. The nurse said it seemed like an attention-getting scheme. In other words, typical Peter."

"Do you feel better now that you know?"

She nodded. "I hope you understand—I only asked Freddie to look into it because I wanted to know if he was dead or alive. That's it."

"Sam, honey, I know you don't have feelings for him. How could you after all the shit he's pulled on you—on both of us? He took six years away from us, not to mention everything he took from you."

"It threw me when he listed me as his next of kin and wrote me a letter and all that."

"Of course it did. You wouldn't be human—you wouldn't be you—if it didn't. But now you know it was more of the same, so don't give it another thought." She reached for his hand and linked their fingers.

"I won't."

"I hate how you have so many things in your life that

cause you angst. How you manage to stay so balanced and sane is amazing to me."

"Am I balanced and sane?"

"Extremely."

A knock on the door had her dropping his hand and turning to face the doorway.

"They're in the cell, Lieutenant."

"Thanks, Beckett. Sorry you had to spend your entire tour babysitting stinky pants."

"It was pretty gross," he said, grimacing. The young man was in his first year on the job. "I had no idea pee could smell that bad."

"Welcome to police work, where the offensive aromas never end."

"Good to know," Beckett said with a smile. "See you tomorrow."

To Nick, she said, "Five more minutes, Senator, and then I'm all yours."

"Get to it. I'm running out of patience. It's time for you to take your punishment for making me wait all day for you and your idea of funny text messages, not to mention having to stand by silently while you receive compliments from your not-so-secret admirer."

Sam's mouth fell open and then snapped shut, making her gasp from the pain. Astounded by the game they were suddenly playing, she bit back the snotty retort that was sitting on the tip of her tongue, aware of him watching her as she walked away. The rational, feminist side of her said she really shouldn't let him get away with a statement like that, but the other side of her, the side that was ridiculously turned on by their game, told the rational side to shut the hell up. She couldn't deny she was painfully curious to see where this night might lead.

Downstairs, in the city jail, she greeted the sergeant on duty.

"Your boys are in cell three, Lieutenant," he said as she went by.

"Thanks, Sarge."

As she approached the cell, she heard Jerry and Porter whispering to each other but couldn't make out what they were saying. The cell contained two narrow cots, a small sink and a metal toilet between the beds. She could smell Porter from the hallway and choked back a gag.

"Gentlemen," Sam said, clapping her hands loudly as she approached, making them jolt. She loved that. "I'd like to remind you that you have the right to remain silent." She pointed to the cameras mounted in the corners of the cell. "Anything you say can and will be used against you in a court of law. You have a right to an attorney. If you cannot afford one, an attorney will be provided for you. Do you understand your rights in this matter?"

Glowering at her, they both nodded.

"I'm going to need you to say, 'Yes, I understand my rights.'" She pointed again to the cameras.

"I understand my rights," they said in flat-sounding voices.

"Can you find him some new clothes?" Jerry jerked his thumb toward a red-faced Porter. "He fucking reeks."

"I believe he was offered a jumpsuit, which we're happy to provide, but he refused it."

"Take it, you dickwad," Smith said. "I don't want to smell your piss all night."

"Boys, boys," Sam said condescendingly, "let's try to get along."

"I'll take the jumpsuit," Porter said through gritted teeth.

"I'll have one brought to you."

"I have to change here?"

"Where else?" Sam said. "This isn't exactly the country club." She called for the guard and asked him to bring Porter a change of clothing. "I'll be back in the morning," she said to her prisoners. "Hopefully, your lawyer or lawyers will be here by then so we can have a chat and get you arraigned. I can't imagine what's keeping them." She shrugged as if it was no consequence to her, which it wasn't.

They had a long, hard night ahead of them. With any luck, before the sun rose on a new day, they'd put two and two together and realize they'd been cut loose by the Patterson organization.

"Sleep tight," she said as she walked away, smiling when Jerry muttered, "Fuck you" under his breath. "Fuck you too, you murdering son of a bitch," she whispered to herself as she took the stairs to the pit. "Let's go," she said to Nick, who jumped up at the sound of her voice.

Knowing he was so anxious to get home had a flutter of nerves working its way down her spine as she locked her office door and walked out with him into the sultry night.

TWENTY-THREE

SAM KNEW SHE was in serious trouble when he tossed his suit jacket on the sofa in a move so wildly out of character for her neat-freak husband that she was shocked speechless. Tossing clothes on the sofa was her move, not his.

He continued to astound her when he unbuttoned her blouse, pushed it off her shoulders and let it drop to the floor.

"Who are you, and what have you done with my freakazoid husband?"

"Be quiet, and do what you're told."

Oh my… Since he was stepping so far out of character for the night, Sam decided to go with him, anxious to see where they might end up together. She had no intention of making a habit out of allowing him to boss her around. But this new and unexplored side of her sexy husband had her extremely intrigued. She wouldn't have guessed he had it in him, which, she could now see, was a vast underestimation on her part.

Moving them toward the stairs, he continued to remove clothes, kicking off his wingtips with barely concealed abandon that made her hot and wet and needy. As he snapped her bra free with a move right out of the high school boy handbook, her nipples tightened.

Her pants and underwear followed and somehow her bra ended up hanging from the newel post.

"Up." He pointed to the stairs. "Now."

Sam was almost afraid to turn her back on him. Her bottom tingled at the possibility that he might get down to business on the way up. Tentatively, she took the first stair and then the second. Waiting to see what he would do was almost as arousing as knowing what was coming when they got upstairs.

Her legs felt heavy and clumsy as she made her way up, knowing he was right behind her but not touching her with anything more than his gaze. She had no doubt he was fully enjoying the sight of her ass as she moved up the stairs. Her mouth was suddenly dry and her palms damp as her clit throbbed and moisture pooled between her legs. She'd never been more turned on in her life, and he hadn't even touched her. Yet.

When they reached the second floor, he said, "Keep going."

He wanted to go to their special place in the loft, which he'd created to remind them of their honeymoon paradise in Bora Bora. That he wanted to do this there only ramped up her overwhelming anticipation as she took the stairs to the loft. It felt so decadent to be walking through the house naked, knowing he was also naked right behind her.

The loft retained the fragrance of the beach from the scented candles he'd bought. She was instantly transported to the blissful days and nights of their honeymoon.

He moved around her to adjust the double lounge chair—exactly like the one they'd so enjoyed in Bora Bora—so it was flat. "Lie down," he said. "On your belly."

Acutely aware of him watching her every move, Sam stretched out facedown, resting the uninjured side of her face on the pillow.

"Comfortable?" he asked.

"I guess…" She was nervous and embarrassed and aroused and all sorts of other things she couldn't seem to put words to as she heard him rustling around, lighting candles and turning on their favorite island music.

"Does your face hurt?"

"No."

"Will you tell me if it starts to hurt?"

She had a feeling her face was going to be the least of her concerns in a few minutes. "Uh-huh."

The lounge dipped under his weight when he joined her. She started to raise her head to see what he was doing, but he stopped her. "Don't move. Close your eyes and trust me."

Since there was no one she trusted more, she did as he requested even as her entire body quivered with anticipation and excitement.

His hands glided over her back, warm and smooth as a new fragrance filled her senses. Cedar and spice and flowers. She couldn't place it. Massage oil, she realized as he kneaded the tension from her neck and shoulders before working his way down her back. Realizing he'd obviously put a lot of thought into how this night would unfold only ramped up her desire to unprecedented levels.

After a long period of silence in which Sam desperately wanted to ask him what he was thinking and planning, he said, "I'm annoyed with you."

His playful tone told her he was anything but annoyed. "What did I do this time?"

"I have a long list of grievances, and I plan to punish you for every one of them."

"Is that so?" Sam said, playing along. She wanted to purr from the magic he was making with his skillful hands. Where had he been hiding this skill all these months?

"Uh-huh. Let's start with your friend Avery Hill, who looks at you like he wants to take you home and tie you to his bed and keep you captive for days on end." The slap to her ass was quick and sharp and shocking and so intensely arousing.

Sam gasped and bit her lip to keep from crying out. Heat radiated from the spot where his hand had made contact, and a flood of new moisture had her pressing her legs together, as if that might actually contain it.

"I don't care for the way he looks at you. Not one bit." The next slap landed on the other cheek, followed right after by a slap to the first spot, which now burned and tingled. He rubbed massage oil into both cheeks, cooling the sting but feeding the fire.

The effort to remain still and appear unaffected by what he was doing had her squirming ever so slightly, which caused her nipples to rub against the coarse canvas on the lounge. If he so much as breathed on her clit, she'd go off like a Roman candle. She floated as he started from her shoulders and worked his way down again, giving extra special attention to her ass. His fingers slipped between her cheeks, rubbing oil on her anus and drawing a sharp gasp from her as his finger slid inside.

"Now let's talk about that text you sent me that damn near gave me a heart attack today." Another slap, harder than the earlier ones.

Sam would've laughed but she was too busy trying to breathe.

"I'm also not at all happy about the fact that you've been keeping things from me again." His free hand came down on her ass again as his finger tunneled deeper into her.

"What things?" She squeaked out the words as an orgasm of epic proportions grew and built. The foreign sensation of his finger in her ass sent her out of her mind. She'd had no idea she would like that so much. She'd had no idea she'd like any of this as much as she did.

"That you like this," he said, slapping her other cheek. "And this," he said as he pushed his finger in and withdrew it before pushing it in again.

Sam came harder than she ever had in her life, and he hadn't even touched the spot that usually required focused attention. She cried out from the overwhelming sensations that rocketed through her like an out-of-control freight train. Nothing she'd ever experienced could compare. Keeping his finger firmly lodged in her ass, he drew her up to trembling knees and thrust his cock into her.

Sam cried out from the dual assault on her senses and the near pain of his entry. Had he ever felt bigger or thicker inside her? Not that she could recall. Apparently, this new phase in their sex life was having the same overwhelming effect on him. That thought had her climbing toward another orgasm as he timed the thrusts of his finger and his cock so some part of him was inside her at all times, pushing hard against her with each reentry.

When he reached around to pinch her clit, she went off again, harder and longer than the last time, screaming out her release as he slammed into her and roared with his own climax. Long after they collapsed onto the lounge, he kept his finger and his cock inside her, absorbing the trembling shockwaves that followed two of the most astonishing orgasms of her life.

"Well," he said, as he slowly and torturously withdrew his finger, "who knew?"

Sam let out a wobbly laugh as he pulled out of her and kissed her shoulder on his way to the bathroom. She lay there, still facedown, breathing as hard as she did when she sprinted after a suspect. He had taken her somewhere she'd never dreamed of going, and she'd loved every minute of it. Probably because she loved him so much.

As a woman who prided herself on a hardcore, take-no-prisoners personality, she should be embarrassed by the way she'd let him completely dominate her, but she wasn't. She'd loved it, and she wasn't going to pretend otherwise. Because he was Nick, he fully understood the rules of their game without her having to tell him she'd never tolerate such behavior anywhere else.

He returned to the lounge and stretched out next to her.

Sam curled up to him, resting her face on his chest and listening to his heart pounding as hard as hers was.

"So?" he said after a long period of contented silence.

"So what?"

"Did you like it?"

She laughed—hard. "Two screaming orgasms didn't paint a good enough picture for you?"

He pressed his lips to the top of her head. "They gave me a pretty good idea, but I'd still like to know what you're thinking."

"I didn't know I'd like that," she said.

"I didn't know I would either."

"So you liked it too?"

"Oh yeah. I felt like I was going to explode watching my finger sink into you as your cheeks got redder and redder." His hand slid down her back to caress her bottom, which was warm and tender. "It didn't really hurt, did it?"

"It stung, but in a good way."

"I was worried about losing control and hurting you. I was so turned on. I've never been more turned on in my life."

"Me either." She tipped her head up so she could see his face in the candlelight. "I couldn't have done that with anyone but you. I hope you know that."

"Baby, believe me. I know. If there's something else you want, I hope you'll tell me. I don't want you to ever feel embarrassed to ask me for anything."

"I liked what you did with your finger," she said, her face burning despite her earlier bravado. "I wouldn't mind more of that."

He swallowed hard, his Adam's apple bobbing. "How much more?"

She ran her hand over his belly to grasp his cock, which was hard again. "As much as you can give me." She stroked him to make her point.

Releasing a jagged breath, he said, "Have you done that before?"

She shook her head. "Have you?"

His shrug answered for him. He rarely talked about the other women he'd been with, and Sam was dying for details he clearly didn't wish to share.

What did it matter? He was hers now, and she planned to make sure he never wanted anyone else ever again. With that in mind, she raised herself up and straddled him, sinking down on his erection and drawing a moan of pleasure from him.

He cupped her breasts and tweaked her nipples as she rode him to a fast, hard release that drained the last of her energy. She collapsed on top of him and felt his strong arms come around her as she flirted with sleep.

"I need to go clean up the clothes we left downstairs."

Laughing, she said, "You do not!"

"I can't sleep if I leave them there all night."

"Try. I stepped way out of character for you. Time to return the favor."

Chuckling, he said, "I love you, Samantha Cappuano."

Sam, who had never planned to change her name for any man, loved the sound of her new name coming from him. "Love you too."

SAM'S FIRST STOP the next morning was the city jail, where her two prisoners looked as if they hadn't slept a wink all night. Unfortunately for them, she'd slept like a baby and was feeling energized and ready to rumble after the best sex of her entire life. They'd ended up sleeping in the loft and had engaged in some rather stupendous morning lovemaking. Whoever said married life was supposed to be boring hadn't met her insatiable husband.

"Good morning," she said to the two men, doing nothing to hide her chipper disposition. "Hope you slept well. Did you get your breakfast?"

"If you can call it that," Porter mumbled, diminished by prison orange. Apparently, city jail fare wasn't up to his usual standards. Imagine that? His dark hair stood on end, and his jaw was rough with whiskers. While it wasn't as pungent as it had been the night before, the aura of urine was still present. Once Porter lost his polished veneer, he lost his bravado too, Sam noted.

"We haven't heard anything from your attorneys," Sam said, not mentioning that she'd been elated to learn she'd been right about that too. She'd been right more often than usual in this one, and that was saying something, since she was usually right. She liked being right. Her day had already been made by the news that Crime Scene detectives had found bloody clothes in Jerry's hotel room. Could he be any stupider? It was proof that he'd never expected to be caught. He'd never expected her.

"Is there someone else you'd like us to call?"

They exchanged nervous glances.

"We're not from here," Porter said. "We need to call people in Ohio and get them here."

"I can get you someone from the public defender's office if money is an issue," Sam said.

"It's not," Porter snapped. "We can pay for our own lawyers."

"Speak for yourself, a-hole. Christian and Colton will send someone for me. I'm going to wait."

Porter glowered at Jerry. "They're not going to send anyone, *a-hole*."

She was glad to see that at least one of them had realized they were on their own to face the charges with no help from the Patterson camp. Jerry was still holding out hope.

"Can I call someone in Ohio?" Porter asked. "He'll know who I should call here."

Sam passed her notebook and a pen through the bars. "Give me the number, and we'll do it for you." She watched him process that information and could tell he was once again on the verge of mentioning his rights, but he wisely refrained. According to the officers monitoring the cell, they hadn't said much of anything to each other during the night. *Too bad*, Sam thought. It would've made things nice and tidy if they'd shared a few confidences while they were the guests of the city.

No such luck. While it galled her that they might not nail any of the Pattersons for their involvement in Victoria's murder, at least they had the guy who'd actually murdered Victoria as well as one of his accomplices.

Porter returned the notebook to her. "I don't have his number memorized, but I wrote down his name and address."

"I'll make the call and let you know what he says." She paused before she added, "If either of you is willing to speak to us without an attorney present, we're willing to listen to what you have to say."

They exchanged glances again.

"What do we have to tell you?" Jerry asked.

"The truth," Sam said with a shrug. "We want to know why Victoria was planted close to the Nelson administration. We want to know who was behind the scheme. We want to know who gave the orders, pulled the strings, paid the bills. We want to know it all."

"In exchange for?" Porter asked.

"That'll depend on what you give us."

The two of them stood with their arms crossed and mulish expressions on their faces as they contemplated what she'd said.

"I'll let you think about it," she said with a jaunty wave as she started to walk away.

"What're we supposed to do in the meantime?" Jerry asked with a snarl.

"Chill out and relax," Sam said with another cheerful smile as she headed out of the jail and took the stairs.

Gonzo met her in the pit. "Derek Kavanaugh is waiting in your office with something he said he needs to show you. Looks like he's been crying."

"Shit," she muttered, hoping her good mood wasn't

about to take a hit. She went into her office and shut the door. Derek was sitting in her visitor chair with his elbows propped on his knees and his head hanging between his shoulders. He was the picture of devastation. "Derek?"

He raised his head to reveal a grief-ravaged face.

"What is it? What's happened?"

"She loved me," he said softly. "It was real. We were real."

Relieved and curious and instantly on alert, Sam leaned against her desk. "How do you know?"

He handed her a large white envelope. The address portion contained a printed label with Derek's name and his parents' address but no return address. There was no other information on the envelope except for a registered mail tag.

"It arrived via registered mail to my parents' house first thing this morning. She arranged it in advance in case anything ever happened to her. It's the whole story with a notarized statement in her legal name attesting to the fact that it's from her so it can be entered as evidence in court. There's a note from a lawyer that said he had to retrieve the documents from storage, so it took a couple of days to get them to me. He also said he'd be available to testify to the fact that he handled this matter for her."

"Oh my God," Sam said as she skimmed the letter written in Victoria's own hand, in which she professed her profound sorrow for her involvement in a scheme that had gotten so far out of her control she'd seen no way out of it. Sam read as fast as she could, devouring the details of how Valerie Taft's father George worked as Arnie's second in command at the Patterson Financial Group until he quit abruptly. A few days later, he and his wife perished in a fire at their home.

Authorities had suspected arson, but they'd been unable to prove it. Valerie, who'd dated Colton Patterson in high school, had been working in Pennsylvania after college at Bryn Mawr when her parents died. Devastated, she'd returned home to Defiance. The Patterson family had taken her in, treated her as a member of their family and helped to soothe the raw ache of her loss.

She detailed meeting with her father's attorney, at which time she learned he'd uncovered a massive fraud within the Patterson empire, which was why he'd resigned. The company was nothing more than a Ponzi scheme, a house of cards that could fold at any time. He'd detailed everything he knew and had given the information to his attorney the day before the fire, intending to contact the state attorney general. Her father's attorney suspected her parents had been killed by Patterson to keep her father quiet about what he'd discovered. Shocked and dismayed that people she considered family could be responsible for her parents' tragic deaths, she'd made the egregious mistake of confronting Arnie Patterson about what she'd learned.

The lawyer who'd been so kind to her had been found dead the next day, his office firebombed, leaving Valerie without any of the evidence her father had so carefully accumulated to prove the Ponzi scheme. Arnie had made her a virtual prisoner in his home, refusing to let her leave or contact anyone. After two weeks of lockdown and deprivation, he and his sons had presented her with an ultimatum—participate in their plan to gain access to the top levels of the Nelson administration or they would pin the fraud at Patterson Financial on her father.

They'd made it very clear that they would ruin his good name—and hers—unless she gave them a year of her life and did exactly what they told her to. The only thing the Patterson family had more of than money was ambition.

"I'd once heard Arnie say at a dinner party," Victoria wrote, "that if he had to choose between being president and never having sex again, he'd choose being president because power was the greatest high on earth."

Since she'd been their prisoner at the time, she'd taken the deal, hoping to find a way out once she was free of their estate.

Astounded by what she was reading and trying to process it all, Sam glanced at Derek, who was staring off into space.

"Keep reading," he said. "It gets better." Valerie—now known as Victoria Tate—got the first whiff that nothing was as it seemed when she saw the trouble and expense they'd gone to in creating her new identity. The scheme and her identity had obviously been a long time in the making. That was when she realized they'd planned everything right down to expecting her to confront Arnie about what she'd learned from the lawyer. It had all been part of a plan so much bigger than her she couldn't begin to get her head around it.

Fearing for her own life, she did as she was told and befriended Derek at the gym, beginning a cat-and-mouse game with him that culminated in him asking her out more than a month later. "You took far longer than they expected you to, my love," Victoria wrote.

WE'D BEGUN TO give up on you when you finally asked. It's so important to me that you know that even though we met under the worst possible circumstances, every single thing that happened between us—the magic, the fireworks, the sparks—it was all real. From the first night we spent together, every word I said about how I felt about you and our darling daughter was real. I loved you. I loved Maeve. I loved our life together so very much, which is why I stayed long after the year I'd promised them was up. By then I'd realized they had no plans to let me go until Arnie was in the White House. After that, they probably planned to get rid of me too.

I tried so hard to get free of them. I'd truly made a deal with the devil—and his sons. I realized how deep I was in this thing when my background check came back clean after we were married. I'd been hoping the officer would uncover the truth, but they'd even gotten to him.

If you are receiving this letter, then my worst fears have come true and our life together is over. I want you to know that after I fell in love with you, I gave them nothing of any import that they could use against you or the president you so faithfully serve. I purposely steered our conversations away from your work so you wouldn't inadvertently say something I could potentially use to harm you or the president. If I didn't know, I couldn't report, even if they tortured me. I dried up on them, which infuriated them.

They were never angrier than after I conceived our beautiful baby girl. That wasn't part of the plan, and they tried to force me to have an abortion. I refused, and they made threats against me, you, the baby. I was afraid all the time. I so wanted to tell you what was happening, but I was far more afraid of losing you once you learned the truth about me than I was of whatever the Patterson family might do to me. If you've discovered the tracking device I had implanted in our baby, now you know why I did it. They've been threatening to take her away from me since the day she was born, and there was nothing— and I do mean nothing—I wouldn't do to protect her.

If I'm dead, tell the police to talk to Jerry Smith. He's the one they send to 'remind' me every now and then of my obligation to the Patterson family and how prepared they are to ruin my father's reputation at any time if I continue to be uncooperative. Colton and Christian set the whole thing up with the help of their assistants, Porter Gillespie and Jonathan Thayer. Arnie didn't do any of the heavy lifting, but he was well aware of what was going on. If I'm dead, one of them gave the order and they all knew about it. Tell the cops to take a close look at Patterson Financial. Something is rotten there, and my dad had the documents to prove it. The truth could be uncovered with the right questions.

SAM LOOKED AT DEREK. "Victoria handed us the one thing we didn't have—a direct connection between her role in this and the Patterson family." Sam went to the door, opened it and called for Agent Hill to join them. When he came into the office, Sam told him to close the door and handed him the first two pages of Victoria's letter while Sam read the final page.

I don't have the words to apologize to you, my dearest love, for what I've done to you. The time we spent by ourselves and with our daughter were the finest moments of my entire life. I have scores of regrets, but not one of them is about you or the time we spent together. I love you with my whole heart and soul, and I'll be watching over you and our darling Maeve. I'll wish you happiness and love and success and all the good things life has to offer. Please don't be bitter. Please open yourself up to love again with my blessing and fondest hope for your every happiness. Please find it in your heart to forgive me. Please find a way to remember me with love. Yours always, Vic.

Avery finished the first two pages and took the third from Sam, scanning it and the notarized document that came with it. "I'll get warrants for Arnie, Christian and Colton Patterson as well as Jonathan Thayer. We've got them nailed."

"Thanks to Victoria," Sam said, her gaze fixed on Derek.

"Yes," he said, wiping away tears, "thanks to Victoria."

EPILOGUE

AVERY WAS PACKING up his Washington hotel room and dreaming of Jamaica when his cell phone rang. He didn't recognize the local phone number. "Hill."

"Agent Hill, this is Marcella, Director Hamilton's assistant. He'd like to see you at headquarters in an hour. Are you able to get here then?"

Avery was shocked speechless. A summons to the director's office was unprecedented. He'd been in the same room with the director a couple of times but had never spoken directly to him. He quickly ran through the last few weeks, trying to determine when or if he'd fucked something up. Wouldn't he have heard from his own division director if that were the case?

The bureau had gotten some good press after the Patterson arrests. Hell, the media had done little more than chew over how close the country had come to possibly electing a lying, scheming, cheating, murdering scumbag. It couldn't be that he'd fucked up something on the arrests, could it? His meticulous attention to detail had ensured there were no screw-ups. So it couldn't be that.

"Agent Hill?"

Startled out of his musings, he said, "Yes, of course. I'll be there."

"Thank you. We'll see you then."

He rushed for the shower, grabbing his razor on the way in. Forty-five minutes later, he stepped off the Metro at Federal Triangle and hoofed it through sweltering heat to the agency's Pennsylvania Avenue headquarters. He arrived at the director's suite with two minutes to spare, so he took a moment to mop the sweat off his face and straighten the tie he'd hastily put on before he left the hotel.

Marcella was waiting for him and ushered him straight into the director's inner sanctum.

The entire thing felt surreal to Avery, as if he'd suddenly stepped onto a movie set and he'd find Jack Nicholson playing the role of the director. But it was the real Troy Hamilton who stood and came around the desk to shake Avery's hand. It was the real Troy Hamilton who offered Avery a drink and asked him to have a seat as if they were old pals catching up after a long absence. "Thanks so much for coming in on short notice," Troy said after he poured them each two fingers of bourbon. He was tall and broad-shouldered with close-cropped silver hair and intense blue eyes. The man was a living legend in the bureau, and Avery was downright star struck.

"It was no problem."

"I understand you're heading off on vacation. I hope I didn't mess up your plans."

He had, but Avery would never admit to that either. Flights could be rescheduled. Meetings with the director came along once in a career, if that. "You didn't."

"I asked you to come in because I wanted to personally thank you for your work on the Kavanaugh case. I understand from Chief Farnsworth and Lieutenant Holland that you played an integral part in building a case against the Pattersons and their associates."

Reeling from the fact that Sam had commended his

work, Avery wasn't sure how to reply. "Thank you, sir. That's nice to hear."

Troy propped a large foot encased in a black loafer on the coffee table. "I also heard from Mrs. Bertha Ray, who wanted me to know that you saved her life and showed exceptional compassion when you called with the news of her son's death. She was afraid you'd get overlooked in all the madness that followed the arrest of Arnie Patterson and his sons."

"Oh," Avery said, astounded. "She said that?"

Troy nodded and took a swig of his drink. "Her e-mail said she was concerned that if she didn't write to me, I might never know what an outstanding agent I had in you. But I already knew that. You've been on my radar for a while now."

"I have?" Avery wanted to shoot himself with his own gun. He sounded like such a jackass, but he hadn't expected this day to unfold quite this way. He'd expected to be on his way to his favorite beach by now, not listening to Director Hamilton compliment his work. He would've guessed the director had never heard his name.

"Yes, you have. Were you aware that Loring is retiring at the end of the month?"

The director referred to the agent in charge of the Criminal Investigation Division at headquarters. "No, sir. I hadn't heard that."

"I'd like you to take his place."

Avery stared at him as the implications spun through his mind. He'd have to move to Washington. He'd be in regular contact with the MPD and a certain lieutenant, and he'd have to give up his plans to move far, far away from her.

"Agent Hill?"

"I'm sorry, sir. You've caught me off guard."

Troy smiled at that. He went on to describe his goals for the division and his lofty aspirations for Avery's career.

While Avery listened intently, all he could think about was remaining in Washington near the woman he loved but couldn't have. Would he be better off using his new-found cache in the agency to request a transfer to the hinterlands, where he'd never have to see her? Or should he put his career first and do his best to keep his distance from her?

"Agent Hill?"

"I was wondering, sir, would I still be able to do some fieldwork?" The idea of sitting in an office all day made him cagey, and it hadn't even happened yet.

"You could organize your unit any way you see fit."

Avery's mind whirled as his plan to get the hell out of Washington was upended by an unexpected promotion.

"Can I count on you to take on the CID?" Hamilton asked.

Avery's better judgment was urging him to cite personal reasons and request a transfer, ideally to the West Coast, where there was no chance he'd ever see her again. But while his brain was sending that message loud and clear, Avery's heart was telling him to stay where he might cross paths with her once in a while. It was better than nothing, or so he told himself. He couldn't believe he was basing the biggest decision of his career on a woman who'd never be his. If he'd been looking for proof that he'd lost what was left of his mind, there it was.

The word "no" was on the tip of his tongue. But that wasn't what came out of his mouth.

"Yes, sir," he said. "I'd be honored."

"Excellent. Your first order of business will be briefing the president on how Arnie Patterson and his organization managed to infiltrate the Nelson camp. He's
looking for an assessment of the damages to his campaign. Are you prepared to report on the case?"

As images of his favorite beach in Jamaica flashed
through his mind, Avery said, "Yes, sir."

THE ROAR OF the crowd was so deafening Sam could barely
hear herself think, let alone hear what Nick was saying.
Luckily, she'd heard the speech so often in the last couple
of weeks that she had it memorized. The roar, she told
herself, meant it was being well received.

Terry O'Connor flashed a big grin and a thumbs-up to
Sam and Christina. Graham and Laine had been forced
to sit out the convention after they were hit with the flu.
Nick and Terry had joked earlier about what a mood
Graham must be in to be missing out on being there for
Nick's big moment. "Better Mom is babysitting him than
me," Terry had said, making them all laugh.

"This is crazy," Scotty said to Sam, his grin a mile
wide as he stood next to her in the wings, waiting for
their signal from the stage manager.

"You're sure you're up for going out there?" Sam
asked, not at all sure that she was. Trying to imagine
walking across the huge stage to join her husband in front
of all those people had kept her awake the last few nights.
She'd pictured breaking a heel and sprawling on her face
in front of the thousands in the massive ballroom and
millions on TV. She'd taken an endless amount of grief
from her colleagues at the MPD about her prime-time
debut. For that reason alone, falling wasn't an option.

"I'm so excited," Scotty said. "This is the coolest thing I've ever gotten to do."

What did he have to worry about? He wasn't wearing the three-inch heels that Shelby had talked her into in a moment of supreme weakness. At least they weren't pink. Sam was thankful for small favors. The red dress the Nelson campaign stylists had chosen for her would complement the red stripes on Nick's tie and Scotty's. People were actually paid to think of such details. How boring their lives must be compared to hers.

Her name had been all over the media—again—after she'd helped to take down the Patterson family and Arnie's campaign. The twenty-four-hour news cycle had devoured the story of a campaign so driven by ambition they'd plotted and schemed and killed to get a leg up. The SEC was poring through the records at Patterson Financial, and parallels had been repeatedly drawn to Watergate. Arnie's comment about sex and power was broadcast over and over and over again until Sam reached the point where she'd actually gotten sick of hearing about the Patterson family.

However, she never got sick of watching the footage of the FBI swooping down on the Patterson estate in Defiance, where all three members of the family had been arrested, along with Christian's top aide, Jonathan Thayer. That was some of the best TV she'd ever watched. Hill had offered her a spot on the FBI's plane when he'd left with the team that had been dispatched to arrest the Pattersons, but Sam had declined. She'd done her part and didn't feel the need to be there when the arrests were made. Since it was none of Hill's business, she didn't bother to mention that flying terrified her. She'd been glad to see the last of the bothersome agent.

Instead of going to Ohio, she'd stayed home to support her husband as he prepared for the biggest moment of his career and to mother the child who'd been staying with them for two of the most spectacular weeks of her life. They'd been to see the Red Sox play the Orioles at Camden Yards in Baltimore, they'd seen the Federals play at home several times, had attended Freddie's "surprise" thirtieth birthday party and had enjoyed Scotty's pleasure in the baseball camp that had been deemed righteous, especially after the visit from the Federals' star center fielder Willie Vasquez.

Sam's heart would break in two when they had to take him back to Richmond, and she knew Nick was equally despondent at the thought of Scotty leaving. They'd loved every second they'd spent with him, and he seemed equally thrilled to get so much uninterrupted time with them. He'd even told them they got the exact right mac 'n cheese and chicken nuggets, which had pleased them to no end.

The only thing that had marred their time together were the threats Arnie Patterson had made against Sam and her family, leading the Secret Service to offer protection to Nick for the remainder of the campaign. Because they were worried about some of Patterson's supporters going rogue, Sam had urged Nick to accept protection while she'd refused it for herself—much to her husband's dismay.

She might be willing to take her colleagues' ribbing about being on TV, but she wasn't at all willing to be trailed by Secret Service agents, as if she couldn't take care of herself. At this very moment, her service weapon was holstered to her leg under the glamorous folds of the red dress. She'd insisted on a dress that could be worn with the gun she never left home without, especially when some douche-bag murderer was threatening her family.

Nick's speech, which was supposed to have been twenty minutes in length, was now at thirty minutes as he'd been interrupted so often by rousing applause. Taking Terry's advice, he'd gone with a speech similar to the one he'd given at John O'Connor's funeral, drawing on his humble beginnings, the academic scholarship that'd landed him at Harvard and the friendship he'd struck up with the son of a senator.

As he talked about John O'Connor's tragic death and the impact it'd had on him, a hush fell over the crowd, and Sam blinked back tears. The pain of his loss was still so raw, even all these months later. Watching him take a long pause to gather himself, Sam ached for him. Then he rallied and ended by talking about his hopes for a second Nelson administration and his optimism for the country's future that drew a final, thunderous round of applause.

"He killed it," Terry said euphorically.

"Totally," Christina said. "This'll catapult him into the big time."

Sam wasn't sure how she felt about him being catapulted anywhere, especially the big time, so she focused on watching for the signal from the stage manager as her heart beat fast and erratically. Nick was always so there for her. She wanted to be there for him and prayed to a God she didn't much believe in to let her make it across the stage without calamity.

The stage manager waved for them to proceed.

Sam reached for Scotty's hand, thankful to have him as her escort. "Ready, pal?"

His grin nearly split his handsome face in half. "So ready. Let's go!"

As if they were attending a Sunday picnic in the park, she and Scotty strolled onto the stage to join Nick as the applause rose past deafening to whatever level came next. Sam kept her eyes fixed on Nick, who waited patiently for them to the left of the dais. When they reached him without incident, he put an arm around both of them and bent to kiss Sam's forehead.

"Can you believe this shit?" he whispered in her ear. Somehow she was able to hear him over the roar and smiled up at him. The lights on stage were so bright she couldn't see beyond the first few rows. Taking their cues from Nick, she and Scotty waved to the audience, and she tried to forget that millions of people—including her coworkers—were watching at home.

They'd talked about this ahead of time, about how the media would latch on to the fact that Scotty had been out there with him. They'd ask who he was and what he meant to them. Sam and Nick had wanted to be sure he'd be okay with the scrutiny.

"I'll be fine with it," he'd said with twelve-year-old confidence.

"Are you sure?" Nick had asked. "They can be relentless when they think they've got a juicy story, and once your face is broadcast across the country, you may need security too, which will be no fun."

"It'll be fine," Scotty assured them.

"How do you know that?" Sam had asked.

"I'll tell you later," he said with an adorable smile. "After the speech."

He'd left them to wonder what he had to tell them as they'd gotten dressed in their carefully chosen clothes.

They were sharing a hotel suite across the street from the convention center, and Nick had promised Scotty ice cream sundaes from room service after the speech.

For ten minutes, the crowd roared and chanted. Sam couldn't figure out what they were saying until the chant crystalized, and she heard exactly what they were saying: Cappuano for president.

She looked up at him, and he shook his head in amazement.

He gave one last wave to the crowd and then ushered them to the wings. The minute they were clear of the stage, Nick reached for her and gave her a bear hug.

Sam returned the embrace, thrilled for him that it had gone so well.

"That was awesome," Scotty said. "I've never seen that many people in one place—ever!"

"Neither have I, buddy," Nick said.

"And they were all cheering for you. That's so cool."

Nick ruffled his hair. "Glad you thought so."

"You were amazing, and I'm so proud," Sam said.

"Thanks, babe." Nick leaned in to kiss her and wiggled his brows to let her know he'd do better later. "Let's get back to the hotel. I promised a boy an ice cream sundae."

"Don't you have stuff you need to do?" Sam asked.

"Nothing more important than keeping my promise to Scotty."

"I could take him back if you need to stay here for a while."

"I'd much rather be with you guys. Let's go."

It took an hour for Nick to break free of the masses who wanted to shake his hand and share in his moment of glory. By the time the Secret Service detail escorted them across the street to the hotel, darkness had descended upon the city of Charlotte. The oppressive heat was almost a welcome relief after hours in the frigid convention center. Sam couldn't wait to kick off her shoes and get comfortable with her guys.

They wandered into the hotel, where more well-wishers awaited them. Twenty minutes later, they cleared the lobby and made it onto the elevator.

"You're crazy popular," Scotty said, summing up the madness in three simple words that made Sam and Nick laugh.

"It wouldn't have been any fun without you guys there with me," Nick said as he loosened his tie and released the top two buttons on the light blue dress shirt that had been deemed more suitable to the bright lights than white would've been. He wore a new dark navy suit with a subtle pinstripe, and Sam would venture that he'd won the vote of every woman in America tonight—a thought that sent an odd stab of insecurity to her belly.

"You'll be staying in for the rest of the evening, Senator?" one of the agents asked.

"Yes, we will."

"Have a nice evening. We'll see you in the morning."

"Thank you."

Nick gestured for Sam and Scotty to proceed ahead of him into the room and closed the door behind them, leaning back against it and closing his eyes. He let out a deep breath, which was the only sign of nerves he'd shown all day. He was one cool, collected customer.

"Can I order the ice cream now?" Scotty asked.

"Go for it," Nick said.

Scotty scampered off to his room.

Sam went over to Nick and unbuttoned the rest of his shirt buttons, kissing his chest. "Glad it's over?"

"How can you tell?"

"The deep breath was a big giveaway," she said with a smile as she planted more kisses to his chest and neck. Turning to him, she said, "Unzip me. I want out of this getup. Immediately. And the next time Shelby talks me into three-inch heels, she is so fired it's not even funny."

He took his own sweet time unzipping her, planting a few strategic kisses on the way. "Will you put the shoes back on later?"

"Really? You like them?"

Nodding, he did an impression of a panting dog that made her laugh. "Hot. Seriously, hot."

When he reached for her, she dodged him. "Not with the boy in the next room, Senator," Sam said, smiling at him over her shoulder and leading him by his tie into their room to change into sweats and T-shirts.

"So that's a yes on the shoes for later?" His hands landed on her hips and his lips on her neck, sending a shiver of need rippling through her. Things between them had been hotter than ever after the night in the loft, where they'd spent a lot of nights since Scotty had come to stay with them, as it was on the other side of the house from where he slept.

"We might be able to negotiate something."

"It'll be here in ten minutes, you guys," Scotty said, knocking on their door. "Hurry up. You can do all that gross kissing stuff later." He loved to tease them about all the gross kissing that went on in their house. He'd commented that he'd had no idea how much kissing they really did until he lived with them. Of course there'd been more kissing than usual, as they'd been making up for lost time since her face finally healed to the point where kissing no longer hurt.

With that in mind, Sam planted a long, slow wet one on him, to tide them both over until later, when they could be alone.

"To be continued," Nick whispered as they went into the sitting room to join Scotty.

"Can we get a movie?" he asked.

"Why not?" Nick said. "We're celebrating."

"Definitely," Sam said. "But I want something with guns and lots of explosions."

"You would," Nick said, rolling his eyes at her.

Scotty glanced at Nick, did a double take and busted up laughing.

"What's so funny?"

"You," Scotty said, laughing so hard he had tears rolling down his face. He pointed to his own mouth. "Lipstick looks good on you. I knew you were kissing in there."

"Whoops," Sam said, wiping the residual lipstick off her husband's lips. "Busted."

"So busted," Scotty said, mopping up his tears.

"Glad we're available to amuse you," Nick said, "but I'll remember this when you start getting girlfriends and come home with lipstick on your face."

Scotty shuddered at the thought of it. "Ewww, gross."

"Talk to me in a year or two, buddy," Nick said smugly. "Now how about that movie?"

"Before we do that," Scotty said haltingly, "could I talk to you guys about something kinda serious?"

Instantly on guard, Sam said, "Sure you can. Anything you want, but we're not quitting the gross kissing no matter what you say."

Scotty laughed, which seemed to ease his tension. "I wondered if, you know, what you asked me a while ago…

About coming to stay with you for good… I mean, I know I said I wasn't sure if I should do it, but after being here for a couple of weeks, I can't imagine leaving like ever, and if you still wanted me to stay… I mean, if it's okay with you… I um… Well, it would be okay with me too, because I really love you guys a whole lot, and I think you really love me too—"

"Yes!" Sam laughed through her tears as she threw her arms around him and hugged him harder than she'd ever dared to hug him before. "Yes, we want you! Yes, we love you! We've been *dying* over the thought of you leaving next weekend."

His brown eyes went wide with amazement. "You have? Really?"

"Dying," Nick said gruffly, putting his arms around both of them.

"What about school and everything?" Scotty asked tenuously.

"Details," Nick said, waving his hand. "We'll work them all out."

"Will I still be able to see Mrs. L and my friends in Richmond?"

"Any time you want," Sam said, smoothing the hair off his face and kissing both cheeks. He made a cringing face at the kissing, which made her laugh.

"Are you sure about this? It's a big deal to take on a kid who isn't yours—"

"How could you be any more ours than you already are?" Nick asked, drawing a smile from Scotty. "You know how the speech tonight was kind of a big deal?"

Scotty nodded. "It was a really big deal."

"This is *soooooo* much bigger."

Sam reached for her husband's hand and linked their fingers. "So much bigger," she said.

"Bigger than all those people saying your name?"

"Much, much, much bigger. I've never had a son before. What's bigger than that?"

"So you'd like adopt me or something?"

"We'd love to adopt you," Nick said. "If that's what you want."

"Would I have to change my name?"

"Only if you want to."

Scotty rolled his bottom lip between his teeth. "I've been kinda thinking about that. What if I kept Dunlap as my middle name and used Cappuano as my last name?"

Nick tightened his grip on Sam's hand. "That sounds like a great idea to me. Don't you think it's a great idea, Sam?"

Sam was trying very hard not to cry like a baby. "It's the best idea I've heard in very a long time."

Scotty leaned into her embrace. "It's been a very long time since I had a real family," he said. "I barely remember my mom or my grandpa."

"You have a great big family now that loves you very, very much," Sam said. "Grandparents and aunts and uncles and cousins who'll be thrilled to hear you're staying for good. But no one loves you more than we do."

"Thanks, Sam," Scotty said, swiping at a tear. "That's really nice of you to say."

A knock on the door had Scotty flying out of Sam's arms and running to let in the room service waiter.

"Did that really happen?" Nick asked quietly as Scotty signed for the ice cream the way Nick had taught him that morning when they ordered breakfast.

"It really did."

"I think it's possible my heart stopped for a minute there."

"Mine too."

"Come on, you guys! It's melting."

The tray had three bowls of vanilla ice cream with side dishes containing all the fixings.

"I'll make them," Scotty said.

"Ladies first," Nick said.

Sam considered her options. "I'll have caramel, nuts, M&Ms, whipped cream and a cherry on top."

Scotty made the sundae and presented it to her with a flourish.

"Thank you, sir."

"Nick?"

"Make it a double."

Scotty made Nick's and then covered his own ice cream with caramel, hot fudge, sprinkles, M&Ms, nuts, whipped cream and a cherry. He brought his full-to-overflowing bowl to the sofa and plopped down between them.

"I believe this calls for a toast," Sam said, holding up her bowl.

Scotty flashed the grin that so reminded Sam of Nick and held up his bowl, getting into the spirit of things.

"To the Cappuano family," she said, gazing into Nick's gorgeous eyes.

"Hear, hear," Nick said, as he clinked his bowl against theirs. He looked happier than she'd ever seen him. Knowing Scotty would be staying for good was a big load off their minds and hearts.

"Hear, hear," Scotty said, taking his lead from Nick, as always.

Sam hadn't yet been able to give Nick the baby they both wanted so badly, but now he had the family he'd never had before. It was a start.

* * * * *

Turn the page for a new,
never-before-published bonus peek
into Sam and Nick's life,
AFTER THE FINAL EPILOGUE.

AFTER THE FINAL EPILOGUE

It took a long time for Nick to come down from the huge rush of the day that had just ended. Between the excitement of the speech, the blast of sugar from the ice cream and the monumental decision they'd made to officially become a family, they were all flying high—no one more so than Scotty, who seemed relieved after initiating the conversation about his future.

At one a.m. Nick told him it was time for bed.

"But the movie isn't over."

"We'll watch the rest in the morning."

Primed to protest further, Scotty apparently thought better of it. "Okay." He got up, leaned over to hug Nick and then kissed Sam, who was sleeping with her head propped on Nick's leg.

"See you in the morning, buddy. Sam and I might be gone when you wake up because we have to do TV interviews. Order what you want for breakfast, and we'll be back as soon as we can. The agents will be here."

"Okay." He started to shuffle off toward the suite's second bedroom, but turned back. "Hey, Nick?"

"What's up?"

"That thing we talked about earlier?"

Nick wanted to laugh. That "thing" was only one of the most important *things* he'd ever talked about with anyone. "What about it?"

"I was really nervous about talking to you guys about

it, and afterward, I realized I had no need to be. I just wanted you to know that. Thanks. And stuff."

Easing Sam onto a pillow, Nick got up and went to him. "Don't ever be nervous about talking to us about anything. We love you more than you'll ever know."

"Yeah, still getting used to that."

"You've got the rest of our lives to get used to it." Nick hugged him and Scotty returned the fierce embrace. "Get some sleep."

"You, too."

Scotty went into his room and closed the door.

Nick stared at that door for a long moment, thrilled that a decision had been made and Scotty had decided to stay with them permanently. He and Sam had been stressed out for weeks about how they might handle it if he decided to return to the state home for children in Virginia.

And now they didn't have to worry about that anymore, and the relief was profound. He went to the sofa to kiss his wife awake.

Her eyes fluttered and then opened, a smile stretching across her lovely face.

"You never wake up smiling."

"I do when I have a dream that we fell in love with a boy and he decided to stay with us forever."

"I'm very pleased to report that it wasn't a dream." Nick held out a hand to help her up and then led her into the bedroom. He loved her like this, soft and sleepy and happy.

"You, my friend, are going to get very, *very* lucky tonight."

"I get lucky every night because I get to sleep with you."

"Tonight is going to be a whole other level of lucky."

"There's another level?"

"Damn straight. This is a def-con-delta level achieved only after we become parents for the first time and you make an incredibly awesome speech. I was so proud, I thought I'd burst. And I was seething, too."

"Dare I ask why the seethe?"

"Women everywhere are going to be lusting after my guy."

"If I didn't know better, I'd think you'd been drinking."

"Because I'm talking about your supreme hotness?"

Nick rolled his eyes at her, as he always did, when she said things like that.

"Get naked."

The two words, bluntly stated, made his blood boil. He pulled the T-shirt over his head. While it was covering his face, she went to work on his sweats. Before he could recover from the surprise, she was pushing him onto the bed and coming down on top of him.

"Hold onto your hat, Senator. This is gonna be hot."

"I'd rather hold on to you, and P.S.? It's always hot."

THE NEXT MORNING, he and Sam made the rounds of the network morning shows, beginning with Wake-Up America, where they were asked about the young boy who appeared on stage with them the night before.

Glancing at Sam, Nick said, "He's our son, Scotty Dunlap Cappuano."

"Oh," the host said, "I wasn't aware that you had a son."

"We're in the process of adopting Scotty out of state custody in Virginia." He went on to tell the story of how he had met Scotty while on a campaign stop, and the immediate bond that had formed over their shared love of the Boston Red Sox.

"After last night, your name is being tossed around for the next presidential race. What're your plans, Senator?"

He took hold of Sam's hand, giving it a squeeze. "I plan to continue serving the citizens of Virginia while my wife and I help our son adjust to a new home and a new school. We've got plenty on our plates, to say the least."

"Any thoughts on your husband running for president, Mrs. Cappuano?"

"That's Lieutenant Holland," Nick said.

"Of course, I'm sorry, Lieutenant."

"No problem. As for Nick running for president, I think he'd be a great president, but like he said, we've got a lot going on now, and our focus is going to be on our son, which is where it should be."

Nick smiled at her, the two of them in perfect harmony, as always.

ACKNOWLEDGMENTS

THANK YOU TO my dear friend and assistant, Julie Cupp, who answers all my D.C. logistical questions, and props me up every day with laughter, friendship and endless support. Thank you to Captain Russell Hayes of the Newport, RI, Police Department who reads every Fatal book and always helps to make the police action more detailed and precise. Special thanks to my husband Dan for the information about how security clearances work as well as the agency that oversees them.

Thank you to my beta readers Ronlyn Howe, Kara Conrad and Anne Woodall. I appreciate your input more than you'll ever know. Thanks to everyone at Harlequin and Carina Press for their commitment to the Fatal Series, and to my agent, Kevan Lyon, for her help with the details. To Alison Dasho—thanks for your help with this book! A HUGE thank you all the readers who've embraced Sam, Nick and their story, especially the members of the Fatal Series Reader Group on Facebook, who cheered me on as I finished *Fatal Deception*—after a nearly FATAL computer crash took the first half of the book. Luckily, I got it back, but that was un-fun.

To answer your most pressing question: YES, there's much more to come for Sam and Nick. And finally a huge thank-you to Sam and Nick, who continue to be such a joy to write. They make me feel lucky to show up for work each day I get to spend with them, and they're so real to me after six books that some days it's hard to believe they aren't alive and living madly in love in Washington. So I choose to believe they're doing just that.

To discuss the Fatal Series with other avid readers, join the Fatal Series Reader Group on Facebook at www.facebook.com/groups/FatalSeries/. To dish about the details in *Fatal Deception*, with spoilers allowed and encouraged, join the *Fatal Deception* Reader Group at www.facebook.com/groups/FatalDeception/. I love to hear from readers! You can contact me at marie@marieforce.com. Thanks for reading!

xoxo

Marie

ABOUT THE AUTHOR

Marie Force is the *New York Times* bestselling author of 50 contemporary romances, including the Gansett Island Series, which has sold more than 2.2 million books, and the Fatal Series from Harlequin's Carina Press, which has sold more than 1 million copies. In addition, she is the author of the Green Mountain Series as well as the new erotic romance Quantum Series, written under the slightly modified name of M.S. Force.

Her goals in life are simple—to finish raising two happy, healthy, productive young adults, to keep writing books for as long as she possibly can and to never be on a flight that makes the news.

Join Marie's mailing list on her website at marieforce. com for news about new books and upcoming appearances in your area. Follow her on Facebook at www.Facebook. com/MarieForceAuthor, on Twitter @marieforce and on Instagram at www.instagram.com/marieforceauthor/. Contact Marie at marie@marieforce.com.